THE REDWING SAGA

BOOK EIGHT

THE POISONED PAWN

SHARON K. GILBERT

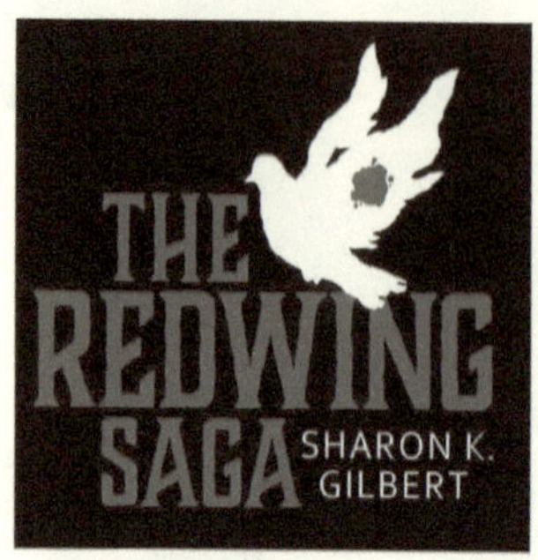

THE POISONED PAWN

BOOK EIGHT OF THE REDWING SAGA
BY SHARON K. GILBERT
WWW.THEREDWINGSAGA.COM

Published by Rose Avenue Fiction, LLC
514 Rose Avenue, Crane, MO 65633

First Print Edition – September 15, 2022
Kindle Edition – September 15, 2022
All Content and Characters © Sharon K. Gilbert
All global and domestic rights reserved.

ISBN-13: 9798986635705

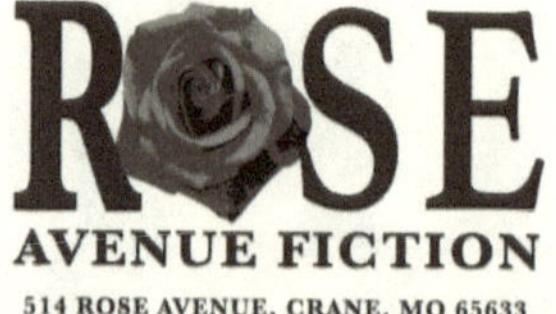

Published by Rose Avenue Fiction, LLC
514 Rose Avenue, Crane, MO 65633

TABLE OF CONTENTS

FROM THE AUTHOR

Writing this book has been a slow, but wonderful journey through time and toil. Originally, as most of you know, I'd planned to release the book in December of 2021. Life, however, had other plans.

In October of that year, Derek and I began to discuss a new phase of our Gilbert House ministry. Our good friend and mentor, Dr. Thomas R. Horn, encouraged us in this, and so we've launched a brand-new website and online store. We've also created a mobile app and resumed filming one of your favorite programs, *SciFriday*. Of course, we're still producing our Sunday Bible study, *Gilbert House Fellowship*, and weekly episodes of *Unraveling Revelation*. The new ministry effort has taken months of planning and loads of energy—all of which diverted time away from writing projects.

And so, after months of plotting, re-plotting, deleting, editing, re-editing, and plotting yet again, I've finally finished *The Poisoned Pawn*. During the draft stage, the book grew longer and longer and longer. Far too long for a single book, and so I've divided the manuscript into two novels. This is part one. Part two will begin Book Nine (*Queen Sacrifice*).

You'll notice, I've chosen to capitalise (British spelling, remember?) 'the Duke', when referring to Charles Sinclair and 'the Duchess' for Elizabeth. I do the same whenever the title 'King' refers to Charles. This is to set our Duke apart from others of similar rank. All other royal titles are in lower case, with the exception of Queen, when it refers to Victoria. Military ranks such as 'major' will remain lower case unless preceding the man's name. Dog breeds are capitalised when referring to a proper name, such as Weimaraner, named for the Grand Duke of Saxe-Weimar-Eisenach. Conversely, dachshund (the German word for 'badger dog') isn't usually capitalised, save for articles written for dog-lovers and professionals. I've chosen to keep it lower case.

And isn't it about time we had a dachshund in this story?

As with the previous seven installments of the series, our main characters find themselves drawn into fallen-realm plots and ploys, but the Lord God Almighty uses these dark plans to shed light upon Himself and upon His Truth. Sometimes, the Shepherd leads us into dark places—even into the Valley of the Shadow of Death—but no matter what, no matter where, *He is always with us*.

Even unto the end of the world.

As always, the spelling is British and antiquated, per nineteenth-century convention. I ask your indulgence for any typographical errors. I've tried to remove them, but one or two—even three or four—invariably sneak it, like crabgrass in the summer. Such is the happy life of a writer.

May you find encouragement and edification in this book. I know I have. Researching historical figures informs my view of current affairs. Sadly, humanity repeats old mistakes. We're walking round and round in circles—as if in a Maze.

May the Lord bless you, dear reader. And remember, you are NEVER alone. Our Lord is with you *always*.

Much love,
Sharon

August 24, 2022

I dedicate this novel to YOU
my patient, supportive readers.
Your encouragement
means more than
I could ever say

Thank you so very much.

For their vine comes from the vine of Sodom
and from the fields of Gomorrah;
their grapes are grapes of poison;
their clusters are bitter;
their wine is the poison of serpents
and the cruel venom of asps.
- Deuteronomy 32:32-33 ESV

But thanks be to God,
who gives us the victory
through our Lord Jesus Christ.
- I Corinthians 15:57 ESV

PROLOGUE

26th March, 1894 – Easter Night

Our story begins on a strange night in March, inside the city of London. That year, Easter was a strange and sober celebration. March blustered in with the promise of flowers, green grass, and warming air. Lambs were born, calves frolicked in green fields, and winter wheat waved upon sunlit hillsides. Then, on the twenty-third, the cruel hag of winter returned with bitterly cold nights and fierce, northeasterly winds. On Resurrection Morning, parishioners shivered in the pews, parsons preached in heavy woolen overcoats, and organists wore gloves whilst playing *Christ the Lord Has Risen Today* and *Crown Him With Many Crowns*.

A few, more modern churches originally planned something called an Egg Hunt, a German competitor to the traditional English Egg Roll. For weeks, church leaders argued over which activity best reflected Christian values. Giving up eggs for Lent was an old tradition. Everyone who stored up the forbidden eggs believed they should be used rather than wasted. Whether to roll or to hide the eggs, *that* was the crucial question. But as the freezing cold descended, debate died out. Outdoor activities were cancelled, due to inclement weather.

Happily, that cold Easter morning soon yielded to a warmer evening. At long last, winter's hag forfeited the field to the youthful child of spring. But the child's warm breath concealed a killer. Traitorous Death had set a trap within the rising mercury. An atmospheric inversion had formed. The colder, heavier air dropped to the ground and forced the incoming warm front to glide o'er top, creating a deadly climatological disaster. This anomalous bowl of fury delivered an otherworldly, poisonous veil across all London.

That evening, whilst happy families gathered round their Easter tables, a relentless grey ghost shaped and draped itself into the clefts and crannies of Seven Dials. It creeped eastward into the Square Mile. It slithered past St. Paul's Cathedral and slinked down the white-stone battlements of London's Tower. It drifted over the wormwood ruins of ancient Roman walls; slipped through busy Bishopsgate; and came to rest in the poverty-stricken boroughs of London's East End.

To the denizens of Whitechapel, Limehouse, and Spitalfields, such a nightly fog felt natural; even familiar, friendly. But not this night. Not this fog. This was different: stinging, tingling, biting—like a *living thing*; as though some malevolent intelligence slithered within the silvery shroud; an insatiable, unseen assassin that cruelly crouched on each poisonous droplet.

Perhaps, Death itself rode the black chimney smoke. Cruel Thanatos, summoning unready souls to judgement.

Might it be his demonic helpers, harsh heralds, belching out deadly daggers, riddled with disease from coal-fired boilers and stinking lime kilns—dreaded harbingers of dark days to come? Not just one man's death, or even dozens, but the deaths of many hundreds, or even thousands.

Wars and rumours of wars. The End of Days.

As Westminster celebrated Christ's resurrection, Death's phantom fingers scrawled a message for Duke Charles Sinclair, written in human blood.

It commenced with a party. That fateful night happened to be the twenty-first birthday of the Right Honourable, Edward D. Maladroit, Viscount Quibbling—an unfortunate courtesy title provided by his father, Lord Ernest Maladroit, 4th Earl of Garashed. Poor Ed's title said it all, for young Quibbling had no idea which way to go on any day or at any moment, yet often complained that life had somehow passed him by.

Ed was tallish with prematurely grey hair, pale grey eyes, and a grey sort of personality. He hadn't wanted a party at all, but his closest friend, the Right Honourable Tommy Elgin-More—styled as Viscount Volonté and heir to the Stratbourne earldom—exerted considerable will upon poor Ed Maladroit and insisted on hosting a grand celebration at his father's Belgravia mansion. Tom's father was presently out of England and knew nothing about it.

Edward and Tom were on a short break from Merton College, and all their Oxford pals attended the party. To add to the fun, dozens of pretty debutantes from fashionable addresses arrived in bustled silk and satin finery. Whilst men played cards, smoked cigars, and sipped champagne, the ladies gossiped, flirted, and danced.

As the party wound down, the mischievous Lord Tommy convinced his quibbling friend to join him for a second party at a less formal venue in London's East End. After bidding everyone goodnight, the virulent Volonté called for a coach and driver from the Stratbourne mews. Tom whispered the destination to an obedient driver, and off went the viscounts through the treacherous fog. As the coach's geldings trotted across the dark city's cobbles, the deadly, inversion-birthed mist swirled and slinked through the brougham's wheels.

The passengers failed to notice. Champagne had dulled their senses, and datura-laced cigarettes blunted their brains. And so, ignorant of their fate, the young men laughed and smoked as if nothing in the world could touch them. Life, they believed, belonged to the rich.

The coach moved farther east, and the unnatural fog thickened into a bleak silver soup, making it difficult to see out the windows.

"Where the devil are we going?" Ed Maladroit asked his friend through a datura haze.

"We, old chum, are heading to a sweet slice of heaven. Remember the place I told you about? The house of secret sins?"

"No," muttered Ed, inhaling the calming smoke. "What house?"

Tom laughed. "Never mind. Just trust in your old pal."

Edward sighed. He had little choice in the matter. After all, Tom was his best friend. His dearest friend. As close as a brother. They were second cousins through their mothers, known one another since the cradle. Tommy, older by a week, was born with a will of iron and always made the decisions. Consequently, quibbling Ed followed behind like a baby duck. This night would be no different.

Tommy Elgin-More drew deeply on the Indian cigarette, his pupils grown large. Ed didn't care for the strange-tasting cigarettes but pretended to like them. Datura made him sleepy, unable to speak properly. Tom saw Ed's complaints as a sign of weakness.

"Women don't enjoy soft men, Ed. They want to be told what to do. Don't worry. I'll look after you, Cousin," he promised. "You'll soon make that girl your own."

"What girl?" muttered Edward.

"The very buxom Lady Alice Featherstone-Bailey, of course. I hear your old man's fixing it up. Marriage, I mean."

"I've not heard anything about it," complained Maladroit.

"It's a good match, Ed. She's rich as Croesus and will give you loads of children. All the women in that family are fertile as frogs," laughed Tom, coughing a cloud of foul-smelling smoke.

Maladroit had no experience with women, but he genuinely liked Alice and found her quite pleasing. Yes, she had a slight overbite and plump arms, but Lady Alice was amiable, bright, and supportive. Ed wished his friend showed a bit more consideration, but then Tom always was a heartless mug.

And he's all I've got, thought Maladroit gloomily.

The black brougham rolled through the City, passing by the reassuring marble pillars of the Bank of England. It trundled along Cornhill Street to Leadenhall and into the darker regions of immigrant-packed Whitechapel. By now, the fog had fallen across the land in a thick blanket of poison. It pierced the window seals of the expensive coach and forced Edward to put a silk handkerchief to his face, trying to block out the smell of smoke, soot, horse muck, fish, and sweat.

"Just where are we going?" he asked Elgin-More.

"To a den of delights. It's not much farther."

The coachman turned the geldings south, down the cobbles of Leman Street. Near the Police Station entrance, stood several young constables, smoking Turkish cigarettes and chatting about crime and women. Not one noticed the brougham.

The coach drove beneath a railway bridge. Maladroit noticed the bright lights of a barrel fire inside the sooty brick arches. Round its flames, stood dozens of haggard, homeless men and women, warming brittle bones in the thick fog.

Finally, they turned left onto St. George Street, where they passed an abandoned brewery with broken windows, the Albatross Public House, and an old brick factory, currently used as a Jewish orphanage.

The crested coach stopped one block past the orphanage, in front of a brightly painted, three-storey wooden house, with seven chimneys and six gables. Above a bright red door, hung a large wooden sign with blue lettering identifying the place as the *Molly-Mae Hotel*. The windows glowed with electric lights. Laughter and piano music filled the foggy air. A thickset watchman stood beside the conspicuous entry, dressed in a blue uniform. He spat out a mouthful of tobacco juice and approached the driver. The two men spoke briefly.

Within the brougham's snug interior, Tom turned to his friend. "We're here, Ed. Tonight, you become a man."

"I'm not sure about this," confessed the other nervously. "I mean, aren't the women in this sort of place riddled with disease? Besides, it's frightfully foggy out there, Tom. Perhaps, we should go back."

"Don't tell me you're worried about fog!" laughed his tow-headed cousin. "Ed, if you want to be a man, then act like one. Lady Alice won't want an amateur on her wedding night. Trust me. I have experience in these matters. I guarantee you the time of your life."

Maladroit sighed. *Have I ever said no to him?* "You're probably right. It'll be fun, won't it?"

"You will never be the same!" declared Elgin-More.

The driver opened the door, and Ed joined his cousin on the foggy street. Tommy told the coachman to wait at the nearby pub. He approached the doorman and offered the man three silver coins. The guardian smiled and opened the gaudily painted door. "Enjoy yerselves, gents," he told them as he pocketed Tom's generous tip.

Despite its dockside location, the Molly-Mae Hotel catered to wealthy businessmen and high-class visitors. Prostitution was all too common in London. Over eighty thousand women, girls, men, and boys haunted London's streets, selling tender wares. Street-workers barely earned a living, but establishments like the Molly-Mae provided lodging, medical services, regular meals, and clean water—but only to the beautiful, talented, and healthy.

The proprietress, Mae Morris, had high aspirations. Until recently, Mae's greatest competition was the Empress Hotel on Columbia Road, formerly managed by Margaret Hansen. In 1889, Hansen decamped to parts unknown, and one of Hansen's older girls assumed management. Then, in December 1891, a suspicious fire destroyed the hotel, making Mae Morris Whitechapel's leading provider of gentlemen's pleasures.

Mae began her nefarious career at the tender age of twelve. Orphaned at eleven during a cholera epidemic, Mae made a living by selling flowers, birds, matches—whatever she could lay her hands on. It was a very rough life. As she neared her twelfth birthday, a Scots-French builder noticed Mae selling matches on the corner of Commercial and Batty. The man bought Mae a hot meal, hastily taught her the harsh realities of life, then sold her to a woman named Iris Lemuel, who billed the pretty protégé as 'pure as the driven snow'.

The greedy punters lined up to pay.

Mae's heart soon hardened to life's cruelties. She saved her earnings in a red-wool sock, concealed beneath the floorboards. When Lemuel died of food poisoning, clever Mae took over the business. She used her savings to renovate the building and changed the establishment's name to the Molly-Mae Hotel, where a man could forget his worries and enjoy partners to suit every taste and every dark desire.

Mae pocketed sixty percent of every sale.

Morris looked young for forty. A tightly laced corset gave her the required hour-glass shape, whilst accenting the fleshy bits that men always liked. She was happy to display herself. But money made her happiest. On that Easter night, the avaricious businesswoman greeted the wealthy young men and imagined a high profit margin.

She recognised Tom Elgin-More as a regular, who tipped generously. "Evenin', sirs," Mae said happily. "What sort o' delights might we offer two such handsome men?"

"Good evening, Mrs. Morris. I wonder if Charity's working tonight?" asked Elgin-More.

"Charity's working in the City this evening, sir. A private party on Wormwood," replied Mae as she stroked the expensive material covering Tom's left shoulder. She avoided speaking his name. Most of her customers preferred the illusion of anonymity. But gifted with a fine memory, Mae kept a mental list of every customer, along with each man's particular tastes.

Elgin-More enjoyed variety.

"We've other delights, too, sir. Perhaps, something more exotic this evening?" she suggested, nodding towards a dark-haired boy, dressed as Aladdin.

"No, not that," Tommy answered as he stuck out his chest to appear more manly. "I'd hoped for Charity this evening. You see, my friend requires instruction, if you get my meaning."

Morris smiled, her manner motherly. "I understand completely, sir. Your friend's a handsome man. I'm sure any of our girls'd be happy to serve him. We've lots to choose from. It is *a girl* you want, right, sir?" she asked Maladroit, nodding once more towards Aladdin.

The embarrassed viscount vigorously shook his head. "No. I mean, well, yes—but no!" he stuttered senselessly. "I mean, that is what I mean to say, ma'am, is I want neither. My friend brought me here without explaining the purpose or destination. Might we just play cards or have a drink? Have you something cold? Perhaps, a German wine? This strange fog's left me very thirsty," Ed finished, mopping sweat from his brow.

Mae laughed. She'd seen unwilling customers before, but in the end, they always succumbed to one or more of her services. She put an arm through his and whispered in a smooth voice. "Of course, sir. We have plenty o' wine, in all manner of vintages. And if it's cards you want, there's a gaming room upstairs. I'll send one of our girls with a selection of refreshments."

"That's fine," said Elgin-More. "And smoking is permitted? Special cigarettes and the like?"

"Of course, sir. And if it's *special* cigarettes, you'll want the Red Salon, my lord. Is that your pleasure? The Red?"

"Oh, yes," answered Elgin-More, remembering a very pleasant night spent there recently. "Send up champagne with the food, will you, Mae?"

"Of course, sir. Do you know the way? Shall I send an usher along?"

"Red Salon? No, no, I can find it. I think," Tommy replied. The datura was causing his words to slur.

"I'll have Lara take you up," decided Morris. "But she's not on for tonight, you understand. I'm saving Lara. She's not available, but still pretty to look at."

Mae called to a waifish girl sitting near the staircase. She had ringlets of dark hair and a tiny waist. The child looked no older than ten. One could only imagine what devilish plans lay in store for such an innocent. "Lara, take these gentlemen up to the Red Salon."

The girl's silk skirts rustled as she offered a polite curtsy. "Yes, ma'am. This way, sirs. Just up these stairs."

Thomas Elgin-More and his captive cousin, Edward Maladroit, followed the girl up two flights of carpeted steps to a second-storey gaming parlour, awash in thick smoke and garish decor. Seated at a collection of tables, lounged half a dozen bankers and peers in evening dress, served by scantily dressed women, whose curves threatened to escape their tightly laced bustiers. Crimson and purple silk covered the walls and framed the windows. Four crystal chandeliers cast soft candlelight across busy tables. Smoke, perfume, and overt sensuality hammered at Maladroit's datura-tilted visual cortex. The world felt foreign, swimmy, off-kilter. To his crawling brain, the room's cast of characters acted out a strange shadow play.

A tiger cub, bound with a velvet-wrapped chain, purred quietly in one corner. A collared spider monkey leapt from chair to chair and table to table, stealing food and pinching cigarettes. In another corner, on the cushion of a basket chair, lay a Siamese cat. Its thick tail twitched as it greedily eyed a caged greenfinch.

Not surprisingly, the bird hadn't the will to sing.

Near the bay windows, stood a William Harper cabinet piano. The musician at the instrument was dressed as Apollo. The make-believe god played music hall tunes to accompany a curious warbler, dressed in gold chiffon, edged in pearls and lace. Something about the vocalist's posture bothered Edward. It seemed 'off'.

"Tom, is that a woman, or a...?" he croaked through the murky haze.

"It's a man, of course," replied a handsome stranger from a neighbouring table. "I believe his real name is William, but he likes to be called Nancy. A nice enough fellow, but don't cross him. Word is, he was once a captain with the British Army. In the North Africa campaigns."

"Nancy?" gasped Maladroit, taking a glass of champagne from a waitress. He gulped it down. "An army captain wants to be called Nancy? And he wears a dress?"

"Oh, yes," the stranger replied. "But the man's very secretive, so keep your distance."

Tommy Elgin-More hated seeming out of touch. He prided himself on leading fashionable thought, so made a pretence of knowing everything. "Ed, this sort of thing's done all over the world. If you travelled more, you'd know. You really ought to expand your horizons, old thing."

The helpful stranger stood and bowed. "You gentlemen will join me, yes?" he asked in accented English.

"We'd be honoured," Elgin-More eagerly answered.

He and Tom took the last empty chairs. Maladroit examined the man's peculiar but interesting appearance. Assuming his senses weren't lying, the man was seven feet tall. Yet, despite the height, he was well-proportioned and exceedingly handsome. Not handsome. *Beautiful.* He wore the requisite evening clothes of a London gentleman, but these were accented with foreign flourishes. His hair was a river of gleaming ebony, ending at a narrow waist. The shoulders were broad. The hands were surprisingly delicate. The man's large eyes were so dark they looked black, with ebony lashes as lush and pretty as any woman's. The exotic beauty was so thoroughly entrancing, Ed felt as though he were falling into a vortex of raw sensuality, towards a dark and bottomless void.

Tommy didn't seem to notice. "I'm Lord Volonté," he said, holding out a right hand for shaking. It was typical of Tom. He loved to flaunt titles. "This other chap's Lord Quibbling."

"Quibbling?" repeated the stranger, offering a toothy grin as he accepted their handshakes. "Is an interesting name, yes? Quibbling. I think I have heard this name. You are from Westminster, yes?"

"Belgravia, actually. Cadogen Place. A monstrous pile at Number 32," bragged Elgin-More. "And you're from?"

"Romania," the tall man replied, pronouncing it *roo-mah-nya* with a heavily rolled 'r'. "*Hoia Baciu.*"

"Hoia what?" asked Ed.

"Is within Transylvanian forest. My castle is there. And my friend here, he is English."

The friend was thin with a sagging sallow face. He might have been handsome once, but sickness or hard times had sapped his youth and left him with yellow skin, that smacked of dark streets and vermin. His teeth looked worn, though relatively straight.

He reached out for handshakes. "The name's Lionel Wentworth. I've no fancy title to brag about, but this gentleman has dozens. I'm a Cambridge man. Silver Spoons, if you know what that is. Might you be Cambridge men, too?" He waited a second, but noticing the tall man's annoyed expression, he added, "Allow me to introduce His Royal Highness, Prince Aleksandr Koshmar. At least, that's the name he's using tonight."

"Lionel enjoys the riddles. He admires my many guises," explained the prince with a sharp glance at his friend. "Lionel, are these not fine-looking gentlemen? Handsome and tasty?" he asked the sallow-faced friend.

Elgin-More blinked. "*Tasty?*"

"Your fine clothes. Your polished manner. This is tasty, yes?" the prince asked with a toothsome smile. "Is right word?"

"I think you mean we show *good taste*," corrected Tom. "And you're right, by Jove, we do dress well. One does, you know. It's required of certain classes. I'm surprised to meet a prince in a place like this. And you're Romanian?"

"For the moment," whispered Koshmar. "Oh, but I do love this London, my lords. Your city inspires me, especially on nights like this, when the fog falls upon humans with such poisonous beauty."

The two cousins glanced at one another. "I suppose fog can be beautiful," suggested Maladroit, wishing he'd stayed in Belgravia.

"What brings you men here tonight?" asked Lionel Wentworth, sensing the need to redirect the conversation. "After all, it's Easter. Shouldn't you be in church, praying or something?"

"I would be, if Pa weren't in Paris," said Elgin-More. "Mum's at our country house, most likely passed out from too many G&Ts. Ed and I are on our own and celebrating his birthday, actually. Twenty-one years today," Tom added with a slap to his timid cousin's shoulder. "He deserves a special gift, so I brought him here, where a red-blooded chap can indulge himself without remorse."

"Remorse!" laughed the disguised fallen angel. "Humans love to indulge, but then construct this annoying emotion you call remorse. Is interesting to me." He leaned close and stroked Edward's baby-smooth cheek. "You are twenty-one, Lord Quibbling? So young. So innocent. And you seek a woman's touch, is right?"

"Call him Ed," said Elgin-More. "Everybody does."

"Is true?" smirked the blood-thirsty Watcher known as Saraqael ben Chosek. "Ed. Is very small name, yes? Tell me, Ed, does our pretty singer intrigue you? Our Nancy?"

The inexperienced Maladroit frowned. He wasn't sure what the prince meant, so he shrugged without answering.

"Ignore him, Ed," said Wentworth. "His Highness enjoys playing jokes. Might you be Cambridge men? I asked earlier, but you didn't answer."

"Oxford, actually," said Elgin-More with a diffident air. "On Easter break from Merton."

"Easter!" Saraqael sneered. He waved his left hand in the air as if to dismiss the notion of a Christian holiday. "Easter makes no sense to me. Why do you celebrate a Jew's death?"

"He didn't stay dead," Ed argued. "The Bible says he rose again. Easter's about the resurrection."

"*Christ,*" snarled the vampire. "Do you believe?"

"My mother does," answered Maladroit. "She's a bit of a Bible thumper."

"And you?" mocked the inquisitor. "Do you also *thump?*"

"Well," Ed gulped nervously. "I'm not sure, but it's a mighty strange topic for a place like this, don't you think?"

"Lord Quibbling, you've no idea how very amusing you are!" laughed Saraqael through the Prince Aleksandr face. "Tell me, my new friends, do Oxford men play chess?"

"Of course, though Tom's a better player."

"Is he? The proud Mr. Elgin-More," Saraqael whispered as he leaned close enough to touch noses with the conceited viscount. "Tell me, my pretty little lord, does a game of chess appeal to you?"

Elgin-More bristled at the implication and answered with a puffed-out chest. "For your information, sir, I've been playing since I cut my eye teeth. And I've won the Varsity Match against Cambridge two years running."

Ed's impaired brain swam in a dreamy soup of datura smoke. He struggled to think clearly, but something nagged at him. The stranger called them Elgin-More and Maladroit. *When did we give our last names? I'm sure we didn't. How does the Romanian know?*

"Your Highness, have we met before?" Ed asked the braggart prince. "You've called us by our surnames, but I don't remember giving them."

"Oh, but you did," Wentworth insisted as he filled their glasses with a dark liquid. "Drink up, gentlemen. This is the last of a very special vintage."

"What kind?" asked Elgin-More proudly. "I know my wines. This looks like a Cabernet."

Wentworth laughed. "Not quite. His Highness owns a stake in the Molly Mae. The hotel's cellars are stocked by Koshmar Imports."

"That's why your name's familiar!" exclaimed Elgin-More, wondering how best to use this new friendship. "It's your company. Koshmar Imports, exotic treats from across the Empire. You must be rich."

"I am very, very rich," the false human told them. "I am, how you English say, *rolling in it*. Filthy with the money. And the chess? You will play with me, yes?"

"Of course," Tom confidently replied.

"Excellent!" Koshmar shouted. "Is good! Or as good as I may be, yes? Now, we make small wager, yes?"

"A wager?" echoed the greedy Elgin-More. "Sure. What are the stakes?"

Koshmar laughed. "Stakes! Is funny! No, seriously, here are rules. If you win, I pay for all your evening here. Anything, anyone you wish to enjoy. Drinks, food, women, whatever companions you choose. I pay for all, yes? One night. No limit."

"I'd say that's a tempting offer," answered Elgin-More. After all, how could he lose? He was the finest player at Oxford.

His cousin wasn't so sure. "And if *you* win, Your Highness? Do we pay for your evening?" asked Ed.

"Oh, I should never expect that," smiled the other. "My evenings are much too expensive. As I say, money is for me to roll in. I have plenty, but I think of something. Lionel, do you require something?"

"Just a warm, nutritious drink," said the pallid wraith with the yellow smile.

"You shall have it, my thirsty friend," Saraqael promised. His ebony eyes grew large and swirled into bottomless pools of midnight as he stared at the humans. "What of this idea, my pretty lords? If I win, you join me on my yacht. Is good?"

"You have a yacht?" Tom asked, practically drooling with envy.

"Oh, yes. A racing yacht," Wentworth told him. "The finest on the Thames. It's called the *Sange Proaspat*. It's Romanian design, of course, and quick as a blade. The *Sange* came in second in the Royal Thames last May."

Saraqael smiled through the fleshy Koshmar carapace. "I could have taken first, but I felt compassion for the Prince of Wales and allow him to win," replied the prince in a cool voice. "*Britannia* is quick, but *Sange Proaspat* is throat-cutter."

"It's *what*, sir?"

"She cut through waves, yes? She is pretty sloop, moored at very nice marina, that caters to my kind."

"Your kind, sir?" asked Maladroit.

"Aliens. Travellers. Otherworlders."

"How's that again?" repeated Ed.

"Foreigners," said Saraqael with a sly wink. "Here is wager. If I win, I pay all. If you win, I bring you aboard the *Sange*, and we enjoy caviar and champagne until you say stop. How that sound to you?"

"Sounds like we'd be winners no matter which way the hammer falls," Tom told his cousin. "Either we get our night paid for, or we're fêted aboard a fancy racing yacht. Ed, are you in?"

Maladroit's eardrums picked up the sound vibrations of his friend's question, but the language was ominous. Ed had a very bad feeling. Why would the stranger be so generous? Still, those black eyes were magnetic. *Am I falling?* he wondered. *I'm dreaming. Yes, that must be it. I'm at home in bed, dreaming.*

"Whatever you say," was all Ed could muster. His tongue felt thick and dry; it stuck to his teeth.

The Romanian clapped his hands together gleefully. "Excellent! We prepare the table." He waved his left hand to summon a pleasingly plump girl, dressed as a shepherdess. "Sweet Belinda, clear the plates and glasses. Bring my board."

Belinda curtsied and did as the prince commanded. After clearing the table, she opened a carved ebony chest and fetched a black-and-cream chessboard. Once she'd set it before them, the exceedingly tall prince kissed her hand. He lingered long, sniffed the girl's skin and licked it lightly.

"Belinda, you taste delicious," he whispered. "Go now. Leave me to work. I see you tomorrow."

The girl giggled and crossed to the same corner as the cat and greenfinch.

The cage was empty; the bird gone. The cat smiled.

"This is a fine-looking board, sir, but there aren't any chessmen," observed Elgin-More.

"That is because I carry my own," Koshmar told the human. The pretender produced a velvet bag from the deep recesses of the voluminous coat. "I carry them for luck, you understand," he added. "You set board, Mr. Elgin-More. I am always black."

Tommy poured out the beautifully carved pieces. The white were made of bone; Elgin-More presumed elephant or whale. The black were obsidian. Each king and queen had multiple sets of wings and tall crowns that looked like delicate tree branches. The knights rode snarling dragons; the bishops were magicians. The rooks weren't castles at all, but birds. Most disturbing of all were the pawns: twisted creatures that looked like gargoyles, with ruby eyes and lolling black tongues.

"I'll be damned!" Elgin-More exclaimed. "What sort of pieces are these?"

"Oh, yes," muttered Lionel. "Damned is the word."

The prince chided his companion. "Now, now, we must be cordial, Mr. Wentworth. Is understandable. Set is unusual to Englishmen. These are made by *Szyékely* craftsmen in my home country. You English call them gypsy people, I think. Travellers. The set is unique for many reasons. Created through special rituals."

A shiver ran down Ed's spine. "Rituals?"

"Is not right word?" asked Saraqael, feigning innocence.

"I think, you mean *traditions*, sir," suggested Wentworth. "The pieces represent Romanian myths."

"Yes. Is so. Lord Tommy, you are white. You make first move," said the vampire.

Without a moment's thought or contemplative strategy, Tommy Elgin-More moved a pawn to the KP-4 square.

"This is move?" asked Saraqael with a sardonic smile. "King's Gambit? You cannot know how amusing that is!"

"King's Gambit's a standard opening," answered Elgin-More confidently. "It's difficult to challenge without opening yourself up for early capture, old man."

"Hmm," the disguised Watcher muttered. "Perhaps, but I am most skilled at chess."

"No matter, sir. I'm afraid you're doomed to lose."

Saraqael's crimson mouth spread outwards, the pointed teeth startlingly white against full, flushed lips. "Then, I shall play my best game, Mr. Elgin-More. But no matter the outcome, I *never* lose."

And so it was, that on that foggy Easter night, the Honourable Thomas Elgin-More, Viscount Volonté, learned a very hard lesson. It would be his last lesson—in this life, at least. Never a believer in anything other than himself, the boastful viscount would soon take a final, wide-eyed gasping breath before opening his eyes to an eternity of utter regret.

The fate of Edward Maladroit would prove different. Saraqael let the birthday boy live.

Was it pity that stopped the trickster from drinking every drop from the young man's plump veins? Hardly.

Was Maladroit a survivor? Or was he left as a *poisoned pawn*; a piece offered up to trick an opponent?

After killing Elgin-More, Saraqael bled the boy a little, then scrawled a coded message on Maladroit's back with an other-world weapon.

"I can't read that. What does it mean?" asked Wentworth.

"It is secret, but he'll decipher it," answered Saraqael, whilst Wentworth licked blood from Elgin-More's corpse. "Another will help."

"Who, sir?" Lionel asked. "Who'll decipher it?"

"Charles of Haimsbury, of course," said the trickster. "England's very own Shadow King. Then, the games begin anew. Won't that be fun, Lionel? I'm sure he's missed me these past five years."

The human shrugged and nodded. He carefully arranged the victims into an interesting pose, then covered both to keep away rats.

Saraqael had already gone; vanished like always.

Certain no one had seen him, Lionel Wentworth returned to the Molly-Mae, where he'd sleep till midday.

But someone had seen: A boy dressed as Aladdin, hidden in the shadows of a nearby boat shed. He'd seen it all, and now shivered from cold and fear. He remained in the shed till the way was clear, then the terrified child ran all way to the Leman Street Police Station.

The games were indeed about to begin.

CHAPTER ONE

London, Below Ground – Easter Monday

Charles Sinclair, 1st Duke of Haimsbury, awoke that Monday morning to alarming headlines, printed in tall letters beneath every newspaper's masthead: JACK IS BACK. GOLEM RETURNS. MAN DRAINED OF BLOOD. DEMON OF WHITECHAPEL BACK. FOG OF DEATH. CREEPING KILLER. PEASOUPER POISON. INVISIBLE HAND OF DEATH, and so forth.

Most of the dead were poor Whitechapel folks, primarily prostitutes and beggars. Their eyes bulged; hands clutched at their throats; the skin of nearly all turned black. No one understood how fog could alchemically alter into a poisonous haze, but thankfully, the combination of morning sun and southerly winds soon banished the ghostly killer into vaporous memory.

Like most in London, Charles took Easter Monday as a holiday and planned to spend a quiet day with his wife and four children. Elizabeth had only just returned from a three-week trip to Vienna, and Charles thought they might visit their friend, Dr. Henry MacAlpin, in Fulham.

Sadly, that drive would never happen, for as Lewis Carroll's White Rabbit once summoned an unsuspecting Alice to adventure; so it was that a portly man in a Regency-style suit appeared without warning to summon our Duke into a labyrinthine world, beneath Whitehall's busy streets.

Sir Reginald Parsons arrived at the Duke's new home at half past nine, completely without warning, and convinced Haimsbury to abandon his pleasant plans. They'd driven to Whitehall in an unmarked brougham, entered a nondescript door behind old Scotland Yard, and descended into a twisting tour through polished tunnels.

Charles and Parsons had been walking for a quarter hour and travelled a fairly long distance through the Whitehall tunnels. The passages were beautifully formed and neatly finished. Well-spaced gas lamps, set in brick walls, offered ample illumination, but the stonework floor showed signs of rats. Once they even chanced upon an abandoned nest.

"I'll see a rat-catcher's sent down," Parsons told Sinclair. "Not much farther now, sir. The room's just ahead."

Sir Reginald's official title was Head Clerk at the House of Lords. Unofficially, one might call him a government rat-catcher, for the plump politician had a knack for ferreting out information to use as plum or poison, depending on his goal. Consequently, the garrulous Sir Reginald was both loved and feared. Yet, despite the rat-catcher reputation, the gentleman nearly always smiled.

"Here, we are, my lord," he told Sinclair as they reached a set of blue doors. "The good lady awaits within."

"I'm to go in?" asked Sinclair, who'd come to trust in the peculiar little clerk. "It leads to some sort of room?"

"It does indeed, my lord," promised the man in the strangely flattering suit. The metaphorical White Rabbit unlocked the right-side door and crooked a chubby finger. "This way, my lord. Mind your head as you enter. The doorway's rather low for someone as tall as you."

Sinclair ducked as he passed through the arched opening and emerged into a vast subterranean chamber. The spacious room was dressed and furnished as finely as any at Buckingham Palace. Hanging from the finished ceiling were crystal chandeliers, containing hundreds of wax candles, each cotton wick glowing brightly. Wall sconces and floor candelabra added another hundred to the beeswax tally. The flickering tongues of fire provided light and shadow to the chamber, showing off gold-cloth tapestries.

More to the point, the buttery soft candlelight showed off the face of the diminutive lady, who stood at its centre. The Duke bowed low upon seeing her.

"Charles, my dear," she said as he kissed her hand. "I do love your sweet kisses, but you mustn't bow. After all, you and I are equals. Some in government even say, I should be bowing to you."

"Never, Your Majesty," said Sinclair, smiling. "Never."

"It's Drina, remember?" the Queen reminded him.

He kissed her cheek. "I remember. My very dear Aunt Drina. Now, why has Parsons lured me away from my home so early?"

"Did he lure you? Is that what Reggie did? Well, if so, there's no harm in it. Reggie's forever luring someone or something, isn't he? Yet, I cannot imagine what I'd do without him. Now, sit, my dear. Let me share my mind with you."

Though the chamber was vast, it contained just two chairs, set beside one another. Both were gilded and lined with crushed red velvet, in the manner of thrones. Charles waited for the Queen to sit and then took the second chair.

"I'd no idea there were tunnels beneath Whitehall," he began.

"Didn't you? It's a very old system, built by the Stuarts, or so Reggie says. And they lead to some lovely little oubliettes. You'll want a map, I'm sure. This is part of the section that connects with Queen Anne, and from there, one passage ambles off towards Haimsbury House. Well, to the old one, that is. I quite like your new house, Charles. What's its name again?"

"King's Meadow Court," the Duke replied.

"That's right. It has such a lovely sound to it. King's Meadow Court. Named for the King who resides there?"

He smiled. "Not exactly. As I'm sure you know, we built the new house on land owned by the Branham estate. The tract's been called King's Meadow for centuries. We'll soon be dedicating the house with a ball, Drina. We sent you an invitation. I hope you'll come."

"My secretary takes care of all that, but when is it?"

"May."

"I'm not sure about May, Charles. Surely you remember the Coburg wedding is the nineteenth of April. I hope this grand ball of yours doesn't keep you from coming. After all, you and Beth are top of the guest list."

"I've not forgotten, dear. Our ball is the sixth of May. That gives us plenty of time to return from Coburg and have a short rest before we celebrate. And our absence gives the staff time to prepare the new house without having us under foot."

"The sixth?" she asked, her small mouth sweetly pink. "But the Branham fête is always in early May. You are having it this year?"

"Beth would never cancel the fête, you know that; not unless dire circumstances arose. No, we'll enjoy the ball, and leave for Branham the following day. Say you'll come."

"To both?" she asked, her eyes sparkling mischievously.

"Yes, dear. To both. The ball and the fête. You are family, after all."

"So I am. How nice. I shall have to consult my diary, but I can give you a provisional yes, if that's all right. Tell me, now that you've moved into King's Court, what do you plan to do with the old house? It's not yet fifty years old and considered a very fine example of neoclassical architecture."

"That's true, but the old house has secrets I prefer to remain hidden, Drina. I've not decided how best to use it. We're considering creating a college."

"A college? For what purpose? Whom will you educate?"

"Future ICI and inner circle agents, most likely. It would be a college of spies, I suppose," he laughed.

Drina laughed as well. "My dear, that makes perfect sense! Your family have always served England as spies. And what will you do with Queen Anne? Will you continue to use it as ICI offices?"

"No," he answered. "Beth loves that old home, as does our Chief Inspector Baxter. We plan to return Queen Anne to its original purpose, as the London residence for the Branham heir. Officially, it still belongs to Beth, but one day, when Beth and I are gone, Robby can use it as he pleases."

"May that day be many decades in the future, my dear. Tell me," she continued with an endearing smile, "have you arranged for Robby's future bride yet? It's never too early to think about matches. I could recommend several girls who are two or three years old at present. Many are Scottish, and all have impeccable family lineages. Seriously, Charles, you must plan ahead. After all, you're founding a dynasty."

Talk of dynasties and kingships always made Sinclair uncomfortable. Only six years earlier, he'd been a commoner, or so he believed. He knew no title other than Superintendent with the Metropolitan Police. Back then, he lived simply, in a modest terraced home on the north side of Whitechapel. Now, he could legally claim hundreds of noble titles, including Duke, Prince and Shadow King. Sometimes, the incredible speed at which his life had altered left Charles's mind reeling a little, but he tried very hard to keep a level head; always remembering the house in Whitechapel and the people who lived there.

"Well?" she prompted him. "You're lost in thought, my dear. What about a bride for Robby? And Georgianna, Jamie, and Connor will need matches, too. One cannot leave such an important thing to chance. I've given similar advice to Lord Aubrey, regarding his children. Ian will require a bride, and little Abigail will need a proper husband." Then, she grew more serious. "It is quite awful about their second son. Just six days old and gone with no warning. I cannot imagine it, Charles. I really can't. I never lost my children as babies, but I have lost three adult children now, and know that sort of pain. I imagine, losing an infant is different. I understand Paul's taken his wife to Breitenfurt. Is that right?"

"Yes. Henry MacAlpin thinks Delia will heal better there, away from the London house and the rooms where it happened. She's in a very bad way, Drina. Her spirit's utterly broken."

"As any mother's would be," answered the Queen. "I understand Elizabeth went along to keep Paul and Cordelia company. Did the earl return with Beth?"

"No, he stayed with Delia to help her settle."

Drina grew quiet again, her lined face somewhat haunted. "Yes, that should help. Husbands make a world of difference. But let's discuss children and all that when we've more time, all right?"

"I am ever and always at your disposal, though I'm still mystified as to why I'm here," said the Duke.

"Yes, I imagine you are. Reggie most likely dragged you away from your breakfast table, too. I apologise for not warning you, Charles, but I've several items on the agenda. One reason for our meeting comes from something I learnt only last night. We shouldn't be more than half an hour, but in case you haven't eaten, I asked my staff to send down a few bits and bobs."

"Then we're to have a tea party whilst discussing this last-minute news?" he asked with a raised brow.

"That and a few other things. Besides, I enjoy taking tea with you, Charles."

"And I with you. Shall I pour?" he asked lifting a red velvet cosy from a white-and-gold china pot. "Two sugars?"

"Three, my dear, and a whisper of milk."

He prepared the cups and handed one to Drina. Sinclair took a sip of his. "Branham Blend."

"Of course! I seldom drink anything else these days," the Queen answered. "Beth was kind enough to ask Mrs. Stephens to send me the recipe, which I passed on to my chef with the caveat that he mustn't share it with anyone else. No doubt, he has, but then that's how it generally goes. Trust is seldom honoured these days. There are only a few people I trust implicitly, Charles, and you are at the top of that very short list."

He smiled. "Is my Uncle James also at the top?"

"Oh, yes! James Stuart is tied with you for first place. Now, talking of your uncle, it was he insisted we meet down here."

"James suggested the tunnels?"

"He suggested both the meeting and the location. James said I should tell you about your family's greatest secret. Hence, this very private chamber."

"Funny, how often our family secrets include some underground facility or tunnel," replied the Duke. "Has this secret anything to do with my new home?"

"No, not directly, but these tunnels run beneath parts of all your properties. As I said, they connect Whitehall to Queen Anne House and from there to Queen Anne Mews. One unfinished section runs beneath Haimsbury Drive and comes out near King's Woods."

"Which is on the north edge of our new estate."

"Precisely. An unfinished section sits directly beneath King's Court."

"It does? My architect said nothing about that, and the home's name is King's *Meadow* Court," he corrected her.

"Not so, my dear. You call it that, but everyone else knows it as *King's Court*, which I think is much more fitting. According to Reggie, King's Court is how the house is listed in the House of Lords registry and in Westminster's archives. Therefore, that name is the official one."

"Might the House of Lords entry be written in Sir Reginald's handwriting?"

"Probably," she replied with a sweet giggle.

"He's a bit of a meddler," Charles said with a smile of his own.

"Of course, he is. Parsons is an efficient and much needed meddler, and I should be lost without him. And the tunnels?"

"What of them?"

"I wondered if you might extend them one day?" she asked. "They're yours, Charles."

"Mine?"

"Yes, of course! The system was commissioned by James I, one of your Stuart ancestors!"

"I take it you mean James VI?"

Drina laughed; another sweet giggle that made all the dry wrinkles vanish for a moment. "Ah, yes, your Uncle James is a stickler on that point. The Scottish viewpoint supersedes all others. Let's say *England's* first King James ordered the tunnels built."

"Fair enough."

"Originally, they were meant to connect Whitehall Palace to the Queen's home, now called Queen Anne House, of course. I believe the first tunnels followed the course of an older branch of the Tyburn. Later, after that dreadful civil war, Charles II expanded the system, presumably as a redoubt. I've read he also used them for parties."

"That explains the chandeliers."

"Yes, doesn't it?" laughed Drina. "But beyond parties, he wanted a comfortable hiding place in case of a second uprising from the Commons. There's a warren of rooms down here. One has a deep well with surprisingly clean water, another serves as a cold storage larder—which by the way is kept stocked with smoked meats and cheeses. There's even a wine cellar with some very fine vintages. Albert and I hosted several lovely parties down here."

"What about fresh air? How is that circulated?" asked the mathematician, always thinking of logistics.

"We're breathing now, aren't we?" asked Drina. "Reggie can show you a schematic, if you wish. The tunnels include a series of shafts that lead up to the street. It's remarkably pleasant down here. The rooms stay warm in winter and cool in summer. But I didn't bring you down here for a lesson on London history and topography. As I said, it's to tell you a family secret. I wonder though, might I have another cup of tea and a biscuit first?"

"Of course," he told her, standing to fetch a plate of pastries. "I could invade those finely stocked cellars, if you wish."

"Now, that is a tempting thought, but not today. However, when you do venture down there, you'll find a cask of '36 Drummond Reserve. It's the last I have, I'm afraid, so I've been saving it."

"I'll have a few casks sent over."

He filled their cups, added milk and sugar, and returned to the chair with the pastry plate. She took two biscuits. Charles chose a scone. "And this secret?" he asked, as he sliced the scone open.

"Do you see that table?" she asked, pointing to a long oak table; four feet in height, eight feet in length. The turned legs were carved with gilded lions, and the draping that covered it was fine silk velvet, dyed a deep blue and embellished with the royal *VR* cipher in gold thread. The draping's silhouette formed an intriguing landscape of small hills and valleys.

"I don't suppose it contains casks of Reserve?" he joked.

"If only it did. Nevertheless, the contents are considered quite valuable. Remove the cloth, my dear."

The Duke crossed to the table and pulled away the velvet. Beneath, lay a glittering array of jewelled items: gemstones of every size and shape, each one set in gold, silver, or platinum. He saw crowns and scepters, rings and spoons, bowls and cups; and all of it shone like miniature stars in the chandelier's buttery glow.

"Good heavens, Drina, these are the crown jewels!" Haimsbury exclaimed. "Why on earth would you bring them down here? And why aren't there guards standing over them?"

She laughed, her blue eyes twinkling. "Are they?"

"Are they what?" he asked, dumbfounded.

"Are they the crown jewels?"

Charles stared at the Queen, sea-blue eyes contemplative and still as he considered the question. "I don't know what you mean. How could they be anything else? I'll admit, I've never seen you wear most of these items, but I had the pleasure of viewing the jewels as a collection once; years ago, when I served as overseer for Scotland Yard during your '87 Jubilee. The Tower Jewel House was opened up to tourists, and the collection put on display over the summer. My team kept watch for anarchists and thieves."

"Ah, you were Superintendent St. Clair, then, I suppose?"

"Yes, and we took every precaution. Anarchy was on the rise even then, and we feared a foreign agent might steal them."

"I'm sure everyone thought that," she answered, a smile tugging at her lips. "It's a mercy no one dared try. The last thing we want is a thief uncovering the truth of those jewels."

"What truth?" he asked, looking up from the glittering display of wealth.

"I think you'd best sit down again, my dear. This may come as a shock, particularly as you were put in charge of security back then."

He resumed the throne-like chair, wondering if he shouldn't have looked for one of those casks of whisky. "I'm sitting. What truth don't I know?"

The Queen took another sip of the Branham-blend tea, then set the cup into a floral saucer. "In the middle of the last century, as I'm sure you're aware, England was involved in multiple theatres of war on five continents, all at the same time. Even one war can put a country into financial jeopardy, but five put us into a most precarious position. It was all down to the House of Hanover, of course, which I'm sure you know."

"Yes, I studied all that at Cambridge," he replied. "England joined Prussia, Portugal, and the Holy Roman Empire against France, Saxony, Russia, and Spain."

"It was an awful mess," she told him. "England and France even formed alliances with some of the American Indian tribes. Terrible things were done, Charles. Unspeakable things! Sadly, warfare is a constant in the world of men. And even in the world of women," she added with another pleasing smile. "My ancestors, George II and his son George III, had to oversee it all for the Crown. Most of today's politicians insist it was Hanoverian allegiances that drew us into those awful wars. It's true that England had interests in America and hated losing them, but France and Russia were the real problems. And Russia remains so today. The way they're treating their Siberian prisoners has made Tsar Alexander very unpopular, and rising political competition twixt our two countries will only lead to sorrow. I can see it coming, Charles. Sometimes, it feels as if wars are but pearls on a long string that goes round and round our necks like a beautiful but deadly choker."

"Funny. Beth says that, too," Charles noted. "Did she hear it from you?"

"No," Drina confessed. "I heard it from her, actually. Your wife is quite the philosopher, and she keeps a close eye on politics. You have your spies, but Elizabeth has hers as well, and she draws very clear inferences. If only the pearls on such a strand had value, but sadly, those who love war just make us *think* they do. Beneath the lustre of victory is nothing but worthless paste. Only industrial tycoons benefit from warfare, along with bankers and politicians.

Which brings us to that table," she said, coming round to the point. "England's coffers were nearly empty when George II took us into war. What little money there was dwindled to nothing as we expanded our Army and Navy. Soldiers and sailors require food and clothing, as well as armaments and ships. Those cost money. In 1760, when George III became King, do you know what document he first read?"

"The Magna Carta?" asked the Duke.

"No, dear. The very first document he read and had to sign was the DBA. The Drummond-Branham Agreement. I'm told my great-uncle cursed quite colourfully, when he read it. He asked why the House of Hanover was brought over at all, if England had a more legitimate line of Kings. Apparently, his father and grandfather asked similar questions, but said nothing to him about it."

"I imagine the DBA has surprised many sovereigns," the Duke remarked soberly.

"Not me," she said softly. "James had already told me about it. Sir John Conroy knew as well, which is why he allowed James to visit me at Kensington. Of course, that new King George asked to meet the Dukes of Drummond and Branham. Your uncle's father lived a long and very productive life, as did his father before him. In fact, both houses generally live into their eighties and nineties. I think God smiles on your family, if you must know."

"As he smiles on you, dear Aunt, and may he bring you many more years."

"I hope he does," she whispered. "And though I miss my Albert, I've discovered another kind of happiness in these golden years. And by that, I mean *you*, my dear," she said, taking his hand. "Learning you were alive has brought more joy than I could ever describe." Tears wet her cheeks, and Charles handed her his handkerchief. She used it to dab her eyes. "Haimsbury-Branham," she whispered, looking at the red-and-gold *H&B* monogram. "How lovely. May I keep it?"

"Of course," he whispered. "I'll send you an entire box."

"I'd like that. Ah, but let me return to my story. George III sent for Drummond and had the audacity to *order* him him to take the throne. As you might imagine, such a pompous attitude did nothing to ingratiate the King in Duke Robert's graces. Drummond said no. Then, George turned to Branham, but Duke Richard also declined.

Now, we must be gracious with my poor, Great-Uncle George. After all, he was but twenty-two at the time, and despite first impressions, he and the two dukes formed a lasting friendship. In a very real way, Drummond and Branham mentored the young King."

"No one told me about that," said Charles. "But how are we connected to the jewels on this table? Why bring me here, and how is it a secret?"

She took a sip of tea, then licked her lips; an old habit when thinking through a problem. "I wonder how much to tell you. James said to blurt it all out, but I know your detective's mind chews best on a succession of palatable facts. You like evidence, am I right?"

"Are you offering it?"

A glimmer shone in the robin-egg blues. Drina smiled. "I can see wheels turning in that remarkable brain of yours, Nephew. I haven't lost myself in a maze of memories. Trust me, dearest friend. This moment matters."

"Then, take all the time you want."

"Yes, well, I'll try not to keep you, for I've business waiting for me as well. These debts, I mentioned earlier. They soon multiplied like jackrabbits in spring. George III learnt England was nearly bankrupt, and so he asked the two dukes for advice. The Houses of Drummond and Branham have always made sound choices financially, and that wisdom continues today. James, Elizabeth, and now you, my dear, invest in modern inventions, that are years ahead of everyone else. It's as though you take the pulse of the world before it even beats. As a result, both houses are exceedingly wealthy. King George found the dukes willing to help, not only through financial advice, but with money. Drummond and Branham paid the interest due on England's debt and gave the Crown an additional thirty million pounds to finance the war effort."

"Thirty *million*?"

"Yes, thirty million," she answered. "Sobering, isn't it?"

"Did they give it or lend it?"

Another smile. "And so we come to the items on that table. The financial arrangement began as a simple loan, requiring full payment at the end of twenty years. No interest was ever asked, but collateral was required as security. The government had little of intrinsic value, save land. Branham received over a hundred-thousand acres in

Kent and another thousand acres in and around London. Drummond needed no more land, and so he suggested the crown jewels."

"Wait a moment. Drina, are you going to suggest these were collateral on a loan?" he asked, pointing to the table of wealth.

"Patience. I'm getting to that," she said. "I'll give you a copy of the loan papers, if you wish, but I'm sure the Branham and Drummond archives have their own."

"I'll ask Beth, but if she knows, she's never mentioned it."

"Oh, she knows."

"The debt must have been paid," he reasoned. "After all, the jewels are all here."

Her head tilted and she took up her teacup again. "Are they?"

"What do you mean?"

"Allow me to finish my tale, and it will make sense. As I said, Drummond suggested the crown jewels, but he wanted something else, too. To sweeten the deal, Duke Robert added another ten million, beyond his share of the thirty million. The security he wanted was the Stone of Scone, or as James would say, the Stane o' Scuin."

"The coronation stone? The one used by the Stuarts?"

"The very same. Edward I captured the stone and brought it down to London in 1296 as a spoil of war. And it remained in Westminster Abbey until Duke Robert took it to back Scotland."

"Are you telling me the coronation stone's at Castle Drummond?" asked Charles in amazement. "James has never said a word."

"It's there, but we were never told the precise location; for security purposes, I should imagine. After all, someone in English government might try to steal it back."

"And the loan?" he asked.

"The money was never repaid. When my Uncle William became King, he talked with both dukes and asked them to take the throne, but again both houses refused. The war against Napoleon left our coffers filled with nothing but IOUs, and so the two dukes agreed to extend the loan indefinitely, so long as they retain the jewels and the Stone."

"We *kept* the Crown Jewels?"

"Oh, yes. Branham has most of them," she told him. "Crowns, scepters, hundreds of gemstones, gold, silver, and the original ampulla and spoon for coronations. Drummond holds the Stone of Scone and the St. Edward's Crown."

"The new one or the original?"

"The new one. Cromwell and his lot melted down the first crown and most of the original coronation jewels. Charles II had them remade, and at a very high cost I might add. He modelled the coronation crown on St. Edward's, as he did the scepter, spurs, orb, staff, and sword. It's a mercy Branham took possession of them, for in 1841, the Grand Storehouse, which is next to the Jewel House as you'll remember, caught fire. Those who risked their lives to rescue the jewels had no idea the gold, silver, and a few of the smaller stones are real, but nearly all the gems are glass."

"Which would have burnt or melted."

"Most likely, yes. To this day, the forty-million-pound loan has never been repaid. Most in government think the jewels you guarded are real and locked safely in the Jewel House, but nearly all are imitation. Very fine imitations, mind you, and only a top jeweller could tell the difference. Nevertheless, they are imitation. I learnt the truth shortly after signing the DBA. James and I grew up together, as you know. He and I talked about the loan shortly after I became Queen, and I asked him where the Stone might be. He just smiled in that endearing way of his."

"Yes, I know that look."

"Then I asked if he knew about the jewels, and again I got that darling smile," said the Queen. "To this very day, I've no idea where any of it is."

"Drina, why are you telling me this?" asked Haimsbury.

"Because James said I should. He could have told you, of course, but he thought it should come from me. I'm not getting any younger, and with that bombing at Greenwich last month—well, anything could happen. I leave for Luxembourg tomorrow, and one never knows if travel might go badly. I wanted to make sure you heard all this from me. Not in a letter, but from my own mouth."

"Nothing will happen to you, Drina, I promise. I've assigned men to ride with you to Luxembourg. Beth and I will meet you in Brussels and ride with you all the way to Coburg. We'll all watch your grandchildren get married."

"Yes, I know," she whispered. "I'm glad you're going to the wedding, Charles. And so are Nicholas and Wilhelm."

"Prince Nicholas and Kaiser Wilhelm?"

"Oh, yes. They look up to you, almost as an uncle."

"I enjoy their company," he said. "They're deep thinkers."

"Time moves so quickly."

Charles reached for her hand. She wore black lace gloves, but he could feel her cool, papery skin beneath the crochet. "Drina, is there something you're not saying?"

She dabbed at her eyes again, for they'd begun to fill with tears. "You're very dear to me, Charles. I so wish you'd take the throne."

"As I've already told you, I have no desire for..." he began, but she held up a hand and shook her head.

"My dear, I know what you're going to say. You protest and demur at any suggestion you become King, but surely you've noticed the rising tide of public sentiment that supports that very thing?"

"I try to ignore it. The papers carry such stories nearly every day. Are you behind those?" he asked.

"No, dear. Your popularity is entirely due to your own actions and your own self. It's nothing to do with me. The people of England love you, and they love Beth as their own dear Duchess."

"She loves them in return, but the people will always love you, Drina. Always." The Queen began to cry again. "What is it, dear? Have I said something to hurt you?"

"Of course, not," she answered, blowing her nose. "Charles, my dear, you are a tonic to my old heart! Just wait until you're my age. If a woman, who's less than half your own age, ever calls you darling, it will touch your heart as well."

"Only if that woman is also my daughter," he answered carefully. "And I'm always happy to call you darling. Six years ago, I never imagined sitting here, with the Queen of the British Empire, having such a conversation."

She giggled; the strange mood having passed. "Neither did I, my dear. Neither did I! Ah, I do feel better for telling you all this, Charles. But let me tell you the rest of my news, then we'll ring for Parsons. He'll escort you back through the tunnels to Whitehall. I imagine you entered through the Foreign Office. Or did he choose Scotland Yard's door?"

"The Yard. Parsons thought it fitting and even placed emphasis on the *Scotland* part of the name. I've known about that locked office since I became a detective. We used to joke about it, wondering what secrets lay behind the mysterious, locked door. I never realised it was the entrance to a system of tunnels."

"You'll be given a key to that door tomorrow. Now that the Yard's moved to its new headquarters, I imagine the entrance will need to be watched."

"I'm told the Yard's mews will remain for the present. And I'm happy to say Yard activities no longer concern me. The despatch boxes you insist I receive each day contain plenty work as it is. Wait, you mentioned something else. What else did you wish to tell me, dear?"

"Dear?" she giggled, her cheeks pinking again. "I shall have to tell Beth, if you keep offering me such pleasant endearments."

"She already knows and approves."

"Does she? Yes, well, she is my god-daughter, after all. But to this other thing. I've heard troubling news regarding a possible alliance of certain German and American organisations. Avian groups, I mean. One black, the other white. Is this true? Should I be concerned about it?"

"If you're referring to Blackstone and America's White Council, I'm not sure," he explained. "Redwing still keeps offices in Chicago and New York, but the White Council appear to be overcoming them through their own brand of mergers."

"Mergers?"

"Violent takeovers," explained Haimsbury, "Not civil, corporate alliances, but open warfare."

"And will these wars spill blood onto our streets?"

"That is a constant worry," he told her, "but let me handle it."

"Yes, of course. You will tell me, if you learn anything that affects my family, won't you? Especially, if there are any birds planning to attend the wedding next month?"

"I promise, Drina."

She grew quiet for a few minutes. He could see worry in her eyes; they clouded into grey-blue orbs, rimmed in sagging flesh. Alexandrina Victoria was mortal, after all.

"Drina, we can handle this," he said, taking her hand again. "I will not allow anyone to harm you or your loved ones."

"Yes, I know," she whispered, "but I'm worried about something else. I asked if these birds might be flying together. The reason is because of a letter I received from Emperor Franz Josef."

"Austria-Hungary's ruler?"

"He rules today, yes, but for how long? These avian anarchists nest everywhere, Charles. They grow and flourish."

"Does the letter say so?"

"Not directly, no, and the message isn't actually for me. He penned a short note to me, but the package contained a second letter, addressed to you."

She reached into a quilted handbag and withdrew a buff-coloured envelope, perhaps six inches by four. "Read this when you are alone. Franz's words are likely to be sensitive. Why else send it to me in a sealed envelope?"

He took the letter and placed it into an inner-jacket pocket, opposite a shoulder holster. "I promise to read it before I talk with James tonight. Drina, do you want us to return the jewels? Shall I try to find the Stone of Scone?"

"Of course, not," she replied. "And I might add that Bertie, my philandering son and heir, has no knowledge of this, nor will he until the day he becomes King. However, should *you* accept the throne, he'd never *need* to know, now, would he?"

Charles sighed, his eyes on the table of gold and imitation gems. "It's really quite remarkable."

"Becoming King?"

"Yes, well, no. I mean the workmanship of the stones is remarkable. They look absolutely real."

"A few of the small ones are real, but not the majority. See the two largest stones, set in the Imperial Crown? Those are the Stuart Sapphire and the Black Prince Ruby. Both are beautiful but made from coloured glass. I should love to see the real ones, but it's unlikely I ever shall. James is Plantagenet and Stuart to his bones, and that ruby's a Plantagenet prize."

"How so?" he asked.

"You don't know the story? Well, Edward the Black Prince won the jewel from Don Pedro of Seville; I think, in 1366. Edward helped to put down a revolt led by Don Pedro's brother; you see. I'm sure Elizabeth could tell you all about. Your wife has a marvellous head for history. The Branham family keep detailed records of all family histories in their archives. And though your wife is generous, she's as staunch a Plantagenet as James, and would never part with that ruby. It's doubtful the Crown will ever see them returned. Unless you take the title, that is."

He finished the tea and returned the cup to its saucer. "Let's talk of other things. I prefer not to consider anything that requires losing you." He kissed her hand and added, "You are England's greatest jewel. We need no other."

The old Queen smiled; her eyes bright with tears. "Charles, you are always so gallant! But promise me you'll consider it. Bertie has no head for ruling, nor does he want to, and with the loss of our darling Prince Eddy, Bertie's heir is now George, and he doesn't want the throne either."

"I promise to consider it, but for the present, the crown of Shadow King is heavy enough."

"I shall take that as a possible *yes*, then," she answered with a wink. "Well, my dear, I should love to stay and share all the family gossip, but I'm afraid I've a meeting with Lord Rosebery in half an hour. The man's as punctual as he is dull. To the extreme on both counts."

The Duke helped her to stand, and then offered a warm hug. The Queen clung to him for a long time, her head against his chest. Charles stroked the silver hair and whispered, "I love you very much, Alexandrina Victoria. All of us do."

"Oh, and I love all of you! Very much! Ah, but I must return to work," she sighed as she left the embrace. "If you'll just ring that silver bell for me, Parsons will come and take me out. Then after, he'll return to guide you."

"You're trusting me with these jewels?"

She laughed. "Oh, my darling, that is quite funny! After all, your family already own the genuine stones."

He rang the handbell. The door opened, followed by the entrance of the man in the Regency suit.

"Ma'am, I take it all is finished and correct?"

"Yes, Parsons, all done. If you'd take me back, Charles will remain until you return. I'm sure he'd appreciate a guide for the return trip."

"Of course, ma'am," said Parsons as he offered the Queen his arm. "Your Grace, I shan't be more than ten minutes. There's whisky in a decanter on the lion table, should you require it."

"I'm content, Parsons. Goodbye, Drina. We'll meet you in Brussels."

Drina smiled. "Promise you'll read the Emperor's letter before you firm up your travel plans. Regardless, I shall see you in Coburg." The Queen and Parsons chatted as they left, passing through a door on the opposite end of the magnificent chamber.

Once alone, Sinclair gazed at the table of precious metals and masterfully crafted paste. Such false gems were created from a type of polished lead glass, tinted with a variety of pigments to simulate coloured stones. Somewhere, the Drummond and Branham families kept watch on the real royal gems. The most important was the Stone of Scone; no doubt, hidden away in some deep Drummond oubliette or priest hole. In a very real way, possessing the coronation stone gave their families even more control over England.

"Why me?" Charles asked aloud. "I'm just a policeman who enjoys mathematics. How did I get here?"

"You are here, because the One wills it," replied a deep voice from beyond the long table. "The Shepherd has led you to this place, Charles Robert. Never forget that."

"Do you often lurk beneath Whitehall?" the Duke asked the Russian prince. "How long have you been standing there?"

"I do not lurk, but come when ordered. And I have been here for quite a while," the angel replied.

"Spying?"

"Watching. You are never alone, Charles Robert."

"So you keep telling me."

"I say it, because it is true," Anatole replied.

"I thought you were out of the country."

"I've been travelling," said the Russian, "but I cannot remain long. Other duties soon take me to Africa."

"Africa? Why?"

"To protect the future," the angel answered in typically vague fashion. "I come now with a warning. In Whitechapel last night, one of my fallen brethren murdered the son of an English earl."

"Is that what's behind those horrible headlines? Which brother? Who?"

"One you have encountered before," replied Romanov. "He sometimes goes by Prince Aleksandr Koshmar, but you will not find him, for he's left London. Be careful, Charles. He is a trickster and hopes to ensnare you by setting out human bait."

"You're saying this Koshmar murdered a man as *bait?* Has this creature no compassion at all?"

"Saraqael detests humans."

"Saraqael," Charles repeated in a deep groan. "That's the devil that murdered my father."

"Indeed," the elohim said, placing a comforting hand on the Duke's shoulder. "This murder in the East is but one move in a very long game. You must follow the clues. Read the Emperor's letter, but a second letter will guide you further."

"Drina only gave me one."

"The second will arrive in today's post. It is from the Lady Adele."

"I don't understand. Della's letter will guide me?" asked the human, but the enigmatic elohim had already vanished.

Alone again, Charles tried to sort through Romanov's cryptic messages. He'd go to Leman Street and talk with Reid. All plans for a day with family had vanished.

Moments later, Parsons returned, his round cheeks pink from the exertion of a brisk walk. The clerk fanned his fleshy face, a smile lighting the pale grey eyes. "I ask you, why are there are so many stairs in these old buildings? I'm glad you and the Duchess installed lifts in all your homes, Your Grace. It's far kinder to ageing knees. Shall we go, or do you wish to linger a while and get to know the items on this table?"

"If you're referring to the coronation regalia, I prefer another head wear that crown, Parsons. But should we leave them here? Unguarded?"

Parsons laughed. "Very droll, sir. No, you needn't worry. Two of Lord Carrington's men are on their way. They'll return it all to the Jewel House. As I'm sure you're aware, Carrington is Her Majesty's Lord Chamberlain; though his assistant, Lord Kresmore, generally does the real work."

"I've not heard of Kresmore."

"Few have, sir. He's a newly titled viscount. He's Lord Carrington's cousin by a second marriage. Kresmore's a fine young man. He loves the Lord and the Queen, in that order. You know, sir, you might consider him for your own *circle* of friends."

Just then, footsteps echoed along the floor of the deep chamber. Charles wondered if Anatole had returned, but the boots belonged to a human. He carried a silver candlestick.

"Morning, Sir Reggie," said the slender gentleman.

"It's good to see you, Lord Kresmore. All is well?" asked Reggie.

"All is well, sir, and all is glorious," came the reply.

"Lord Kresmore, allow me to introduce you to His Royal Highness, Duke Charles of Haimsbury and Branham. I'm sure you've seen His Grace at the House of Lords now and then."

The young man bowed. "It's a very great honour, sir. We all look forward to your weekly reports in the Lords. I know you and Lord Aubrey are cousins. Please, offer the earl my deepest sympathy on the tragic death of his son. The baby's name was Liam? Is that right?"

"Liam David Andrew Robert Stuart," replied Haimsbury. "Poor lad died at just six days old. Just before Christmas."

Kresmore shook his head. "Tragic! I've known the Lady Cordelia since we were children, sir. Truly, I cannot imagine how such a thing might affect her."

"It's caused very great distress," replied Charles tactfully. "I'll convey your condolences to Delia and my cousin, when I see them next."

Charles knew it could be weeks before he saw Cordelia Stuart again. Liam's death had sent Delia into a deep and troubling depression. After weeks of consultation with Henry MacAlpin, Paul agreed to send his wife to Breitenfurt, a special retreat near Vienna. The family hoped to keep the truth from the public, but such truths had a habit of being discovered.

"You know, Kresmore, it occurs to me that you and His Grace have a great many things in common," said Reggie. "Perhaps, you and His Grace might talk again soon?"

"I'd like that very much," said Kresmore eagerly.

"Contact my secretary. His name's Gerald Pennyweather. He works from Queen Anne House," the Duke told the viscount. "If Parsons insists we spend time together, then I must pay attention."

The young man smiled and bowed again. "Thank you, sir. I'll write to Mr. Pennyweather today."

Parsons and Haimsbury left through the double doors and passed into the tunnel. “How are your children doing, sir?” Reggie asked the tall peer.

“Well and healthy. Doctors tell me Robby will exceed my height one day. Georgie will be petite like her mother. Both are bright as buttons! Jamie and Connor have their mother’s eyes, but they’ve inherited my height, it seems. They and Adele are the true jewels in my crown, Parsons.”

“I hear your crown will soon have another gem, sir.”

Sinclair turned towards the clerk in mild surprise. “How on earth did you find out? Beth only just learnt about it herself a few weeks ago.”

“Then my information is correct?” the inquisitive Parsons asked with a cherubic grin.

“Yes, but who told you?”

“I cannot divulge sources, sir.”

Charles began to laugh. “Well, then you should come work for me. Yes, Beth’s with child again. Due in late October, if not sooner. My wife’s already blossoming.”

“Perhaps, it’s another set of twins?” suggested Parsons.

“Do your mysterious sources tell you that, too?”

“Just intuition. We go right up here.”

“How much farther?”

“Not too far. Oh, but do forgive me, sir. I’d completely forgotten! You had a very bad experience in a similar place to this, didn’t you?”

“Yes,” answered Charles softly. “Quite bad.”

Sinclair had come to detest tunnels. They reminded him of the tortuous journey through the Time Maze in late ‘89. He’d spent nine weeks there as a captive; six of those weeks in a mysterious sleep induced by Alphonse Theseus, and three weeks, finding his way through the horrid Time Maze. After reaching the centre and confronting Legion, he’d somehow escaped, but Charles had no memory of how.

In truth, he recalled very few details of his captivity; though, he sometimes dreamt of tunnels and alternative versions of his life. The nightmares always left him nervous and sweating on waking, and he dreaded sleeping.

After his rescue on the seventeenth of October, the Duke lay in a strange and lingering sleep that lasted over a fortnight. When he awoke, the first sight his weary eyes beheld was his wife's face. Charles had somehow known Beth sat nearby, and that she held his hand and read to him. He vaguely remembered hearing her play the piano and singing, but other times, she wept and fervently prayed.

Much later, Charles learnt that Anatole had placed him into the limbo sleep to give his mind and body time to rest. The ordeal had taken a heavy toll on Sinclair, physically as well as mentally. He'd lost more than two stone, but Branham's cook, Mrs. Stephens, soon helped the Duke regain the weight through a regimen of tasty, high-calorie food. Once the Duke grew strong enough, Paul Stuart helped to restore his cousin's lost muscle by sparring with Charles each day, followed by running through the estate's bridle paths. As a result, Sinclair was now fitter and more muscular than before, requiring slight alterations to all his suits and shirts. His dear friend, Martin Kepelheim, enjoyed every minute of the task.

Parsons allowed the Duke to walk in silence; as if the astute clerk recognised Sinclair's need for it. Eventually, the government official cleared his throat. "Tis a sullen sort of place, don't you think, my lord? After your experience, I imagine you prefer to remain above ground."

"I'm all right," the Duke replied. "Reggie, might you know a man named Alphonse Theseus?"

"The alienist? Of course, sir. Why?"

"I've been trying to find him for over five years, but he's vanished. Another man runs Pollux Institute now, and all three locations of Theseus's private practice have shut down, with no forwarding address."

"Have you spoken to Prince Anatole?" asked Parsons.

"Just now?" Sinclair asked.

"I'm not sure what you mean, sir."

"Never mind. Yes, I've talked with Romanov about Theseus. His answers are typically vague, implying Dr. Theseus will reappear when the time is right."

"Then, I'm sure he will, sir."

As they turned again, Charles decided to ask about the murder Anatole mentioned. "What can you tell me about this crime in the East?"

"Which crime, sir?"

"A murder that may involve an unnamed peer."

"Ah, *that* crime," Reggie said, his voice lowering. "There isn't much information yet. Do you plan to investigate?"

"If a peer's involved, I shall have to," Charles answered.

"Be sure you're armed when you go, my lord. My sources say the people of Whitechapel are angry about the rise in crime there, and some are quite violent. Those same sources tell me Romania's Ambassador Balaçeanu's been called to Scotland Yard to answer questions. One can only speculate as to why."

"It looks as though my family outing is well and truly cancelled," Charles sighed.

The Duke was right. Before the hour was out, Charles Sinclair would be standing over a body in Leman Street's dead room.

CHAPTER TWO

Breitenfurt Retreat – Outside Vienna

Paul Stuart had never liked goodbyes. After years spent as a spy, pretending to be someone else, the Scotsman rarely had to announce his departure. The thought of leaving his sensitive, broken wife dragged at his heart like a millstone round the neck of a drowning man. Following Beth's departure, he'd spent five extra days at the retreat, hoping to ease his wife's transition to a new and healthier season. Now, he sat in the office of Dr. Vano Pyramis, the man he hoped would bring Cordelia back to him.

The earl rose as the physician entered. He shook the shorter man's hand. "Thank you for meeting with me, Dr. Pyramis. I've a few final questions before I leave."

Vano Sándor Pyramis grew up in Lucerne, the only child of an English baronet and a Romani ballerina. He was youthful for forty, with wavy black hair and intelligent brown eyes. His beard was dark and neatly trimmed into a stylish Van Dyke. He wore glasses to read. Pyramis preferred fashionable clothing with high, starched collars and narrow ties. Paul recognised the look as Oxbridge and scholarly, yet the earl suspected the man's true essence went far beyond expensive cologne and bespoke silk suits.

Paul prayed his instincts were wrong.

"Please, Lord Aubrey, sit," said Pyramis. "I promise to address all your questions, but I should like to ask a few of my own, if you don't mind. Tea? Coffee?"

"No, thank you," the earl answered as he took the nearest guest chair.

The doctor sat behind a large, oak desk. The enormous piece of furniture must have cost hundreds of pounds. It was carved on three sides, with woodland scenes from Teutonic mythology: imps, faeries, satyrs, dwarfs, and sprites. Standing above these lesser creatures, the artist created a nebulous leader, sporting curved horns and a forked tail. This leader's body looked unfinished. Paul struggled to make out a face, but the head seemed to move and shift, even as he looked at it.

I'm tired, he told himself. *I need a good night's sleep.*

"I see you've noticed my desk. Interesting, isn't it?" asked Pyramis.

"I think it's very strange imagery for a man of science."

The alienist laughed and poured himself a cup of coffee. He dropped in four sugar cubes and began to stir. "I have a sweet tooth, inherited from my father. My mother eats very few sweets. She's a retired ballerina and says sugar ruins the figure and causes feet to ache. My feet ache regardless of how much sugar I consume. Strange images? Yes, I suppose they are, but the artist was one of my patients, so I could not refuse the gift. The desk represents his dreams, you see. They plagued him right up to the last."

"The last?"

"Oh, yes, to the very last. The poor man died quite unexpectedly. His name was Heinrich Müller. I've never told his wife, but it's my belief that Müller died of fright."

"Fright? Is that even possible?"

"Entirely possible. Müller was an excellent carpenter with a fine talent, but he suffered from night terrors. I thought allowing him to carve the desk might help to externalise the bad dreams. Sadly, it is my one failure, which is why I keep the desk here. It is a daily reminder of my own limitations. Now, then, how may I ease your mind?"

Paul sighed. Where to start? The desk and the peculiar story only amplified his suspicions, yet a part of him longed for resolution. He'd lived with Cordelia's illness for years, but her periods of lucidity had become so very rare now, he feared she might hurt herself or their two children. Henry MacAlpin insisted Vanu Pyramis could work miracles.

If only, he could.

Aubrey took a deep breath. "Since we arrived here ten days ago, you've spent many hours with my wife, but I've had little opportunity to speak with you in private. You did talk with my friend, Henry

MacAlpin. He speaks highly of your ability to plumb the depths of human thought. How did you and Henry meet?"

Of course, Paul already knew how Pyramis and MacAlpin met; at least, he knew Henry's version. It was an old spy trick. Paul hoped Pyramis would verify MacAlpin's account. *Am I looking for a reason to take my wife home? Perhaps. But before I leave, I must know she's safe in his care.*

The man smiled, apparently oblivious to his guest's inner thoughts. The alienist's brown eyes crinkled at the corners, making him look wise and slightly older. "I like Henry very much, Lord Aubrey. He's a genuinely kind man and a very fine alienist. How did we meet? It was in Paris, at a conference on hypnosis and the Breuer method. This was—oh, let's see, '92? '93? No, wait. It was definitely 1892. Are you familiar with Josef Breuer?"

"A little," Paul answered. "I enjoy reading about scientific advancements. I've studied a variety of disciplines, including alienism. Dr. Breuer discounted traditional hypnosis in favour of a milder, cathartic approach."

"You've read his treatise on hysteria?"

"Not entirely, no, though I understand the basics."

"I can give you a copy, if you like. You'll find it quite insightful. You know, Breuer lives nearby, in Vienna. He often comes here to talk with our guests."

"With the patients, you mean?"

"You might call them that, Lord Aubrey, but we see them as guests. Each is free to leave, if he or she wishes, and each is special. Back to Henry, though: he and I happened to sit next to one another at the Paris debates. They settled nothing. In fact, it all ended in a catfight, I'm sorry to say. I fear, the behaviour of my colleagues did little to bolster the public's view of alienism. Henry thought it all amusing, and we spent the next few evenings exchanging ideas. He's a good sort of chap; a competent sailor in a sea of scholastic pirates."

"I'm sure Henry would find the metaphor amusing," said Aubrey. "I've known him since childhood. He and I are cousins. Tell me, what is your view on hypnotism?"

The doctor took a sip of coffee, then added another cube of sugar and a dash of cream. "Still too bitter. Now, the term hypnosis is overused, and its precise mechanism inside the brain remains misunderstood. I find Breuer's relaxation method helpful. Are you asking if I plan to use hypnosis with Lady Aubrey?"

"Yes. Do you?"

"At present, I cannot really say," Pyramis answered with a practised smile. "My initial impression leads me in that direction, but time will tell, as they say. Time is an all-important factor in the equation of Life, don't you think?"

"You might say Time is Life," Aubrey answered.

The alienist's smile widened, and the dark eyes blinked twice. "I wonder, if Life would continue without Time? Another philosophical discussion, yes? Now, Lord Aubrey, I should like to ask you some questions. Is that agreeable?"

"Of course. Ask me anything."

"And if these questions are, shall we say, personal?"

"Doctor, my wife's welfare is of paramount importance. If asking personal questions will help, then ask all you wish."

Pyramis leaned forward. The disarming smile vanished, replaced by a frank coldness that startled the earl.

"Your wife's welfare is paramount to you? Yet, you arrived here three days after Lady Cordelia. It was Lord Salperton and the Duchess Elizabeth who brought your wife here. Isn't that so?"

"No, it isn't," said Paul, his voice hinting at irritation. "I travelled the entire way with my wife, Henry, and Beth. The journey took us three long days, during which time my wife slept very little."

"Yet..."

"Allow me to finish," the Scotsman insisted. "As I say, I rode with them until we reached Vienna, but as soon as we arrived, I received an urgent telegram. It was sent by England's War Office two days after we left. The telegram instructed me to follow up on a diplomatic issue. That is why you didn't see me the first few days."

"Ah," Pyramis said. "I've heard that you are a spy, Lord Aubrey."

"If I were, I wouldn't tell you. That's how spying works, Dr. Pyramis."

The other man laughed; the brown eyes flecked with points of black. "Well put! But I confess, it was your wife who mentioned your covert duties. Lady Cordelia isn't indiscreet, just proud of you, sir. She says England relies on your remarkable abilities. I'm sure it helps to ease her mind, when you're away."

"I try very hard to avoid leaving her, Dr. Pyramis. And I came here as quickly as possible."

"Seventy-two hours to correct a diplomatic problem?"

Paul's first instinct was to argue with the frustrating man, but he could hear an echo of his father's voice, speaking inside his head: *Son, hold your temper. You must control yourself, lest your enemy control you.*

The earl took a deep breath and pictured a block of ice. An old trick to redirect his thoughts. He counted to five before saying, "You're right, though I'm not permitted to tell you what I did in those three days. Doing so would place both England and Austria in perilous positions. I've explained it to my wife. Delia understands."

"I see," the other said in a smug sort of whisper. "Your wife has lost, how many children?"

"Surely, you know the answer, Doctor. You've been with her for ten days."

"Yes, but I wish to hear it from you."

The tenderest part of Paul's heart ached when thinking about his children. Telling a stranger about the ones who died felt like a stab to that tender heart. Paul pictured the ice block. *One, two, three, four, five.*

"We've lost three," he told Pyramis, managing to keep his voice neutral. "Two miscarriages and a cot death. Liam was six days old."

"When did the losses occur?" asked the alienist, who'd begun to take notes.

"She gave birth to our first child, Ian, in October of '89. He was healthy, though nearly born breech. Delia conceived again in mid-1890. She suffered the first miscarriage in January of '91."

"At how many months?"

"Seven. A little boy with curling blonde hair."

"Did you name him?"

"Of course. James David Paul," replied the earl, that block of ice still sitting firmly inside his mind. "He's buried in our family cemetery."

"Your next child was born safely?"

"Actually, there may have been a very early miscarriage in August of '91. Delia experienced no signs of pregnancy, yet she suddenly became quite ill and bled profusely. She took to bed for several weeks afterward. It was then she began to suffer from the old visions again."

"August '91, you say?" he asked, scribbling notes.

"Yes. I remember, because it was about that same time Elizabeth and her husband announced she was with child again."

"Again? How many children do the Sinclairs have?"

"Four. The twins, Robby and Georgianna, are nearly five now. Eleven months later, Beth delivered a second son, Jamie Sinclair. Then, there's Connor, the baby. My son was born about the same time as Jamie. He and the twins have formed a very close bond with our Ian."

"Tell me about Ian. What sort of boy is he? Active? Artistic? Does he favour you or Lady Cordelia?"

"He favours us both. Light auburn hair and blue eyes. He's tall and strong for his age. Active? Very. He's only four, yet rides a Welsh pony with ease. He'll be a grand horseman one day."

"And your daughter? What of her?"

"Abigail?" Paul responded with a proud smile. "She's my sweet lassie, Dr. Pyramis. Abbie's a beautiful combination of Delia and my late mother. Fair hair, blue eyes, and my wife's perfect nose and mouth. Ian loves his sister dearly. He takes very good care of her."

"When was Lady Abigail born?"

"November of '92."

"And Liam?"

The ice block shivered, ready to melt. Paul's internal struggle must have shown, for the doctor made a note of it. "His full name was Liam David Andrew Robert Stuart," the earl whispered. "He was born five weeks early. He seemed healthy and ate well at first. He interacted with us and had a strong grip. Then, on the fourth day, he started to decline."

"Decline how?"

"He stopped eating, developed a high fever, and slept most of the time. We had round the clock medical staff, but on day six, Ian passed to Jesus."

Ames's pen stopped. "To Jesus?"

"Yes. Our son is with the Lord now."

The alienist made a quick note. "Interesting. Tell me, does Lady Cordelia share your faith?"

"Of course, she does. Don't you?" he asked boldly.

Pyramis set down the pen and steepled his hands as though commencing a classroom lecture. "I believe in science, Lord Aubrey. I do not discount the possibility of worlds beyond human senses. After all, my mother is Magyar. Hungarian gypsy. Her father was a *táltos;* what you and I might call a shaman. He had six fingers on each hand, and six toes on each foot. When such a child is born, the elders proclaim him a *táltos.*"

"Six fingers?"

"Oh, yes. My mother's hands and feet are normal, as are my own, I'm pleased to say. Grandpapa Lakatos performed many strange rituals, and my mother, Magda, is a fortune-teller. She can read your palm and tell your future. She'd be right almost a hundred percent of the time. I asked if I might study her powers for a future project, but she refuses to teach me. I am not *táltos*, you see."

"What about your father? Is he a man of faith?"

"Ah, now that answer would fill an entire book, Lord Aubrey. My father climbed the ladder of Western Enlightenment. You probably know he was a baronet. 4th Lord Pyramis."

"You speak of him in the past tense. Did you inherit the title?"

"Very perceptive. Yes, my father died last year, and I took the title, but seldom use it. English baronetcies mean very little in Viennese society. My mother remarried recently, and she's retired from the ballet. But she still reads palms and takes spirit journeys, as she calls them. Her new husband is climbing the ladder of influence, just like my father did."

"Is he also English?"

"Scottish. Well, very nearly Scottish. He's from Cumbria. Sir Colin Davies. He's handsome enough and tolerates my mother's quirky behaviour. They live in London. Magda loves to conduct seances and has many high-society clients. You should invite her to your home sometime." Pyramis smiled in a knowing sort of way as he poured another cup of coffee. "You're certain you don't want any?"

"I had three cups at breakfast. Thank you."

The alienist stirred sugar and cream into the refilled cup. "Who was it first added sugar and cream to this beautiful drink, I wonder? They are such tasty additions. Additives create something new, don't you think, Lord Aubrey? My mother's beliefs rose to new levels after her remarriage. Sir Colin attends meetings at one of those enlightenment societies that my late father so loved. Every morning, at ten on the dot, he and others meet a club on Pall Mall. Sir Colin's visiting Vienna presently. There's a branch of that society here."

"It's an international organisation? Is it religious or philosophical?"

"Both from what I can tell. What is that society called again? It's on the tip of my tongue! They follow all sort of teachings, but lately Sir Colin's been prattling on and on about the writings of Saint Germain."

"Saint Germain?" Paul asked, his voice revealing surprise. "That name has a very dark, even occult history."

"Oh, yes, I'm aware of that. My stepfather finds dark ideas irresistible. He's like a child sometimes. You should meet him. Life of the party! He's become a favourite with many of the Imperial courtiers, but I'm not sure the Emperor approves. They discuss Saint Germain's notions, especially the search for the Elixir of Life. Have you visited the Emperor's court? There are some very peculiar people there; people I should love to examine more closely—get inside their heads."

"I'm familiar with most of the courtiers," Paul answered flatly. "In fact, I spent a great deal of time with Emperor Franz Josef before I came here."

"Ah, well, that explains those three lost days, then," Pyramis said with a wink. "But I wonder if you might believe in Saint Germain's ideals? You're a man of traditional faith, yes?"

"I believe Christ died for our sins."

"Really? What sin did your son commit to require dying so young? Or your living children? Your son and daughter. What sins have they committed that they require saving?"

"Shall we debate the doctrine of original sin, Dr. Pyramis? I'm happy to oblige you, but it could take a few hours—if not days."

"Uh, no," the other responded. "Not today. But tell me, is the Lady Cordelia of similar faith?"

"She is."

"And is she close to Duchess Elizabeth?"

"Very close. They're like sisters, why?"

"Sisters are often jealous of one another, no?"

"I've seen no jealous behaviour twixt them. Only love and compassion."

"Compassion? That's a very interesting word, but I'm glad to hear they're close, for I'd like to invite the Duchess to return for a short stay. Might she and Duke Charles be travelling to Vienna soon? Will they attend the wedding next month?"

"They plan to go," Paul replied warily, "but my family try to keep Charles's movements secret."

"Why is that? Why protect *him* especially?"

"Security reasons," the earl replied, his suspicions growing stronger by the second. "Charles and Beth have been targeted before. Anarchists have struck at many such, high-value people. Only last month, a man set off a bomb at the Greenwich Observatory."

"Yes, but wasn't there another incident? One not reported by the press?"

"Not that I can discuss," Paul answered carefully.

There had been two additional anarchist events: One at Queen Anne House, when a gardener found an explosive in a storage shed. The device hadn't exploded, thanks to bad wiring. A second, much larger bomb was discovered beneath the library windows at Loudain House, where ICI agents kept offices. For reasons unknown, the explosive failed to detonate. God's plans. God's ways. Neither Paul nor Charles had told their wives.

Vano Pyramis kept digging. "Charles Sinclair is an intriguing man, don't you think?"

"He and I are like brothers, Dr. Pyramis. If you intend to speak against him, then..."

"No, no! Not at all!" the alienist exclaimed. "I admire him, as does everyone else, so I understand."

"Charles Sinclair is a rare sort of gentleman."

"He's England's Shadow King, no? An interesting term."

Paul pushed back the chair and stood. "We're done, Dr. Pyramis."

"I've overstepped."

"One might say so, yes. If my wife's to remain here, then you will treat her well. If not, she leaves. Do you understand me? I have friends staying nearby. They will keep careful watch on her. I expect daily letters, written in her own hand."

"Of course, of course, but not the first few weeks. We discourage early outside communication, to allow our guests time to integrate into our community."

"No, Doctor," Paul said flatly. "Delia will write to me whenever she wishes. And you, sir, will report to me twice a week. Is that clear? Twice a week, or she leaves."

Pyramis stood and smiled as though nothing were wrong. "I shall happily comply, sir. The Breitenfurt Retreat is here to serve and heal." He reached for the peer's hand. As they shook, Paul had the unsettling sense he'd sealed a pact with a devil.

"I'll say goodbye to my wife now. Again, I expect regular reports, and she *will* write to me. Anytime she wishes. In her own hand. You will not deny her that basic right. If you fail, my agent will come and remove her."

"We'll make an exception in Lady Aubrey's case, but only if she chooses to write. I shall not force her. And don't worry, Lord Aubrey; your wife will be quite content."

Aubrey left the ground-floor office and climbed two flights up to his wife's suite. Delia was one of twenty-four guests seeking healing in the peaceful surroundings of the retreat's dense woods. His wife's door stood open. Paul could see her sitting on the small balcony. The nearby trees looked close enough to touch. A pretty bluebird sat on an oak branch; its feathery head tilted to one side.

He crossed through and approached quietly, his heart already breaking. "*Mo bhean?*" he called, using the Scottish pet name. "Dee, I have to leave now."

She turned. So often of late, Cordelia Jane behaved as though she barely knew her husband, but now she ran into his arms. "Oh, my darling husband!" she cried happily. "Thank you for bringing me here. Thank you! Henry's right. Oh, yes, he's right! It's like a paradise, isn't it? And everyone here is so nice. May I stay, Paul? Please? Mrs. Fischer said I may. She speaks English very well, as does everyone else. I met a lady from Kent this morning, who knows Elizabeth. Her name's Hermione something or other. She's here to take the waters. I'm told the spring water here is quite miraculous. Have you tried it?"

"No, dear, but I've heard that as well," he told her, holding her close. "I shall miss you, *mo bhean*. Miss hearing you breathe next to me at night, miss your cheerful little face across the breakfast table, miss your laughter, your perfume. Delia, you're my heart and soul. Do you know that?"

She nodded; her cheek pressed against the pearl buttons of his waistcoat. "And you're mine, darling Paul. Promise you'll take care of Abbie and Ian for me. Say their Mama is taking the waters in Vienna and will come home soon." She looked up at him, the light eyes filled with trust. "I shall write every day."

"As will I," he promised. "Darling, if you ever want to come home, if you ever doubt staying here, for any reason, you must write and tell me. I'll be on the very next boat across the channel."

"A boat, three trains, and how many coach rides?"

"I lost count," he smiled. "Four, I think."

"It's a very long trip, isn't it? Will Della write?"

"I'm sure she'll be a faithful correspondent."

"And Charles will come see me, won't he?" she added. "He'll be in Vienna soon, I think. Tell him to come, please."

Aubrey paused, wondering why she might make such a statement. "I'm not sure he's planning to visit Vienna, but if he does, I'm sure he'll come see you."

"Oh yes, he's coming," she said matter-of-factly. "The angel said he was. Angels never lie."

He stroked her cheek, wondering if she'd had another of her visions. "No, the holy angels never lie. Darling, if you're ever afraid or want to come home, send me the code word. Do you remember it?"

"The code? Do you mean the poem?"

"Yes, dear, the poem. Send me that. Just the title will do, and I'll see you're brought home. You're not alone here. I have men nearby, and the embassy in Vienna will keep in touch."

"And there are angels, too. They'll look after me," she said wistfully.

"Yes, darling. There are angels, too."

A tall woman in a blue dress and white pinafore knocked. "Lord Aubrey, your driver says you'll be late, if you don't leave right away."

Paul kissed her sweetly. "Keep these warm for me, all right?" he asked, touching the curve of her upper lip.

"I will," she giggled.

"I'll come see you soon. Write, darling. Promise?"

"I promise," she said. "I love you, Paul."

"I love you, *mo bhean*," he said. "I'll come back soon. I promise."

He left, his heart torn in half, but the earl had vital government business pressing down upon his broad shoulders. He hastened to the ground floor and out the main entrance, where a black landau waited in the crescent-shaped gravel park. The driver spoke in English.

"Rail station, my lord?"

"No, Lambert, take me to the British Embassy."

"Very good, my lord."

Paul left Breitenfurt Retreat behind and headed northeast towards the magical city of Vienna. The team of four horses pulled the coach quickly through the whispering woods. A thick woolen rug lay on the opposite seat. Suddenly, he felt cold to his bones. The earl reached for the blanket, but as his hand touched the wool, he heard a voice speak:

"Pyramis is an odd one, don't you think, Lord Aubrey?"

On the very spot where the crimson rug had rested, sat a tall man, dressed in bespoke finery. He wore lavender gloves and a pinstriped suit. The right hand rested casually atop a silk top hat, whilst the left curved round the handle of a rosewood cane.

"Who are you?" asked Aubrey.

"A friend," the intruder replied in a lilting voice. "Forgive the unannounced visit. It isn't my usual style, but you should be warned about a few things."

"You've brought me a warning? I hope you're come armed with more than that stick, sir; for I don't respond well to threats."

The stranger laughed. He had dark eyes, and shoulder-length ripples of ebony hair. "You are clever! This should be fun."

"Fun for whom?"

"For all involved, I should think, but most particularly me."

"I detect an Eastern origin beneath your smooth words," the earl challenged the visitor. "Russia? No, it's more obscure than that. Transylvania? Moldavia?"

The man's black eyes glinted with flecks of yellow. "Moldavia and Transylvania are fine guesses, but no country is my home, for I travel the entire world. If my accent is unusual, it's because I am unusual."

Paul prayed inwardly. *What do I do, Lord?* The creature had popped into existence out of thin air, meaning he had no native corporeality. Unlike Charles, Paul's experience with otherworld creatures was decidedly limited. He'd been visited by a messenger angel at the Branham fête in '89; and after, an angel supernaturally protected him during an attack on Leman Street, when, a runaway coach—possibly from Hell—tried to kill him. Paul believed the protector angel pulled him out of the real world for a moment. Whilst there, he beheld that same angelic warrior, fighting against an army of black-winged devil birds.

Whose side does this one serve? God or Satan?

"You said you came to warn me," said Stuart to the intruder. "What about?"

"Hmm," mused the opponent. "You're not accustomed to visitations, are you? I bring this warning: War is coming, Lord Aubrey. Your wife and children are at risk. Your entire family are at risk. The chessboard is set. Are you ready for the battle?"

Paul had the sense he'd met the creature before, but he couldn't quite recall the circumstances. Was it the eyes? The cane?

The other smiled and leaned closer. "You're confused, aren't you? You imagine us as fixed points, but we manipulate matter and perception." He removed the gloves, and Paul noticed the creature had six fingers on each hand. "Hear me, Paul Stuart. Your government intends to despatch you to Africa. That is why the Embassy has summoned you. Now, I happen to know who runs that part of the world, and *she* is very territorial. You'll be invited to witness a special ceremony on your last night there. You'll receive a gift, but beware, Lord Aubrey. That territorial ruler I mentioned will use the gift *against* you. If you value your life, then avoid the ceremony. Do NOT go. In fact, I advise you to avoid Africa entirely. Steer clear of Lady Moon."

With that, the strange fellow vanished. On the empty coach seat, he'd left a calling card, printed in white ink on black cardstock:

PRINCE DMITRI KASADYA

TRAVELLER OF THE WORLD

CHAPTER THREE

Leman Street Police Station, Whitechapel

"Chief Inspector Baxter to see His Grace," a tall man told the desk sergeant. To reach the booking desk, Baxter had passed by a long line of angry citizens, and they shouted at him for jumping to the head of the long queue.

"You say you're a detective?" asked the uniformed sergeant, somewhat annoyed.

"As I'm called Chief Inspector, one might assume it were obvious," answered the former butler. Cornelius obliged by showing the sergeant a warrant card. "You can read, I presume?"

"That's a right good joke, sir, but that don't look like a Yard warrant card. Wrong colour."

"It is the correct colour for this organisation, Sergeant. I work with His Grace at the Intelligence Branch, which supersedes Scotland Yard. If you'll kindly call Inspector Reid, he'll vouch for me."

"We got lots o' folks what wants ta talk wi' the inspector, sir, but he's busy just now, which means, you'll have to wait your turn, I reckon. There's a chair by the door. I'll give a shout, when a real detective comes back up."

Baxter had never met this particular policeman before, and so endeavoured to achieve his purpose laterally. "Real detective? I see. And I'm to wait until he comes *up?* Meaning, these real detectives are presently *below* stairs. Thank you, Sergeant. I know the way to the Dead Room."

Cornelius started towards the south stairwell, intending to descend to the morgue, but the persistent desk sergeant grabbed Baxter's right coat sleeve. "I can't let ya do that, sir. As I say, iffin you'll take a seat, I'll call yer name once I get a chance."

"Baxter!" cried a friendly voice from the other side of the lobby area. Inspector Edmund Reid was coming down from his second-floor office, carrying a thick sheaf of papers. He came up to the desk, saying, "Sergeant Calvert, you've never met this remarkable gentleman, but Cornelius Baxter is one of the Duke's finest detectives. Come with me, Neil, I'll take you downstairs myself."

Baxter offered the embarrassed desk sergeant the same, sharply raised brow-and-frown combination, given to many a footman during his years as head butler. "Thank you, Inspector Reid. I'm quite sure Sergeant Calvert will remember me the *next time* I come to the station house. Won't you, young man?"

The chastised policeman gulped a throaty, "Yes, sir."

Neil and Edmund left Calvert to deal with the remonstrance and the unruly crowd, whilst they hastened down the steps to a flagstone floor. "I imagine you're here to meet up with Haimsbury."

"Yes, sir, but as it's officially an IB case, let's refer to him as Superintendent Sinclair."

Edmund smiled. "Always proper and correct, aren't you Neil? I've always respected that. The Superintendent's with Sunders right now. And I apologise for Sergeant Calvert. He's a little flustered this morning. The lad's just taken over the desk and never experienced a full-scale revolt from our citizenry. Unfortunately, he'll soon get used to it. We're down this way now. We've relocated the Dead Room to a larger facility since you were last here."

The two men followed a brightly lit hallway to a set of windowed doors; their wood painted a rich blue. Through the window-glass, Baxter could see a dozen or more uniformed officers and plain-clothes detectives, drinking coffee and talking inside an office. Reid pushed on one of the swinging doors, admitting them to the new Leman Street morgue.

The antechamber office was twenty-by-twenty, with four oak desks and four filled bookcases. A large blackboard was mounted to one wall. A list of current cases was written in a neat hand. Each entry included the victim's name, examining surgeon, and presiding detective. Presently, the chalk list contained twelve names. The present case would make it thirteen.

Neil Baxter had never been a small man, even when young. He'd shot up to six feet by the time he reached sixteen, when he began putting on muscle instead of inches. He had bushy eyebrows, dark eyes, silvering hair, and a barrel chest. Every servant at Branham knew his deep voice, and every member of the Sinclair family loved and respected him. Duke Charles Sinclair had come to rely on Neil's experience and discernment.

The IB detective followed Reid into a second room, lined with bright white wall tiles over a green-and-white floor. A dozen more detectives stood near a stainless-steel table. Around the table's perimeter, ran a two-inch deep channel that directed blood and other fluids into a collection chamber directly beneath. The room smelled of blood, alcohol, and chemicals. A body lay on the dissection table, covered from the groin downwards in cotton draping. The visible skin was a pale, ashy grey. Charles Sinclair stood at the victim's head, next to Anthony Gehlen and Thomas Sunders. Dr. Gehlen held a scalpel in his right hand.

"Glad you could make it," Haimsbury told Baxter. "I hope the crowded streets didn't impede your arrival."

"My coach had to slow at several points, sir, but our Mr. Trout drove. He's more than competent in such situations. Do we know this gentleman's name, sir?"

"You don't recognise him?" asked Edmund Reid.

"Should I?"

"Possibly not, but I assumed you knew everyone in the peerage classes."

"Are you saying he's a lord?" asked Baxter.

"We think he's the son of an earl," explained Charles.

"*Think* is the operative word, sir, for he had no identification papers when found," Reid continued. "A boy reported the crime. Sadly, our desk sergeant failed to enter the child's name, so we're unable to interview him further. When our men reached the scene, they found two victims. One survived; however, he's in poor condition, and we cannot say how long that will prove true."

"The second boy's at the HBH," Charles told Baxter.

"Boy, sir?" asked Neil.

"Both victims are twenty or so. That's a boy to me," smiled the Duke. "Our survivor was conscious but rambling on arrival. He kept repeating the same name, over and over. That's what brings Lord Pencaitland to us."

The Earl of Pencaitland, also known as Dr. Anthony Gehlen, nodded to the Chief Inspector. "I'll not shake your hand, Baxter, for I've not washed mine yet. As to why I'm here, I was staying overnight at the HBH to keep an eye on a post-op patient, when Matron Gilchrist came to fetch me, regarding a new arrival. When I examined the man, I recognised him. If I'm right, then he's Edward Maladroit."

"If you're right, sir?" asked Baxter.

"I met him just the once, but I've a pretty good memory for faces. Still, whoever the patient is, he's in a very bad way. Massive blood loss. We nearly lost him but managed to transfuse enough blood that he's fairly stable. That miracle's down to Emerson's cross-matching method."

"And did this gentleman mention a companion?" asked Baxter. "Might he know our dead man's identity?"

"No, as I said, the patient has no memory," answered Gehlen. "But if he is Edward Maladroit, then his father is Lord Palmore. Edward runs with a cousin. Lord Thomas Elgin-More. He's the son and heir of Lord Stratbourne."

"Good heavens!" Baxter exclaimed. "He's our ambassador to France!"

"Precisely," said Gehlen. "Which is why we must all tread carefully."

"Before we send for Stratbourne, I want verification," Charles told the assembled men. "I've despatched Arthur France to Stratbourne House to ask about the son. If Lord Thomas is accounted for, then we look elsewhere for the identity of our dead man."

"Dear me, this explains why reporters keep ringing your home, sir," said Baxter. "I stopped by King's Court before coming here, just to let my wife know of my plans. Mrs. Baxter mentioned several dozen telephone calls from the press. The Duchess is handling it all very well, though."

"My wife has a way of dealing with persistent reporters," said Charles proudly. "She's less gentle than I. Now, to business. There were other deaths in Whitechapel overnight. Do the other victims show similar signs? Was any of them drained of blood?"

"Is that what happened to this gentleman, sir?" asked Baxter in shock. "Drained of blood? Is it happening again?"

"We don't know yet, Neil, but possibly. It's but a theory."

Next to Gehlen, stood Dr. Thomas Sunders, a steady, experienced hand. At sixty, he'd seen nearly every common cause for a man's death, and since joining H-Division, he'd grown accustomed to Reid's more unusual cases.

"The other deaths you asked about, sir, died of respiratory failure," Sunders told Haimsbury. "I've examined six bodies now: three men, two women, one male child. Their lung tissue indicates an intake of poisonous fumes, very likely, caused by last night's fog. I've sent several of Gehlen's medical students round the borough to collect any precipitates."

"Any what?" asked one of the Yard detectives.

"Precipitates," Sunders explained. "Solid matter that floats inside a fog and clings to surfaces once the fog lifts. Fine coal ash, bits of wood, brick dust, fecal matter, that sort of thing. The lime and brick kilns have been going for days, and they produce toxic fumes as well with their own precipitates. But whatever caused last night's cloud of death has nothing to do with this man's loss of blood."

Charles turned to the non-ICI detectives. "Gentlemen, if you don't hold an IB or ICI warrant card, then I must ask you to leave. We're about to discuss sensitive information, which must remain internal for the moment."

"I reckon you mean this Golem, right, sir?" asked a well-dressed man to the Duke's right. "The Whitechapel Horror?"

"You will not use those terms again, Sergeant," answered Sinclair firmly. "And if I hear that any one of you has spoken to the press or referred to this man's murder as unnatural, I shall see that man cleaning Reid's latrines with a wire brush by end of day. Is that clear?"

The detectives nodded and slowly began to leave the room, except for one young man in a checked suit. "Did you hear me, son?" asked Haimsbury. "If you're not IB or ICI, please, leave."

"I would, sir, but this is my case," the snappy dresser argued. "I was first on scene, Your Grace."

"I see. You may remain for the moment, but I prefer you refer to me as Commissioner Sinclair, Detective Sergeant. My authority on this supersedes both Yard and Home Office, therefore you will obey me without question. Is that clear?"

The man refused to back down. "I reckon you're due respect cause o' yer reputation and great title, my lord, but beggin yer pardon, sir, that don't cut no mustard with me. You ain't Whitechapel, sir. My responsibility is to the people who live and die here."

Reid started to intervene, but Charles put up a hand. "Go on, Detective. Why don't I cut the mustard, as you say?"

"I mean no disrespect, sir, but I grew up in Whitechapel. I know these streets. Why should I stand down, when it's my neighbours what's dyin'?"

Charles listened carefully. He knew the other dismissed men from previous cases, but this lad was new. He had a point, and he fearlessly defended it. "What's your name, son?"

"Wheelwright, sir. Len Wheelwright. My dad's got a pawn shop over on St. George, next to Porter's Inn. I got two brothers still livin' with my dad, above the shop."

"I see," the Duke answered. "How old are you?"

"Twenty-two, sir."

"And already a Detective Sergeant? That's a quick rise."

"Might be, but I earned it, sir. I know 'bout your career. You done a lot o' good whilst at the Yard, but I ain't convinced 'bout your current authority to dismiss me, sir. I got a stake in this, too."

"You've made your point, Mr. Wheelwright, but you're beneath Inspector Reid's command. I'll let him decide," Charles turned to the Leman Street boss. "You know the sensitive nature of what we're about to discuss. If you want him gone, then say so."

"Yes, I do know, sir," Reid replied. "Wheelwright's a good man, and it's why I recommended him for CID. He's already solved six murders." The inspector turned to the young detective. "Son, the reason the Commissioner dismissed everyone else isn't because he doesn't trust them, but because the ICI tracks down killers that don't fit your idea of normal."

"I got a brain, sir. I can see this man's death ain't normal."

"Then, what killed him?" asked Anthony Gehlen.

"If I say it out loud, you'll send me away, sirs."

"Try us," said Charles.

Leonard Wheelwright had an inquisitive nature and a pragmatic worldview. His personal faith was a quirky mix, based on a Jewish mother who considered herself enlightened, and an Irish-Catholic father who saw angels on every corner. The dichotomy cut him down the middle, half in, half out.

"Well, sirs, if I'm to speak my mind, then I reckon this man died from somethin' my Jewish mum would call a Dybbuk. It's sort o' like a ghost that feeds on energy or blood. My dad calls 'em vampires."

Everyone grew silent. Sunders, Reid, Gehlen, Baxter, and Sinclair all looked at the young detective's honest face.

Charles broke the silence. "The killer is a vampire? That's your professional assessment?"

"Yes, sir, it is, and I won't budge from it, lessin' you can give me evidence to the contrary."

Sunders smiled. Gehlen did, too, and eventually they all began to laugh. "You certainly have nerve, I'll give you that," Anthony told the young man. "Not many have the bald-faced gumption to spin such a tale to Charles Sinclair."

"I'd spin it to anyone, if I thought it was true, sir."

"Good," said Haimsbury. "In that case, you may stay, Mr. Wheelwright, but lock the door. Your notion of a supernatural killer is closer to the mark than you could possibly realise. As of this moment, you're on my ticket as a probationary member of the Intelligence Branch."

CHAPTER FOUR

Vienna, Austria

The remainder of Paul Stuart's journey to Vienna passed without incident. Once inside the ancient city, the earl asked the driver to park on *Dorotheergasse* and wait. Aubrey entered a four-storey, baroque-style building known as the *Palais Starhemberg*, located in the 1st district of the inner city. The former palace was officially listed as the Ministry of Culture and Education, but it actually served as headquarters for Britain's covert operations, particularly those considered off-book and *very* unofficial.

A smartly dressed gentleman rose from a small desk as the earl entered the waiting area. The man crossed the floor and spoke in a whisper. "Lord Billington is waiting for you, sir. If you'd follow me?"

The secretary led Aubrey up a flight of marble-and-ironwork stairs to a second-storey office, situated near the northwest corner. The room overlooked a narrow street, choked with carriage traffic, flower-sellers, and well-dressed pedestrians. The office's sole occupant was Sir Rupert Stentforth, 7th Earl of Billington, a portly gentleman with a droopy moustache and an equally droopy countenance. He rose to shake his visitor's hand.

"Well, now, if it isn't the infamous Lord Aubrey in the flesh! Good of you to come at short notice," he said in polished British. "Sorry to drag you here without preamble, particularly as my War Office colleagues summoned you only a week ago. Since then, a rather sticky situation's developed in West Africa. Gold Coast problems again, I'm afraid. And as you cleared them up so neatly last time, our new P.M. thought you might be good enough to do so again. Please, sit, sir."

Paul had paid a similar call to this very building at the beginning of his Vienna visit, only then with a different War Office representative—often, the right hand had no idea what the left was doing. Aubrey was accustomed to War Office inconsistencies and so took a chair opposite the desk, ready to receive new orders.

The fleshy-faced ambassador filled two crystal glasses with whisky. "I'm afraid it isn't Drummond's stuff. We ran out of that weeks ago. Truth be told, we're lucky to get any whisky these days. I'm afraid politics and import tariffs go hand-in-hand, even for Her Majesty's loyal servants. I don't suppose you brought any? No? Ah well, perhaps, next time."

"I'll wire my uncle's distillery and instruct them to send you half a dozen casks on the next ship. Now, what's going on in West Africa?"

Billington returned to the sturdy wooden chair, sipping the whisky thoughtfully. "That is a long story, and I'm very glad you happened to be nearby, as you're the only one for the job. I talked with Simon Galway last night. He said you brought your wife here. Is she all right?"

"Yes," Paul answered simply. "And thanks to Galway's little problem, I wasn't with her for the first three days."

The moustache drooped further. "Yes, well, Simon felt sick about causing that delay, but it couldn't be helped. If only all our agents were as reliable as you. Your wife's all right, I hope? I'm told she's at Breitenfurt Retreat," he continued. "Jolly good place. I know dozens of chaps whose wives have taken the waters there. My Sarah stayed at Breitenfurt for a month. Best thing we ever did! Our children are all grown now, and so the nest is empty. Women get melancholy, when they've no one to nurture, you know. What's your opinion of the fellow in charge? That Pyramis chap?"

"Arrogant, but then most physicians are. My friend Salperton likes him; though, I'm not sure Henry knows the man all that well. They're colleagues by way of a conference."

"Is that so?" asked Billington. "Yes, well, these fellows always bolster one another up, don't they? Alienism is a lonely sport, but there's a fellow hereabouts that's making a go of it. He's quite famous with the ladies. Jewish chap, but still all right."

"Does his religion matter?"

The politician shrugged and poured himself a second whisky. "Not to me, but some consider it a professional handicap. This fellow sometimes calls down at Breitenfurt. I'm told, he and Pyramis are thick as thieves. Sigmund Freud's the name. Ask Salperton about him. Odd fellow, but then most are."

"Most doctors?" asked Paul, taking a sip of the whisky.

"Yes, but then so are most of us men!" laughed the other.

"Lord Billington, why am I here?"

"Call me Rupert."

"Thank you. Rupert, why am I here?"

"Ah, yes, that," replied the droopy-moustached politician after taking another swig. "I know you've asked us to take you off the rolls, but with your good lady well cared for at Breitenfurt, we hoped you'd go yourself to the Ashanti and speak with their king. It's a very maternalistic society, so most likely, it's his mother you'll need to impress."

"Are the Ashanti rising up again?"

"Not yet. They're busy skirmishing with other tribes, but the king seems to think he can take us on again."

"Britain's military campaigns never go well there, Rupert. Please, tell me Rosebery isn't planning another war."

"He prefers to avoid one, but he needs to reset the current relationship in England's favour. And he's willing to let you lead the charge."

"Reset it? In what way?"

"With rising tensions in Europe, England must secure our colonies. Despite the Berlin Treaty, France may yet seek to out maneouvre us by expanding westward from the Sudan. We need exclusivity to Ashanti ports and mines. Rosebery promises to be generous with King Prempeh. He can maintain tribal rule, and in return for exclusivity, English warships will guard his coastline from foreign attack."

Paul shook his head. "Prempeh will never accept that."

"Yes, I understand, and I'm sure if you were Foreign Secretary, all this would be different. Your late father detested colonialism, but it's a fact of life. Will you go?"

Aubrey finished the whisky and set the empty glass on the desk. "Only if I can negotiate the treaty on my terms. I'm well aware of the powder keg waiting for us down there but sending in soldiers to talk peace will guarantee another war. Let me do it my way, or else find another spy to do your dirty work."

Billington grew silent. He stroked the moustache with a pale, wrinkled hand. Like Stuart, the sixty-one-year-old was raised on the milk and meat of government life and foreign policy. Diplomacy was in Billington's bones, just as he knew espionage was in Aubrey's.

"Could you manage it quietly and quickly? If not, Baden-Powell's men are ready and, I daresay, eager for another round. That would make a very big noise, I'm afraid. The army want war, Paul, but we prefer to partner with the Ashanti, not destroy them."

"Britain's fought three wars against them already, Rupert. The king will see himself as winning a fourth. He may want a war."

"Yes, but he cannot win. Not this time. The king may have rifles and hardened men, but we have Maxims. Baden-Powell and his marksmen will shred the king's warriors like so much tissue paper. Neither of us wants that."

Aubrey hated war, and he'd always found the African peoples intelligent, hospitable, and friendly. He preferred an open hand, to a closed fist. Though trained as an expert in self-defence and espionage, at thirty-nine, the Scotsman was becoming a pacifist, just like his late father.

"Very well," he decided. "Plot a route that allows me a stop in Paris to collect a few things. I want to make sure my aunt and sister are safe first. I'll take one of our circle trains down to Nantes and set sail from there."

"Excellent!" Billington shouted happily, his heavy moustache lifting at last. "You'd make your father proud. Robert Stuart had a wonderful knack for avoiding war, and I see that same trait in you. We'll wire ahead and get you a spot on one of our naval ships out of Nantes. I know you prefer to go in disguise, but the Ashanti queen mother likes foreign visitors to put on a great show. Take her son an expensive gift but make hers bigger and much more important. She likes horses. Let me know what you need, and I'll see you get it."

"I can wire my cousin for that gift. He keeps stallions near Paris. They can be shipped to Nantes as well. I will need a place to stay when I arrive. It's bad form to presume I'd be invited to the palace. And I'll get in touch with our circle men there, as a backup residence, just in case."

“I knew you’d be the one to ask, Aubrey. Good man! You can leave tomorrow morning. Come by my home this evening, and we’ll work out the details. Eight o’clock. Oh, and come dressed for dinner. My Sarah loves company. When she learns you’re joining us, she’ll no doubt invite all her friends just to show you off.”

CHAPTER FIVE

Haimsbury-Branham Hospital, Whitechapel

Charles Sinclair arrived at the HBH a little after four that afternoon. Most pubs had shut for Easter Monday, but the hospital lounge was open, and he decided to stop for coffee before examining the vampire-attack survivor. He met Ida Stanley on his way in.

"Good afternoon, Mrs. Stanley," he said happily. "Or do I call you Sister? I see by your uniform insignia, that you're a supervisor now. Congratulations."

Ida Ross Stanley had aged very little since she first met Charles Sinclair. In 1879, she'd been a child harlot, not yet fifteen. The next nine years were spent in the thrall of an abusive and sinister man named Sir William Trent. Then, in 1888, desperate and alone, Ida pondered suicide in the River Thames, but Anatole Romanov intervened, telling Ida that her future was bright. The angel's promise had certainly come true. Since that day, she'd married Elbert Stanley and given birth to two children, a boy and a girl. A bright life, indeed.

"Thank you, sir," the thirty-one-year-old nurse replied softly. "Elbert's up on the second floor with that poor young man. It's something quite awful."

"Murder is seldom otherwise," Charles told her. "I wonder if I might have a sandwich or some soup? I know it's not your job, but if you could ask one of the cooks to prepare a light meal, I'd be very grateful. All I've had today is tea and half a scone."

"Of course, sir," the willowy nurse answered. "I'll have a plate sent up to the patient's room. He's on the second floor. Room 222. You're alone, sir? Or is there someone else who might be hungry?"

"I came alone. I thought the gentleman might be more inclined to speak with fewer faces round his bed."

"Yes, sir. I'm sure he would. We all just worry about you, my lord. Considering the recent bombings and all."

He smiled. "That's very thoughtful, but I'm accustomed to danger. Have you talked with him?"

"Not very much, sir. I'm an instructor now and spend a lot of time marking papers and writing out lesson plans. But I love my job, Your Grace. I'd not change my life one bit."

"It shows," said Sinclair proudly. "I've never seen you so radiant."

She blushed. "Well, now, that might be my condition, my lord. Elbert and I are expecting again—in about six months."

Charles's smile widened. "Congratulations!"

"Thank you, Your Grace."

"Six months? You'll be on a similar schedule to my wife. We've not said anything publicly yet, but Beth's due in October."

Ida's eyes brightened. "Really, sir? Congratulations to you as well. This will make your fifth?"

"It will," he replied, eyes alight. "Watching you women carrying a child amazes me. You exemplify honour and glory. It's truly miraculous, don't you think?"

"God's miracles never cease, my lord. I see them every day."

"As do I, Ida. As do I. I'll go up now. If you'd be good enough to organise the lunch?"

"I'll go right now, sir. Shouldn't take more than fifteen minutes. Maybe less."

Charles left, still smiling at Ida's good news. He loved and admired the Stanleys. Both Elbert and Ida had surmounted terrible circumstances, and when they found one another, each helped the other to heal the wounds left by supernaturally driven experiences. In the intervening years, they'd become like family to all the Stuarts and Sinclairs.

Charles rode the lift up to the second floor and followed a bright corridor to Room 222. He knocked. Elbert Stanley opened the door. His lean, beardless face widened into a grin when he saw the Duke.

"Great heavens above, sir! I sent word to the ICI, but never imagined you'd call in person, considering how busy you are. Are you alone?"

"All alone," Charles answered.

"Lord Aubrey didn't come?"

"My cousin is elsewhere presently, though I'm sure he'll want a full report. I talked with Ida downstairs. She told me your good news. Congratulations, Elbert."

"Thank you, sir," answered the ICI liaison. "We've you and God to thank."

"Just thank God," whispered Charles. "He's working all things together for good, remember?"

"Yes, sir, that he is. Even the things done against us can be worked for good, which is why I'm keeping an eye on this one. He might be another man marked by the enemy.

"Has he said anything? His name, for instance?"

"No, sir, not yet. I was told his name's likely Edward Mal..."

"Don't speak the name," warned Charles. "Gehlen admits he could be wrong. As Sherlock Holmes would say, we require more data."

Sinclair left the doorway and crossed to the room's solitary occupant and began to examine him forensically. "He's led a semi-sedentary life," he observed by lifting the arm. "Not much upper body muscle. The fingertips and palms are soft."

"Not a manual labourer, then," said Stanley. "Nor a factory worker."

"No, though he might wear gloves when performing manual tasks." The Duke removed the sheets to expose the patient's legs. "Now, here's a contradiction, but one I've seen before. Despite the lack of upper-body development, the thighs show signs of moderate physical activity. Horseback riding?"

"Not polo, though," Stanley observed. "Otherwise, his shoulders and arms would show it."

"Indeed," murmured the experienced peer. "His skin's clear and clean, apart from the bruises. The hair and scalp are in good condition as well. He's about the right age for Gehlen's best guess. Twenty or so. Probably a student at one of the elite schools. Cambridge or Oxford. He doesn't look like a scholarship student, which means he probably comes from gentry. Perhaps, a peerage or banking family." He turned the man over and found Saraqael's message. "Good heavens, Elbert! Did he come this way?"

"Gracious heavens, sir, that is hideous! I'm not sure when this happened. It's the first time I've seen it. We could check the intake record. It's hanging inside the green cupboard, sir."

The Duke opened the medicine cabinet and lifted a brown clipboard from a metal hook. He scanned through the notes. "There's nothing about his back. Perhaps, no one thought to turn him over. It certainly doesn't look like a typical wound."

"Might it be writing of some kind?" asked Elbert.

Charles stepped close to examine the scratches. "They look familiar. I've seen something like these before. Elbert, do you remember the strange carvings left on the bodies of Round Table members back in '88 and '89? The ones we thought were killed by Raziel?"

Inspector Stanley visibly shivered. He'd suffered more than most at the hands of William Trent and his malevolent Round Table. Trent and the Castor Institute scientists used an unknown 'germ plasm' from *Sanguis, Ltd.* to alter Elbert's mind and body. The experimental goal was to create a human-wolf hybrid, and it worked. Only the intervention of Prince Anatole Romanov and God's wonderful miracles had restored Elbert's humanity and soul.

"I've not thought about the Round Table for years, sir. Are they still active?"

"No one knows. If so, then they've found a very deep hole to hide in. And we still don't know who or what left those indecipherable messages on the victims' bodies."

"Didn't some of the symbols refer to you, sir? Or am I misremembering?"

Sinclair shook his head. "Perhaps. I've tried to forget those awful days. What do you think these symbols mean? Are they words?"

"It's hard to say, but they look a bit like branding. You know, sir, when a manufacturer burns his name into leather."

Charles leaned down to examine the scars more closely. "Yes, it does look a bit like that. There's a faint smell of burnt flesh, too, and it looks as though the wounds were instantly cauterised. Is the attending physician here today?"

"Dr. MacKey? Yes, she's here somewhere, sir."

Lorena. I've not talked to her in months.

"Where is she now?" asked Sinclair.

"Not sure, sir, but I can go look, if you want. Will you be all right on your own? I'm aware of the threats you've been receiving, sir. I've read the ICI memoranda."

Charles smiled and opened his dress coat to reveal the very serious pistol beneath. "I always take precautions."

Stanley laughed. "It's nice to know royal life hasn't changed you, sir. I'll go find Dr. MacKey."

The door closed behind the departing detective, and Charles drew a chair close to the bed. He stared into the unconscious youth's ashen face. Anatole's warning echoed in his thoughts. Had Saraqael done this? If so, then why? And to what purpose? What did the savagely burnt letters on the poor man's back mean?

It was then, Charles realised he'd forgotten all about the Emperor's letter. "I don't suppose you'd mind if I read?" he asked the unconscious man. "No?" He reached into his coat and withdrew the envelope Drina had given him. The cream linen bore the personal crest of Emperor Franz Josef, head of the powerful Habsburg Dynasty. The imprint included a crowned Austria-Lorraine shield, flanked by two griffins, one with the head of a lion, the other an eagle. Beneath the crest, ran a royal ribbon, emblazoned with the Emperor's personal motto: *Viribus Unitis*. With United Forces. Each word of the Emperor's letter was written quickly. The hasty penmanship revealed angst and worry, as though the man's own fear mixed with the midnight-blue, India ink.

Though Charles was fluent in German, he had no need for translation. The Emperor had written in English.

> 24th March, 1894
> Schönbrunn Palace, Vienna
>
> My Dear Friend Duke Charles,
>
> I send this letter, sealed inside another, for I know Drina will see that you get it. I do not trust anyone else. It is long since we saw you in Paris, my friend. My darling Sisi sends much love to your sweet wife, the dearest Duchess Elizabeth. Our wives do so love one another, which makes me bold to ask something of you which will place you in grave danger. For this, I beg your Elizabeth's forgiveness, but you are a man of both thought and action. You will understand.
>
> Charles, I require your expertise. I know this asks a lot, but if you agree to meet me, I shall explain the precise nature of my problem in person. I cannot write it in a letter that might be opened and copied.

Select a date and time, but make it soon, please! I shall meet you at St. Stephen's Cathedral. All must be done in secret. Not only for political reasons, but for your safety as well as my own.

If you agree, then wire one word to me: MOZART and the DATE you can come. That is all. Just MOZART and the DATE. Then, I shall know your answer is yes.

If you must answer no (which I pray you do not), then send SALIERI as your reply. That alone will suffice, though it will make me quite sad, for I do not know where else to turn. If you agree to help, then you'll be doing a service not only to me, but to all Europe.

I await your answer, my dear friend. Wire me at once. If you come, I shall arrange for you to stay at Schönbrunn Palace. It is always best to hide a secret mission in plain sight; therefore my court will announce your arrival with great fanfare.

Charles, I pray you send MOZART.

May God guide you to HIS answer.

Your very dear friend,
Franz

The Duke re-read the letter, then folded it back into the envelope and returned it to his pocket. The hospital had a telegraph room. He'd compose a reply and send it today.

Anatole said I'd be leaving London. How did he know?

"Huh—huh—who are you?" slurred a weak voice. "Wuh, wuh, where am I?"

Charles reached for the young man's hand and held it gently. "You're in hospital. I'm Charles."

The man's pained expression lengthened into bleak shock. "Hospital? Hospital! Wuh—*why?* What hospital?"

"The HBH in Whitechapel. You've been injured. It looks as though someone may have attacked you. Could you tell me who you are?"

"Yes, of course, I'm..." he began, but the dry mouth grew still, and the face paled. "I'm... I mean, my name is... Wait. I don't... I don't know. Shouldn't I know?"

"Sometimes a head injury affects more than just our bodies. The memory can suffer, too. I've been there myself."

"What did you say your name is? Charles?"

"Yes. Charles Sinclair."

The patient's grey eyes blinked, then rounded. "Not *the* Charles Sinclair?"

"I suppose so, yes."

"Duke of Haimsbury and Branham? The one with the monstrous pile near Queen Anne House?"

"Monstrous pile?"

"A huge marble house near the woods. Brand new. What's it called? King's Palace?"

"King's Court, actually, but how is it you remember details about me and my home, but not your own name?"

The man threw back the yellow-and-white quilt and tried to sit up. "I need to go. I shouldn't be here."

"Hold on, my friend. You mustn't exert yourself. Lie back," Charles cautioned him, easing the man back into bed. "You've suffered some very serious injuries."

"Injuries? What happened? I can't remember anything." His face twisted with pain and confusion. "Something's crawling inside my head, and my back aches like it's burning."

"Yes, I imagine it does. You sustained a few scratches back there," the Duke answered softly. "You've suffered some sort of accident or attack, and you weren't alone."

"Someone was with me? Does he know who I am? Is he in hospital, too?"

"Do you recall someone named Elgin-More?"

"I'm not sure," said the pale patient. "It sounds familiar. I'm so very tired. Why am I in Whitechapel?"

"As I said, an attack. We're not sure of the details."

The door opened, admitting Elbert Stanley and a well-proportioned woman in a blue silk dress and matching jacket. Her auburn tresses were fashioned into an elegant chignon, and the slender nose supported a pair of gold spectacles. Lorena MacKey's natural beauty shone through the sedate appearance, and the music of her voice augmented the pleasant effect.

"I see our patient's awake," she said, reaching for the man's hand.

He yanked it back. "Who are you?"

"Sorry to surprise you. I'm your physician. Dr. MacKey."

"You're a—a *doctor?*"

"She's a very fine doctor," Sinclair explained. "One of the best in England. Good to see you," he added, speaking to Lorena.

"You, too," she answered with a bright smile. Then, to the patient, she said, "Sir, I just need to take your pulse. Might I have a moment of silence to count?"

The room grew quiet. Once done, MacKey wrote down the number. "Seventy-nine and a bit irregular." She placed a stethoscope against his chest. "Your heart's a little weak. Have you a headache?"

"Yes. A peculiar crawling sort of pain in my head."

"Where?" she asked, touching his forehead. "Here?"

He nodded. "It goes all the way round. Like it's squeezed from the inside."

MacKey used shorthand to record the patient's words in a brown leather notebook. "Any backache?"

"A terrible one, yes. Like it's been scoured and burnt," he answered. "What happened to me, Doctor? Why am I here?"

"We don't know yet, but Duke Charles is very good at investigations. He'll find out. What do you remember?"

"Remember?" asked the patient.

"About the attack?" she asked again.

"You're really a doctor? I don't know any women doctors."

"I'm a qualified surgeon, certified by the Royal College, and I have a doctorate in chemistry. That's a dangerous combination for a woman, isn't it?"

"I suppose so," he muttered. "And I'm in hospital? In Whitechapel?"

"The Haimsbury-Branham Hospital," she answered. "The hospital's founder is sitting beside you. Duke Charles of Haimsbury and Branham. He and the Duchess built this place."

"I must be dreaming," the patient muttered. "Dukes and women doctors. It's all a bit mad."

"I'm sure it will make sense soon," Lorena told him as she continued the examination. "Look up for me now. Yes, that's it. Good.

Now, close your eyes. Open them. Shut again. And now open." She watched the pupils carefully and observed how well his eyes worked together. "Does moving your eyes hurt?"

"Yes. Look, will someone, please, tell me what happened?"

"I'll let the Duke deal with that, but first, I need to get a bit personal, sir. May I have a look at your legs?"

"My legs?" he asked in a shocked voice. "But you're *a girl*."

"A woman, actually, but I see your point. In all honesty, I've seen your legs already; earlier, when you came to receiving, but I need to take another look. Do you want my medical opinion or not?"

Charles enjoyed watching Lorena MacKey's bedside manner. Since they first met in '88, she'd become a well-respected physician. Back then, Lorena worked with Sir William Trent and his secretive Redwing group, the Round Table. Then, she'd served a fallen deity, imagining she would gain power through blind obedience. Now, Lorena served only God Almighty and loved the Saviour with all her heart, mind, and soul.

Once, she'd shown an obvious attachment to Charles. Paul Stuart believed Lorena had fallen in love with Sinclair. The truth behind their relationship was much more complicated. Charles admired Lorena. He'd come to think of her as a little sister.

Despite all, memories of *another* Charles, another version of himself, entered his thoughts from time to time—when, he'd encountered the mirror-shard alternate in a locked room of the Time Maze. There, he'd watched another version of Elizabeth die. That *other* Charles had loved Lorena physically, and Beth had tumbled down a flight of stairs, because she'd seen Lorena kiss him—as though *he* were that alternate Charles Sinclair.

The mirror-shard version of Beth died because of the fall, after giving birth to twin boys. A tragedy caused by a stolen kiss. Now, this Beth, HIS Beth, was pregnant again. Should he worry? Was it possible she carried twins again? Could there be a repeat of that mirror-shard catastrophe?

Rest in the Lord, came the answer. *Rest in Him.*

Charles pushed aside the worrying thoughts and returned to the present. Lorena had turned the patient onto his side and was lightly pressing against the charred skin. "No one mentioned these marks in your chart," she said. "It's unclear what might have caused them. A tool of some kind? Certainly something hot. Tell me, does this hurt?"

He screamed. "Yes! Yes, it hurts! Why the devil would you...? Wait. Wait! I was on the docks. Fish. I can smell fish. And river water. There was a boat. A chess match. And... And TEETH! For God's sake, what happened to me?!"

He began to thrash wildly in panic. Charles held the man down while MacKey injected a strong dose of morphine. Slowly, the patient grew quiet.

"There," she said. "This should dull the pain. Just try to relax and let sleep take you. Rest is healing. I'll come back later to look in on you in a few hours."

Lorena returned the hypodermic assembly to its case and placed it in a bright red bin marked 'TO STERILISE'. Then, the experienced physician led Charles from the room. Once in the corridor, she saw Ida coming up the corridor. MacKey called to her softly. "Mrs. Stanley, would you keep an eye on our patient whilst I talk with Duke Charles?"

"Yes, ma'am," answered Ida. "Your food tray's on its way, sir. Chef O'Leary was just packing it up."

"Thank you, Ida."

"Oh, Ida," added MacKey, "I've given our patient some morphine, but I don't want him left alone. If you must leave, see there's someone to take your place. Is Elbert still here?"

"He's with Inspector Reid. I think the inspector's come to fetch the Duke, actually."

"Then, we'll go down and meet him," Lorena answered decisively. "I'll make sure His Grace is fed."

MacKey led Haimsbury to the lift. Once in, Charles shut the heavy iron cage and turned the handle to 'G' for ground floor.

"Anthony thought the dead man might be Lord Thomas Elgin-More. Is he right?" she asked.

"Possibly. Elgin-More's father's a very powerful earl. He's presently in Paris, but once I know for certain, I'll send a telegram. It's a heartless way to learn your son's dead."

"Yes," she whispered. "It's been a long time since we last talked, Charles. How've you been?"

"Busy, but then, that's usual for me. Beth's with child again," he added, instantly wondering why he'd blurted it out.

Lorena's smile was genuine. "Charles, that's wonderful. I'm very happy for you both. Does Adele know yet?"

"No, but I'll see her soon. I'll tell her then."

An awkward silence followed. Charles had no idea what to say next. He often dreamt of that other-world version of his life; nightmares of the whole, dreadful experience and how it ended. Seeing Lorena in the light of reality brought the nightmare back full-force, as though it happened only yesterday.

She touched his hand. He pulled it back.

"Are we on bad terms?" she asked. "Have I done something wrong?"

He shook his head. "No, not at all. It's complicated."

"I'm a very good listener."

"Yes, I know."

The lift stopped. Charles drew back the metal cage. They stepped onto the busy, main-floor reception area; now crowded with waiting patients. Near the lobby doors, stood a group of reporters, peppering two gentlemen with questions. Edmund Reid was barking short answers, clearly angry.

One of the journalists recognised Sinclair. "Your Grace! Is it true the dead man's a peer's son? Is the Golem back? Will we see more murders?"

"Gentlemen, come with me, and I'll answer your questions outside," the Duke answered in a quiet, commanding voice. "The HBH is a place of healing, not a Fleet Street pub."

Just then, a uniformed man in a slightly stained apron pushed his way through the throng. He bowed his head, then gave Haimsbury a large, metal dinner bucket, painted with the HBH symbol.

"Beggin' yer pardon, my lord, but Sister Stanley told me ta bring this to you. I didn' know what sort o' sandwich you like, so I put in one o' each. There's pickle and chips as well, with a jar o' milky tea. And six fresh biscuits. I hope it's all right, sir."

Charles offered the beleaguered man a grateful smile. "You're O'Brien?" The chef nodded and bowed again. "Thank you very much for being so thorough," the Duke told him. "I've been rather busy today, and there's been no chance to eat. This will go a long way towards helping my brain to function."

Charles offered the chef a tip, but the man refused. "I can't take them coins, sir! This hospital's yours, sir. You pay my salary. But my kitchen's available to you and yours anytime, my lord. Day or night.

Any time at all." He bowed again, lower this time. "It's a right great honour to serve you, Yer Highness."

"That's very kind of you, Mr. O'Brien. You and your team are the engine that keeps the hospital clockwork moving."

The chef bowed once more and then left. Reid and Stanley herded the reporters through the doors and onto a sidewalk that ran north along Mansell Street. The Duke leaned down to whisper into Reid's right ear. "I need to have a look at the crime scene. Might you and Stanley keep these men busy?"

"Happy to help," said Reid. He handed Sinclair a slip of paper with the address. "Be careful, Charles. That nest isn't called the Devil's Den for nothing."

"I've been there before, Ed. Let's pray the name is just a metaphor," said Sinclair. "Join me, if you can get rid of this lot. If you can't, we'll meet up again at Leman Street."

"Glad to help," smiled Reid.

As Charles started to leave, one of the reporters shouted, "Your Grace, have you no comment for *The Star?* You did insist we gather out here. Have you nothing to offer?"

It was the persistently annoying gadfly, Michael O'Brien.

"No, Mr. O'Brien. Talk to me tomorrow." Then, Charles turned to MacKey. "Care to visit the Devil's Den?"

"As what? Another set of eyes? If so, then, I'd love to come. It's a very strange place, Charles. You say you've been there before?" she asked.

"Long ago," Sinclair replied as they walked towards an unmarked black coach. Hamish Granger, a burly Scotsman with a bushy red beard, stood nearby. The driver bowed his head, then opened the door.

"Where to, sir?" Granger asked.

"The Devil's Den."

"The Devil's what, sir?"

Charles smiled. "It's what the locals call it, but you know it as Wilson's Marina at St. Katherine's Docks."

"That sounds more like it," said Granger. The Scotsman helped MacKey into the coach, then waited for the Duke to follow before shutting the door. "Looks like you might have some riff-raff taggin' along, sir. Shall I take care of it first?"

Charles smiled. "That would be most helpful, Mr. Granger."

Three reporters had hired a hansom, intending to follow, but Hamish approached the hired cab and offered the driver some words of advice. Satisfied with the results, Granger returned to his own coach and climbed up to the driver's seat. The horses responded to instruction, and the black brougham rolled forward.

"Your driver's certainly capable," Lorena said.

"Granger's far more than a driver. He's also one of our ICI detectives," Charles answered as he unlatched the dinner bucket.

"Charles, have I done something to hurt our relationship?"

"Not at all," the Duke answered. "Hungry? There's enough food in here to feed at least three. And there's plenty tea in the jar. Also, I believe, Granger keeps a picnic box somewhere with a set of glassware. Let me see if I can find it." He reached beneath the seat and removed a storage box. The lid was made from tufted red leather with large buttons, rimmed in gold.

"Mind if I steal your rug?" she asked, seeing the fringed edge of a woolen blanket inside the box. "I left home without an overcoat."

"What?" Charles asked, his mind on finding the glasses.

"It's a bit cold in here. May I use the blanket?"

Sinclair straightened up, suddenly aware of his rudeness. "Sorry. Yes, of course, take whatever you want. I can have Hamish drive you back, if you prefer. The weather's turning cold again."

"No need to go back. The rug's plenty warm enough, and I'm glad for the chance to talk. I assume you want a medical person with you at the marina."

"Not really."

This surprised her, and MacKey grew silent. She watched Charles bite into a ham sandwich, but his mind was clearly somewhere else. "Charles, what's wrong with you?"

"Wrong?"

"You're acting quite strangely. Would you rather I go back?"

"Of course not. Really, Lorena, it isn't you at all. It's just..."

"Just?" she prompted.

"Troubling memories."

"Memories of what?"

"That place," he whispered.

The Duke leaned back; his eyes shut. Sometimes, when he least expected it, the Time Maze crashed through into reality, bringing back every smell, every touch, every turning of its horrid halls. And each time it happened, he relived Beth's death, heard the twin boys crying, saw Paul rush past on his way upstairs, felt Lorena's warm mouth on his: that unwanted kiss that killed his wife. If only he'd pulled away sooner, Beth might not have fallen. If only. If only...

"You will leave this world, but not before your heart is broken," Romanov warned him. And it was true. Horribly, agonisingly true. Seeing Elizabeth die had drained all life from his heart.

"What memories, Charles?" the real-world Lorena MacKey asked again. "What place?"

Tell her, a voice whispered.

"It's a long story."

Tell her.

"I have two ears to listen, Charles."

He sighed. "It happened in '89, when I was gone. Do you remember?"

"We all remember, Charles. You were missing for weeks and weeks."

He reached for her hand, noting its warmth. "They abducted Adele. I ran to the coach and tried to help, but Flint and the others took us both prisoner."

"Della's safe now, Charles," she said, gripping his fingers. "She's happy and strong. But you're not. Tell me."

He took a deep breath. "Something happened to me there."

"Are you talking about the Time Maze?" she asked.

"Yes, did someone tell you about it?"

"Charles, I attend most of the circle meetings, remember? I've heard you mention that place, but you seldom say more than a passing comment. I once heard Theseus talk about it, though."

"You know Theseus? What has he told you? When did you last see him?" he asked, releasing her hand and sitting back against the leather seat.

"I met him a few years ago, at Castor Institute. He was visiting Trent. My skin crawls whenever I have to speak that man's name. Trent's name, I mean. Alphonse Theseus was actually quite a kind person, considering."

"Considering his attachment to Redwing?"

"In a way. You do know he's a hybrid?"

"Yes, and he's quite proud of it."

She nodded and reached into the lunchbox, removing half a sandwich. "Those chips smell good. May I?"

"Yes, of course. Go on, if you don't mind."

She poured them both glasses of the milky tea. "Alphonse believes hybrids possess superior abilities. They can enter other worlds, as though standing on a metaphysical bridge. Charles, did he torture you?"

"Not in the usual sense of the word. In fact, he tried to be my friend. I think Theseus sees the Maze as a proving ground."

"A ground to prove what?" she asked.

"Suitability, I suppose. Apparently, I passed the test. Ever since then, Redwing's left us alone."

"I wouldn't consider it a permanent condition, Charles."

"I pray you're wrong," he whispered, his hands tightening round the small glass.

"Charles, what happened there? What memories drag at you so? I can sense deep pain in you, as though you're grieving."

He glanced out the window to hide his face. Just thinking about Beth's final breath caused tears to well up, and a heavy weight to form round his heart. They'd reached St. Mark's School, with its limewashed walls and a gravel playground. Overhead, ran the Royal Mint railway split, an elevated, y-shaped track, used by the London and Blackwall line. Every day, hundreds of cars carried passengers and goods from St. Katherine's to the City Terminus. Beneath the brick arch, he noticed children at play.

"I watched her die," he said at long last, the deep voice just a whisper. "Beth died in my arms. The Maze had areas Theseus called locked rooms; each filled with an alternative reality, like shards of a broken mirror. I entered several and lived the lives of *other* Charles Sinclairs. Sometimes, the experience lasted a day, other times much longer. In one, Elizabeth..." He took a deep breath, praying he wouldn't break down weeping. "Beth fell down the stairs. The fall caused her to give birth prematurely. Two tiny boys who almost died. They lived, but she... Elizabeth didn't."

Lorena almost reached for his hand, but realised he needed time to compose himself, so she remained still. "I cannot imagine how awful that was, Charles, but it wasn't real. The Maze is designed to play with your head. You said Beth's pregnant again, yes?"

He nodded.

"And you're worried because of what happened to this other version of her. Beth's strong, Charles."

"Yes, I know, but it's different this time. I can't explain why. It isn't logical. I just *feel* it! Have you ever had a dream so real that, many years later, you still remember it, almost like a real event?"

She nodded. "A few times. One dream was about you, actually. Not inappropriate, you understand; and it was before we became such good friends. I'm ashamed to say I was still part of Redwing at the time. You probably don't remember what you said to me in Scotland, but it made a profound impact on me. You were the first man who ever really cared about me. Not physically, *spiritually*. You urged me to turn away from Redwing and seek the true God. Your kindness planted a seed. I ran away from Castle Drummond the next day, do you remember?"

"You stole one of James's best horses."

"I've since made up for that," she said, smiling. "I returned the horse and sent him another as an apology. Shortly after I returned to London, I had this dream. In it, we were close friends, and I interacted with your family as though I were one of you. Charles, that dream was the closest I'd ever felt to being part of a real, loving family. The dream still feels real to me. That dream may be why I started loving you."

His head snapped towards hers, eyes round. "Love?"

"Don't panic," she whispered. "I love you as a friend. Nothing romantic. Not now, anyway. I admit to flights of fancy at first, but the Lord redirected me towards a kind of love that's far better. Charles, your friendship means more to me than any romance ever could. I mean that. You are one of my dearest friends in all the world. Like a brother."

He relaxed, for her words rang true. "The truth is, I feel the same, Lorena. Forgive me. I'm being peculiar, aren't I?"

She laughed softly. "Considering all you've been through, I think you've earned the right to be peculiar now and then. Did I tell you about Anthony?"

"Anthony Gehlen?"

"Yes."

"What about him?"

She blushed slightly. "You know that we've been seeing one another, right?"

He stared at her. "I know that you work together. I suppose that requires spending time in one another's company. Am I missing something?"

She laughed, her green eyes sparkling. "A fine detective you are! Tony and I've been walking out together every Sunday for six months. He's proposed."

The brougham stopped, but Charles barely noticed. A part of him felt joy at her good news; another part of his psyche wanted to interrogate Anthony Gehlen.

"He's proposed?" he asked, failing to conceal concern. "Isn't it a bit sudden?"

"Are you worried? I meant to talk with you about it, but you've been so busy the past few months. And my own schedule makes meetings difficult."

He grew thoughtful. "Have you given him an answer?"

She nodded. "We're to be married in June. At Pencaitland Chapel."

"I don't understand, Lorena. When did all this happen?"

"Are you jealous?" she asked.

"No, of course not. Your welfare means a great deal to me. You said you see me as a brother. Well, I think of you as a sister, and I want to look after you."

A small crowd had formed round the coach. Despite the lack of any crest, the popular peer's face was visible through the windows.

"Now's not the time for this, is it? We'll discuss it later," she said, pleased to know he cared so much.

Granger jumped down from the driver's seat. He gently pushed back the crowd and came round to open the door. The sounds of river traffic rushed into the interior. "This is it, Your Grace. Wilson's Marina. It's a wee bit crowded, though. Should we come back later?"

"I imagine Reid's policemen are still guarding the scene. Granger. We'll be fine."

The Duke exited and helped Lorena to step down. Granger remained close, his sharp eyes on the milling crowd. "Might be pickpockets about, sir. Mind your valuables."

Sinclair managed to smile. "I'm in my old neighbourhood, Mr. Granger. Pickpockets are a familiar nuisance. Keep a sharp lookout for reporters, though. They're far more dangerous than any pickpocket."

The three of them left the coach on Nightingale Lane and followed a wide jetty towards North Quay, and from there to Wilson's Marina. Within the numbered slips, floated a variety of colourful pleasure boats: sloops, luggers, catamarans, and square rigs. Four constables and a plain-clothes detective conversed near a large sloop, painted in red with the name *Sange Proaspat.*

Sinclair motioned to the detective. "Are you in charge?"

The man wore a checked suit and bowler hat, which he tipped politely. "You with the press, sir? I'm afraid we're not giving interviews, and the crime scene's off limits."

"This is Duke Charles of Haimsbury and Branham," said Granger. "Commissioner of the Intelligence Branch."

The newly minted detective removed the hat and bowed nervously. "Sorry, my lord. I mean, Commissioner, sir. No one said you were coming."

"No problem, Detective. And you are?"

"Ames, sir. Wally Ames. I came over from D-Division last week. This is my first murder."

"Then you've jumped directly into the fire, Sergeant. Or is it Detective Inspector?"

"Sergeant, sir. And aren't you Dr. MacKey?" he added. "I've seen you at the HBH a couple o' times. Dr. Gehlen told me your name."

"Dr. MacKey is here in a professional capacity, Sergeant. Ames. If you'd show us the scene?" Sinclair said in a business-like tone.

"Of course, sir. The body's already gone."

"I've seen it," Charles told him. "And now I need to see the crime scene. Have your men keep this crowd back, Mr. Ames, whilst we take a look inside. None of them has been aboard, I hope?"

"Just the owner. He was here about two hours ago. He wanted to fetch some important papers from the cabin, but I made him sign for everything he took. I hope that's all right, sir."

"The owner's name?" asked Haimsbury.

The detective looked down at his notebook, wishing he'd dressed more smartly that morning. No one told him he'd be meeting a duke. "Another titled gentleman, sir. A foreigner. Prince Aleksandr Koshmar."

The telling tingle of impending danger buzzed along every nerve of the Duke's back and arms. "Koshmar?"

"That's the name he gave me, sir. You know him?"

"I'm afraid I do. Has anyone interviewed him yet?"

"Just briefly, sir. He promised to talk with Inspector Reid later today. He has an alibi, though. Koshmar and a friend were at Molly-Mae's all night."

"So he claimed," Charles responded.

"I thought of that, sir, so I talked with the proprietress. She backs him up. I reckon the dead man was trying to steal something on board the boat and got caught out by the other fellow. The one at the HBH, I mean. Is Inspector Reid with him now? Has he been arrested?"

"I doubt my patient's a murderer," said MacKey. "Did anyone at the marina see him last night? Have you discovered evidence to implicate him?"

"No, ma'am. Not that anyone'll admit, anyway. Folks round here keep quiet about such things. They don't grass on each other."

Charles stepped onto the moored boat. The *Sange* was larger than ordinary yachts. It resembled the British Navy's 'sloop-of-war' class, with three masts, ample storage, sleeping quarters for crew, and a sizable cabin. A trail of sticky blood led from the mainsail to the cabin's door. A constable stood on either side. Both saluted as the Intelligence Commissioner approached and entered the crime scene. MacKey followed.

"Does this qualify me for a warrant card?" she asked as they began to inspect the blood-soaked scene.

"This doesn't bother you?"

"Charles, I see worse than this every day in medical practice. I've not examined the body, though I've heard a bit about it. The man was exsanguinated, correct?"

"To the very last drop. Lorena, what can you tell me about Aleksandr Koshmar?"

She tried to keep out of the way, to allow Charles room to examine the area. "He's an enigma. Koshmar attended a few Redwing meetings, or so I heard. I never met him at any, though I did see him recently at the HBH."

Sinclair's head jerked upwards. He'd been bending over the rumpled bed. The mattress and sheets were soaked with oxidising blood. "You saw that devil at my wife's hospital?"

"Yes," she said, moving close enough to whisper. "You're right. He is a devil, but you might want to temper your tone around these policemen. They haven't the experience to understand."

"I think Whitechapel police understand better than you could imagine. And they're frightened, Lorena. Ripper's work was bad enough, but if we return to those awful days of the Golem and the White Lady, then..."

"You think Koshmar's responsible for those crimes, too?"

"I'm sure he is, and he uses many names."

"You talk as if you know him," said the physician.

"That creature has haunted me since I was a boy, if you must know."

She touched his arm. The Duke pulled back. "I'm fine," he said in a voice a bit too detached and cold. "I've seen all I need to see here. I'm going back to Westminster. If Koshmar's involved, then I want to make sure my family are all right."

As they left the sloop, Charles found Hamish Granger talking with Michael O'Brien near the jetty. The six-foot-five coachman loomed over the thin American reporter. Still, O'Brien managed to snap several photographs of Charles and Lorena as they came towards him.

Granger grabbed the expensive camera. "None o' that now," the Scotsman said sternly.

Charles took the camera and removed the film roll. He searched O'Brien's pockets and found two exposed rolls, which he confiscated. "This is a crime scene, Mr. O'Brien. It is closed to the public and to all newspaper men."

"But not to physicians apparently," argued the American.

"Dr. MacKey is here as a police consultant. You are not. I'm keeping this camera and the film rolls. Send a receipt to Queen Anne House, and the ICI will reimburse you."

"It won't cover the real loss, though, will it?" the American grumbled. "Nor will it hide the truth, Your Grace!"

The Duke ignored the reporter and returned to the coach. Once inside, Charles took a moment to breathe. He shut his eyes. He felt dragged down and heavy. The familiar tingling screamed down every neural pathway.

Something is coming. Darkness. Death.

"Charles, are you all right?"

"Yes, fine. I don't like any of this," he muttered as the coach rolled away from the marina. A crowd of admirers ran alongside: men waved hats, and women threw kisses to demonstrate affection and loyalty for the Sinclair family.

"They love you, Charles."

"I don't deserve it."

"That humility is why you'd make a great King."

"I don't want to be King," he told her. "Not now, not ever."

"Still, you'd make a fine one," she said, smiling. "So, what do we make of the boat? If it belongs to Koshmar, then he's a prime suspect, right?"

He nodded, trying to ignore the nagging dread growing in the pit of his stomach. "Yes."

The coach turned onto St. George Street. Beyond it lay the railway bridge, where children still played beneath the open brick arches. One little girl had dark hair and looked a bit like Georgianna. Charles shut his eyes, trying to reason through the clues. *What does Koshmar want? Why leave one of the victims alive? Why write a message in the man's skin?*

"Those symbols on the boy's back," he said after a long silence. "Did you recognise them?"

"They looked like burns, probably from a cauterising instrument of some kind. Why?"

"Because they're intentional."

The girl with the dark curls ran towards the coach. She waved happily, her face and hands covered in dirt and soot. Nearby, two men waved moth-eaten caps, shouting, "Long live our next King!'

The Duke waved and managed to smile.

Lorena sat as far back as possible, hoping to avoid being seen. "There's no denying it. They do love you, Charles, and with so much darkness in the world, these people need to believe in something good."

"Let them love their Queen. What about the message?"

"You're a very stubborn man, Charles Sinclair."

"So I'm often told," he said, half smiling. "Did you recognise them?"

She shut the window drapes. "If the marks are intentional, then they might be..."

"Might be what?"

"Their basic shapes remind me of something I read about long ago. If I'm right, it makes this murder even more disturbing."

"How can a vampire attack be any more disturbing?"

"It's to do with Trent, Charles."

"Go on."

"When Trent was grooming me for membership in the Round Table, he gave me a book of ancient writing to memorise," she explained. "The *Liber Loagaeth*, written by Dr. John Dee."

"*The* John Dee?" he asked. "Queen Elizabeth's soothsayer?"

"Some have called him that," she replied. "Dr. Dee believed he'd discovered the original angelic language, spoken by Adam. I consider the book evil now, but when I was under Trent's spell, I thought it mystical and wise. That it revealed long-hidden truths of the universe."

Charles turned to gaze into her face. Lorena Melissa MacKey had once used powder, kohl, and rouge to enhance the God-given beauty of her natural features. Now, she preferred a simpler life. The emerald eyes sparkled more brightly, and the copper hair gleamed with auburn richness. *Is this what Anthony fell in love with? Her innate beauty? With our Saviour's help, she's become an honest, redeemed soul. She radiates God's love now.*

He reached for her hand and took it firmly. "Lorena, forgive me. I've been distracted and often rude to you today. I truly am a plod sometimes."

She laughed. "I'm not sure what you mean, but I accept, nonetheless. And you're never a plod. A policeman, yes, but never a plod. It's strange, though, isn't it?"

"What?"

"The way our lives have changed since that first meeting in Glasgow. Back then, I was helping the Round Table with a long ritual, and now I'm helping you to fight them."

Sinclair noticed traces of tears forming in those pure green eyes. "No, I really am a plod, and again I apologise. I'm glad for your friendship, Lorena. I lost my sister long ago, but I've come to think of you in that way. As an adopted sister."

"I once told Tony that you're like my older brother," she confessed. "You lost a sister? Was that Charlotte?"

"Yes. She was stolen as an infant."

"And Adele's her daughter, right?"

"How did you know?"

"I realise it's a family secret," she answered. "Paul told me about her a couple of years ago. He and I've become good friends, too. Let him know that he's in my prayers, will you? Tony said Paul's in Vienna. He didn't specify much, but Henry and I are close, and he mentioned Cordelia's state of mind. I've heard good things about the retreats in Vienna. I'm sure Delia will be well again very soon." She paused for a moment, then added, "Charles, regarding those symbols; if they're Dee's language, then I might be able to translate them. I'd need to take another look, though. I only had a glimpse."

He withdrew a leather notebook from an inside coat pocket and used a pencil to sketch out a series of lines and circles. "They looked like this."

"How can you remember them, if you don't understand the symbols?" she asked.

"Photographic memory runs in our family."

He passed her the paper, and she studied it carefully. As they neared Mansell, Lorena knocked on the coach's roof to signal Granger, telling Charles, "You can drop me off at the hospital. I need to check on our John Doe—or rather, Lord Edward, assuming that's his name. He'll need our prayers, too."

The coach slowed, and Charles took her hand once more. "Be careful, Lorena. If Koshmar's involved, then we're all in danger. I need to leave London quite soon, and I'll be gone for several weeks. Be sure Anthony keeps close. And you can call on circle men any time. You do know that, I hope?"

"I do, and I will. Are you off to attend the royal wedding in Coburg? It's been in all the newspapers."

"Yes, but I have a job to do in Vienna first. City of music and Mozart."

Her face paled.

"What? What is it? Did I say something out of place?"

"No," she answered, dread filling the pit of her stomach. "It's just that... Well, I think the symbols you've drawn might be phonemes. Sounds, I mean. Smaller than syllables. They don't spell actual words, but form parts of words."

Is she trembling? "Lorena, what is it? What do the symbols mean?"

"If I'm right, the sounds form the word Mozart."

Suddenly, every nerve in the Duke's body screamed.

Mozart. The code word Emperor Franz Josef had asked him to telegraph as a positive reply to his letter.

Mozart.

How could Saraqael know?

Because he'd planned it all.

Dear Lord, what hell awaits me in Vienna?

CHAPTER SIX

King's Court - The Duke's Study

At that very moment, on the opposite side of London, in the southwest corner of the newly built mansion, a woman set to work. With four storeys and two hundred rooms, the master wing consumed nearly all of the home's southern elevation. On the second and third floors, lay the Sinclair nursery, with ample work and living space for a tutor, governess, nurse-maids, footmen, and chamber-maids. The wing included separate dining, kitchens, a formal state room for private audiences, and a suite for the Duke and Duchess. That apartment included three baths, a library, two drawing rooms, a parlour for napping, a music room, dressing chambers, and his-and-her studies.

That morning, the larger of these studies was in use, not by its owner but by his wife, Elizabeth Stuart Sinclair. Beth had been raised in peerage luxury, but sheltered by her family's secretive group, the *inner circle.* Despite her high rank and privilege, Beth's grandfather and his inner-circle veterans instilled in her a love for humanity and a strong sense of duty. It was this sense of duty that brought her to occupy her husband's study on that particular day.

The Duke's study overlooked the south gardens, with a spectacular view, enjoyed through a long wall of French windows. Contained within the study's comfortable interior, were Sinclair's diverse collection of books and sheet music, a Bösendorfer grand piano, eight leather chairs for meetings with his inner-circle core, and at that particular moment, a pair of snoring dogs. One was a small black-and-white spaniel, the other a pale-yellow Labrador retriever. The dogs snoozed peacefully on a braided rug, close to a crackling fire. Ten feet away, sat Elizabeth Sinclair, a gold fountain pen clutched in her small hand, as she composed a series of letters. Since her husband's desk and chair were designed for his tall frame, the petite Duchess looked childlike in the massive oak chair. But she loved sitting here, for the room reminded her of Charles. It was almost like having him with her.

Almost.

She gazed at a recent portrait of her husband, hanging on the north wall, opposite the French windows. The artist, Sir Percival Winslow, had painted the extraordinary likeness the previous year, to celebrate the Duke's fifth year as heir to the Drummond ducal title. As such, Charles wore a kilt in the Drummond-Stuart tartan with all the requisite trimmings.

Since their wedding in November of '88, Sinclair had come into his own as a popular and powerful member of British aristocracy, treated like the next King Charles. He even looked a bit like a Stuart Cavalier, with curling black hair that brushed his shoulders and a neatly trimmed beard. Beth loved the long hair but wasn't sure about the beard. Charles originally grew both to cover scars left by a terrible accident in '88, when an explosion nearly killed him on their wedding night.

"You're very handsome, Captain," Beth said to the portrait. "Beard or no, nothing can diminish the impact of your perfect nose and wonderful eyes."

She'd always called his eyes 'sea-blue', shaded like the Mediterranean Sea near the French Riviera: a mixture of delicate azure round the pupil, that graduated to a deep cobalt at the outer rim. They were piercing, intelligent eyes, that could issue commands with a single glance or delight his children with a cheerful wink.

A knock interrupted. "Yes?" she called.

A panelled door was opened by a lean man in military dress. "Forgive me, my lady, but I thought you called."

"Good morning, Major March," Elizabeth replied. "Did I call you?"

"I'm not sure. I was standing nearby and heard you talking, thus I presumed so. I've brought the despatch boxes from Mr. Pennyweather. He asked if the Duke could finish them before tomorrow. Apparently, the Cabinet members are on a tight schedule."

"I see," she replied. "If there's a rush, I could look through the boxes. My husband might be some time yet. You know how these criminal cases often go."

The military man smiled, his lean cheeks widening. "Yes, ma'am, I do."

"I am perplexed though, Major. Why the rush? Surely, no one's working today. It's Easter Monday."

"I cannot say, my lady, but allow me to ring Mr. Pennyweather and offer him your thoughts."

"Mr. Pennyweather's working, too?"

"Very few of us take the day for leisure, ma'am. Duty never ends. After all, my lady, you are working."

She smiled. "I see your point."

He stepped closer. "Your Grace, as to its being Easter Monday, I wonder, if I might discuss another matter with you? I'd hoped to ask His Grace about it, but as he's away, might I have a moment?"

Before March could continue, the door opened again, this time to a male servant in Haimsbury livery.

"Oh, Major March!" the servant exclaimed. "I wasn't aware you and Her Grace were in a meeting." He bowed politely to the Duchess. "My lady, I've brought your morning tea."

"Thank you, Mr. Sugden. Just set it on the tray by the windows. Mind the dogs as you walk past. I prefer they remain asleep, if possible. They were up all night with our eldest son."

"Of course, my lady," said Sugden as he crossed the large room to set the tray near the French windows. "Is Lord Anjou unwell, ma'am?"

"He's cutting another tooth," she replied as she finished the letter and signed it. "That and mild growing pains."

"Sugden, are the crowds still out there?" asked March in a whisper.

Sugden hesitated. "Ah, well, I'm afraid they are, sir."

"The same number?"

"More, sir, and increasing by the hour."

Beth folded the letter she'd just signed and placed it into an envelope. "What crowds are those?"

Major Aleister Andrew March was a leading officer with the Haimsbury Guards and presently served as Duke Charles's equerry—a sort of private secretary and personal bodyguard combination.

Previously, March had served as aide-de-camp to General Sir David Wilson. He'd first joined the Haimsbury household in April of '91 as the Duke's attaché, then was given the equerry position in late '92.

The ranks of the Haimsbury Guards were drawn from old inner-circle families; each man trained in combat and spy craft by Paul Stuart and other ICI instructors, then assigned to various roles within circle households. Some guarded, others patrolled. Those most trusted lived inside the house itself.

With strong circle ties reaching back for three centuries, Aleister March fell into this last category. The family trusted him completely. "Ah, yes, the crowds," the Major began, wondering how to explain a security matter to a woman. "Nothing to worry about, my lady. Just a few curious individuals by the gates. The Duke's Guard will handle it, I'm sure."

"And if my husband were here, you'd say the same to him, I suppose?" she asked.

"Naturally, my lady. The very same."

She turned to the footman. "Mr. Sugden, what is your estimate regarding the number at our gates? You said they're increasing by the hour. Shall I go myself and count them?"

The footman gulped. "No, ma'am. There's no need of that. I'd say there's only a dozen, perhaps two."

"And do I sense three dozen in your unspoken thoughts? Or even four?" she asked, rising from the desk. "Tell me, gentleman, why are there people at our gates? Are they visitors? Do they have a message for us? Should we admit them?"

"No, ma'am!" March answered quickly. "Hardly, ma'am! That would be a breach of security, and we cannot know what temperament these people hold. Remember, my lady, it wasn't that long ago that a man tried to explode a bomb inside the Greenwich Observatory."

"He didn't just try," she countered. "The man blew himself up, if you'll recall. He died, Major."

March glanced at Sugden. Both knew anarchists inside London had done far worse than detonate a bomb at the Observatory, they'd also planted devices in Queen Anne Park. Only the Haimsbury Guard's quick thinking had kept that bomb from exploding. The Duke insisted they tell his wife nothing, therefore March could not elaborate further.

Beth shrugged. She suspected March of keeping secrets but decided to let the matter drop. "It's clear you men have your orders. I shan't countermand them. Not today," she added with a raised eyebrow. "Have the morning papers arrived yet? I should like to see what crime my husband's investigating."

"Most are here, Your Grace," said Sugden. "I believe Mr. Willoughby is bringing them up along with the second post."

"Willoughby?" she asked. "Do I know him?"

"He's the new underbutler, ma'am."

"I see," she said. "And if I've not said so, thank you, Mr. Sugden."

"For what, my lady?"

"For taking such good care of us."

The servant smiled as he bowed, his grey eyes alight with pride. "You're most welcome, Your Grace. Tis an honour to serve here."

Major March retrieved two governmental boxes from the doorway and placed them on the desk's edge. One box started to slide off the edge, but March reacted quickly and kept the box from falling. However, the sharp sound roused the sleepy spaniel. Lady Napper, whose name was most fitting, left the fire to sniff at March's trouser leg. Apparently satisfied he wasn't an intruder, she crossed to the tall windows and began to paw at the glass.

"Does Lady Napper require a visit to the lawns?" asked Sugden, who still stood near the door. "I'm happy to take her out, ma'am."

"That won't be necessary," Beth answered. "She and Aramis went for a long walk not more than half an hour ago. I'm told Aramis chased a rabbit."

"Ah, yes," remarked March dryly. "Those animals are in abundance just now, my lady. Hares are engaging in their spring rituals, I believe."

"I imagine they are," laughed the Duchess. "Mr. Sugden, I have all I need for the moment. Would you send up the newspapers when they're ready?"

"Of course, ma'am. Shall I pour your tea first?"

"I can do that, but it's kind of you to offer."

The footman bowed, then left quietly.

March stationed himself close to the fire, next to the sleeping Labrador.

Beth stared at the two despatch boxes, their rich colours contrasted with the deep green of her husband's desk blotter. Government boxes such as these had been used since the sixteenth century. The iconic leather cases were made exclusively at Barrow, Hepburn, and Gale in Bermondsey. Most were dyed red and bore the current monarch's royal cipher on top in gold, with the title of the recipient stamped on the edge just above the brass lock.

Duke Charles received two boxes each morning, one made of traditional red leather with COMM. INTELLIGENCE BRANCH on the edge; and a second box, dyed royal blue, its top stamped, not with the Queen's cipher, but with the Haimsbury-Branham cipher: an entwined H&B beneath the Plantagenet crown of Henry V. Above the lock, the gold lettering stated: HRH, THE DUKE.

The Duke. Plain and simple. No other identifier was required. Everyone in government knew precisely who *The Duke* was: Charles Robert Arthur Sinclair III, heir to the Plantagenet and Stuart dynasties, and England's Shadow King since January of 1890.

Elizabeth unlocked the blue box and began sorting through tied bundles of parliamentary laws and treaties. She arranged them into two neat stacks: domestic and international.

March cleared his throat. "My lady?" he asked. The forty-year-old soldier had grown up Castle Drummond and spoke in a lilting Scottish brogue that often belied the dry, military delivery. "I know you've a great deal to do, but might I have a moment?"

"Of course," she answered, glancing up from the desk. "Is it to do with me or my husband?"

"In a way it's you, my lady. May I sit?"

"Yes, of course! Please, forgive my manners, Major March. My mind's elsewhere. I've spent most of my life doing paperwork of one kind or another, and I find it familiar. Almost comforting in a way. Please, have a chair. Would you like tea?"

"No, thank you, ma'am. No tea," said March as he pulled one of the smaller chairs to the desk, opposite the Duchess. "Your Grace, it's been three years, almost to the day, since the Duke asked me to serve in his household."

"Three years already? To the day?"

"Not to this day, ma'am, but next month. The tenth."

She smiled. "April tenth? That's two days after my birthday. I shall remember that, and you've done a splendid job, Major. Just splendid. Are you about to ask for a pay rise? I should be happy to offer one, particularly as your list of duties continues to grow, but that's my husband's decision."

The Scotsman shook his greying head. "No, ma'am, it isn't that. A pay rise, I mean."

"Regardless, I'm sure the Duke would give you one. Shall I mention it to him?"

A smile played at the man's stiff upper lip. "That's kind of you, my lady. And no doubt, Mrs. March would make good use of it."

"Mrs. March is a lovely woman and very pennywise. We've come to know your children well. They're bright as pennies!"

"That's kind of you, my lady. Our boys enjoy spending time with your children. However, our newborn is too young to offer an opinion."

"She's two months?"

"Three, my lady. Becky turned three months yesterday."

"Children are such a blessing!" she said happily. "You know, it seems to me that you work very long hours, Major. Up at dawn and here long past dusk. I'll mention that pay rise to my husband and also suggest he provide you with an assistant. Or would two be better?"

A faint blush rose to March's beardless cheeks. "That is very generous of you, my lady."

"Nonsense. You're like family to us, Major."

"Thank you, my lady. I appreciate your generosity, but my work arrangements aren't why I asked to speak with you. There's another matter on my mind. During my years with the British Army and your family's inner circle, I've learnt a little of how an anarchist's mind works. I've seen the result of their devilish devices, and I don't wish for King's Court to suffer another Greenwich affair."

"Nor do I," she answered. "Have you a solution?"

"I'd planned to discuss it with His Grace, but as you and he make household decisions together, I wonder if I might have your permission to work with Mr. Miles and Chief Inspector Baxter on a household manual?"

"What sort of manual?"

March paused, trying to reorder a prepared speech, meant for the Duke, and make it fit for the Duchess. "Well, ma'am, the British Army have manuals regarding conduct and job descriptions. I'm sure His Grace is familiar with police procedural manuals and hierarchical charts. Both the Met and Yard publish them. Am I making sense thus far?"

"Yes, of course. I've read the Met manual, you know. And despite my femininity, I found it quite interesting, particularly the section on criminal investigation. I've also read the Duke's ICI manual."

"I must admit to surprise, my lady," he replied, his eyebrows raised. "Please, forgive me, if I've offended you."

She laughed. "Not at all, Major. No offence taken! And I often surprise men. I take it, this household manual would lay out the hierarchy and conduct expectations in military style?" He nodded. "To whom would it apply?"

"Staff. Servants. Groundsmen. Anyone not part of the Guards, ma'am. We have a manual of our own."

"Yes, I imagine you do. Well, I think it's a fine idea, but it's quite likely Mr. Miles already uses such a manual, though perhaps not as specific as you're describing. Have you consulted him yet?"

"Yes, but the Haimsbury-Branham household grows by the day. Since opening King's Court, we've added nearly fifty new staff, and new hires can lead to infiltration."

"Are you saying our home might be infiltrated?" she asked, her face paling a little.

"I'm not saying that. Not yet. Forgive me for alarming you, my lady, but I must consider all possibilities. That is my job. May I begin the process, or do you prefer I speak with His Grace first?"

The Duchess folded her hands, her dark eyes turning towards the tall windows as though expecting invaders at any moment. She didn't like thinking about such matters, but she knew March's motives came from a loyal heart.

"Yes, all right. If you think it necessary, begin the process at once, but do be gentle with our older staff, Major. They are loyal to the core and love us. Mrs. Paget and Mrs. Anderson, for example. Those gentle-hearted sisters are easily bruised, and I will not see either of them them hurt. Mrs. Partridge is another. She's a proud woman and might well bristle if she isn't part of your organisational meetings. Also, you might wish to consult with our new head chef, Mr. Farrell. He's come down to us from Briarcliff and knows all the inner-circle rules. Before you detail any of his responsibilities or those of his staff, I recommend you speak to him first."

"Of course, my lady. With Chief Inspector Baxter and Mr. Miles to guide the project, I'm sure we can write a clear and concise manual that benefits everyone without bruising anyone's pride."

The Labrador awoke and began to whimper, his thick tail held high. "What is it, Aramis?" Beth asked the dog.

"Perhaps, he and Lady Napper want to enjoy a bit of sunshine, ma'am. Though still cold out, it's sunny. Shall I take them?" asked March.

"That's kind of you, Major, but they've both been out within the past hour, and obedience rules apply to canines as well as people. Come, Napper, Aramis!" she called, clapping her small hands. The dogs responded immediately, and Beth rewarded them with scratches behind the ears. "Good dogs. Now, go lie down whilst I work. We'll all go for a walk in half an hour." Both animals returned to their previous spots, on the hooked rug near the fireplace.

"I think Lady Napper misses Adele," she told the equerry. "And Aramis definitely misses Mr. Blinkmire. They're very close friends. Regarding your manual, it occurs to me that rules require boundaries. Will there be a list of consequences for infractions?"

"I'd planned to include them, my lady, but will confirm any and all elements with you and His Grace."

"Be sure the rules and their consequences are fair and just."

"Of course, my lady. I shouldn't imagine it any other way."

"Is there anything else?" she asked. "These boxes take an hour or more to do, and I hope to take the children for a drive this afternoon."

"Ah, driving," he muttered, taking a deep breath. "Are you and His Grace attending the Coburg wedding next month?"

"Yes. We're travelling with Her Majesty."

"And your departure date, ma'am?"

"Well, that's a bit complicated, Major. Her Majesty's off to Luxembourg first. Tomorrow, I think. We're to meet her in Brussels on the third of April, which means the Duke and I must leave London by week's end."

"I see," the soldier replied, his orderly mind performing mental calculations. "I don't wish to press you for details, but arranging protection along so many rail routes takes time."

"Yes, I imagine it does," she said softly. "I'll discuss it with the Duke when he returns, but I've no idea when that will be. These criminal investigations sometimes take days to pursue. Let's talk tomorrow morning—all three of us."

"Thank you, ma'am."

"Is there anything else?"

"No, my lady. I'll go downstairs and talk with Mr. Miles." The Major bowed and left.

Beth had only just begun to work again, when another knock sounded. "Will I ever get to work?" she asked the dogs. "Yes, come in!"

A pleasant looking young man entered, dressed in livery similar to that of the mansion's head butler.

"Good morning, Your Grace. I've brought the second post and the morning papers," he began. "Most of the lead stories are about that murder."

"It's Mr. Willoughby, isn't it?"

"Yes, my lady."

"You've been with us a few weeks, I think. How are you settling in?"

"Quite happily, ma'am. King's Court is pleasant, well-run, and efficient. I'm honoured to be here." He placed the newspapers on the desk, then produced a small domed plate. "Chef's sent up some warm cherry rolls, ma'am. He allowed me to taste them first. They're quite good."

"They smell wonderful," she replied, glancing at the plate of iced pastries. "I must look very hungry this morning, Mr. Willoughby. Chef's already sent tea and biscuits, and now pastries. Set the tray on the other side of the desk, if you don't mind. Away from the boxes." Elizabeth put down her pen. "Mr. Willoughby, are you related to the family that used to serve at Drummond Castle?"

"Malcolm Willoughby? No, ma'am, but my old Auntie used to work in Lord Granddach's kitchens. I spent a great deal of time there as a boy."

She smiled. "The Earl of Granddach was a dear man. It's hard to believe he passed five years ago. Time certainly flies. My husband's to take the Granddach title soon, according to the late earl's will. Odd though. Your accent isn't Scottish. Do I hear Northumberland?"

"Yes, ma'am, though I've tried to polish it up. I was raised near Tweedmouth. Tis a very great honour to work here, my lady. Shall

I pour you a cup of tea, or do you prefer coffee, ma'am? I could bring some up."

"Tea, please. Three sugars, a little milk." She stood and stretched her small arms upwards, letting out a sigh. "I sometimes wonder if age isn't creeping up on me, Mr. Willoughby. Not yet eleven o'clock, and already I require a break. Would you mind taking the tea out to the balcony? The fresh air will do me good."

The young man smiled, flashing bright teeth and a single dimple in the right cheek. "I'd be happy to, my lady. Tis a very pleasant day, though somewhat chilly. Shall I bring you a blanket?"

She nodded. "Oh, yes, that's good idea. Thank you."

He left to fetch a woolen throw. "Ma'am, we received a telephone call from Mr. Kepelheim a little while ago," he said upon returning. "He asked if he might come by this afternoon."

"To see me or the Duke?" she asked, setting the blanket across her silk skirts.

"I believe he asked for the Duke, my lady. Do you know when His Grace might return?"

"Not really. What time did Mr. Kepelheim wish to call?"

"Four o'clock, ma'am. Shall I ring back and make other plans?"

"No, I'll ring him," she answered. "My husband was thoughtful enough to provide a telephone for his desk. If I need to make a call, I can ring our operator."

"Of course, my lady." The underbutler carried the tea service through to a small wrought-iron table, then bowed and left.

The balcony spanned the entire south elevation, allowing every room to enjoy a spectacular view of the gardens, as well as the estate's southern gates. Lacy ferns and potted palms decorated the Portland-stone veranda, providing beauty as well as privacy.

The dogs joined their mistress in the fresh air, and Elizabeth glanced down at Lady Napper. "Shall we have a look at the post?" she asked them. "Perhaps, there's a letter from Lady Cordelia."

The sunshine cheered Beth's soul, and the blanket warmed her knees. On the grounds below, she could see dozens of gardeners, busily planting herbaceous borders and rose bushes.

"Looking good, gentlemen!" she called down with a little wave. "Quite splendid!"

Seeing the Duchess, the supervisor removed his cloth cap. "Mornin', m'lady! We'll get these done up afore week's end! It's all goin' to plan!"

The petite peeress waved once more before picking up the teacup. She'd been sitting quietly for several minutes, when the sound of soft footsteps caught her ear. Elizabeth turned to look into the study. The new underbutler had returned and seemed to be searching through the papers on her husband's desk.

The windows were still open, and so she called through, "Is there something you need, Mr. Willoughby?"

Her voice surprised the young man. He froze, a blue paper clutched in his left hand. "No, ma'am. Sorry to startle you. I was just looking for one of my cufflinks." Then, as if to cover his activities, he set down the paper and joined her on the balcony. "Sorry to startle you, my lady. I should have alerted you to my presence. As I'm here, shall I refresh your tea?"

"That would be very nice," she replied, keeping her response cheerful whilst inwardly trying to sort through the man's odd behaviour. The servant prepared the Duchess's cup, and as he poured, she noticed H&B cufflinks on both wrists. "It looks as though you found it," she said, a little worry settling into her heart. Perhaps, his story was true. After all, Willoughby was hired by their long-serving butler John Miles, who never made an error in judgement.

"Yes, ma'am. I did," Willoughby replied smoothly. "It was on the Duke's desk, not far from the blue despatch box. I must not have fastened it properly this morning. Cherry roll?"

"Not yet, thank you. Was that all of the post?"

"All that's come thus far, ma'am, yes. I noticed you've written some letters. Shall I take them down? The postman's due back in about an hour."

"No, I'll send them down, when I'm finished. Would you ask Major March to come see me? I've had a thought about our earlier conversation."

"Of course, my lady. At once," the underbutler answered.

As he left, Elizabeth watched to make sure the man truly exited. Then, she crossed back through the Duke's office and put an ear to the door. She could hear muffled conversations in the corridor: parlour maids chatting with the handsome underbutler. One of the girls asked Willoughby about a Saturday party. Beth couldn't make out the man's answer. Finally, after waiting several minutes and hearing nothing else, she joined the dogs on the sunlit veranda.

Napper was nosing the cherry rolls hungrily.

"You're not to have those," Beth told the spaniel. The small dog sat up, whining and begging with her paws. Aramis paid no heed to Napper's efforts. He was busy keeping an eye on the gardeners.

"Very well, just a wee bite," the Duchess told the begging dog. She tossed a pinch of pastry towards the spaniel. Lady Napper snapped it up and gobbled it down, then fixed two dark eyes on her mistress's hands as if to beg again.

"No more. Della says I'm not to spoil you. Now, go lie down with Aramis."

The spaniel complied, circling several times before choosing the best spot in the mid-morning sun. Very soon, both dogs had fallen asleep.

Elizabeth took a sip of the tea, noting an odd taste. The new chef may not have used Branham Blend. She'd visit him later and ask. The morning post sat nearby, and she reached for the stack. Most were from estate managers, lawyers, or clerks. Two of these were posted from New York. Many others were invitations to spring balls at fashionable London homes or solicitations from charities. Tucked amongst all the letters, Beth discovered a very welcome missive in a yellow linen envelope, scented with hints of lilac. The return address made the Duchess smile. She used a pearl-handled letter knife to release a red wax seal of a trumpet swan resting on a water lily—Adele Sinclair's personal emblem.

Inside, Elizabeth found three scented pages, covered with line after line of her adopted daughter's artistic handwriting:

> Lady Della Stuart Sinclair
> Schloss Meggenhorn Ladies Academy
> 24th March, 1894
>
> My Very Dearest Father and Mother,
>
> I received your most recent letter an hour ago, and I'm rushing to add my reply to today's postbag. It was so lovely to see you last week, Mother. I'm glad that all of you stopped on your way to Vienna, but it breaks my heart about our sweet Cordelia. How

> weary and worn she looks! And my poor brother is so very worried about her.
>
> Couldn't he find her a proper place to recover, closer to London? May she not live at Montmore with Henry? I hate to think of Dee all alone in Vienna. Can we trust the people at Breitenfurt Retreat? My brother insists we can, but I've a strange sense about it all.
>
> Am I being too suspicious, Holmes? (I ask this of Father, of course)

Beth smiled at Adele's reference to Charles as 'Holmes'. He and Della loved to read Sir Arthur Conan Doyle's books and often discussed the various cases.

The letter continued:

> Whilst on my walk with Henry, I asked him about Cordelia's condition and the need for a retreat. He said Dee's too close to him for objective therapy (whatever that means). He said, it sometimes takes a stranger's touch to reach so deep a wound in one's heart.
>
> Can that be true? Surely, a stranger would only compound the problem, wouldn't he? After all, Dee's just lost a child. She's a mother in mourning, not a medical curiosity for strangers to examine.
>
> Yes, I know. It isn't my decision to make. Seeing Paul and Delia under such obvious strain made your brief stop a little awkward, though it was nice to see all of you. I pray every day that Dee and Paul will come through this stronger and happier, but then marriage doesn't always go as planned, does it?
>
> Mother, are you all right? You looked somewhat peaky whilst here. And just so you know, my concern arises because of a local outbreak of influenza. The illness has infected several of my fellow students, and one of the instructors nearly died last month. (I'm very glad to report she's now fully recovered.) It's a dreadful illness and strikes with no warning.

Please, take care, Mother.

Elizabeth sighed. She'd said nothing of her weariness and morning sickness whilst visiting Adele. *Has she guessed I'm with child again?* Henry knew, of course, as did Paul, but they'd decided to say nothing to Cordelia. Having just lost a baby, any happiness Beth felt might have the opposite effect on the fragile young woman's condition and cause her to deteriorate further.

She returned to the letter:

> Did you know Dr. Holloway is teaching at a nearby military academy in Lucerne? It's an elite school called the Eagle Institute, and boys study all manner of topics, not just battle planning and military history. Seth teaches linguistics and Middle Eastern history. I'm sure you're aware how close he and I became during my stay at Montmore in '89, and our friendship continues to grow. Dear Seth writes daily and has visited me twice.
>
> And talking of school, our present term ends soon, and so I've a favour to ask. I've received an invitation to attend the Coburg wedding. It's quite official, for it was Prince Alfred of Edinburgh that extended it. You remember him, Mother. His father is Auntie Drina's son Prince Alfred, and he's the new Duke of Saxe-Coburg. Alfie's very nice. He and I ran into one another last November, whilst I was shopping at Bucherer Jewellers. (That's the shop where I bought Father's Christmas present.) Alfie was standing at the stationery counter and recognised me. We'd met several times before at various occasions and always got on well.
>
> May I attend? There's nothing inappropriate about our friendship, I promise. Prince Alfred is a perfect gentleman; and besides my heart tends elsewhere, as you both know quite well. Also, Alfie holds a special fondness for another lady, whom I may not name, because, sadly, his parents don't approve.

Elizabeth noticed the dogs had raised their heads, growing interested in the groundskeepers. Aramis began to bark. She set down the letter and stood to have a look round. She wondered if the tutor might have brought the older children outdoors for a nature lesson. A tall stranger lingered near the south gates: a lanky, shadowy gentleman with a stovepipe hat and long coat. He looked out of place. Beth decided it must be one of the 'people' mentioned earlier by March.

Returning to the chair, she took up the letter once more, only now her mind was divided: half on the stranger, the other on her daughter's interest in men. Adele was nearly seventeen. She might soon become engaged, but to whom?

Beth continued reading:

> Now, I must address this next portion to Holmes (my father, of course). There's another reason I should like to go to Coburg, and I appeal to that detective aspect of your remarkable brain, Father. It's to do with a deep mystery there. Prince Alfie told me the story that day, and he asked if I might relay the details to you. The local police despair of solving the matter, but I'm sure you'd find no trouble. Of course, you'll need to consult your Watson, and so it's vital that I attend the wedding.
>
> (Yes, Holmes, I can picture your smile right now.)
>
> Here is the gist of the great mystery: As you know, Alfie's father had been Duke of Edinburgh for years, but when he inherited the Dukedom of Saxe-Coburg and Gotha last year, the family were required to leave England and live in Germany. At first, they found everything quiet and typical for a rural village. Then, last November, a girl was reported missing. Her name is Editha Rutche. According to Alfie, Miss Rutche is a virtuous milkmaid, who works at Schloss Rosenau, one of his father's two palaces there in Coburg.
>
> On the night Editha vanished, she'd prepared a stew for her father, then left to milk and bed down the cows. She never returned to the house. Her poor father searched the barn and the surrounding land, of

course, but found no sign of his daughter. The cows hadn't been milked, meaning she disappeared soon after leaving the house.

I can just picture you, dear Father; already asking a number of questions.

Allow me to pre-emptively answer:

- No, she didn't run away with a young man.
- No, there'd been no argument with her family.
- She was, by all accounts, a virtuous maiden.

This happened on the eleventh of November. In December, a second girl vanished in like manner, only she was a shepherdess, not a milkmaid. This occurred on the ninth. I give you the dates, because both were dark nights with no moon. Do you see, Holmes? I try to take note of these things.

In January, the seventh to be precise, a third girl disappeared. On the fifth of February, a fourth; and another girl on the seventh of March. All occurred on nights with no moon. All girls were of the same type: beautiful, virtuous, and flaxen-haired.

Father, the next moonless night is the sixth of April, and it's quite possible another young woman might vanish. Surely, this pattern suggests a diabolical design, yet Coburg's High Constable shows no interest. He told Alfie's father that 'these simple girls often run away on dark nights'. What utter nonsense!

I know you're very busy, Father, but will you look into it, please? Alfie's dreadfully worried, as is every parent in the area. It distresses me terribly to think what may have befallen these girls. Are they still alive? Held captive somewhere? I dare not think what else might have happened to them!

Our term ends in a few days, and I'll take the train down to Auntie Tory's home, for I've promised to visit. Tory's been very helpful these past few years, and I miss Auntie Dolly and Uncle Richard, too. Might you stop by the château and collect me? You'll need your Watson, after all.

I close this with lots of kisses to my brothers and sister, and also to Paul's children, Ian and Abigail. How time has flown! It seems like only yesterday that I first held Robby and Georgianna in my arms. Soon, the twins will be five, and I'll be seventeen. And Father, you will be thirty-nine. Just one year shy of forty, a very Biblical number, I think. Not to say you're old, Father. Hardly. Those silver strands at your temples are quite distinguished, and my dear friend, Lady Florence, likes the grey. She says it makes you look even more like a King. (In truth, I think Florence has a bit of a crush on you, but then so do most ladies. But we shan't even mention the many gentlemen who stare at Mother, right?)

I send lots of kisses and hugs to both of you! Please, tell my sister and brothers I'll see them soon. For now, I must close and rush this to the post bag. I cannot wait to see the new house. All the papers call it King's Court Palace.

I'm sure it is.

– With greatest love from your very own Della

P.S.
Please tell Lady Napper how much I miss her. It's a shame the school won't allow us to keep our pets. And give my love to Mr. Blinkmire and Count Riga. Oh, I miss everyone so very much!

Sealed with love and kisses
– Your curious and loving daughter,
Adele Marie Sinclair (i.e. Dr. Watson)

Elizabeth wiped happy tears from her eyes as she returned the pages to the scented envelope. Della's love and respect for her father shone brightly through every word. The two had forged an unbreakable bond, almost from the moment they met at Castle Drummond, when he'd teasingly searched her coat for 'pocket heads'.

Would Della be marrying soon? When Beth and Charles were lost in the Stone Realms, their unborn twin children had helped them find the way home. That was in 1888, but for the twins, it was 1899. Georgianna told her father they were on their way to Briarcliff to meet Adele, who'd be bringing the *new baby*. Georgie never revealed the name of the baby's father, which begged the question: who will it be?

Of course, Elizabeth had noticed Adele's blossoming friendships with Seth Holloway and Henry MacAlpin. Both demonstrated obvious affections towards Della, yet only Seth had asked permission to court her. The auburn-haired viscount had spoken with Charles before accepting the teaching position in Lucerne. Seth worried that being in the same city as Adele might appear inappropriate, and so sought the Duke's approval.

Henry MacAlpin had said nothing to Charles thus far, but his affections were written all over his face each time he spoke Adele's name. He, too, had fallen in love with the willowy young woman. Holloway was a fine man. He'd make a faithful, loving husband, but Beth believed her daughter preferred a future with MacAlpin. Both men loved her. Both loved Christ. Each had an established career. Both were respectable with stable incomes.

Did Della's letter imply a third possibility? Drina's grandson, Prince Alfred? Yes, Adele had insisted they were only friends, but many successful marriages began with a friendship. Beth's own, for example. Even now, she and Charles were best friends with a love that would outlast Time itself.

Perhaps, Adele would find such a love.

In the previous year, Charles had fielded dozens of marriage proposals from peerage fathers, each seeking a match for his son. Adele had matured into a beautiful young woman, the equal of any royal in Europe. Her bloodline was impeccable, and she enjoyed financial independence, thanks to a generous inheritance from Paul's father, the 11th Earl of Aubrey.

"What do you think, Lady Napper?" Beth asked the spaniel, who'd joined Aramis near the balcony rail. Hearing her name, the dog turned. "Shall I ask Charles to stop in Paris and visit our girl? Perhaps, he might even bring her to the wedding. Shall I talk to him about it? Yes?"

The dog's tail began to wag. Beth laughed. "Napper, you always say yes, if there are treats nearby. Aramis, what do you think?"

The Labrador's large head turned towards the human for a second, then quickly swiveled back towards the gates. He barked several times, then growled.

"Never mind," Beth told the dogs. "I'll consult with Charles when he gets home, whenever that is. I do hope he doesn't spend all day in Whitechapel."

The Duchess decided to try one of the cherry rolls. The spiral pastries were filled with sticky preserves and iced with a vanilla glaze. The filling was tart but sweet, and the buttery pastry melted in her mouth. Their new chef, Robert Andrew Farrell, was an inner-circle Scotsman, raised by his uncle in France. Farrell had an easy, jovial temperament; a good fit with the rest of the staff. He was tall and commanding in the kitchen, yet gentle as a lamb with the Sinclair children. Robby, their eldest, had quickly discovered Chef Bobby Farrell was an easy touch.

Beth swallowed the small bite. *What is it about that underbutler that bothers me?* she wondered. *Should I say something to Major March? Talk to Charles about him?*

She decided to wait and discuss it with her husband. Let the 'Holmes' part of Sinclair's great brain deal with it.

The late morning sun grew stronger, and Beth enjoyed the warm sensation on her face and hands. The previous night, she'd retired early and fallen asleep within minutes. Consequently, she'd missed witnessing the acidic fog that crept through the area. Nor had anyone mentioned it to her thus far. Yet, a tiny dread dragged at her heart.

What's wrong with me? What's gnawing away at my mind? It's been quiet for years. Just let it go, Beth! Let it go!

Why had Charles left so early with Reggie Parsons? Then, as soon as he returned, he rushed off to Whitechapel without saying goodbye. Were the two events connected? Might Parsons be part of a new ICI investigation?

Below the veranda, the new herbaceous border was taking shape. And in another part of the gardens, four gardeners fussed with piping for a fountain. She noticed the tall stranger in the stovepipe hat lingered near the south gates.

Suddenly, both dogs jumped up and began to bark. Aramis scratched and pawed at the marble railing, as if trying to clamber over it. “Down! Down, now!” Beth cried, startled at the animal’s frantic behaviour. Napper’s high-pitched bark drew Hat Man’s attention. He stared up at the Duchess, his face in shadow. Then, to her amazement, *he waved.*

At the very same instant, an intense wave of nausea overwhelmed Elizabeth. It might have been morning sickness, except for the smell: a mouldy sort of pungency that reminded her of childhood dreams.

Is that music playing? A piano?

Her vision dimmed. Chaotic glimpses of black mirrors and damp stone tunnels flashed through her mind. Elizabeth gripped the railing to keep her balance. As though sensing the human’s thoughts, the dogs stopped barking and drew near. Aramis nuzzled the human’s hand. Napper pawed at her silk skirts. Elizabeth slowly regained her balance. She took a deep breath and blinked. Reality returned. The dizziness, nausea, and troubling vision had all passed.

The Duchess searched the south gates for signs of the stranger, but the shadowy Hat Man had vanished. Beth scratched the Labrador’s large head, whispering, “Sorry to worry you. You’re both such very good companions. Come, let’s go back inside.”

Beth and the dogs returned to the Duke’s study. She shut the French windows, then sat in the oversized chair and began to work on the despatch boxes.

Outside, Hat Man left the south gates. He walked along the estate’s perimeter fence, limping slightly on the left leg. As he toured the property, he whistled a song that Beth and Charles knew all too well.

It was Beethoven’s *Moonlight.*

CHAPTER SEVEN

King's Court, Main Gate

The bells of St. Katherine's Church rang out the hour with ritualistic pomp and punctuality: twelve bells, midday hour on Easter Monday. As the chimes finished, a black hansom deposited a well-dressed father, a demure wife, and two bouncing children on the sidewalks of No. 7 Haimsbury Drive. The happy group had driven in from their home on Compton Street in Bloomsbury, just to visit the Duke's new house. As they mingled, husband and wife chatted with other curious visitors and shook their hands.

"A lovely Easter Monday, isn't it?" asked one.

"A bit breezy," replied another. "But glad of the winds, for they've driven away that awful fog!"

"I heard it killed some people out East," said one man.

"I heard it were dozens," said a workman in overalls. "Glad for them winds."

"Glad for the sun," said a woman in a pink bonnet.

"Just look at the gardens!" exclaimed another in blue.

The first tourists had arrived at nine. They'd missed seeing the Duke's fine carriage pass through the main gates, bound for the tunnels beneath Whitehall. By half nine, the curiosity seekers' numbers swelled to several dozen and now, the crowd numbered over a hundred.

Amongst these, was a very tall man who claimed to be a journalist. He said he'd travelled all the way from Hastings to get a look at the fine new mansion. He had a very odd manner, though his clothing was expensively cut. Despite the bespoke finery, he wore a strange hat: an old-fashioned stovepipe style, that was terribly out of date. He introduced himself as Justice Ravenhill, an independent writer, who sold lifestyle stories to a variety of British and American magazines. Though handsome and youthful looking, he leaned upon a cane and hobbled ever so slightly, favouring a bad, left leg.

Seeing the young family arrive, Ravenhill approached the newcomer's son. "Good day to you, young master," he said politely in an accented voice. "My name is Ravenhill, and I write news articles. What made you come here today?"

"Well, sir, it's Easter Monday," replied the boy with a wide smile. "My father's off work today, and it's a good thing, too."

"Why is that?" asked the man in the hat.

"Because the flag's up!" exclaimed the boy.

"Flag? What flag is that?"

The lad's father replied in a cultured voice. "He means the Duke's flag, sir," he explained, pointing towards the roof. "See up there? On that tall mast, opposite the weathervane? The flag's flying. The Haimsbury-Branham flag only flies when His Grace is here."

"Is that so? But why would he ever be away?" asked the reporter. "After building so fine a house, I'd expect him to live here permanently, wouldn't you?"

"I suppose you and I might, but that's not how upper-rank peers do things," the father replied patiently. He started to continue, but the boy drew his attention. The child had removed his gloves and was picking any flower that leaned through the fence. "Jack! Jack, you mustn't do that. Those are the Duke's flowers, not ours. And put your gloves back on. Please, don't remove them again." He turned back to address the reporter. "I do apologise, Mr. Ravenhill. Even good children need a moment's attention now and then. As I was saying, the Duke and Duchess have country homes in Kent and Cumbria. They spend time there as well. Land holdings require upkeep, and seasonal events such as the Branham fête require their personal attendance. Did I hear you say you're from Hastings? How did you know to come today? The Duke might have been out of the city. Was it because of Easter? Did you read they were in residence to attend resurrection services?"

A faint shadow squirmed across the man's face for a second. "Easter? Resurrection?" repeated Ravenhill as though the very words were poison. "No, not because of—not because of *those*," he mumbled. "Let's just say I had a keen intuition. One might say a little bird told me to come. Why did you come today?"

"Truthfully, because of the Easter Monday holiday," replied the gentleman. "I don't work today, you see. Last evening, we feared today might be similarly foggy, but God's given us a beautiful day, hasn't he?"

Another shadow flitted through the reporter's otherwise pleasant features. "*God*," he said with a choking sort of voice. "Yes, I suppose one might see it that way. Today's a day for leisure, then? And you've brought two fine children, sir. Aren't they about the same age as the Duke's oldest?"

"Somewhat older than the Haimsbury twins," said the man. "Our son is named for me. He's John, but we call him Jack, so there's no confusion. Jack just turned six, and our Mary is eight."

"Eight and one quarter, Papa," corrected Mary sweetly.

"You have funny hands," Jack blurted out to the reporter.

"Do I?" asked Justice Ravenhill.

"I'm so sorry, sir!" exclaimed the father. "My son doesn't always keep his thoughts to himself."

The stranger smiled, and the peculiar eyes crinkled beneath the old-fashioned hat. "I take no offence, sir," he told the father. "My hands are funny. I was born with six fingers on each. I can't imagine having just five, as this is all I know."

"Funny hands," the boy repeated.

"So, they are!" laughed Ravenhill, bending down to the boy's level. "And I've a spot of trouble with my left foot as well. I wear a special shoe, but finding gloves is nearly impossible. A seamstress makes them for me."

The petite wife had been quiet the entire time, but suddenly came to life, crying out, "John, look! Is that someone coming? Is that the Duchess? Oh, my, but she's so very pretty!"

"Why, you're right! It is the Duchess!" replied John cheerfully. "See there, Jack? Mary, do you see? That petite woman with the tall gentleman is Duchess Elizabeth, and she's coming into the gardens. How exciting!"

"Is that the Duke beside her?" asked another.

"No, ma'am," replied a rather portly gentleman in a stylish morning suit. "I've had the honour to meet His Grace. In Whitehall. He's taller and never wears a Regimental Guard uniform. Besides, I have it on good authority, the Duke left quite early to investigate a crime in Whitechapel. However, that is most certainly the Duchess.

I believe the gentleman with her might be Major March. He's the Duke's equerry and head of security."

Strangely, rather than ask questions (as any reporter would), the mysterious Justice Ravenhill stepped to one side to observe the crowd's reactions. The six fingers of his left hand twitched upon the silver head of a rosewood cane, and the agile mouth twisted into a satisfied smile. Ravenhill slipped away to a quiet spot beneath an ash tree, and with everyone's attention on the gates, he very neatly *vanished.*

To stave off the chill, Elizabeth Sinclair wore a Sinclair tartan shawl over her shoulders. Aleister March walked one step behind, and to his left, trotted Aramis and Lady Napper. Always sympathetic to public sentiment, the Duchess had decided to talk with the crowd, rather than leave it to March and the Haimsbury Guards. She failed to notice the stranger she thought of as Hat Man, for Justice Ravenhill had cloaked himself in a shadow of invisibility.

The Duchess and Major March approached the uniformed guards. March spoke to them briefly, explaining that the peeress wished to talk with the visitors. Both guards bowed their heads politely, then one ordered the porter to throw a switch inside the gatehouse. The brass switch closed an electric circuit, initiating a complicated mechanism of interlocking gears that released the locks. Each guard took hold of his side of the enormous ironwork gate and swung the doors open, just wide enough for the little Duchess to pass through.

The crowd bowed low, women curtsied, and men removed their hats. Then all began to cheer, crying out 'Long live our Duchess!' and 'Hail our future Queen!'.

Beth took the sentiments with good humour. She offered them a bright smile and said, "You're very kind. This fine gentleman beside me is Major Aleister March. He keeps an eye on our family, and he told me of your visit."

Another round of accolades rippled through the hundred-strong crowd, and Beth raised her hands to ask for quiet. Once the murmurs died out, she added, "The Duke is away presently, but I'm sure he'd be pleased to see you as well."

"His Grace isn't home today?" asked a woman near the gates. "But the flag's up."

"No, he isn't here, not at the moment," replied the Duchess. "Yes, the flag was raised when my husband returned from Cumbria, but he's working elsewhere today."

"You've a right nice home, Yer Grace," said a woman in a yellow coat. She'd come alone, and her shoes looked worn, but neatly polished. The old coat was mended and carefully pressed.

Elizabeth stepped close and touched the woman's gloved hand. "You're very kind to say so. I like your coat."

The woman blushed. "Thanks, Yer Grace. It ain't much."

"The colour suits you very well. Tell me, madam, have you come just to see our home?"

"I have, my lady," she answered, curtsying again.

"How thoughtful," the Duchess replied. "And all of you?" she asked the rest of the crowd.

"Oh yes!" exclaimed the group in joyous unison.

Jack, the Bloomsbury man's son, shouted, "I like the dogs!"

Elizabeth motioned to the boy and bent down to his eye level. "You like my dogs? So do I. Tell me, did you come alone?"

"No, my lady. That's my dad over there, and my mum's there, too."

"And your sister!" cried Mary.

"And my sister," mumbled Jack. "You're our next Queen, aren't you, my lady? My Aunt Sadie says so."

The Duchess laughed. "That's what everyone keeps telling me, but I'm content to be Duchess of Haimsbury and Branham. Would you like to come inside and see the gardens?"

"Oh, yes, please!" exclaimed the boy's eight-year-old sister. "Are your children here, my lady?"

"They're in the nursery with their nanny," Elizabeth said, "but I can show you where they like to play. Come, all of you. We've a very pleasant seating area just the other side of the fountain." She motioned to a man who stood several feet away. He'd apparently followed her out. It was Willoughby, the new underbutler.

"Mr. Willoughby!" she called. "Please, come here!"

The servant stepped briskly along the walkway until he reached the peeress. "Yes, ma'am?"

Beth whispered a set of orders, to which the underbutler nodded, then left. She turned back to the crowd. "I've asked our Mr. Willoughby to arrange some refreshments. Nothing fancy. Just hot cocoa and biscuits to stave off the chill. Major March, would you and your men show our guests inside?"

"Really, Your Grace?" asked Jack's father before allowing his children to enter. "We're hardly invited guests, ma'am."

"Nonsense. It's Easter Monday, isn't it? Come inside and sit for a short while, won't you? Ignore Major March. I'm sure he thinks me quite mad."

March did think her reckless, and he planned to discuss it with the Duke later, but for now, he said nothing.

"All of you are welcome," the Duchess added, winking at the flustered equerry. "Please, sit anywhere in this area. We'd hoped to host a garden party soon, but we're still finishing the landscaping. Perhaps, later this summer. For now, we'll call this an Easter Monday surprise."

Her heartfelt words warmed the hearts of all the onlookers, and the portly man in the morning suit shouted, "God save our Duchess!"

Another added, "God save our next Queen!"

A boisterous chant followed as the crowd passed noisily through the gates. March and the regimental guards led them through the northeast gardens, towards a small sitting area beside the fountain. The ragstone benches and willow lawn furniture soon filled with men, women, and children—most dressed in shades of blue or grey, with a few wearing spring colours of yellow, pink, and lavender.

Beth looked upon the group with happy eyes. If Charles were to accept the throne, then these dear people would be his subjects. And though she doubted he would ever accept public sovereignty, his role as Shadow King made him answerable to the people of the British Empire.

Each and every one of them was important.

She took her time and milled about, talking to this person and that. Willoughby returned in short order, accompanied by four footmen, each pushing wooden trollies, laden with copper urns, porcelain mugs, and dozens of cloth-covered baskets. The servants distributed cocoa, pastries, and freshly baked almond and chocolate biscuits.

Elizabeth sat with the Bloomsbury family. As they enjoyed the refreshments, she asked the boy, "Tell me, young sir, do you live nearby?"

"Up by the museum, my lady," he answered cheerfully.

"Oh? I love museums. Which one?" she asked.

"He means the British Museum, Your Grace," John's father explained. "I'm one of the curators there. Assyriology. Dull stuff to most people."

"Not to me," she replied with a bright smile. "I find such topics very interesting. In fact, my husband and I've visited your section of the museum many times."

"Really? That's quite surprising. Your Grace, should you or His Grace ever wish to see the stored exhibits, I'd be pleased to guide you through. They're locked away, you see."

"That's kind of you," she replied. "I'll mention your offer to my husband."

"Please do!" exclaimed the young curator. "The museum would be honoured. And may I add, your generosity today is beyond all expectations, Your Grace. Letting us in and even offering us hot drinks, I mean. The truth is we're intruding. You have every right to clear us off."

Beth smiled. "Why would I do that? I'm not quite sure why you've chosen to visit our house this morning, but I'd be a very poor hostess if I drove you away."

"It's kind of you to see it that way, Your Grace," said the curator.

"And you are?" she asked.

"Oh, do forgive my manners! I should have introduced myself. It's John Perry, my lady."

"And as you're a curator, I imagine it's Dr. Perry. Is that right?"

"Yes, ma'am. My son's also named John, though we call him Jack. And this is my daughter. She's Mary, and my wife is Amaryllis, though, she goes by Amy."

Amy Perry had pink cheeks and large grey eyes. Beth noticed auburn hair peeking out from beneath the frilled, lavender bonnet. "It's a very great honour to meet you, Your Highness," Amy whispered. She offered a nervous curtsy. "I don't think we'll ever forget this day."

The Duchess responded with her very best smile. She felt a kinship with the young family, for her husband had once lived as a commoner. Had Albert St. Clair lived, the boy might have behaved just like these precious children. Beth found herself drawn to their honest simplicity and genuine love for one another.

"You're very kind," she told the bashful woman. "Your daughter favours you, Mrs. Perry. And you, Master Jack, do you plan to follow in your father's footsteps and study Assyriology?"

"Not sure, ma'am. I might be a doctor. The kind that looks after animals, I mean. Those are nice dogs. Is the white one a Labrador, ma'am?"

"Yes, he is," she told the lad. "His name's Aramis, and the smaller one is Lady Napper. She belongs to our eldest daughter Adele."

"How old is she?" asked eight-year-old Mary.

"Do you mean the spaniel? She's about five and a half."

"I'm sorry, my lady," the girl answered. "I meant your daughter, ma'am. How old is she?"

"Ah, well, Adele will turn seventeen this June. She's at finishing school presently, and the headmistress doesn't permit dogs or cats. And so, we've been looking after Lady Napper."

Mary sighed. "It must be wonderful for your daughter. Finishing school, I mean. I'd like to go to school one day, but they accept only boys."

"I know of a few schools that accept young ladies," said the Duchess. "Tell me, Mary, what would you study, if you could go?"

"I'd study numbers, my lady. Mathematics and the stars!" she blurted out eagerly with wide eyes.

"Ah, now, my husband would enjoy talking to you about numbers, I'm sure. The Duke read mathematics at Cambridge. He finds numbers quite satisfying."

"We saw a man with six fingers," the boy blurted out.

"You saw what?" asked Beth.

"A man with six fingers. I'm not making it up. Papa saw him, too."

Beth motioned towards March, who was talking with one of the guards. "Major March, I'd like you to hear what this young man has to say. Jack, would you repeat your comment for the major?"

The boy nodded. "I said, we talked to a man with six fingers. Six on both hands. His gloves are special made, and his shoes are different, too. Well, one is. He's very strange. He came all the way from Hastings."

"And is that gentleman nearby?" asked March. "I should very much like to meet someone with six fingers."

"He's over there," said Jack's sister. "Not inside with us. He's by that big tree. It's an ash, I think. Is that right, Papa?"

"Yes, Mary, that's an ash tree. We talked with him, too, Your Grace, but I don't see the man now."

Beth looked towards the ash tree. Ravenhill allowed his human form to flicker in and out of reality. He was testing Elizabeth's spiritual eyesight. The fallen spirit behind the human guise wanted to learn more about her abilities.

The Duchess stared at the tree. For a moment, it seemed to shimmer with intricate sparks. The fleeting vision caused dread to overwhelm her heart. It filled Beth with terror. Not for herself, but for her husband.

Something is coming. Something is about to happen.

Young Mary Perry set down her cocoa and pointed towards the gates again. "Don't you see him? He's sort of hiding, I think. Like he's playing a game. Funny sort of man, isn't he?"

"I'm not sure, Mary. You're right. He might be hiding. Could you describe him for me?" Beth asked the child.

Jack jumped in to answer. "He's like a big black shadowy man. Hugely tall, and he uses a cane to walk. He has a bad left foot. He talks a lot, too."

The father had been talking to the portly man in the morning suit and turned to intervene. "That's quite enough, both of you. I apologise for my children, Your Grace. I don't know what's gotten into them. There was a man, that much is true. He told us his name is Justice Ravenhill. He's a journalist or something like that. And he did say he drove up from Hastings, but he must have left. Odd, don't you think? Driving all this way, then leaving the instant you came to the gate? Very strange behaviour."

"No, Papa," insisted young Mary. "He didn't leave. He's still there. Can't you see him? He's by the ash tree!"

Beth felt cold—as though ice pellets formed round her heart. *Come find me,* a voice whispered inside her head. *I've brought your little dolly. Don't you want to play with her? Shall I give her to your children? Georgie might like a little dolly.*

The Duchess felt faint, but the mention of her children melted the ice pellets in one fiery blaze of maternal anger. No one would harm her children! She turned to the girl. "Mary, could you show me where the man's standing?"

She nodded. "I can take you to him, if you want, ma'am."

Beth smiled at the sweet child's enthusiasm. *Do I dare involve this girl in our troubles? But she can see the creature, when I cannot. Why is that?* "You're very helpful, Mary, and you have keen eyes. Dr. Perry, might I borrow your daughter for a moment?"

"Yes, of course, Your Grace," the curator replied. "Shall I go, too?"

"If you wish."

Beth took the child's hand, and Mary led her father and the Duchess past the fountain and towards a section of the fence, just south of the main gates. "He's right there," she said, pointing to a tall ash tree.

From his hiding place, Justice Ravenhill laughed in a deep voice. He stepped slowly out of the parallel world of *Sen-Sen*, but remained within the inter-dimensional portal, as though standing in a doorway: neither in nor out. The spirit's human guise caused the real-world light to bend. Very few natural eyes could perceive it, but Jack and Mary saw him.

And now, so did Elizabeth.

"Stay here, Mary," she said, intending to confront the creature. Major March remained close. "Dr. Perry, you should take your daughter back to the seating area. Thank you for your help."

"Come, Mary. The Duchess and Major March will deal with this," said Dr. Perry. The antiquarian had an odd feeling about it all; as though he'd just witnessed a thoroughly abnormal interaction. He'd spoken with Ravenhill for several minutes, yet the man had simply vanished.

Or had he?

March followed the Duchess towards the ash tree. Aramis's fur stood straight up, forming a high ridge of warning along his long back. His ears pinned back, and he began to growl. Aleister March had the urge to grab the peeress by the hand and drag her back to the house, even though he saw nothing out of the ordinary. The ash tree looked evil now: a dark void of sorts.

"Your Grace, we should go back inside," he told her.

"I'll be all right," she assured the equerry.

Both dogs barked and growled. As Beth neared the tree, Aramis shot forward in a quick flash of white. He ran through the gates and rushed directly at the tree. Beth watched the animal leap at the flickering creature. The brave dog's teeth ripped into the Shadow's polydactyl hands.

"Aramis!" March called as he chased the dog.

The equerry reached for the animal's collar, but in the process, touched the Shadow's hand. A shock coursed along the soldier's forearm, and a voice whispered into his thoughts.

Tell your master that it's our move, Major. Tell Sinclair that Legion is coming. Legion is watching. Time is running out. Tick tock!

March nearly fainted as he pulled back the hand. It stung as though cut with a knife.

Beth ran towards the ash tree. She could see the Shadow Man fully now; dressed all in black with a stovepipe hat. Justice Ravenhill stared at the terrified Duchess; his lips curled. He started towards her, but Aramis and Napper joined forces and leapt at the otherworldly enemy. Beth heard a howling scream—a deep-throated wail from another world. Aramis had bitten into the creature's hand and drawn a strange sort of ooze from its flesh. The creature screamed and retreated through the portal. Aramis continued to bark and snap at the shimmering air, assisted by Lady Napper.

"Good dogs," Beth told them firmly, though her heart was in her throat. "And thanks be to God for protecting us! Come, now. Aramis, Napper, let's all go back inside, and we'll find you a nice biscuit."

Beth stopped as she reached the ironwork gate. She felt a little dizzy again. March took her arm, and Dr. Perry offered his hand as well.

"My lady, are you all right? You look as though you've had a dreadful shock!" Perry exclaimed.

With concentration, Elizabeth kept her balance. *Don't let them see weakness, Princess,* she could hear her grandfather's voice say. "I'm all right, but thank you for being so kind."

March kept imagining the Duke's reaction when he heard about this incident later in the day. No doubt, someone would tell him. Aleister decided he must be first to tell this tale. "Your Grace, let's return indoors," he insisted. "His Grace would be most upset were he here."

"Yes, of course. You're right." She turned to the curator. "Thank you again for your help, Dr. Perry. I should like to call on you at the Museum, if you're available. Do you keep regular hours?"

"Ten until six, Monday through Saturday. We're shut on Sundays," the man answered. "As it's Easter Monday, the museum's closed today. My wife and children wanted to see your new home. We never imagined we'd be sitting in your garden or enjoying your cocoa. You've been most generous, my lady. Generous beyond our fondest hopes."

"You're kind to say so," she told him. "And I've enjoyed our visit." Then, turning to the rest of the group, she added, "Thank you all for coming today. The Duke will be most upset that he's missed meeting you. However, it's unlikely we'll make a habit of opening the gates. For security reasons. I hope you understand."

Everyone nodded and smiled. The woman in yellow called out, "Of course, we understand, Your Grace. We'd never want anything to happen to you or the Duke! Or to the children!"

Beth smiled at her, imagining herself in that situation. The woman looked proud but kindly. Worn through just like her clothes. She made a mental note to talk with Charles about setting up a clothing charity, not only for adults, but for children as well. "Thank you, madam. I'm glad you understand, for we've had a few, rather upsetting events happen to us since our marriage. That's why we keep men like Major March and our brave regimental guards nearby."

"May I say something, Your Grace?" asked the woman in the mended, yellow coat. "None of us expects this sort o' hospitality again. You're a gentle, generous soul, if I may say so, my lady. And we've imposed on you far too much. I'll certainly have something to tell my grandchildren. I can't thank you enough for that."

The Duchess took the woman's gloved hand and said, "May God grant you many healthy grandchildren, madam."

"Thank you, my lady. Thank you very much." The woman curtsied deeply, as she might to the Queen herself.

The valiant dogs started to follow Beth towards the house, but then Aramis turned about and stared at the spot where Justice Ravenhill had stood.

Another entity stood there now.

A different sort of being. This one was taller than the other. A majestic figure with long hair of midnight black. He carried a fiery sword in his right hand. He looked friendly and had *ice-blue eyes.*

If dogs could smile, Aramis the Labrador would have beamed with joy. He liked the shimmering visitor. The gates had shut, so the animal ran to the fence and jumped onto the ironwork balusters, closest to the ash tree. His thick tail wagged furiously from side to side.

From beyond the fence, the long-haired figure bent low and scratched the faithful Labrador's head.

Good dog, the being whispered. *You have clear eyes, Aramis son of Briar. Go now. Return to your mistress. Stay close to her, Aramis. Let me deal with Ravenhill and all his wicked brothers.*

CHAPTER EIGHT

The Inner Circle Gathers at King's Court

During the new estate's construction phase, Duke Charles asked the architect to include a large private library for inner-circle meetings with sound-proof insulation in every wall and even up the chimney stack, to keep discussions secret. It was young Robby Sinclair who named the room. Originally, the plans blandly listed it as 'The Red Library', but the four-year-old wisely suggested any room used by his father's advisers should be known as the 'King's Council Library'. At first, they'd all joked about the boy's innocent suggestion, but the name soon stuck; sometimes shortened to a succinct acronym, the KCL. The name's irony wasn't lost on Sinclair, who hoped to avoid any future where he was publicly crowned. Yet, even his son seemed resolved to the fact.

The King's Council Library sat directly above the home's main foyer, a vast entryway appropriately named Tree Hall. As the men and women arrived that evening, each was greeted by John Miles and his underbutler Mr. Willoughby, who directed a team of footmen to hang cloaks, hats, and wraps.

The first to arrive was Martin Kepelheim. Originally, the tailor asked to meet with Sinclair at four, but Charles changed the time to seven, when he issued the urgent call to London's members to assemble and discuss the murder in Whitechapel—as well as Beth's strange experience at the eastern gate.

"Welcome to King's Court, sir," said the elegantly attired head butler as he took Kepelheim's coat and hat. "This is your second time, I believe, sir? Or is it the third?"

"Fourth, actually," the tailor replied, "but each visit's even better than the first. This house is beautiful, Mr. Miles! I saw it during various phases of construction, of course, but the impact of the finished home is extraordinary. A veritable feast for the senses! Tell me, Lord Salperton," he said to his travelling companion, "is this your maiden voyage?"

"Not exactly," the alienist answered as he passed his overcoat to Willoughby. "Third time, actually, and I wholeheartedly echo your sentiments, Mr. Kepelheim. This house has no equal in England. Nor in Scotland, I should think."

"I'm told the trees are made of steel," observed a tall man with grey whiskers as he joined the two men. "Shaped, then wrapped in a veneer of marble. Is that right, Henry?"

"Yes, that's right, Dr. Whitmore," said MacAlpin. "Is Lady Victoria with you?"

"As usual, my wife's bringing up the rear," replied the amiable physician. "Tory's a constant dawdler. An old habit, I've come to realise."

"Ah, but we do love her habits, don't we?" jibed the tailor. "Did you know that Tree Hall represents Beth's dream? Charles saw it, too, didn't he, Henry?"

"Oaks and willows," the alienist whispered, his nut-brown eyes on the magnificent corridor of marble trees. "Charles explained its meaning to me on my first visit here. It's simply breathtaking, don't you think, Mr. Kepelheim? I mean, what other house has a grand foyer, lined with oak trees made of marble?"

"None," the tailor declared. "The willows by the staircase are my favourites. They're so very graceful. And all the trees' leaves are formed from coloured glass. Truly, this home is a palace."

Just then, Charles Sinclair appeared at the top of the tall staircase, waiting for his guests from a broad landing, set twixt the glass-leaved willows. "This way, everyone. The library's up here. Where's James?"

"Dawdling with Tory," called Whitmore as he headed towards the stairs.

"How many are we tonight?" Kepelheim asked as he climbed the marble steps.

"As many as possible," replied Charles. "I sent for everyone in London. And I see our chief inspector's arrived. We're up this way, Neil!" he called to a tall man below.

Cornelius Baxter waved as he handed a stylish overcoat to Willoughby. Since retiring from household service to become an ICI detective, the former butler had grown a thick beard of silver and black, that added to his aura of dignity and wisdom. As with the other circle gentlemen, Baxter was dressed in evening clothes: a black tail cutaway, white waistcoat, and tie. John Miles took his friend's silk hat.

"Tell me, Mr. Miles, how do you like serving in so grand a house?" Baxter asked.

"Chief Inspector, I should be happy to serve the Duke and Duchess in any house, as would you, I'm sure. But this house is something quite special. It outshines all others."

"Shall we call it King's Court Palace, then?" Baxter suggested with a wink. "Good evening, Duke James," he said to the next man in line. "I imagine you've been here many times. What do you think of calling it King's Court Palace?"

James Robert Ian Stuart IV stood six feet tall with a muscular build. At seventy-five, the Scotsman still had a physical presence that caused ladies to swoon and men to worry. The 10th Duke of Drummond had dark brown eyes, sun-burnt skin, and laugh lines round the mouth and corners of each eye. Whenever he smiled, which was often, a set of deep dimples creased the sun-flushed cheeks, and rays of Scottish sunshine glistened in the dark eyes.

"Aye, Mr. Baxter, it's true," Drummond answered in a Scottish brogue. "I've been keeping watch on the wee bairns whilst Charles was up north and our Beth was wanderin' about Europe with this one," he added, referring to MacAlpin. "We'll be wantin' a full report on that trip, Henry. And an explanation as to why Paul's not come back with you."

"I'll be pleased to explain all that I'm able," said MacAlpin. "But the earl's reasons are often muddied by international intrigues."

Next to her brother, walked the typically chatty Victoria Stuart Whitmore. Tory had just arrived from the home she shared with Reggie in Paris. As was often the case, she looked annoyed.

"James, have you any idea why we've been summoned? I'm happy to come, of course, but a last-minute edict is highly unusual. I was planning to leave today for Paris. Has something happened to Beth or one of the children? The telegram was irritatingly vague.

Come at once. Seven o'clock. And written in code, no less! Does Charles think someone's intercepting his messages?"

"I've no idea, Tory. Say, there's Mac! Good to see you again, MacPherson. How was Ireland?" called Drummond to the next man to enter the main doors.

"Ireland's still there," answered the cleric.

Dr. Edward Andrew MacPherson had recently retired from teaching at Westminster Seminary and just returned from a research sabbatical in Dublin. "I'll tell you all about it over a brandy. I found out a great deal about those strange incidents from Stoker's childhood. Oh, hello, Henry. Good to see you, son. Does anyone know why we've been called? Has the long quiet ended?"

"I'd say it has," Drummond answered soberly. "And here's our Edmund Reid. Welcome, Inspector. I hear you're planning to relocate to Herne Bay, is that right?"

Reid was just handing a brown overcoat to the underbutler. He brushed back his thinning hair with a gloved hand. "Well, yes, Your Grace, I've been looking into it. How did you know that, sir?"

"A wee birdie," answered Drummond. He noticed his nephew motioning towards them. "Yes, I know! We're dawdling," he called to the younger duke. "We're coming, Charles!"

As they all climbed, each marvelled at the paintings and murals. The landing depicted a painted prophecy of Christ's future kingdom in Jerusalem, with a split Mount of Olives on one side, and the throne of God on the Temple Mount. Beyond this, the circle members passed through a decorated corridor that ended in a set of beautifully carved doors. On the walls and overhead, the corridor's murals portrayed the promised resurrection of saints, as told in the Bible. Using the plaster and paint of an artist's brush, Charles Sinclair made it clear to one and all just where he placed his faith: in Christ, and Him alone.

The Duke led his friends through the carved doors and up to a second-floor corridor that featured portraits from Stuart and Sinclair family history. Faces of Plantagenets, Stuarts, Bourbons, Capets, and Valois stared back at them. Farther on, a series of interconnected state rooms led the gathering through to the majestic doors of King's Council Library.

"Son, this house is grander than any of my homes," his uncle confessed. "I'll have to hire that architect of yours to re-do Drummond House. What's his name again?"

"Sir Anthony Breville, sir. Lord Ailesleigh recommended him. But you'll have to wait until he's finished with our projects first. Breville's redesigning the old Haimsbury House as an educational facility for the ICI. Come in, won't you, everyone? Miles and Willoughby have laid out refreshments. Beth's asked us to convene without her this evening. She's still recovering from her recent travels."

"Will she come down for supper?" asked Tory. "I've not seen Beth since they stopped in Paris. I hope she's not ill again."

Charles turned to look at his aunt. "Beth was ill?"

"Only briefly, but I'm sure it was nothing," Victoria added. "I may go up after we meet, if that's all right. Is she taking supper upstairs?"

"Yes, but she's fine, Tory," Charles answered. "As I say, she's tired. Do eat, everyone. Our new chef's provided us a fine meal, with food to please even a discerning Scotsman."

"I'll tuck in, then, shall I?" asked his Scottish uncle.

"Help yourself, James," Charles told him with a hug to the older man's shoulder. "It's good to have you here, sir."

Before them, stretched an oak table, long enough to host fifty. Porcelain vases filled with fresh flowers provided colour, and six silver candelabra offered lighting. Each side of the table was set with H&B china, rimmed in gold. On two large sideboards, the staff had arranged hot and cold foods. A third table contained water, wine, and after-dinner spirits. Beside it, stood a three-tiered cart, laden with tempting desserts.

"We're letting the staff take the night off," Charles explained. "They've worked very long hours to get the house open. I hope no one minds self-serve buffet."

"I prefer it," said Drummond. "Are we all here?"

"Yes, I think so," Charles answered, glancing at the group. "Miles, if you and Willoughby would secure the outer doors, I think we'll be fine on our own. Go enjoy your evening off."

"And what of the cloaks and hats, sir?" asked Willoughby.

Miles gave the answer. "Mr. Willoughby, you'll find that His Grace's companions are quite adept at caring for themselves." Then to his employer, said, "We've arranged them in the foyer, just as we discussed, Your Grace."

The underbutler looked perplexed. "It's contrary to everything I was taught in my training, but I'll be glad for the night off, my lord. Thank you, sir."

The servants bowed and left. The inner-circle membership found places round the table.

"Before we fill our plates, may we pray?" asked Charles from the head of the table. "James, you've served as leader of this assembly for many years. As we begin our first night of service in this new house, I'd like the opening prayer to be yours, sir."

Drummond stood to his nephew's right, and he placed a hand on Sinclair's shoulder, eyes bright. "Son, you make this old man very proud. Thank you for asking. Everyone, let's bow our heads, shall we?"

Each man and woman in the company lowered his or her head and took the hands of those nearest. Drummond's deep voice filled the room as he began to pray.

"Lord of all the world, creator of angel and human alike, we gather here this evening for the first time as a company, in a household dedicated to you and your eternal kingdom. If some call it King's Court, then let it be King Jesus who rules here. Our King, Redeemer, Creator of all. Each member sitting here this evening believes that..."

Knock. Knock. Knock.

James paused and raised his eyes towards his nephew. "Shall I continue? It might be important, son."

Knock. Knock. Knock.

"Charles?" asked Drummond again.

KNOCK, KNOCK, KNOCK!

"Whoever it is must need you right away, sir," said Baxter. "I'm closest. I'll go." The barrel-chested chief inspector crossed the tiled floor, to the imposing doors, but they opened on their own, revealing John Miles with the Duchess.

Elizabeth Sinclair's face was ghostly pale.

"He's gone!" she wailed; her arms thrown wide.

Charles took his wife's hands. "Who's gone? Beth, what is it?"

"Robby!" she cried in a pitiful voice. "He left the nursery a little while ago to visit me, but never arrived. We've searched the entire master wing. Charles, he's gone!"

"He must be here somewhere, darling," said the Duke gently. "He's probably gone down to the kitchens for biscuits. We'll find him. Don't worry. Miles, let's organise a search party; and, James," he continued with a glance at Drummond, "would you mind helping down here? Beth, try not to worry. He can't have gone far."

The Duchess looked as though she might faint, and Henry MacAlpin hastened to help her to a chair. "Come, Beth, sit. That's doctor's orders."

"I can't sit!" she cried, her eyes red with tears. "I have to help! He's gone, I tell you!"

"No, you need to sit," MacAlpin insisted. "Let Charles and the men look. They'll find him. I'm sure of it."

The circle members formed four parties. And soon, France, Baxter, Kepelheim, Whitmore, Reid, and every able-bodied gentleman and lady were racing down the long corridor to begin the search. Beth could hear a variety of voices as teams split up to cover more ground. With nearly a thousand rooms, the estate was a vast labyrinth for a small child to hide in.

Sinclair knelt before his wife and kissed her trembling hands. "We'll find him, little one. I promise. Tory, stay with her, will you? Aunt Louisa, if you'd stay, too?"

Both women nodded, and Charles Sinclair ran from the grand setting of King's Council Library to search for his eldest child.

Somewhere, near the woods...

Robby Sinclair had fallen asleep at half past seven, happy but exhausted after spending a long day hiking with his tutor, Dr. Simon Bettenhouse. Usually called just 'Dr. Simon' by the Sinclair children, the eager instructor had taken Rob and and Jamie on a nature walk round the estate's west gardens. Not surprisingly, as Robby fell asleep that evening, he dreamt of their hike. The dream's plot followed reality, but with a few exceptions. In the dream, his cousin Ian Stuart, Paul's son, had joined Rob and Jamie on their outing. Ian was four months younger than Rob Sinclair, but far more energetic and brash.

In the dream-world, Bettenhouse led Rob, Ian, and Jamie on the nature hike, teaching the boys about bird life and native grasses. The expanse of land to the west of King's Court included King's Meadow, Anjou Lake, and the remains of Castle Anjou. To the north, an informal garden marked the edge of King James Woods, named for James I, who'd built Queen Anne House. In reality, Bettenhouse had discussed springtime rituals and nesting habits of the lake's trumpet swans; but in the dream, Rob's mind refashioned the lecture as a staging ground for something quite sinister.

This is how the dream went:

As Dr. Bettenhouse described the natural world round the lake, Rob found it difficult to concentrate. He was distracted by a variety of birds, squirrels, and the occasional deer near Castle Anjou. But then a fox caught his eye; a monstrously large fox with pale blue eyes. The sly animal stared at the child, fixing the boy's gaze and drawing him into a trance: a dream within a dream.

"Come on, sleepyhead!" a female voice called. "Let's explore!"

It wasn't the fox, but his sister that spoke. This dream-world version of Georgianna Sinclair looked very different to the real one; taller, more grown-up, and she acted most peculiarly.

"Come on, Rob!" the dream Georgianna called. "Let's explore the woods. It'll be fun!"

The dreaming boy tried to follow his sister, but she'd already vanished within the trees. Rob stopped at the edge of the dark woods, fearful of entering. He'd heard strange tales from the servants about King James Woods: Stories of shadowy people who lived inside; ghosts of men, who were hanged by the old Stuart kings; vengeful, dreadful apparitions with sharp knives and fiery swords.

"Georgie!" he called to his twin from the wood's edge. "George, where are you?"

He heard no answer. There was no one in sight. Nothing but the wind and thick darkness. *What happened to the sun? When did it go down?* he wondered. *And where is everybody?*

Behind him, from the other side of the lake, Rob could hear Dr. Bettenhouse continuing his lecture. He could see Ian and Jamie sitting beside the tutor. Rob cupped his hands and called out, but no one answered. No one looked his way.

It was though Robert Sinclair had become a ghost.

"Where are you, Georgie?" he asked aloud, praying his sister would return and help. "Georgie, please! Where are you?"

He'd definitely heard her voice and he'd seen her, though, she did look quite different. Older somehow. Where had she gone? He called again. "Georgie! George, answer me!"

Still no answer. Only the whistling of the rising wind.

The fox appeared again; the monstrously large grey fox with the ice-blue eyes. The animal's eyes narrowed as it stared into the boy's face. Rob was pulled into its gaze. The animal slowly moved towards him.

One step. Two steps. Then, three long steps.

Then, it stopped.

The dream felt completely real, and yet unreal. Familiar and exceedingly strange. Per his mother's suggestion, Rob had begun recording his dreams, each entry written in a child's faltering hand with a mechanical pencil he'd received from his Great-Grandfather Drummond for Christmas. Along with the pencil, he'd received a leather journal with cream linen pages. He'd already filled half the book, and though Rob had no memory of it whilst dreaming, he'd written about the fox many times before.

Always large. Always grey. Always with pale blue eyes, like angry orbs of arctic ice.

In *this* dream, however, the strange grey fox ran into the woods. Rob remained at the edge, calling over and over for his sister. The boy feared the woods, yet felt a keen sense of responsibility for his three siblings. Though petite, his twin Georgianna possessed a fierce personality that Rob admired. He worried about her, constantly making sure of her safety. He did the same with Jamie and little Connor.

Jamie's safe, the dreamer told himself. *Cousin Ian is safe. Connor's inside the house with Mrs. Baxter. But where has Georgianna gone?*

"Georgie!" the dreaming child shouted over and over. Despair filled his spirit, and his voice grew hoarse. Rob still stood at the woodland's edge. The fox appeared again and tempted him to enter. Still, the boy hesitated. There were ghosts and horrid people inside it, right? The sly fox waited, its glacial eyes glittering.

Near his feet, Rob could see the imprints of small shoes in the mud. And from up ahead, he heard the sharp *crack!* of breaking twigs amidst the soft footfalls of running feet.

"George! Please, Georgie, this isn't funny!" he moaned. "We're not allowed to go into the woods!"

The fox stood beside the shoe prints. It blinked at the boy; then—*like a shot!*—it bolted once more into the woods.

Rob wanted to cry. If he didn't follow now, he'd lose sight of the fox. But if he did go into the woods, what might happen?

"Robby!" his twin sister's voice called from deep within the trees. "Come on, Rob! Come find me!"

With a quick prayer, the boy dashed into the dark woods. He ran and ran, for the longest time. It felt like hours and hours, but he found no more footprints. From time to time, his sister called again; her voice leading him deeper and deeper into the thick trees.

"George, it's dark! We have to go back! Where are you?"

Young Robert Sinclair was exhausted. He had to stop and catch his breath. His right side ached—just as side muscles do, when you've overtaxed your lungs, for even in a dream, the dreamer feels pain and loss. He could also feel fear. Rob was tired and *very* afraid.

He'd reached a clearing. Most of the trees were English oaks, as broad as they were tall, their swaying canopies crowded together as though discussing some great matter. The thick twigs and ambling branches inter-wove into arms and fingers, closer than any thicket. It was a compact copse of conspiring trees.

What now? the boy wondered. Not only had he lost his sister, he'd also lost track of the fox. Other animals chattered within the conspiring copse. Hares, badgers, and birds. Then, from high overhead, came a rush of sound; the sort of sound a flock of geese make when they sail through the air, seeking a new home or water.

Rob turned his eyes skyward. He saw no geese, only a great gathering of birds of a different sort. Perched within the upper branches of the trees, perched an assembly of the biggest blackbirds he'd ever seen—even in picture books. But they weren't actually blackbirds, nor were they merlins or grackles.

No, these were *ravens*.

Bigger and noisier than any bird the sensitive boy had ever seen in waking or dreaming memory. One stood out as special. Perhaps he was their leader, Rob reasoned. This bird occupied the lowest branch of the woodland web. The oak bough swayed beneath its great weight. It had startlingly yellow eyes, that glittered and gleamed in the darkness like a pair of yellow garnets.

"Who are you, and why are you here, tiny human?" the bird asked.

Rob swallowed the fear that overwhelmed his small heart. He felt dizzy, unnerved, strange; all his limbs were cold. *Where's my coat? I've no gloves or shoes. I had a coat when I left the house, didn't I? And shoes, too.*

He struggled to sort truth from lies. *Am I dreaming?* he wondered. Then he remembered Georgianna.

"Where's my sister?" he asked the talking bird, finding a voice at last.

"Do you mean the pretty one?" responded the yellow-eyed raven. "With eyes as dark as the abyss?"

"Yes, she has dark eyes. Where is she?"

"Did I say I'd seen her?" parried the cruel bird. "I've described her, yes, but admitted no visual contact. Not recently, anyway. How did you get past the gate?"

"What gate?" Rob asked, his head whirling round to scan the area.

"What gate? What a silly question! How did you get past *my* gate?" asked the bird. "This is my domain, and you entered without permission. Who sent you? How did you get past my guards?"

Rob thought of his father. He wondered how the great Duke of Haimsbury might respond to such a question. The boy admired his father and hoped to be just like him one day, so he stuck out his chest and feigned bravery.

"*Your* gate?" Rob challenged the bird. "You don't own anything here. This is King's Woods, and my father owns it. There aren't any gates."

The large bird fluttered down from the branch and strutted close to the boy. It stood six feet in height and looked down upon the shorter child. "That might be true in the human realm, but you've passed into *my* world, boy. All of that you see is MINE."

"Nonsense. How can it be yours?"

The bird bent low and stared into Rob's blue eyes. Its breath stank of rotting meat and sulphur. "You look familiar. It's your eyes,

I think. They look like ones I've seen here before. Eyes of someone else from long ago. Some call them *sea-blue*."

"Get away from me!" Rob commanded in his most imposing voice.

The raven leapt backwards, startled by the boy's bravado. "Hmm. Interesting."

"Why would you say that? Why am I interesting?"

"Did I say that *you* are interesting?"

"I believe you did. Just what sort of bird are you?"

"Hah! Now, that is a very fine question!" the bird squawked. "A most intelligent question!"

"If you like questions, then answer this," Rob said. "Where is my sister?"

"Sister? I see no sisters here," the raven replied. "But tell me why you look so very familiar?"

"I don't know."

The raven walked round the child in slow, deliberate steps. It grunted now and then in birdlike fashion, then cried out in a loud voice, "I have it! You're his son, aren't you? The other boy of blood. I've seen you in the *asaru* stones. The stones never lie. I shall have to tell the Queen about this."

"Go ahead and tell her!" Rob shouted. "I'm not afraid of you!"

"You're quite feisty for a little boy."

"Tell me where you've put my sister!"

The raven's yellow eyes blinked several times. "Sister? And who might that be?"

"You know who she is. You said she has dark eyes. Her name is Georgianna Sinclair."

"Sinclair! Hah! I'm right!" the raven exulted. He leaned in close, spewing and spitting the foul breath. "I know your father, boy," it said slyly. "I kept him with me for a very, very long time. He's walked through Time itself. Some call him King. Are you like him, boy? Shall I bring you inside and test your blood? Would you like to tour my domain?"

"I want my sister. I heard her voice. She called to me."

The bird shrugged its midnight-black wings. "If you've lost a sister, don't blame me. Twas you who left her behind, assuming she was ever here at all. Perhaps, you're dreaming."

"I don't know. I might be. But I saw my sister pass, and she came in here. Where is she? Where is Georgianna!"

"If she came in here, then she's probably dead," suggested the devilish bird.

Now, young Charles Robert Sinclair was tall for his age. Very tall. He'd already passed forty-eight inches and was on track to be six-foot-five, if not taller. But at that moment, in an exhausting dream-world, the boy felt tiny, tired, and entirely overwhelmed. His head ached, and his feet felt as though they were growing roots, like those of the conspiring old oaks. The very thought that his sister could die, even in a dream, struck at the very centre of the boy's heart and sapped every last ounce of his strength. Pain stabbed at all his limbs, and his blood ran cold.

The cruel bird laughed. "And Eluna claims your bloodline is perfect. Bah! Your blood is weak, boy! Do you even know where you are?"

Rob shook his head. He tried to separate truth from lies, reality from dreams. "I'm not sure. Why is it so dark?"

"Because the moon is angry with you, boy, that's why," the bird sang back gleefully. "But Princess Eluna might know where your sister is. Why not ask her?"

"Who is she? How do I talk to her?"

"See the stone walls up ahead?" tempted the bird.

Rob's eyelids drooped. His vision blurred. "Stone walls?"

"Those lovely, old bluestone walls. They form part of a magnificent maze; just there, at the end of the path. Look past the reclining statues, and you'll see them. That, boy, is your destiny."

The yellow-eyed raven reached down with one wing and touched the boy's hand. A deadly shudder ran through Rob's bones, as though he'd fallen through a crack in a frozen pond and begun to drown.

"I can't move," he said with a shudder. "Why can't I move?"

"Perhaps, your blood's impure. If it's not the right *kind* of blood, you'll die."

"Die? Why? Why am I here? Am I dreaming?"

"No, boy. You're not dreaming. You are almost DEAD."

With that cruel remark, the bird transformed into the shape of a man with spikey hair and a black cloak made of feathers.

"What happened? Who are you?" Rob asked through chattering teeth.

"I'm your escort," the bird-man told him with a mocking bow.

"Why am I so sleepy? Why does it feel like I'm falling?"

"Because you are dying," the creature whispered.

"Why? What have I done?" Rob begged.

The tall bird-man hopped towards the child and bowed down, a glinting blade in its left hand. He lifted the knife, ready to strike. Rob pulled back in fear, praying for help...

"HOLD!" thundered a booming deep voice from beyond Rob's eyesight. "Leave that child alone, Uriens, son of Mischief, or I will roast you for my dinner!"

"Why? Why! Why must I do so?" the raven asked angrily. "I have every right to slay him. He is in my domain, and in my world. I have every right!"

"You have no right, and you've frightened the child long enough. No more, Uriens. No more, or I'll pluck out all your feathers."

"Why? Why? *WHY?*" the bird-man shouted. "You have no power here! Be gone, or I shall pluck out your eyes!"

"Really? I doubt that. I have power everywhere," came the answer. "I go where I please, and I do what I please. Now, leave him!"

Uriens spat on the ground, then flew swiftly upwards, high into the tree. "Eluna shall hear of this!" he cawed angrily after returning to raven form. The piercing yellow eyes stared down at Rob with such rage and hunger, that Rob's heart very nearly stopped.

Then, a tall figure stepped into the boy's view. He was handsome beyond description, with perfect proportions and beautiful features. The hair was long and black as midnight, and the eyes twinkled like bits of starlight. His cloak was midnight blue and covered all over with shining stars. He reminded Rob of a storybook character. *The Pied Piper of Hamlin.* He'd always liked the Piper, for he seemed trustworthy and kind—when not double-crossed by Hamlin's town council. But the Piper liked children.

How could such a beautiful man be anything but helpful?

Soon, Rob Sinclair would realise that this version of the Pied Piper, though exceedingly beautiful and seemingly trustworthy, was a cruel liar. Indeed, this dream-world version of the Pied Piper was *terrifying.*

"Who are you?" the boy asked, his voice small.

"Which name shall I tell you, Child of Purpose? I have many. But you're right to ask. Names matter. And they tell a story. For example, your name is the same as your father's, which is the same as his father's, and so on."

"Sir, I only care about my sister. Have you seen her? Her name's Georgianna. Please, tell me, if you have. Is she all right?"

The Piper bent low, his stardust eyes an inch from Robert's own. "Perhaps, but first, I have a message for father."

"I don't understand."

"No, but he will," replied the Piper. "Tell your father—tell the Time Walker, I've not forgotten. WE'VE not forgotten!"

"We? Please, I don't understand," Rob muttered, his brain on fire. "Who are you?"

"Hasn't your father told you the story?"

"What story?"

"The story of the Time Maze," whispered the Piper as he limped forward. Only now, did Rob notice the heavy chain round the Piper's left ankle.

"Are you all right?" Rob asked politely. "Someone chained you."

"Yes, someone did. A TRAITOR chained me! My own brother!" the Piper told the boy. "Tell your father, he must return and pay for his crimes."

"I don't understand. Who are you? What has my father to do with you?"

"He cheated," the Piper whispered. "He didn't finish the test. Tell your father he must return to the Maze, or else we'll come after you. And we'll come for your sweet sister, and all your brothers. We'll come for every last one of you, and we will *EAT YOU UP!*"

The dreadful Creature lurched at the boy with outstretched hands—each bearing six fingers—but the strong chain held fast. The Piper screamed in agony and tore at the chain with his fingers. He shouted, "Get him! All of you, get this boy and kill him!"

A roaring sound buffeted the air like a mighty explosion, and suddenly, every head of all the reclining statues groaned and creaked sideways to look at the boy; each stone face filled with murderous rage. The granite mouths widened, revealing long stone fangs. The once-frozen hands gripped the hilts of swords. Ancient weapons were drawn. The ground shook and shivered. They all screamed in unison—a high-pitched, berserker sort of scream that sliced through the cold night air.

Rob could hear their heavy, stone feet pounding the ground. High overhead, a sickly pale moon glowed blood red. The red light engulfed the trees. An enormous shadow rushed towards him. The bloodthirsty stone army was led by a monstrous dragon, enveloped in a sea of black. The dragon's shadow blotted out the trees. Within the rushing swirl of black, Rob could see were a pair of crimson eyes, racing towards him.

Closer. Closer. *Closer....*

Then, everything went black.

When he awoke, Rob Sinclair was lying at the edge of the woods. A waning moon shone bleakly overhead, drifting within puffs of silver-grey clouds. The terrified boy could hear men and women calling his name, but he hadn't the strength to move.

Young Charles Robert was exhausted.

He could feel a persistent nudge against his right hand. Rob slowly turned to look, using only his eyes, for he hadn't the energy to move his head.

It was a white owl.

Now what? Rob thought gloomily, fearing the dream wasn't over. To his astonishment, the owl grew larger and larger. Its white wings began to glow with a blinding light.

"Stop, please, it hurts!" the child cried. "The light hurts, please, please, stop!"

Rob began to weep, softly calling for his father.

Warm fingers touched his forehead. A healing sensation radiated down his arms and torso. His heartbeat slowed and strengthened. His muddled mind cleared.

The piercing light slowly faded into a softer glow, and a deep voice spoke from within the gentle light.

"Fear not, Charles Robert Arthur. You have come through a very great test, in a land, that is but a shadow of things to come."

"I don't understand. Am I still dreaming?"

"The dream is past, child. Your father will very soon find you. You must write it all down, Rob, for your mother's sake and yours. Write down the dream and *remember.*"

"But where's my sister? Do you have her? Please, sir, your light is so bright! It still hurts!"

"Forgive me. Allow me to fix that."

The being's light dimmed even more, growing smaller and smaller, cooler and cooler, until it no longer hurt the child's sensitive eyes.

Now, Rob could see the person who'd rescued him. He looked like a man, though much taller than most. He was handsome, with long dark hair and kind blue eyes. He wore white raiment, girded by a golden belt; and hanging from the belt, Rob could see a jewelled scabbard and fiery sword.

"Do I know you?" he asked. "Have we met before?"

"Indeed, we have," said the angel. "But I wear different clothing when I visit your father. Rob, you must tell your father about the dream. Tell your mother, also. Will you do that?"

"Yes, sir. I will. I promise. Who were those men? The bird and the Piper?"

"Ah, now that answer requires more background to understand, but I promise to visit you whilst your father is in Vienna, and we'll discuss it. Would you like that?"

"Yes, I would, sir—but wait. Wait, I know who you are!" Rob cried suddenly. "You're my father's friend. You're Prince Anatole!"

Romanov laughed. "Yes, young sir, that's right. You and I will share many hours together in the coming years. And one day, you and your children will change the world."

The sounds of men's shouting grew louder. Rob wanted to ask more questions, but the light had already vanished. Anatole Romanov, loyal soldier of the One, was gone.

As promised, Rob's father found him near the woods. Duke Charles Sinclair held his son close as he carried him back to the house, whispering words of reassurance with every step. The sleepy child pulled close. He could hear his father's comforting heartbeat. It sounded strong but fast.

"Did I frighten you, sir?" Robby asked as they neared the west entrance.

"Yes, son, you did. Did you come out here on your own?"

"No, sir. I think, the dream brought me here. Prince Anatole saved me."

"Anatole?" asked the Duke in amazement.

"Yes, sir. He's much nicer than the other one. The Piper, I mean. I must write it all down. And remember it."

"You can tell me all about tomorrow, but now you need rest. Your mother and I will tuck you in together."

"But what about your meeting, sir?"

Charles kissed the child's face. "The meeting can wait, son. Nothing in this world is more important than you. Not one single thing."

CHAPTER NINE

Whitechapel

Aside from Charles Sinclair, the modest police station at 76 Leman Street rarely hosted anyone of high rank or great wealth. Sir Thomas Galton or Sir Percy Smythe-Daniels might stop in to interview a suspect. Dr. Anthony Gehlen, the 8th Earl of Pencaitland, occasionally helped with an autopsy, when Thomas Sunders needed a second opinion. Today, a flustered desk sergeant wore a pasted-on smile as he brought a cup of unappreciated coffee to an overbearing West-End peer.

"Just when will your station head arrive, young man?" the Earl of Stratbourne demanded. "I've not endured a rough crossing and even rougher drive up from Dover, just to drink your blasted coffee!"

Sergeant Peter Troughton sighed. He'd only recently been promoted and hoped to join Reid's famous CID team. For the present, he'd need to prove his worth by coddling a jumped-up, overdressed muckety-muck.

"I'm sure the inspector will be here soon, sir. Would you like a sandwich? We could send to the Brown Bear, if you like."

"I should like to see Edmund Reid!" the man shouted.

Poor Troughton bit his tongue. He'd nearly reached the end of his tether, when the station's big blue doors opened to a trio of very welcome faces: Edmund Reid, Elbert Stanley, and Cornelius Baxter.

It was the last of these gentlemen who spoke first. "Good morning, Lord Stratbourne, I'm Chief Inspector Baxter of the Intelligence Branch. Thank you for coming. If you'd come with us?"

"Why am I here?" shouted the peer. "Are you Reid?" he asked Stanley.

"No, sir, this is Inspector Reid," Elbert answered, pointing to Edmund. "But it's Chief Inspector Baxter who'll be heading this investigation, so if you'd..."

"Baxter?" echoed the pompous peer. "And your rank, sir?"

"Chief Inspector," Neil answered patiently.

"I seem to recall a Baxter who worked in service for the Branhams. Are you related? You look familiar. Have we met?"

"Yes, my lord, we've met. I'm the same man, only now I serve Duke Charles in a different capacity. I investigate crimes connected to espionage and anarchy. Hence, my rank with the Intelligence Branch. I'm quite sure you're aware of our existence, Lord Stratbourne. After all, as part of the Foreign Office, you receive daily updates from us. If you'd come this way?"

Without waiting for an answer, Baxter turned and walked towards a stairwell that led to the lower levels. He didn't care if the arrogant earl followed or not, for Neil intended to pursue his directive, regardless of the man's egregious behaviour. Ed Reid did the same, as did Stanley, forcing the perplexed peer to fall into line and bring up the rear, muttering and mumbling the entire way through to the morgue.

When they arrived in the forensic suite's outer offices, Stratbourne stopped. The pungent smells of alcohol, wax, and blood mixing with chemical stains and fixatives hit the man's olfactory bulb like a shot. Bile rose to the back of Stratbourne's throat, and he leaned against Elbert Stanley's shoulder.

Baxter paused and gazed at the man. "Are you unwell, sir? Your face is pale... Dr. Sunders, quickly!" he shouted into the next room. "We need you!"

Tom Sunders was sixtyish and pragmatic. He'd seen many a man faint when faced with death. Sunders drew the pallid government minister to one side and helped him to a sturdy chair. "Put your head down, sir. As low as you can. That's right," he said softly.

The man obeyed like a frightened child.

Baxter placed a firm hand on Stratbourne's back. "The spell will soon pass, my lord. We've all experienced it when first entering these rooms. Tis a different domain." Neil filled a glass from a nearby tap and brought the water over. "Small sips, sir. We've no bourbon nor brandy down here, but I could send for some, if it would help."

"No, no, I'll be all right. It's just that the smell reminded me of something else. Constantinople, long ago. Forgive me. It's an embarrassing way to act round you men." He sipped the water and used a handkerchief to wipe sweat from his eyes. "I worked there, you see. In a hospital during the '50s. Dreadful stuff! Bits of men lay all about the wards. There were saws and bandages. Blood everywhere, even up the walls sometimes. Tell me my son's body isn't like that, Chief Inspector," he begged, his pale eyes turned towards Neil's. "The Paris papers are filled with stories of this Golem creature. Is that what killed my Thomas?"

Baxter drew a chair close, to be on the same level as the earl. He spoke gently. "We don't think so, sir. And he isn't torn up. Not that way. Shall we go inside, sir?"

"Yes, yes, all right." He put out a hand, and Baxter helped ease the man to his feet. To the surprise of all, the proud Lord James David Bryan Elgin-More, 16th Earl of Stratbourne, leaned heavily upon Neil's shoulder, allowing the former butler to guide his steps into the dead room.

Inside the chilled space, two morgue assistants wearing leather aprons and sleeve protectors stepped aside to allow the pale peer to approach the body at the room's centre. A cotton sheet draped the dead man's body, now resting upon a waist-height steel gurney. Sunders walked round to the head of the table, assuming charge.

"Whenever you're ready, my lord," he told Stratbourne.

The earl nodded. "There's no getting ready for such a thing, Doctor. Go ahead. Do it."

James Elgin-More's fleshy face tensed. A second later, it melted into a drooping puddle of grief. "Yes," he whispered. "That's my son."

Sunders waited a moment, to allow the man to fully view his son's body. He'd done this with a thousand grieving family members during his time with the police force and could sense the most natural moment to put it all away; when best to block the offending truth within a pale, dead face.

The sheet returned to its former position, and the old man's eyes closed. Baxter took hold of the earl's elbow. "Would you care to sit, my lord? We could go upstairs, or down to the Brown Bear?"

"Is that a pub? Yes, yes. A drink is called for. Thank you, Chief Inspector."

Fifteen minutes later, Neil Baxter sat across from the well-dressed peer in the comfortable snug at Danny Zuschlag's popular pub. Elbert Stanley and Edmund Reid filled the other two chairs, and as lunchtime neared, each man ordered a sandwich and soup. Lord Stratbourne stared at the glass of whisky, his breathing slowly returning to normal.

"It's never easy," he said after Zuschlag's pretty waitress had taken their orders and shut the door. "I've tried to keep Tom on the straight and narrow, but he refused to listen. Preferred women and that Hunt Club set. And I don't refer to any foxhound pursuits, sirs. I fear the club my son joined is far different."

Baxter's silvering brows arched. "I shall want to hear more about this club in a moment, Lord Stratbourne, but I wonder if you might know the identity of your son's companion last Sunday night? I've a photograph of the gentleman, taken on Monday morning. We think we know his identity, but lack confirmation, as the boy has no memory. Would you mind taking a look at the photo?"

Neil took a brown packet from his inner pocket and withdrew a four-inch print of the mystery patient's face. The packet held other photographs, of course, but none he intended to show to outsiders. These reproduced the injuries to the young man's back and arms; particularly the curious writing that MacKey translated as phonetically spelling out 'Mozart' in John Dee's so-called Enochian language.

He passed the print to Stratbourne. "Is this gentleman familiar, sir?"

A shock ran along the earl's already weakened facial muscles. "Good heavens, yes! That's Garashed's son! Edward Maladroit!" He wiped his eyes again, panting heavily. "Poor fellow. Ed goes to Merton with Tom. They're cousins, through their mothers. No, I mean, they *were* cousins. Oh, dear Lord. Will it always be like this? Talking in past tense? Gone and dead and all of it over?" Stratbourne gulped down the whisky. Tears welled up in the puffy eyes, and the earl blew his nose. "Maladroit's my nephew, Chief Inspector. Where is he?"

"The HBH, sir," Baxter answered. "Haimsbury-Branham Hospital, the finest medical facility in the country."

"Yes, so I've heard," muttered the peer. "May I see him?"

"Eventually, but not yet, my lord," Baxter cautioned. "We'll want to talk with his physicians before permitting any visitors, but

I imagine it would help his recovery to see you, sir. Now, might you have any information regarding your son's activities on Sunday night?"

"You may as well as ask me about the Queen's activities, Chief Inspector. My son never told me a thing. Just took my money. Oh, he wasn't all bad, you understand, but I'm afraid Thomas has, no he *had* a stubborn streak. He was like his mother in that." The face sagged again. "I shall have to tell her, won't I? My wife's in the country now. Meg never goes to Paris with me. She's at Stratbourne Manor." He wiped his face again and blinked. After clearing his throat, the earl asked, "And Haimsbury? Will he be running the show on this, or is it down to you, Chief Inspector?"

"His Grace wanted to join us, my lord, but he's been called to Vienna. As you're no doubt aware, two of the Queen's grandchildren are marrying in a few weeks. The Duke will attend, of course, but a pressing problem arose that requires his personal attention. He intends to deal with the matter on his way to Coburg."

"Ah, yes, I see. Vienna, you say?"

"Yes, sir."

"I wonder if it's to do with the Emperor? Things nearly went south there recently, but I thought Aubrey took care of it." Seeing the puzzled faces on the others, Stratbourne shook his head and added, "It's all Foreign Office troubles, gentlemen. I imagine Haimsbury will follow up on it all. But as the Duke places great faith in you, then I'm content with you running the show. I'd planned to attend the wedding with Rosebery, but it looks as though my wife and I shall be planning a funeral instead. A funeral," he sighed. "If we're to plan a funeral, we'll need Tom's body. Inspector Reid, when may I take him home?"

"I'm afraid it isn't up to me, sir. I must wait until the Intelligence Branch grants permission," Edmund answered. "If we're to name his murderer, then Dr. Sunders must finish all his tests."

"Yes, of course. That seems logical."

The door opened again. The waitress brought their meals. She served oyster chowder, beef stew, a ploughman, and a plate of sandwiches, along with Scottish ale and a fresh glass of whisky for Stratbourne. Before leaving, the girl bent down and whispered to Baxter. "A man gimme this note fer you, Mr. Baxter. Right nice-lookin' fella."

Neil took the note, read it, and smiled. "It looks as though you'll get to eat my stew, gentlemen. I've been called away. Lord Stratbourne, here's my card. Ring me, should you have any questions or concerns. I promise to give you daily updates."

Baxter nodded politely towards the peer, placed a stylish grey Homburg on his large head, and left to hail a hansom. His drive took a mere ten minutes from the Bear. As he exited the hansom, he looked both ways, half expecting a reporter to be lurking in the shadows. The sign over the establishment's door read *Molly-Mae Hotel*, and a bulky man in an ill-fitting green suit waited nearby.

"Yes, sir?" asked the doorman.

"I'm here on a police matter."

"Nobody gets in without my mistress's say so."

"Sir, you will step aside, or else spend the next few days in Leman Street's cells—if not in hospital. You may choose."

"Ain't no need ta get all rough 'bout it," answered the man. "I's just doin' me job."

"Indeed," Baxter observed as he passed through the doorway.

Inside the bawdy house, all was quiet. Two young women in satin bathrobes lounged on a flowered sofa. Their faces were bruised, and one wore a bandage on her right hand. Neil heard voices coming from a narrow corridor, just to the left of the staircase. He strolled its length until he reached a large kitchen. Inside the warm room, stood an oval table. Sitting before a well-laid breakfast banquet, was a buxom woman of middle age, dressed in a flowered silk peignoir over a gauzy nightshirt. In the next chair, sat the man who'd sent the note, Lord Charles R. A. Sinclair, Commissioner of Intelligence.

"I see you got my message," said Sinclair to his friend. "Allow me to introduce you to Mrs. Molly-Mae Morris, proprietress of this establishment. Mrs. Morris, this well-dressed gentleman is one of my top investigators, Chief Inspector Cornelius Baxter. Join us, Chief Inspector."

Neil removed his hat and set it on the closest chair. He took a seat near the end of the table and removed a leather notebook from his overcoat pocket. "It's very good to meet you, Mrs. Morris."

"I reckon it's the same here, sir, though I'd much rather be talkin' about other matters on such a day."

"Such a day?" asked Baxter, as he began to write. "Is this day particular?"

"It's Easter week, so I reckon so. I ain't religious nor nothing' like that, sirs, but such things can alter customer activity."

"Mrs. Morris was just explaining how a recent investor has also altered her customer activity," explained the Duke. "And there are two workers here I intend to remove. We'll be taking them with us, Chief Inspector."

"I never said yes to that," Morris objected.

"And I never asked permission," Sinclair replied without a blink. "Both children are underage, but more to the point, the boy's mother works for me."

"You know 'im? You never said!" she wailed.

"Nor did I need to," the Duke answered flatly. "That girl Lara's not more than ten, and the boy's barely nine. By keeping them here, you're in violation of the Criminal Law Amendment Act and England's sodomy laws."

"Sodomy? That boy's never done any such thing! He sweeps up, tha's all. No 'arm done."

"Judging by the Aladdin costume, I sincerely doubt that," Sinclair parried back. "The boy's name is Matthew Porter, and his mother works in the HBH women's dormitory. Both he and Lara are leaving with me."

"The prince ain't gonna like that, sir. That lad's a real favourite o' his."

"A favourite for what, Mrs. Morris? For illicit acts?"

"Conversation," she answered with the same cool smile she always gave to coppers. Morris leaned forward, allowing her peignoir to slip a little in the front. "We don't need no courts involved, now do we? Let's you an' me talk. I'm sure we can reach a fair settlement."

Baxter cleared his throat. "Put it away, woman. Your assets mean nothing to this gentleman. He is very happily married and above reproach."

She sat back and closed the robe, her expression turned sour. "Like I said, the prince ain' gonna like it, an' from what I know 'bout gentry an' such, a *prince* outranks a *duke*."

"Then, might I inform you, Madam, that this particular Duke is also a Prince?" Baxter countered. "Though that matters little, for you've broken over a dozen laws by my reckoning. If you wish to avoid a long sentence at Holloway, I suggest you stop trying to find a way out of this predicament and cooperate."

"Prison? I ain't done nuffin' wrong!" she huffed.

"You've broken the law, Mrs. Morris. You're looking at ten years at least. If you wish to avoid that future, then help me," Charles said in a kinder voice. "To begin, who is this prince you keep mentioning, as if he's a magical being?"

"No one you know."

"I know a great many royals, Mrs. Morris. Is he English?"

"No."

"French? German?"

"None o' them."

Using a Faber pencil, Baxter scribbled the entire exchange in shorthand. "Might this gentleman be from Eastern Europe?" he suggested, looking up at the flustered madam.

"Eastern Europe? How can I say, sir, when I got no idea what you mean?"

"Mr. Baxter refers to lands closer to Russia. Romania, for example. Or Hungary."

"He might be from one o' them. I promised to keep his name out o' the papers."

Charles was growing impatient. He had a great many things to do before leaving London. "Do not test me, madam. Tell me his name or else, I shall arrest you."

Morris gulped. "I can't, sir. He'd kill me."

"I doubt that," said Sinclair. "In fact, I'm sure he wants you to tell me. After all, he left me a calling card."

"What card is that, sir?" she asked.

"A rather gruesome message, written upon a man's back. Tell me this prince's name."

"He goes by a whole lotta names, sir. Koshmar's the one he uses down by the marina, but he's got others. I could tell you more, but I need protection."

Koshmar? Anatole was right. Saraqael is back, thought the Duke. But could it be some other prince with the same name? Of course, not. Still, Charles had to know for certain, and he was running out of time; his train was waiting at Victoria Station.

"Koshmar?" he asked.

"Yeah, that's right. Prince Aleksandr Koshmar. And my protection?"

Charles wanted to scream, but instead used Paul's old trick of picturing an ice block and counting to five. It worked.

"I'll ask the men of Leman Street to keep watch on your house," he managed in a calm voice. "How did you meet this prince? When did he invest in this place?"

"Gimme a minute," she said. Molly left the table and crossed to the stove, where a large copper kettle had begun to sing. She poured the boiling water into a warmed china pot, then wrapped the teapot with a knitted cosy. After bringing the tea to the table, she sat again, but her body language had changed. Morris tightened the sash on the filmy peignoir and ran her hands through thinning hair.

Suddenly, she looked twenty years older.

"He first come after I took over. Four years ago, I reckon. After the fire at the Empress."

"I remember that fire," Charles said, thinking of his former neighbour, Margaret Hansen. She now lived in quiet safety in Fulham. "Go on."

"Business picked up after that fire. One evenin', this gent come in an' said his master wanted to invest in my place. The man was dressed nice an' all, but sorta run down."

"His name?" asked Baxter, still scribbling.

"Lionel Wentworth."

Charles managed to maintain a disinterested demeanor, but the mention of Wentworth's name threatened to melt the ice block. *One, two, three, four, five.* The block remained firm.

"Tell me about Mr. Wentworth."

"Clever little fella. Real gobby. Wanted the girls fer free. He weren't like that at first, just got that way later. He used to bring me money in a big leather bag. Lots of it."

"How much?" Baxter enquired.

"The first week, he brung a thousand pounds," said Morris, emphasising the large amount.

Baxter whistled. "That's a great deal of money, madam."

"That were jus' the start, weren't it?" she bragged, sipping the tea. "A week later, he brung another o' them bags wif two thousand in it. It gimme enough to do up this place nice, like you West-End gents expects. An' I were able to procure the best girls, too. If you know wha' I mean, sir."

"I'm aware of the concept, Mrs. Morris," Charles told her. "I haven't always lived in Westminster. I grew up in Liverpool and later in Lambeth. After university, I worked as a police detective, stationed right here in Whitechapel. I lived opposite the Empress."

"That was *you*, sir?" she asked in amazement. "I thought it were a Yard man, name o' St. Clair. You related?"

"I was once called St. Clair, Mrs. Morris. But when I learnt the truth of my birth, I took my original name."

"Sinclair," she said in a whisper. "I never knew 'bout your old name, sir. Strange. He used to talk about a St. Clair. Back then, when he first come here."

"Who talked about it?" asked Baxter.

"That prince, sir. Prince Aleksandr. Pretty sort o' man. Lovely eyes, though they can drill a hole through you, iffin he ain' happy. He used to talk about a boy name o' St. Clair. But the prince left, so there ain' no use tryin' to find him."

"He's gone?" asked Charles, that old tingle beginning along his hands.

"Tha's right, sir. His rooms is empty. Baggage gone."

Charles struggled to picture the ice block.

Two nights earlier, Rob had told his father and mother all about the strange dream. Afterward, Charles and Elizabeth joined hands inside the circle meeting, and the group prayed for guidance. What spirit had masqueraded as this Piper? And why did Rob dream of the Stone Realms? Had he really been there? The Whitechapel murder and Rob's dream were somehow connected.

Something dreadful is coming.

The ice block shivered.

"Mrs. Morris, did the prince return here on Sunday night?"

"Return, sir?" she asked.

"Yes, return. He took the two West-End gentlemen out to visit his yacht, but did he later return? When did he pack his bags and leave?"

Her lips pursed into a firm pout. "I got no idea."

"Then, how do you know he's left?" asked Baxter.

"Cause o' Mr. Wentworth. He come an' fetched the prince's bags an' all. Said they'd be flyin' off to Europe somewhere."

"Flying?" asked Baxter in amazement. His hand stopped writing, and his dark eyes stared into the woman's face as though probing for answers. "He used that word? Flying?"

"Oh, yes, sir. The prince talks about flyin' a lot. Made us all laugh, he did. But then he's a magician, I reckon. Like them music hall men, with them spirit boxes an' all."

Charles stood. Baxter did likewise and shut the notebook.

"Where is the prince's apartment?" Sinclair asked.

"Upstairs, sir. Come wi' me. I'll take you up."

The proprietress led the men up to a third-floor room. She unlocked the door. "This is it."

The Duke stepped in. The walls were red, and the room stank of dried blood and death. In one corner, stood a cupboard. Baxter looked inside and discovered a brown crock, filled with half-eaten rats. The disgusting suite included two bedchambers, a water closet, and a small parlour. The smaller bedchamber held an unmade four-poster bed, dressed in rumpled sheets and a damask quilt. Charles searched every corner, every cupboard, and even beneath the bed, but found only a collection of IOUs from gambling establishments, written in the name of Lionel Wentworth. Sinclair gave these to Baxter and continued to the second bedchamber.

This room was much larger, with three windows that overlooked the river. From here, Charles could see Wilson's Marina, where he and Lorena had searched the prince's sloop. Unlike the previous bed, this was tidy, as though seldom or never used. Charles pulled back the sheets. They were clean and smelled fresh, even pleasant—a complete contrast to the room used by Wentworth. Why would Koshmar keep a depraved wretch as a companion? Had Lionel always been such a lowly person? Was Wentworth a criminal or another poor victim?

"Baxter, I want you to locate this man Wentworth. Sir Thomas Galton and Dr. Gehlen can help, if you require any peerage weight, though I doubt you will. With me away and Lord Aubrey out of the country, the investigation falls to you and your team. Elbert Stanley will coordinate with the police, but you're in charge. You have total authority in all matters. I'll put that in writing, if you want."

The former butler laughed. "No, sir, I don't believe that's necessary. The men know my worth and my habits. We'll see that all is done properly. Mrs. Morris, when the prince mentioned flying away, did you see him depart by any chance?"

Morris smiled. "Just in a dream, sir. Me and some of the girls had the same one, but it were just that. A dream."

Charles stepped close to examine the woman. Morris assumed his advance was of a personal nature and sweetened her facial muscles into a more seductive glance. The Duke took advantage of the woman's mistake and pulled at the silk scarf she kept tied round her throat. Beneath were two puncture wounds, with a worn, ragged look to them, as though something sharp had repeatedly wounded the skin.

"Where did you get these?" he asked.

Morris let out a little scream. She grabbed at his hand and tried to retrieve the scarf. "Tha' ain' none o' your business!"

"Who gave you these marks?" he asked again.

"Nobody give 'em ta me. It's just a bite."

"Do any of your girls have similar bites?" asked Sinclair.

"A few do."

"And might these girls be the same ones who dreamt about the prince flying away?"

The woman's smile disappeared. "I reckon so. We ain' been infected, have we, sir?"

"I don't think so, but to be sure, I'll send a physician to examine you. She'll come by today or tomorrow."

"She, sir? I don' know no lady doctors in Whitechapel."

"Then you've not been to the HBH," said Baxter. "There are two lady doctors there. Dr. MacKey and Dr. Bailey."

"Bailey?" asked Sinclair, who rarely visited the hospital, though Beth made a weekly habit of stopping by to talk with patients and students.

"Dr. Iris Bailey," Baxter told him. "Michael Emerson's sister. Her husband's Sir Harold Bailey, also a doctor. He runs a surgery in Bloomsbury, close to the British Museum."

Sinclair relaxed. "I'm glad you're keeping watch on our lives, Chief Inspector. One more question, Mrs. Morris," he continued, turning to look at the woman. "Did your cleaners look after this apartment?"

"No, sir. No one's allowed up here."

"Yet, you have a key."

"I keep keys to every part of the house, sir, including the cellars."

"Did the prince ever use those?"

"Oh, yes, sir. He keeps his wine collection down there."

"Then, lead the way, Mrs. Morris. I'll survey these cellars, then I'm leaving. Mr. Baxter will remain and finish the interview. Is that all right, Chief Inspector?"

Cornelius nodded; his large head remarkably refined in its grace. "Of course, sir. Shall I take the children to the HBH for you?"

"Yes, thank you. Matthew's mother will be overjoyed. She's been looking for him since before Christmas. I'm sure she'll be willing to look after Lara until we can make permanent arrangements."

They climbed down to the cellars, where the men discovered a large wine and spirits room containing hundreds of vintages. One section even held six bottles of 1891 *Saint Clair Royale Bordeaux* from the Branham-owned company, DuBonnier Winery, in France.

"I see they stock your wine, sir," said Baxter. "The '91 is particularly nice."

The Duke touched the dusty bottles. That same tingle flashed along his hands. *Something is here. A clue? A taunt? What? Lord, help me to see.*

They moved beyond the wine area and found a room that acted as a larder. Inside, hung smoked eels and sides of pork. The shelves contained great wheels of cheese along with tubs of lard and butter. As the coolest part of the cellar, cured meats and dairy stayed fresh for days.

In one dark corner, Sinclair noticed another door. "Where does this lead?" he asked Morris.

"I'm not sure. It's always locked," she told him. "And I don't have a key."

"But you claimed to have keys to every room in the house," said Baxter.

"Not this one. It belongs to the prince. Only he has a key."

For years now, Charles had trained in hand-to-hand combat with Paul Stuart, including classes in *savate*, a French fighting style that originated in Marseilles, where sailors learned to use their feet as weapons against pirates. As a result, the Duke packed quite a punch—even with his feet. He turned to the side and nimbly kicked into the centre of the door. The wood splintered, and the once sturdy door burst apart.

"It appears you had the key, sir," laughed Baxter. "I'm sure Lord Aubrey would be proud."

"Make sure you tell him about it when he returns," Charles told his friend as he entered the closet. "Now, let's see what secrets Koshmar's hidden in here."

The temperature inside the new room was much lower than the larder. Darkness made it difficult to see. Sinclair moved slowly, using his hands to feel for obstructions. The smell hit him first: a sickening mixture of rotten eggs, feces, blood, and mothballs. But another smell stood out. He knew it at once. Decaying flesh.

Charles touched something soft and cold and wet. "Baxter, fetch a candle."

Cornelius stepped back into the larder, where he found a candle table with matches. In less than twenty seconds, he'd returned with the light source. Sinclair struck the match and held the candle high. All three of them gasped as the flickering glow fell upon the area nearest the Duke. He'd touched it.

No, he'd touched *her*.

Or rather, he'd touched her *remains*.

A young woman's body hung suspended from a hook, screwed to the beadboard ceiling. Her tattered clothing fell in long rags round the corpse. Bits of flesh had been removed, as a butcher might strip a hook-mounted pig. The floorboards were soaked with red.

Morris's knees buckled. "It can't be! That's Bridget!"

Baxter caught the woman as she fell. He carried her back through the larder and into the stairwell area, where he set her on the bottom step. "Water?" Neil asked gently whilst taking her pulse.

"No, thank you, Chief Inspector," she whispered in a daze. "Just let me sit a minute."

Sinclair remained inside the secret chamber, surveying the area. Along with the hanging corpse, he discovered skeletal remains of three other women. He used the candle to examine the torn and stained clothing. A bit of white caught his eye, just at the top of the dress pocket closest to him. Charles reached for it. Electric signals coursed along every nerve. He pulled at the white cloth and held it up to the light. It was a man's handkerchief, made from finely woven linen. Along the edge, embroidered in fine gold thread, was a Latin phrase: *Quia Multi Sumus.*

It took a moment for the meaning to sink in, but when it did, the realisation hit him hard. So hard, that Sinclair's knees threatened to rebel. He'd seen the same phrase written on the walls of the final section of the Time Maze, close to Legion's lair.

Quia Multi Sumus, but sometimes just *QMS*.

Translation: FOR WE ARE MANY.

Considering the dark meaning of his son's dream, the Duke hated to leave England, but leave he must, for if Legion and Saraqael were in league with one another, then all Europe could be at risk. Was this why Emperor Franz Josef had written? And was any of it connected to the upcoming Coburg wedding?

Charles whispered a prayer for the dead women and another for his wife and children, then he stepped back through the larder and into the main cellar area to finish the interview.

"Feeling any better, Mrs. Morris?" he asked.

She nodded.

"Who is Bridget?"

"She's—no, I mean, she *was* one o' my girls, Yer Grace. I thought she found a place wi' one o' them gentlemen callers what likes her. Near Lambeth Palace, that's where he lives. She sent me a letter. Sayin' goodbye. I don' understand. Why? Who done this?"

"You're sure the body is Bridget's?" he asked gently.

The woman nodded, dabbing at her eyes with a hankie. "Oh, yes, sir. Tha's her all right. I'd know them eyes anywhere, sir. Violet blue. Like the flowers."

"Let's return upstairs," Sinclair told Baxter. The former butler offered the woman his arm and guided her up the steep steps.

As he ascended, Charles thought of the darkened room. The familiar tingling raged across every nerve now. He knew that soon, rumours and claims of supernatural villains would dominate London's front pages, with claims of the Golem's return or the White Lady murders—perhaps far worse.

Charles knew better. It wasn't a Golem or the White Lady's ghost. All this madness was caused by Legion and his den of evil spirits. And now he'd formed an alliance with Saraqael. Hell was rising up.

Quia Multi Sumus.

For we are many.

It was starting again.

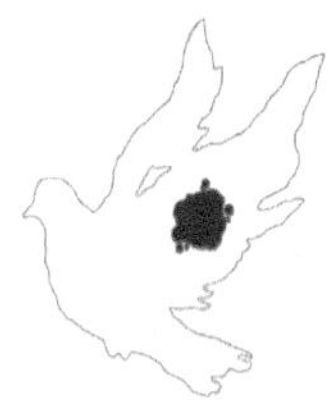

CHAPTER TEN

Nantes, France.

That evening, as his cousin boarded a steamer for Calais, Paul Stuart prepared to board a ship for Africa. The earl sat inside a crowded café, stirring cream into a cup of strong coffee. It had taken two long days and several trains to reach Paris from Vienna, followed by a bumpy coach ride from the City of Lights to the busy Port of Nantes, known to ancient Rome as the *Portus Namnetum*, or Port of the Namnetes.

The Namnetes were a Gallic tribe, rumoured to be the keepers of a magical island filled with strange women who circumambulated their god's temple. Whether true or not, the tribe eventually modernised, intermarried, and became part of Brittany. After Charles VIII married Anne of Brittany, this picturesque river valley was subsumed into the Kingdom of France. And now, mystical Nantes served as one of the country's major ports, where some women still behaved just as wildly as the ancient Namnetes.

One such woman had just entered the café.

"*Bon soir*," she said. "*Salut, beauté. Solitaire?*"

Paul shrugged. "Maybe. Do you speak English?"

"Oui, I mean yes. Of course. You are alone, yes?"

Aubrey spoke fluent French but found it useful to feign ignorance. "Alone for the moment," he answered. "I'm waiting for a ship."

"You don't look like sailor."

"I'm a passenger. And you? Are you looking for sailors or passengers?"

"Both," she answered in a sing-song, sultry voice. "When does ship come?"

"Soon," he answered idly. "Tell me your name."

She smiled and sat into the chair closest to him. "Yvette."

"A very pretty name. In English, it means yew."

"You?" she asked. "I not understand. You? Me?"

He smiled, showing off deep dimples in a smooth face. "Y-e-w. It's a type of tree, used to make bows."

"Beaux? Boyfriends, yes?"

"No, not that. Yew wood is used to make longbows—for shooting arrows," he explained, pantomiming the actions of an archer. "Tell me, Yvette, who are those men?" he asked, pointing to a pair he'd been watching. "They look familiar."

"Those? Just two sailors. They wait for ship, too. Damien say they dangerous. Be careful, m'sieur."

"I am always careful, my dear. And Damien is...?"

"He there," she said, nodding towards the hefty gentleman behind the bar. "Damien is owner. How you English say? Lord of the land."

"Ah, he's the landlord. Yes, I see."

She moved the chair closer and touched his hands. On the right, the earl always wore the Aubrey signet. On the left, a wide gold band. "The rings, they are beautiful, m'sieur. What they mean?"

"This represents my family," he said, showing off the signet. "The other represents my wife. She is very beautiful," he told the prostitute.

She shrugged. "Wives are trouble."

"Not to me. I love mine very much."

"That is why she is trouble," Yvette replied.

Ignoring her attempts at seduction, Paul asked, "Do you work for Damien?"

She bristled at the suggestion. "*Mais non, m'sieur.* Damien is, how you say, *cousine*, yes?"

"He's your cousin. Yes, I understand."

Paul had quietly observed the burly landlord. The one called Damien shared furtive glances with the two sailors. The earl memorised the positions of everyone inside the café, those beyond the windows, and the ones walking on the wharf. He also took note of every possible exit, including the windows.

The woman drew closer. Her perfume smelled heavy and sweet. "You walk, yes? Smell air? Is better than here."

"Yes, of course." Paul dropped several *centimes* on the table and pushed back the chair. "Shall we?"

He took the woman's arm, pretending to play her game. The two men whispered to one another as he left with the blonde temptress. Damien left his place behind the bar.

Outside, the night air was warm and scented with cherry blossoms. The wharf opened onto the Loir River estuary, a massive river mouth, large enough for warships to enter and dock. A railway system crossed over a series of bridges along the estuary, providing transportation for goods and passengers alike. The cherry blossom scent mixed with the smells of fish, exotic spices, fresh baked goods, and human sweat.

The woman took out a brown cigarette. Paul struck a match to light it. The tiny flame set a brief glow against her fair features. She laughed and puffed on the cigarette.

"You leave soon?"

"Soon enough."

"There is time, yes?"

He knew what she implied, and even if the offer were genuine, the earl would never cheat on his wife. Spy craft required flirtation, yes, but never that. Not now. Paul could never do that again. He loved Cordelia far too much.

He glanced at the prostitute. Yvette belonged to someone, too. She had a mother, a father. What dire circumstance had brought her to a life like this?

Then, she repeated the offer, whispering huskily into his ear and offering a soft kiss. "We have time, yes?"

"No, there is no time," he said, holding up the left hand. "This ring represents my wife. She is my only love, Yvette. There can be no other."

The temptress pouted. They continued to walk along the busy dock. A steamship whistle sliced the air; the deep voice of a major vessel.

"That's my ship," he said, pointing to a long, three-stack steamer approaching the dock. The enormous ship ran three-hundred feet by three-hundred-sixty, with a wood and copper hull that looked newly minted. A pair of tall masts rose at either end, crowned by crow's nests. High atop each of these, flew a British flag, and the name H.M.S. *Centurion* was painted in tall, black letters upon the hull.

"That is ship? You go to war?" she asked.

"In a way," he whispered.

"A kiss before you go?" she asked sweetly, her mouth flushed.

The two sailors from the pub had followed them, and they waited, keeping to the shadows. The men made a pretence of conversation.

Shouts of porters, hauliers, and fishmongers sang a rich chorus, harmonising with a nearby concertina.

Paul readied himself.

Yvette rose up on her toes, ruby lips parted. He allowed the kiss, not because he desired her body, but to allow her to spring the trap.

As their lips met, Yvette reached for her victim's wallet. Paul grabbed her wrist with his right hand and produced a revolver with the left. The two sailors rushed at him with such speed, it would have caught any other tourist by surprise.

Not Paul Stuart.

He twirled the girl round and threw her into the first sailor, then kicked at the second with a savate *fouetté*. The first attacker produced a firearm. After the kick, Paul landed with the grace of a dancer, spun round, and shot the man's hand, forcing the gun to drop. The woman screamed and ran towards her bleeding comrade.

She picked up the firearm and aimed it at Paul. "Drop the gun, m'sieur. Your money. All of it. And the rings."

"Or else what? You'll shoot me?" he said, the smoking weapon still in his hands.

She smiled. "Mais oui. I shoot. I am good shot."

"And what if I kill you?" he asked coldly.

Yvette's face tensed. English tourists never behaved this way. She'd played this game a hundred times, maybe more, and the man always paid. Always.

Foot traffic on the wharf had thinned. Hearing the shots, people ran into nearby warehouses and pubs for safety. The two sailors lay on the boardwalk, bleeding and beaten.

"Are they your brothers?" asked the earl.

"Oui. Your money now, m'sieur. I am good shot."

"I think not," came a new voice from out of the shadows. A gunshot sounded, narrowly missing the woman. Her weapon wavered, and a hand pulled it from her grasp.

"You all right, Lord Aubrey?" asked the newcomer.

Paul began to laugh. "Are you following me, Deniau?"

"Of course," replied the French inner-circle member.

A few seconds later, four gendarmes appeared and arrested the woman and her brothers. A third man—an Englishman this time—had brought the policemen. He thanked each for his help. "You nearly bought it, old friend. Whatever would you do without us?" asked Sir Thomas Galton.

"Quite well, I should think," answered the earl with a smile. "Who sent you?"

The English baronet crossed the boardwalk and shook his friend's hand. "Must someone send me? I'm capable of working on my own, you know. But allow me to introduce you to Commandant Albert Laurent. It's his men who are doing your job."

The earl placed the revolver back into its shoulder holster. "It's a pleasure to meet you, Commandant. I'll forgive you for associating with Galton. He's a scoundrel and always cheats at cards."

The Commandant laughed. "A joke, yes? You are good friends. My Lord Aubrey, I know not what is your job, but I am glad to offer the assistance. We keep the watch on Yvette and her brothers. They are known to us. Big criminals. Thieves. I see you use the savate, yes? I am impress."

"Aubrey's footwork is always fancy," quipped Galton. "Commandant, will you need me any further? I see the *Centurion* has docked. I should get our earl on board."

The commander bowed, cap in hand. "M'sieur le Comte. Is great pleasure to meet."

"Mine as well, sir," answered the earl.

One of the *gardiens* walked past with Yvette. She wore steel handcuffs. Paul shook his head. "I shall pray for you, madam."

Yvette spat at him. "I not want your prayers!"

Deniau joined up with them, still dusting off his hat. "I'm not sure prayer would work on her, my friend. Yvette and her brothers would have murdered you without batting an eye."

"Who hired them?" asked Aubrey.

"No one. It is their own game."

Paul shook his head as they walked towards the British ship. "No, that's a bit too convenient. Someone knew I'd be here, so either I was followed, or else someone in the War Office is a traitor."

"Or someone with Redwing?" suggested Galton.

"Yes," muttered Paul, looking back at the woman. "So, am I to travel alone or with company?"

"I am assigned elsewhere, *mon ami*," said Deniau, "but this one go with you."

Galton smiled. "Not all the way, just to Morocco. But the trip should be enjoyable and quick. The *Centurion* can make seventeen knots in calm weather. You'll be there in twelve days or less."

"Still, that's twelve days lost," Paul sighed, thinking of his wife.

"I suppose so," answered Galton. "It's a shame Duke James's work with Daimler isn't finished yet."

"The airship engine, you mean?" asked the earl as they neared the gangway.

"Have you seen it?"

"Last year," replied Aubrey. "They're calling it a dirigible. Basically, it's an engine-powered hot air balloon, capable of being steered. However, the engine's not perfected."

"Wouldn't that be a fine way to travel?" asked Galton as they climbed aboard. He showed his identification papers to a uniformed officer. "Evening, Lieutenant. This man is your star passenger. The Right Honourable and very dangerous Earl of Aubrey."

The officer bowed politely. "It's our honour and pleasure, my lord. Captain Brewer awaits you on deck. Oh, and your luggage is already stowed in your cabin. I'm told Sir Thomas is next door, and the third member of your party has also boarded."

"Third?" asked the earl.

"The Russian, sir. Prince Anatole Romanov."

Paul laughed. "Romanov's on board? Well, now, this will be a very interesting twelve days."

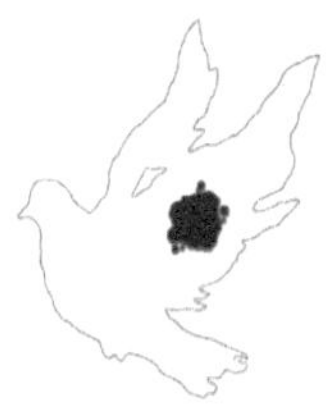

CHAPTER ELEVEN

Goussainville, France

The Duke's channel steamer docked in Calais shortly before six the following morning. Charles had brought Lady Napper to visit Della, knowing how much she'd missed having her sweet doggy. On the crossing, he'd run into Seth Holloway's parents, Lord and Lady Salter. The earl and his wife were on their way to Paris for an antiquarian symposium, and the Duke invited the Salters to share a ride into the city. However, when they arrived in Paris, the Salters discovered their hotel had suffered a fire, causing the business to close. Consequently, the symposium was rescheduled.

Noticing Lady Salter's frailness, Haimsbury suggested the couple go with him to Château Rothesay and spend a few days with his aunt. Circle agent Inspector François Blanchet acted as guide and guardian during the drive from Paris to Goussainville. The Salters fell asleep soon after departure, allowing Blanchet to talk quietly with the Duke. The agent told Sinclair the hotel fire wasn't the first; in fact, there'd been seven suspicious fires, all inside the eighteenth *arrondissement*, six in Montmartre, and one just a block from the place where Adele Stuart Sinclair was born.

"There is more to these fires, my lord," Blanchet added. "A message was found in the ruins of one. Inside a closet, deep within the cellars. The flames, they did not reach, you see," he explained in a whisper. "I think this message is for you, sir."

The agent passed Sinclair a small case. The red leather edges were burnt, but the contents unscathed. Charles shuddered as he examined the note. The paper was made of vellum, and the words written with crimson ink. He'd seen the same phrase in Whitechapel: *Quia Multi Sumus*. For we are many.

"Thank you, François," he whispered, stowing the leather case and its taunting message inside his pocket. "Say nothing of this to anyone else. Let me handle it."

"As you wish, my lord. You understand the words?"

"Yes. François, our old enemies are plotting something new. Promise you'll keep an eye on my daughter whilst I'm in Vienna."

"Of course, my lord. I have men at the Château always. And you as well. We keep the watch."

Haimsbury managed a weary smile. "Thank you. God also watches. He will judge."

The exhausted Duke sat back and closed his eyes, allowing the rhythm of the coach wheels to lull him to sleep. He fell into a fitful dream, filled with dragons and dying prostitutes. Amongst these was Charles's dead sister Charlotte—known once as Cozette du Barroux, Adele's birth mother.

The drive passed quickly, and soon the coach slowed to make the sharp turn onto Rothesay Drive. Spring and all its splendour had arrived at the picturesque castle. Victoria's gardens put on a great and glorious show for the arriving guests. The floral beds looked like an impressionist's painting. One entire hillside was awash in waving tulips, their red-and-cream colours proudly proclaiming ancient heritages, reaching back to the Dutch Lowlands. Bordering the fragrant knot gardens, stood a regiment of magnolia trees with pink-and-white blossoms that scented the air with delicate sweetness. Cherry trees whispered together in a nearby orchard, adding to the heady mix of sight and scent. Weeping willows, narcissi, wallflowers, daffodils, peonies, and irises displayed their dazzling apparel to inspire a Monet, Degas, or Renoir.

A rectangular lily pond divided the long approach into two parallel trackways. As the coach neared the main house, Charles noticed a beautiful young woman standing on the portico. She wore a shell-pink dress, tied with a silver satin bow. Glorious copper-blonde tresses streamed behind her back, shaded by a broad-brimmed hat made of white straw.

The coach slowed, and Charles reached over to tap Lord Salter's shoulder.

The ageing earl shook his head and wiped at rheumy eyes. "What? What's happened?"

"We're here, sir," the Duke told him.

"Ah, so we are. I hope Lady Victoria isn't put out," said the plain-speaking man. "Imogen, wake up," he told his wife. "We're here."

The pale countess took a deep breath and slowly opened her eyes. "Here? Where is here?"

"We're at Rothesay, Lady Salter," said Haimsbury.

The coach stopped. Charles reached out to pick up Napper, but too late. A footman had opened the door, and the dog leapt out. The spaniel eagerly ran towards the young woman in pink. It was clear that both dog and girl were very happy to see one another.

"Napper!" cried Adele as she crouched to pet the dog. "Oh, my darling Lady Napper!" The dog pawed at her skirts, and Adele lifted her up into her arms. "My sweet, sweet doggy. Have you missed me?" she asked, tousling the animal's thick fur and scratching her ears. She walked towards the carriage, her eyes on the exiting passengers.

"Lord and Lady Salter," she said politely as she reached them on the foot path. "What a lovely surprise. It's very good to see you again."

"Ah, Lady Della," said Salter, who walked slowly with a slight stoop. "We've come to impose on you and your aunt. Charles claims we'll be welcome, but will we, I wonder? I hope Tory's not hosting a party or the like. It is spring, after all."

Charles left the coach after making sure Lady Salter was safely on the gravel. Upon seeing her father, Adele lost all sense of propriety—as dictated by her boarding school instructors. She set down Napper and ran into the Duke's arms.

"Oh, Father! Father! It's so very good to see you! We didn't know about the Salters, but I'm sure Auntie Tory won't mind," she jabbered happily. "Tory loves company, though she always complains. It's her way, you know. We're all in back, having breakfast on the veranda."

"Then, we're intruding," said Imogen Holloway. "Ed, I knew we'd be a bother. We should go back to Paris and find another hotel."

"Why?" asked Adele as she took the older woman's arm. "My dear Lady Salter, we have so much food that an army would leave enough to feed a second army. And if there are leftovers beyond that, the cook will make them into a new dish. She's very clever, our Mrs. Marchal. And we've not been here long at all. Tory only returned last night, as I'm sure you know, Father, and we've been here since Monday. Dolly's been chaperoning us, though, so it's quite right and proper. Come this way, all of you!"

"Us?" Charles asked his daughter as they walked. "We?"

"Yes, us and we," Adele answered. "It's my friend from school, you see. She came with me, and I want you to meet her. She thinks you're quite dreamy."

Charles laughed. "You brought a friend who thinks I'm dreamy?"

"You'll see," Adele said as she led them into the house. Then, noticing the circle agent, she asked, "Who's this? Another guest? Flora will be over the moon if it is. She loves meeting young men."

"Forgive my manners," the Duke told his daughter. "This gentleman is one of the circle's newest agents, and you'll probably see him now and then whilst you're here. Inspector François Blanchet, allow me to introduce my daughter, the Lady Adele Sinclair."

Della curtsied. "It's a pleasure, Inspector. I hope you'll join us for breakfast. As I told Lord Salter, there is plenty. Enough for two armies, at least."

"That's kind of you, my lady," the Frenchman said with a polite bow, "but if it's all right with your father, I shall say no this time. And as the Duke say, we shall meet again, my lady." Then he turned to Sinclair. "Your Grace, if I may have a moment?"

"Certainly. Della, show the Salters inside, please. I shan't be long."

The two men stepped aside, finding a quiet spot on a gravel path near one of the many rose beds. Blanchet explained his request as he withdrew a folded note from his pocket. "We received this from Lord Aubrey, sir. I meant to give it to you in the coach, but our conversation regarding the fires and this other message caused me to forget. The telegram is in code, of course. Is it a new one? Even Deniau could not make it out."

The Duke took the sheet of paper and mentally translated the note. "My cousin and I use a separate code. It says he's left for Africa on a British ship called the *Centurion*. François, if you receive or hear anything further, send the entire message, *verbatim*, to me in Vienna. I'll decipher Aubrey's code myself."

The Inspector bowed. "Of course, Your Highness."

Charles laughed. "Is that how Deniau says I'm to be addressed now?"

"Oh yes, my lord. But it was Sir Thomas Galton gave the orders. Be safe on your journey, my lord. Our Vienna contact will meet you at the train station, and other men will keep watch along the route. There are a dozen or more who will ride each link of the rails with you, though you may never see them. It is, as Lord Aubrey calls it, spy craft."

"I'll see if I can pick them out. And thank you, Inspector. I know we're in safe hands. Please, give Chief Goron my warmest regards."

"Of course, Highness. *Au revoir.*"

Once Blanchet boarded the hired coach for the return to Paris, three of the Château's footmen carried in the luggage. Charles asked that his bags remain near the doors for storage in one of Tory's coaches. He'd need to leave by six, he told Russell, the head butler. The Salters' things were to be carried up to an apartment.

Russell showed the Duke through the castle's winding ground-floor interior to the northeast veranda, where Adele, the Salters, and two women waited. A wire-haired terrier barked at the Duke's feet.

"Hello, Samson," he told his aunt's dog. "You're looking a bit greyer since I last saw you."

"As are you, Nephew," said Tory, putting out her cheek for Charles to kiss. "I'm very glad you brought George and Imogen, but why didn't you wire me from Calais? I'd have sent a coach. Never mind. Do sit, all of you. Dolly's famished."

"Where's Reggie?" asked Charles, noticing his aunt's husband was conspicuously absent.

"He's gone off on Queen's Honour."

"Queen's Honour?" asked Salter.

"She's a horse, George," Tory explained. "One of Beth's new fillies, born two years ago, out of Queen's Biscuit by King's Mark. They're White Fell Ponies. Beth's been trying to breed them larger, and it's finally working. Honour's over fourteen hands, but still skittish with a saddle. Reggie's been working her every morning when he's home. Do sit, Charles. Have a croissant. Bacon and eggs are on their way."

"It's good to see you again," he told his aunt. "I'd like to see this new filly, if I have time." He bent to kiss the cheek of a blonde woman in a bright blue dress. "Morning, Dolly. I hear you've been chaperoning Adele and her mystery friend."

"And I'd loved every minute," said Patterson-Smythe, "Well, hello, Napper. Nice to see you back here again. Oh, Della, mind the dog, dear. She'll follow Samson's bad habits and annoy the birds," she said as both animals ran off towards a row of azalea bushes. "There are bluebirds nesting nearby. Where's Flora?"

"Gone back upstairs," said Della. "She's trying on dresses. I think she wants to impress my father." Adele called the dog. "Napper, come!"

The two dogs were sniffing along the petal-strewn ground, near the bottom of an azalea bush. Lady Napper's pedigree descended from the first Cavalier Spaniels, bred at Blenheim as hunting dogs, and she lived up to her breeding. Though Samson barked the loudest, it was Napper who caught the prize. In the animal's soft mouth, chirped a terrified ball of light grey fluff with large black eyes.

Adele knelt down, her pink skirts touching the ground. "Napper, you must drop it!" she commanded the dog. "Drop! Now!"

Reluctantly, the animal deposited her trophy. Della cupped the tiny bird in her hands. "Oh, I'm so very sorry. What do we do?"

The Duke helped Della to her feet and glanced over his daughter's shoulder. "If we can find the nest, we can return it. Poor tiny thing."

"My silver stars, is that a bird?" asked a newcomer. Charles looked towards the open French windows. A girl about Della's age stood within the framework. She wore a lilac-coloured dress with a white sash. Auburn curls spilled out from beneath the brim of a white straw hat. "Your Grace, I hadn't realised you were here yet!" she exclaimed as she sashayed close to Charles and offered a low curtsy. "It's an honour to meet you."

Sinclair smiled, and the girl blushed brightly.

Still holding the bird, Adele said, "Father, allow me to introduce Lady Flora Appleton."

The young woman's actual name was Alice Antonia Appleton, but she'd been called Flora since childhood. Miss Appleton hailed from an old Devonshire family, dominated by very tall people. However, that generous attribute had somehow skipped this particular descendent. Still, five-foot-nothing Flora made up for short stature with a freckled face, copper hair, a pert nose, and giggles galore. Young men followed her about like ducklings, and she'd learnt to use coquettish manners to her advantage.

Della's left brow arched sharply as Flora curtsied again. "That's probably sufficient. You've been introduced," she whispered. "End of story."

"But he's gorgeous," the girl sighed in low voice.

"And very happily married, Flora, don't forget."

Charles was smiling to himself as he crossed to the azalea bush to search for signs of a nest. "Ah, here it is," he said, pretending ignorance of the young ladies' conversation. "There are other babies here. Let's pray the mother doesn't reject this one." He took the fledgling from Adele and placed it in the small nest, then returned to the table. "Might there be a water closet nearby? I should probably wash my hands."

"Oh, and I should as well," Adele realised. "Mr. Wellborne, might you have a wet cloth?"

A middle-aged footman with silvering hair approached and bowed. "I keep one with me at all times, Lady Adele. Allow me." He used the damp white cloth to wipe the young woman's hands, then turned to the Duke. "Sir?"

"Thank you, Wellborne," Charles said, taking the towel and cleaning his own hands.

"Now that it's all taken care of, may we finally eat?" asked Dolly. "Poor Imogen looks as though she might fall asleep!"

Salter turned to his wife and gave her a nudge. "Come on, old girl. Let's have a bite, then we'll go upstairs, and you can have a kip whilst I talk to Charles and Reggie."

"Eat? Oh, yes, sorry," Imogen said sleepily. "Thank you. Good of you to have us, Tory."

The footmen began to serve, and everyone dug in. Breakfast conversation commenced with small talk, but quickly turned to news from London. "The Paris papers are full of this awful rot," moaned Victoria. "As if Paris has nothing to write about. Why are people so fascinated by murder?"

"That's a question to ask Lord Salperton," said Salter. "Henry's become a good friend to our son. Great sort of fellow. You know, Imogen, I might ask Henry to take a look at you, when we're back in London."

"Why?" she asked. "Isn't Henry a mentalist?"

"No, not a mentalist," her husband said, laughing. "But he does work with minds. He's an alienist."

"Isn't it the same thing?"

"Not really, though some might claim it's so," Dolly commented after taking a bite of a chocolate-filled pastry. "Oh, this is good, Tory. Ask Marchal to send my cook the recipe. It's so rich! I wonder where she gets her cocoa?"

Victoria sighed. Dolly Patterson-Smythe often pretended to be a trifle light in the brain department, but the baronet's wife was sharp as the proverbial tack. Tory knew her friend used sudden interjections about food, music, anything at all to divert conversations. Dolly's cleverness allowed Victoria to steer talk towards less gruesome topics. The two women formed an effective team.

"And Beth's feeling well?" Victoria asked her nephew.

"Yes, I think so," Charles said after buttering a croissant. "Henry's keeping an eye on her. He'll be travelling with Elizabeth to Coburg. They're to meet Drina in Belgium."

"The Queen's been in Luxembourg, I hear," said Dolly. "Flora, doesn't your mother have family near there?"

"Near where?" asked Flora, who couldn't take her eyes off Adele's father. Up until now, Miss Appleton had only seen photographs of the famous Duke, but seeing him in person, up close and in the flesh, was something quite different. Duke Charles had a charm about his manner that captivated the girl, and his deep resonant voice was absolutely thrilling. She even loved the way his mouth moved when he chewed.

The Duke pretended not to notice.

There was no such pretence with Dolly. "Flora?"

"Oh. Yes, Lady Dolly?" muttered the sixteen-year-old.

"I asked if your family have relatives in Luxembourg?"

"Yes, I think so," the girl replied, then returned to adoring Della's father. "Your Grace, is it true you're passing through Lucerne on the way to Vienna?"

"Yes," said Sinclair. "I have a business meeting there that requires overnighting at the Grand Hotel."

"And Vienna?" she asked, hanging on every syllable.

"Well, when I get there, I shall call on the Emperor, but only after stopping to visit Lady Aubrey."

"Ah, yes, I see," Flora whispered to herself. "But surely you'll stay here, overnight at least. It's just that Lady Dolly's throwing a party tomorrow, and we hoped you might join us."

Charles glanced over at his adopted daughter. "I wish I could, Lady Flora, but I'm afraid my train leaves at six o'clock this evening."

"Really?" asked the girl. "Is it a sleeper?"

"Not the first train, no, but tomorrow's train will be. I'll travel overnight and into the morning to reach Vienna in time for my appointment."

"Why Vienna?" asked Flora.

Tory interrupted. "You needn't interrogate the Duke," she said. "Charles, as your plans are secret, we'll defer to your discretion. I wonder, though, with all this dashing about, are you still planning to host a ball at King's Court?"

"Yes, that's our plan," he told her whilst setting down a coffee cup. "The staff don't really need me there to prepare. The invitations will be hand-delivered or posted next week."

"Good. I'm glad. Reggie and I look forward to trying out the dance floor in the new ballroom," she answered whilst stirring sugar into her coffee. "And the fête's still on?"

"Tory, you know my wife. Beth would never cancel the Branham fête," Charles assured her. "Adele, you're able to come, I hope?"

"Of course," she smiled as she set down the linen serviette. "And I hope all our friends will be there, too."

"I imagine, they will," he told her, wondering just which 'friends' she meant. "Della, as you've finished eating, let's take a walk together. I'd hoped we might talk before I leave this afternoon. Ladies, would you excuse us?"

Adele rose from the table. Flora started to join them, but Dolly took the girl's hand and whispered something inaudible. Whatever was said, Flora sat again. "We'll look after Napper, dear," Dolly told Adele. "Enjoy the walk. Charles, you might stroll near the long pond. There's a wonderful view of Goussainville's bell tower."

"That sounds quite nice, Dolly, thank you. Lord Salter, we'll speak more when I've returned. Lady Salter, I pray you feel better soon. I know how migraines affect my wife."

The Duke bowed politely to the ladies, then took his daughter's arm, and the two of them left the veranda.

Both Salters were road-weary and pale. Lady Salter, had suffered from a series of illnesses since '89, and looked as though a stiff breeze might knock her down. She was thin and drawn. Her husband leaned close and touched the countess's forearm. "Let me take you up, Imogen."

The two antiquarians apologised for leaving so soon and then followed Wellborne back through the winding passages and up the stone steps to their apartment. As they reached the landing, a sleek black cat dashed past the countess's legs. The poor woman nearly collapsed.

"What is it? It isn't him, is it, George?" she asked her husband.

"No, dear, it was just a cat. What you need is a nice, long lie-down. I'll wake you when the Duke is ready to leave. That gives you nearly seven hours."

"Yes, yes, I might do that," said Imogen. "Was it a real cat, George? Truly? A real one?"

"Yes, dear. Just a cat. Mind your feet, Ginny," he said, using her nickname. "We'll need to climb a bit."

"Oh, yes, of course. It's very French here, isn't it? All these armaments, shields, and tapestries. I suppose beneath it all is old stonework. I wonder if anyone's ever excavated here? We had cats in Egypt, didn't we, George? Lots of them. Big black shadowy things."

"It was just a cat, dear," he repeated as they reached their rooms. "Here, now. Have a nice rest, and I'll come back in a few hours." The earl turned to the footman. "Thank you, Wellborne. Tell Lady Victoria, I'll join her again shortly."

The footman left, and George Holloway helped his wife to undress and prepare for bed. She'd gone downhill so quickly after the recent fevers. *Why is she seeing that cat again?* he wondered.

"Meeting Charles was lucky, wasn't it?" his wife said as she removed her jewellery.

"Yes, wasn't it?" George repeated, his eyes on the retreating figures of Haimsbury and Adele as they walked beside the long, rectangular lily pond. Oddly, enough, the large black cat trailed along after them, weaving in and out of bushes, as though spying.

CHAPTER TWELVE

It rained that afternoon, forcing the Château guests and their hosts to find entertainment indoors. Adele suggested a piano concert. Imogen Holloway awoke at three, and by four, everyone gathered in the music room, ready to enjoy an impromptu performance. Adele and Flora thumbed through music books. Haimsbury and Salter chatted about government work.

"I take it all is not well in Vienna," said the earl as he poured them both a glass of brandy.

"Honestly, George, I'm not sure," answered Charles. "Franz Josef seldom asks for outside help, but his letter sounded urgent. I couldn't say more, even if I knew."

"Yes, those are Drummond's rules, too," George said. "Spying is your family business."

"I imagine it is. George, is everything all right with Imogen?" Charles asked in a whisper. The countess took no notice. She sat several feet away, discussing Egyptian mummies with Victoria and Dolly.

"She's beginning to wind down, I suppose," sighed the elder peer. "Ginny suffered from a number of mystery fevers on our last expedition. We had some rather odd things happen, too."

"Where was this?"

"Northern Palestine. We were asked to look over some of the territory covered during Warren's survey. Our sponsors hoped we might uncover another stela like the one Sir Charles found back in '69. It was a damned strange trip! Forgive my language, but everything that could have gone wrong, did. On the way down from Constantinople, our train's brakes failed, and we very nearly ran headlong into another train, travelling in the opposite direction."

Reggie Whitmore joined the two men, a small brandy in one hand. "Nice to have you here, George. Forgive the interruption, but did I hear something about Constantinople and a train?"

"Yes, I was telling the Duke about our last trip down to Palestine. Hellish, simply hellish!" George exclaimed. "First, there were the mechanical problems, then a near-crash, and when we finally reached Damascus, the new Pasha insisted our papers weren't in order. We were forced to remain under lock and key at a small hotel. The lodgings were pleasant enough, but somewhat of a cat haven. Everywhere we turned, huge black cats followed us. Poor old Imogen is generally rock solid in the field, but even she was spooked. Soon after, she took to bed with a fever, further delaying our journey. I wanted to send her back to England, but she refused to go alone."

"Was it malaria?" asked Whitmore.

"We thought so, but quinine did nothing to help. We always carry it with us, as you can imagine. After a fortnight in Damascus, we finally made it to the dig at Mt. Hermon. But then heavy rains delayed most of our activities. I did manage to uncover several new finds at Caesarea Philippi. Several statues of cats, oddly enough. Then my wife's fever returned, and those damnable cats came back, slinking and slithering all over the encampment. Ever since, Ginny panics at the sight of a black cat. I noticed you have one here. Poor old girl nearly lost her nerve when she saw it run past."

"Cat?" asked Reggie. "There's none that I know of, but then Della picks up all manner of animals when she's here. Lady Flora does the same. Now that her dog's here, perhaps Della will stop looking for creatures to feed and tend."

Charles smiled. "I doubt it. My daughter loves animals."

Tory had been sitting near Countess Imogen, but she rose and crossed the room to speak to Charles. "Now, then, Nephew, since you're using my home as a stop-over inn, you had best give me a very good explanation. I'd hoped you might stay a day or two before gallivanting off to who knows where."

"I promise to stay a week next time, Aunt. But I hear no music. Weren't we promised a piano concert?"

"You're changing the subject, Charles. Typical of you. Very well, if you're going to be obstinate—Della, are we to have music?"

"Of course, Auntie," answered Adele. "Just give us another few minutes." The adolescent huddled with Flora.

A shadow crossed just behind the two girls. The countess suddenly jumped from the couch and began to scream. "Get it away! Get it away!" she cried, scurrying about the room as though running from an assailant.

Sinclair reached Imogen first and took her hands. "It's all right. It's fine. If there's a cat, we'll see to it, Lady Salter. Here now, let's go back to the sofa."

He drew the panicked woman from the piano and placed her beside Victoria. "Dolly, would you sit here as well? Then we'll have three beautiful women, all in a row. Della, let me know when you're ready to play."

The ladies sat together whilst Charles pulled Whitmore and Salter to the doorway. The three men held a quiet conversation, away from the piano and Imogen Holloway.

"George, this is more than just a migraine. Shall we have Reggie take a look?" asked Haimsbury. "Her hands are like ice."

"Forgive me, Charles. Yes, it's the result of those strange fevers. I've asked her to see a doctor, but Imogen refuses, claiming they're all charlatans," Holloway replied. He ran a hand through his pale, thinning hair. The movement sent dull wisps of golden-white flying upwards like bird feathers. The earl swallowed hard, fighting against emotional scars. "Yes, you're right. Reggie, would you take a look at her?"

"Of course," said Whitmore. "Might she have eaten something poisonous in Damascus? Some poisons have long-term physiological effects."

"No, not that I can remember. She tends to eat sparingly, but then Ginny's always watched her weight."

Whitmore's bearded face filled with worry. "She looks too thin, if you ask me, but then I prefer a woman with a bit of meat. Look here, let's talk more later. I can walk Imogen upstairs, if you wish."

"That's kind of you, Reggie," said Salter, "but if Della's going to play, we should remain, don't you think? Ginny, would you like to hear Lady Della play?" he called to his wife.

The countess was sandwiched twixt Dolly and Victoria. She quietly nodded. Adele joined them and spoke softly to Seth's mother. "I shall play whatever you choose, Lady Salter," the young woman told her. "Pick one, and I'll do my best."

"Let's all have a seat," suggested Haimsbury. The music room clock was approaching the hour of four. He'd need to leave soon. "Ladies, we apologise for delaying you," he told Della and her friend. "Who's playing first?"

Flora volunteered, and Adele turned pages. The Appleton girl played several Brahms pieces, followed by a less than perfect rendition of Chopin's *Nocturne, Opus 9*. Charles knew the piece by heart. He'd played it dozens of times, and his eidetic memory made it easy to remember every note and musical instruction. The nerves in his fingers wanted to move and correct the girl's mistakes, but he watched patiently, smiling now and then.

Next, Adele sat down, whilst Flora Appleton turned pages. Adele Marie had finer interpretation and greater agility than her friend. Her long hands reached beyond an octave, and she brought a great deal of maturity to each selection. Once she'd finished, her proud father rose to his feet, applauding and calling 'Brava!" Then Charles quickly added, "Very well done, both of you! Bravissimi!"

Adele offered a deep curtsy of appreciation, as did Flora—though not quite as deeply, nor as gracefully. Della crossed to her father's chair. "Well? What did you think?"

"The Brahms was perfect. A shortened version of the No. 3, wasn't it?"

"I knew you'd recognise it. I shortened it on my own. You've such a good memory."

"Usually, but what was the last song you played? I've never heard it before."

"At last, I've surprised you, Holmes!" she giggled. "Prince Anatole introduced me to a new composer named Rachmaninoff. He's Russian, as you might deduce, and the piece is called *Morceaux de Fantaisie*. It's a collection of five pieces, but as you're leaving soon, I played just the *Elegie*. Quite nice, isn't it?"

"Lovely. I shall buy the music."

"I've already bought it for you," she whispered, offering him a little kiss. "I wish you didn't have to go so soon." She smiled, but Charles noticed a hint of worry as she whispered, "Father, what's wrong with Lady Salter? Is she ill?"

"I don't know, darling. Probably just overtired. Reggie will see to her recovery. He's a very fine doctor. Shall we take one last walk before I go?"

"Yes, I'd like that, for I've a favour to ask."

Charles stood with his arm through that of his daughter. "It looks as though the rain's stopped, Tory. I think we'll walk over to the stables and see that new filly."

"Fine, but don't dawdle, Charles. Your coach will be ready at six. Just as you insisted."

"I shan't forget," he promised. "Ask Russell to have my luggage ready to load. Come, daughter. Let's enjoy the air."

They left Flora and the others behind and exited the castle by way of the south doors. Father and daughter wound along a series of brick pathways, through rose beds, knot gardens, and finally headed northeast towards the stables. Beth kept breeding stock here and shipped the best stallions and mares back to Branham.

The skies began to sprinkle again, and Charles led his daughter into the first stable, a relatively warm building with brick walls and concrete floors. A groom started over. "Your Grace, is wish to ride?" he asked in accented English.

"No, thank you, young man," he answered. "My daughter and I thought we'd look at the horses. Please, go about your duties."

The young man bowed, his dark hair tumbling from beneath a grey gabardine cap. Charles noticed a quick glance twixt the two young people. "He's a rather handsome boy."

Della laughed. "He's twenty, Father. Hardly a boy."

"Twenty's a boy to me. What's the young man's name?"

"Emile Deniau. He's André Deniau's son."

"That explains it then. I thought he looked familiar. He favours his father."

"Do I favour you?" she asked.

He kissed the top of her head. "In many ways. Your colouring is like my mother's, but your eyes come from my Grandmother Stuart, the late Lord Aubrey's twin sister."

"Flora says your eyes are quite unusual. I told her Mother thinks they look like the sea."

"Is Flora interested in anyone her own age?"

Adele smiled. "She thinks Seth's quite nice. He sometimes visits, when he's in Lucerne."

"Is her admiration serious or mere flirtation?" he asked, smiling. "Shall I warn Seth?"

This made Adele laugh. "No, Father. Flora's engaged to be married. Or at least, she's promised to someone. Budgie Bingham. Do you know him?"

"Budgie? Like the bird?"

"It's a silly nickname, but everyone calls him that. His father's Lord Palmore. Budgie's real name is Edward Simmons, the Viscount Silverdale."

"And does Budgie take their engagement as lightly as Flora?"

She grew serious. "I don't think so, but, Father, Flora can't help being a bit flighty. Nearly all the young ladies at Meggenhorn are like that. She's actually quite intelligent, beneath all that pretence."

"I hope you don't behave that way."

Della smiled up at him. "Of course, I don't. I feel sorry for Flora. She wants everyone to like her but doesn't know how to behave. I don't think she really wants Seth's attention; not long-term, that is."

"And what about you?" he asked as they reached an area with a long stone bench. "Come, let's sit. I'd like to speak seriously for a moment."

"About Flora?"

"No, darling, about you. What attention do you hope to receive from our dashing viscount?"

Her eyes grew still and serious. "Are you asking if I love Seth?"

Charles nodded. "You've spent the past four years getting to know him. I realise he's older, but such arrangements often work quite well."

Della sighed. "Yes, I know that, and I do like Seth very much. Flora thinks he visits Meggenhorn on account of her, but he's really there to visit me. Seth's called on me four times since he took the position in Lucerne."

"Has he? Did you know he accepted the position just to be close to you?"

"No, but I suspected it," she replied. "Are you certain of that?"

He nodded. "Quite certain. Seth asked my permission before he took the position."

"Really? Does he talk about me?"

"Often," Charles told her. "I've gotten to know Seth well in the past five years. He's become one of my closest friends. The man's honest and true, Della. I've come to respect and admire Holloway.

And his scientific expertise is invaluable to the inner circle. In fact, he's just become one of our ICI agents, with the rank of Inspector."

"Yes, he told me about that, which is why I want to ask you this favour."

"Ah, yes, you mentioned that. What favour, darling?"

Her grip on his hand tightened. "You asked me how I feel about Seth. He and I talked the day before Flora and I left Meggenhorn, and he—well, he mentioned marriage."

Charles smiled. "And how do you feel about that?"

"Honestly?"

"Yes, dear, honestly."

"I'm not sure. Marriage is a lifelong thing, and I want to make the right choice."

"An admirable ambition."

"I see you're smiling, but I'm serious, Father."

"Forgive me if it seems I'm taking this lightly. Della, I promise, I understand it all too well."

"How could you?" she asked. "You and Mother are so perfectly matched."

"Yes, but my first wife and I were a very poor match."

"I'd forgotten you were married before. How long?"

He took a deep breath. "When Amelia died, we'd been married for almost ten years. I don't blame her for leaving me. It was my fault for jumping into that relationship. But after Amelia died, the Lord brought me your mother. I still consider it a miracle." He noticed tears welling up in her eyes. "What can I do to help, little one?"

She leaned against his shoulder, the tears falling on his coat. "Little one," she whispered. "I've not heard you call me that for months."

"Even when you're old and grey, I shall call you that. You are my pride and joy, Adele Marie. How can I help?"

Della turned to face him, eyes glistening. "Well, if you're willing..." she began.

"If it's in my power, I'm willing. Ask me."

"You said earlier that you intended to stop over in Lucerne for the night."

"Yes?"

"And afterwards, you're going to Vienna. Is it to do with a murder?"

"It might be, but tell me, Watson, why would you mention murder?" he asked, tweaking her nose.

"Elementary, Holmes. You are the finest detective in the world, and murder is the greatest of all crimes. Is that why you're going?"

"I'm not sure, but even if knew, I couldn't speak of it publicly."

"My brother's gone to Africa. Did you know?"

"Yes, Paul sent me a telegram," Charles told her. "Why?"

"He stopped to see me on his way down to Nantes," she continued. "Whilst he's away, you'll need someone else to act as a second set of eyes and ears. A faithful companion, like Watson is for Holmes."

He shook his head, assuming she wanted to come. "Della, that is quite impossible. I'll admit, your mind is just as sharp as your brother's, but I need someone who's able to fight when required. This assignment could be dangerous."

"Yes, Father, I understand," she said, "but I'm working on that. I'm quite good with a pistol now, and I do a bit of fencing. However, I'm not suggesting myself. Truthfully, I've no desire to live 'on the edge', as Seth calls it. I prefer a more cerebral approach to crime, I suppose. I've more of Mycroft in me than Sherlock."

He put his arm round her shoulders. "As do I, little one. Becoming a policeman forced me out from the safety of my mathematician's box. But if not you, then who should I take to replace your brother?"

"I thought you might take Seth along."

"Seth?" he asked, thoroughly surprised. "No, wait, let me use my detective skills a moment and see I can deduce your reasons for this interesting suggestion. You are fond of Seth, correct?"

"Correct."

"And he's made his feelings clear regarding marriage?"

"Yes, he has. He didn't actually propose, not yet, but he said he wished to court me."

"Yes, as I said, he asked me for permission to do that, but I deduce that you need time to consider other options first. Am I nearing the mark?"

She leaned against his shoulder and let out a loud, long sigh. "Very near the mark. Do you think me foolish, Father? Am I wasting my energies? I'm sure Henry has feelings for me. Why can't he just speak up and tell me?"

"Henry MacAlpin?"

"Yes, of course, Henry MacAlpin!" she said with another loud sigh. "Am I being foolish?"

"Little one, that is a very tricky question, and I'm probably not the one to answer it. I was married to Amelia for ten years, but most of those years, we were separated. She'd given her heart to another, and I doubt she realised I'd fallen out of love with her."

"And you'd fallen *in love* with Mother, right? When did that happen?"

"I'm not sure. Our relationship is complicated yet simple, if that makes sense. However, it was '84, when I first realised the depth of my affections. I'd no idea she felt the same way until we met again in '88. That long separation whilst she lived in France nearly killed me, Della. Truly it did. I'd no idea I was heir to the Haimsbury estates. I assumed a duchess was beyond my reach, and it ate at my heart. But sometimes, the Lord allows us to walk through a sort of emotional desert. Even after Amelia died in '86, the Lord kept saying no. Then, finally, in *his* timing, God allowed us to find one another."

"Father, do you think Henry might love me, silently, the way you loved Mother back then?"

Charles took her hands and kissed them. "My darling daughter, I *know* Henry loves you, for I can see it written upon his face every time I mention your name. And when he asks about you, I see the same light in his eyes that shone in mine, whenever I talked about your mother."

"Then why doesn't he declare it? Why remain silent about it all?"

"Do you want my honest opinion?"

"Yes. Please, tell me!"

He took a moment before saying, "Please, don't take this the wrong way. MacAlpin does love you, but I believe he thinks he's too old for you."

"Too old? Why?" she asked, tears sliding down her face. "He's only four years older than Seth. If he isn't too old, then why should four more years matter?"

"Yes, but, Della, you're only sixteen."

"I'll be seventeen next month, and in August, I'll graduate from Meggenhorn. Wouldn't that be a good time to marry?"

"Yes, and Henry will be forty. Perhaps, to him, the difference is too great."

"Do *you* think it's too great?" she asked him pointedly.

"Perhaps not. In peerage families it isn't at all unusual."

"No, it isn't," she answered. "Did you know, the late Lord Aubrey married Abigail Stuart when she was barely sixteen, and he was forty? They had a wonderful marriage. Right up until the moment she died, Robert Stuart loved and adored her. And Henry's father was over fifty and his mother just twenty when they married. They were very happy, despite the difference."

He kissed her cheek. "You're right, but it's Henry who must decide. Shall I speak to him for you?"

"Oh, no, please don't!" she begged him.

"Then how can I help? If I don't talk with Henry, then what? Shall I talk to Seth?"

"Not exactly. I wondered if you might take him along as your Watson? He's very good with a pistol and with a sword, and he's clever, Father. You said so yourself. As he's an inspector now, it can be official, right?"

He smiled; his eyes filled with admiration. "I suppose, it could also help you to decide if he'll make a good husband or not? Is that it?"

"It might," she whispered.

They sat together silently for quite a while, enjoying being in one another's company. The large black cat watched them from an oak beam—high overhead, its tail flicking back and forth. Finally, with time slipping away, Charles and Adele headed back to the castle, and the Duke prepared for the long trip to Lucerne.

Left alone, the cat's ice-blue eyes blinked as it smiled.

See you in Vienna, whispered the disguised entity inside the cat. *We'll be watching, Time Walker.*

All of us.

For we are MANY.

CHAPTER THIRTEEN

Breitenfurt Retreat – Outskirts of Vienna

Cordelia Stuart sat before an ash writing desk, pen in hand, paper at the ready. She wondered just what to say to her mother. Five years earlier, the Dowager Baroness Constance Wychwright had married the 15th Earl of Brackamore and become modestly wealthy as Constance Palmer-Newhouse, Countess of Brackamore. Ever since, Connie splashed the earl's money round London's shops and tea rooms. She'd even redecorated Brackamore House three times, since becoming an influential countess, explaining the actions by the need to host endless parties and afternoon teas. Delia's mother hadn't even said goodbye when she left London, yet the young woman felt compelled to write, though she had no idea what to tell her harsh and inconstant mother.

Just write, mo bhean, she imagined her husband saying. *Tell her how you really feel.*

> Dearest Mama,
>
> Well, we arrived. Our small entourage took a scenic journey to Vienna, and though long, the route was quite pleasant. I apologise for not sending postcards, but we spent only one night at each railway stop, and there wasn't time to visit any of the shops. The hotels Paul chose were lovely and modern, and all the employees quite nice. Elizabeth came with me, as did Dr. MacAlpin. There were several of Paul's other friends on board, too (those he sometimes calls agents), and some have remained nearby. I'm told they're lodging at a small inn about two miles away.

Breitenfurt Retreat is even nicer than the brochures make it out to be, Mama. It's in Liesing Valley, in the famous Vienna Woods. The Retreat was once a hunting lodge, used by the Habsburg Emperors, so you can imagine how splendid it is. My rooms are spacious and airy and beautifully decorated. There's even a balcony overlooking the woodland valley, and from it I can watch birds, deer, rabbits, and foxes. Birdsong fills the air all day long, and the sweet scent of flowers accompanies their chorus.

I'm sure you wanted to come with us. I overheard you and Paul arguing about it the day before we left. He means well, Mama. I hope you've forgiven him by now. Paul's a very fine husband and only wants the best for me—but also the best for us: myself and our two children.

Yes, I know our Liam is gone, but even now, it kills me to write his name. He's with God now. I realise his death isn't my fault, not really. I'm very sorry for how my mind fails sometimes. I try not to let it happen, but then it does, and there's no way to stop it. Dr. Pyramis says I must admit my failings, if I'm to rise above them. It's difficult to do, but he is a specialist, and his reputation is without blemish.

He's actually quite a handsome gentleman. (I say this only because so many of the other ladies here comment on his looks), but he's more than handsome, Mama. He's also very kind. Dr. Pyramis lets me talk about Liam all I want. For hours and hours. He says it's like lancing a deep wound. Once the wound is clean, and the incision heals, then my mind can heal, too. I'm not sure what all that means, but he's the professional, so it must be true. Mustn't it?

I cannot spend too much time on a letter, as the doctor's coming to talk with me shortly. I promise to write again soon. Much love to Lord Ethan and to you, of course, dearest Mama. Please, tell my brothers that I love them with all my heart. I'm very glad Ned's working for Duke Charles now. Perhaps, Thomas will find his calling, too.

I wonder though, what happened to William? I can't seem to remember much about him. Isn't that strange? Oh, I hear the doctor coming! I really must finish and get this in the post.

Hugs and kisses,
Your Little Delia

Cordelia folded the pages and placed them into a linen envelope. She'd just sealed the letter, when Vanu Pyramis knocked on the door.

"May I visit?" he asked politely, standing in the door frame.

"Oh, yes, of course!" Delia said, flushed with excitement. "I was writing to my mother. I'm sure she expected a letter sooner, but I hadn't the time."

"Mothers are like that," said the handsome alienist. "I've ordered tea, if that's all right. I thought you might be growing hungry."

"Hungry?" she repeated, her cheeks pink and warm. "Do you say that because of my problem? Mama says I overeat when I'm emotional. She's right, I suppose. But I'm emotional so very often, that I'm nearly always hungry, Dr. Pyramis."

"We'll discuss that shortly, but calling me Dr. Pyramis is so very formal. Why not call me Vanu? Or even Van, which is how my wife calls me."

"Van? I'm not sure. Van seems rather informal. I am your patient, after all. May I call you Dr. Van?"

He smiled, and the deep, dark eyes sparkled with mesmerising wonder. To many of the female residents, Vanu Pyramis seemed terrifyingly handsome, even seductive.

Delia felt herself falling into those dark eyes.

Tea? Did he say something about tea?

Pyramis stepped closer, almost touching her hands, but then a uniformed servant arrived, pushing a silver cart.

"Ah, yes," said the charming doctor. "Here's our tea."

An oval table stood near the balcony windows. The young man dressed the table with a flowered cloth, then laid out china plates, cups, a variety of small cakes, crustless sandwiches, fruit, water, coffee, and tea.

"Will that be all, sir?" he asked Pyramis in perfect English.

"For now," Pyramis replied, also in English. "I'll let you know when to clear it. Thank you, Michael."

The waiter bowed and left, shutting the door.

"Sugar and milk?" asked the physician.

"Oh, shouldn't I pour?" asked Cordelia. "After all, it's a woman's job, isn't it?"

"Why? Do men not do these things in England?"

"Sometimes, but generally, it's a lady's job."

"But my dear Lady Delia, I am your host. Do you take milk and sugar?"

"Yes to both. Three cubes of sugar, unless the cup is large. Then four. And a little splash of milk. I've an awful sweet tooth. Mama complains about it all the time."

"Why?" he asked, adding four cubes.

"Why what?" she asked, taking the prepared cup.

He repeated the question, his eyes trained on hers. "Why would your mother complain about so small a thing as sugar cubes? Surely, you can afford them, yes?"

"Oh, yes! Easily. We have lots of money. Well, Paul and I do. Mama has money, too, now that she's remarried. But when I was growing up, our finances weren't sound or reliable. Papa had a noble title but very little to go with it."

"And so she limited your sugar?"

"Well, no that isn't why she scolded me about sweets. It's because a lady needs a small waist to catch a husband."

He stirred the tea, then took a sip. "Many mothers often say such things. How did you feel when she said it?"

"Not said, Dr. Van. Mama still says it."

"But you have a husband now. As you say, he is already caught. Does Lord Aubrey scold you about your figure?"

She set the cup into its matching saucer; her large eyes thoughtful. Pyramis could see the glisten of unshed tears near the inner corners. He watched and waited.

At long last, Delia picked up the cup and took a small sip. Her hands were trembling. "I would never call my husband caught, Doctor. Paul's far too clever and important to be caught."

"Forgive me. I use a poor word. My English is not always right. Does your husband scold you?"

"No, not ever," she said, the hands calming a little. "The truth is, Paul says my figure is perfect, and he never mentions anything about my sweet tooth. If I want cake, I eat cake, and he never says a word. If I don't want any cake, then he says nothing. No matter what I do, Paul makes me feel like a..."

"Like a what, Lady Delia?"

Delia smiled, the image of her wonderful husband filling every part of her mind. "Paul says I am his very own Venus, come to life. He calls me his Titian wonder," she added with a soft giggle. "He makes me feel so very special, Dr. Van. But, Mama..."

"Your mama says differently, yes?"

She nodded, old scars and deep-rooted pain darkening her sweet features. "Mama calls me hideously misshapen," Delia began, her hands trembling once again. "She says this treatment will make me thinner. That it's my childish mind that makes me want sweets; that Paul will cease to love me if I fail here."

"Your mother thinks Breitenfurt is a slimming spa? Nothing but a weight loss course of some kind?"

Delia nodded, tears sliding down her cheeks. "Mama has a friend who cried all the time, but after she spent three months here, she'd lost a great deal of weight and was much happier. Will that happen to me?"

"Is that why you came, Delia? To lose weight?"

She shook her head. "No, I don't care about any of that."

"Then why are you here?"

The young woman set the cup and saucer on the table, but nearly dropped it. The tears fell in a torrent. "I just want to stop hurting all the time!" she wept. "I want to stop thinking about Liam. I want to stop seeing things that aren't there! I need to heal, Doctor. For Paul. I have to do it for him and our children."

He reached for her hands and clasped them tightly. "And you will, Delia. I promise. We never fail at Breitenfurt. Never."

Her entire body trembled, and he could see the long tracks of tears as she glanced up. "There's always a first time," she whispered.

"Never, Lady Delia. I never fail. Let's take the first steps together." He kissed her hands, then refilled her teacup. "You mentioned seeing things that aren't really there. What do you mean by that?"

She set her hands into her lap and took a deep breath. A large black bird landed on the balcony railing. Delia noticed it had yellow eyes.

"Lady Delia? Is something wrong?"

"Oh, sorry, no, nothing wrong," she replied in a soft voice. "I was just watching that bird. It is there, isn't it? It's not my imagination? A bird with black feathers?"

"It is really there," he said, turning towards the bird. "I believe it's a raven. We have lots of them here. If I asked you to tell me the bird's name, what would you say?"

"William," she answered without hesitation.

"William? Why that name? Do you know someone by that name?"

She pushed back her chair and left the table, preferring to stand by the window and watch the birds. "He's my brother. I have three brothers. William's the eldest."

"And why would you compare him to a bird?"

"I'm not sure. I don't like to think about him, though."

"Why?" asked Pyramis.

"Because William's in prison. At least, I think he is. I'm not sure anymore. He used to be Baron Wychwright. As the eldest son, he inherited my father's title. He tried to murder my husband, Dr. Van, and then he pushed me down the stairs. That's why he's in prison. For that and—*other* things. I don't like to think about him."

"And your two other brothers? Are they also criminals?"

"No, not at all!" she answered quickly, her head turning towards Pyramis. "Ned's a lovely man. He's Baron Wychwright now, and he works for Duke Charles as steward for his county holdings. Ned divorced three years ago. He's raising two daughters on his own, so working for the Duke helps a great deal. And Ned's very good at his job. Thomas is the youngest of the brothers. He's four years older than I. Tom lives in Paris. Mama used to dote on William, but now she does the same with Tom. He's a painter and lives in Montmartre. He never has any money. He says painting is a difficult way to make a living."

Pyramis laughed. "Yes, I've known such artists. Does your mama extend financial help to this struggling painter?"

"Sometimes. Tom writes to me now and then, asking for a small loan. Paul's been generous with my family, and he's helped Tom once or twice. I think he even got him out of a French jail once. Ned's the good one."

"Come back to the table, please, Delia."

"All right, but I don't want to eat."

"No? The cakes are dark chocolate with raspberry. It's your favourite, so I'm told. Come now, don't make me eat them all. I could, you know. I could eat every last one of them, for I have a very keen appetite."

Cordelia noticed his dark eyes flicker as he said the word 'appetite'. The subtle glint drew her close rather than cause fright. She obeyed and sat again, then selected a cake. Slowly, she sliced off tiny bites with the edge of her fork and let the rich morsel melt on her tongue. After three such bites, she put down the fork. Strangely, she no longer wanted the cake. She only wanted to hear Dr. Pyramis's voice.

"You may eat all you want, Lady Delia. You need only take it."

"Thank you," she answered in a small voice. "I'm not really hungry."

"Good," he replied, taking full charge of the conversation. "Now, tell me about your husband. The earl is older than you, yes?"

She stared at the chocolate torte, wondering why she no longer wanted it. "Yes. Paul will be thirty-nine in October."

"And you? Forgive me for asking, but I'm your doctor. I must ask. How old are you?"

"Twenty-two. I turn twenty-three in December."

"Almost a fifteen-year difference? Does this ever lead to problems? Such a wide gap can make for incompatible spouses."

"Incompatible? Oh, no, not at all," she said, defending her husband. "Paul's lovely. Really, he is! He never makes me feel too young, and besides, Paul's not old. Not like some of his Oxford friends. He's very active. He hunts, plays polo. He's a champion fencer, and he boxes."

"Bare knuckle?"

"I... I don't know," she admitted. "I've never actually watched the matches, but he and Charles box three times a week."

"All these are male activities, Lady Delia."

"Yes, but Paul's a male, isn't he? He and I do things together. We go for drives and horseback riding. Beth's far better at riding than I, though. She's won championships. She and Paul sometime compete against one another."

"Do they?" he asked in a tone that Henry MacAlpin would recognise as clinically significant. "Tell me about their relationship. For instance, why did Duchess Elizabeth come along with you to Breitenfurt?"

"Elizabeth's my friend, Dr. Van. You mustn't think there's anything odd about her coming. She's like a sister."

"I see."

"No, I don't think you do," Delia told him. "There's nothing inappropriate between them. Yes, they were once promised to one another, but it doesn't mean he's still in love with her."

"They once had an understanding? Were they in love?"

Suddenly, Delia's craving for sweets returned with full-force. She forked up a large mound of cake and crammed it into her mouth. After chewing hastily and swallowing, the countess said, "It isn't his fault. When Elizabeth was born, everyone told Paul that she was his responsibility; that he was to marry her when Beth came of age. He did look after her and grew to love her. Of course, he loved her. No, he *loves* her. Yes, that's what I mean. He loves her now, but they're cousins. It isn't romantic."

"Why didn't he and the Duchess marry?"

"Because she didn't want him!" Delia snapped, but quickly recovered. "Forgive me, Dr. Van. What I meant to say, is Elizabeth found someone else. She found Charles. Please, don't think Paul married me just because he couldn't have her."

"And he still loves her. Is that why Elizabeth came along?"

"No. Yes, of course, Paul loves her. Why wouldn't he? But Beth will always love Charles. They're made for one another."

"Isn't Charles the earl's cousin?"

"Yes, but he was lost as a boy."

"Lost?" asked Pyramis.

The yellow-eyed bird had moved. Now, it sat by the windows, staring into the room.

"Is it warm in here?" Delia asked.

"Not at all. Tell me about Charles. How was he lost?"

"His father was killed, and then his mother ran away. She took him to Liverpool. At least, that's what I can remember. You should ask Charles. It was in all the newspapers. I'm sure you've read about his story."

The alienist calmly poured her another cup of tea, adding the appropriate cubes of sugar, and then passed her the fresh cup. "I've read many stories about Duke Charles, but most sound like a faery tale. Is he really such a paragon of virtue?"

"Yes, Doctor, he is," she answered firmly. "I will not hear anyone speak negatively about Charles. Not ever! He's been my friend from the very first. Ever since that, that *incident* in Whitechapel, he's stood up for me. He hunted down the man who did it, and that man's in prison now because of Charles. In Paris."

"What man is that? What incident?"

She swallowed another forkful of cake. "Henry says I don't have to talk about it. Albert's in prison. That's the end of it."

"Albert?"

"Sir Albert Wendaway. He... That is, he tried... He tried to..." Delia's hands began to shake again. "I mean, he tried to take advantage of me. Charles wouldn't rest until he found Albert and took him to court."

Pyramis reached for her hands, his thumb on her wrist. "I cannot imagine how terrifying that must have been, Lady Delia. Forgive me for making you talk about it, but it's my job. Talking will help you to lance the poison from your mind. I'm glad he was caught. Did it take long to find him?"

"Yes, a very long time. Charles finally discovered him hiding in Montmartre last year. As I say, he's in prison."

"Montmartre? Isn't that where your artist brother lives?"

The bird had been joined by a large black cat. The cat had ice-blue eyes. Both creatures stared at the countess.

"Are you all right, Lady Delia?"

She took another bite. "Yes."

"I wonder if your brother ever met this man? What is his name again?"

She gulped the cake down, tears streaming onto the fork and plate. "Wendaway. Albert Wendaway. He told Charles that my mother put him up to it, but how could that be true? Albert didn't even know my mother. He may have been involved in my father's murder, too, though the evidence pointed to someone else. Albert gave evidence against some other man, which is why he only received six years."

"What of your father? What happened to him?"

"Poor Papa!" she cried, using the serviette to blow her nose. "He loved me, Dr. Van. He always loved me so very much."

"Your father's dead? He was murdered?" the alienist asked carefully.

She nodded and finished the last of the cake, then washed it down with sugary tea. "I suppose so. I mean, yes. He must be dead. And William's in prison. He tried to shoot Charles and Paul. Perhaps, he even tried to kill the twins. Poor little things. Poor little Liam."

He took note of the sudden switch to her dead son. "Why do William's crimes make you think of Liam?"

Cordelia left the table and walked back to the windows. Her posture shifted. She began to laugh as though suddenly carefree. "Liam? He's such a beautiful boy. He has his father's eyes and smile. Even his dimples. I'm sure he'll look just like Paul one day."

Pyramis joined the Countess near the balcony window. "Will he? Tell me, Lady Delia, how old is Liam?"

"Liam? Who's that?" she asked in a radically altered voice. This one was higher, more girlish. "Is he a new neighbour? Is he coming to the dance? Papa's letting me go to the dance. It's next Saturday, at Bessemer Hall in Keswick. Sir Allen Bessemer's giving it. He has a son my age. Richard Bessemer. He's tall and red-haired. So very handsome!"

Pyramis moved closer, his hands on her forearm. "How old is the Bessemer boy?"

"Seventeen."

"And how old are you?"

"Everyone knows that. Fifteen, but very nearly sixteen. Mama said I may have a new dress, if I don't eat too much. And Papa promised to buy a new carriage. Our old one is quite run down. Oh, I'm sorry, do I know you?" she asked, blinking quickly, eyes wide as saucers.

"You may call me Dr. Van," he said with a formal bow.

"It's very nice to meet you, Dr. Van. I'm Cordelia Wychwright. I hope you'll forgive me, but I'm very tired suddenly. Do you mind if I sleep? Tomorrow will be very busy."

"Because of the dance?"

"Because we leave for London. It's the last fitting for my new ball gown," she said dreamily. "Will you be there?"

"I hope to attend, yes. I've kept you long enough, Lady Delia. I'll leave you to sleep. Please, give my best to your mother and father."

"I will. I'll see you at the ball next Saturday."

He led her back to the table. Cordelia obediently sat. Her eyes closed, and the head dropped forward, as though the muscles lost all tone.

Pyramis crossed back to the apartment door and pulled it open. He motioned to a nurse, who'd been stationed near the far end of the corridor at a small desk. The woman wore a dark dress, but no cap or pin. She arrived quickly.

"Yes, sir?"

"Mrs. Fischer, will you help Lady Delia prepare for a nap? She'll take a rather long one, I should think."

"The water worked its magic?"

He nodded. "Oh, yes. Warming the lithia water in tea always amplifies the effect. Our new guest made great progress today. And I've learnt a great deal about her family troubles. It's likely she'll sleep for several hours but check on her regularly."

"Of course, sir. I'll have Michael clear the table. Shall I assign one of our girls to serve as the countess's maid?"

"Yes, I think that's a good idea. Someone reliable and discreet. We'll want her to report back to us."

"Of course, sir. I'll assign Miss Wingham. Oh, but there is one other thing, Doctor," Fischer said, as she made notes in Lady Aubrey's chart. "What shall we do about the cat, sir?"

"Cat?"

"Yes, Doctor. A large black cat. We noticed it hanging about her balcony doors. Does it belong to Lady Aubrey?"

The alienist smiled. "Hmm. A cat. Do nothing about the cat for now, Mrs. Fischer. I believe I know its origin, but if you see it again, let me know at once."

As he left the patient floors, Pyramis paused now and then to wave to other resident patients. Moments later, he returned to the office and sat before the massive oak desk. He opened a deep drawer, containing a strange-looking device with a thick metal plate, bearing the engraving: *Volta Graphophone Company*. Pyramis inserted a wax cylinder into the main housing and switched on the recording machine. He gripped the speaking tube and dropped the needle into the spinning wax.

The alienist began to dictate in German. "Twenty-eighth of March, 1894. Patient record for Lady Cordelia Jane Stuart, Countess of Aubrey. Previously stated reasons for admission are melancholia, most probably due to multiple miscarriages and, more recently, the death of a six-day old infant. Per today's session, we may add hysteria, hallucinations, and probable sexual repression, most likely caused by adolescent trauma. Lady Aubrey's husband, Lord Paul Stuart, 12th Earl of Aubrey, is a highly influential member of the Scottish elite and plays a key role in British foreign activities. Lord Aubrey co-leads the secretive inner circle of Stuart lore, and he's cousin to HRH Prince Charles Sinclair, 1st Duke of Haimsbury by birthright, and Duke of Branham by marriage. It's likely Sinclair will one day inherit the title Duke of Drummond as well."

The alienist paused. He heard a scratching sound near the window. Pyramis turned round to find both the raven and the black cat perched on one of his balcony chairs.

Vanu smiled and continued.

"Previous physical examination revealed no sign of organic disease. Subject is healthy and four months post-partum. The loss of the baby at six days old precipitated the countess's admission. Heart and lungs are normal. Auscultation revealed a slight ventricular murmur. Appetite is normal, though subject exhibits a profound sugar craving under emotional duress. She is easily entranced. As in previous trials, lithia water works far more quickly when warmed, as in coffee or tea. From now on, this is how we will administer the Breitenfurt Cure.

"Subject also exhibits sudden, idiopathic dissociative behaviour. During today's session, she regressed to an early point in her life—shortly before her sixteenth birthday—perhaps the initial point of trauma. The trigger for this regression is unknown. I shall continue probing but must tread carefully to avoid sending her into the past permanently. Subject shows high sensitivity to the lithia water. Today, I administered a class one dose to her tea and within minutes, she expressed a strong desire to sleep. I've placed her in the care of Mrs. Hilda Fischer. Cordelia Stuart will require a minimum of six weeks at Breitenfurt, perhaps as much as twelve. She may write to her husband and family, but all correspondence must be copied before it is posted.

"Finally, regarding her husband. I find Lord Aubrey careful and intentionally opaque. I also find him fascinating, a worthy subject of study. The earl's occupation as an intelligence operative may explain his careful manner, but his position within the Stuart/Sinclair inner circle must also contribute. There is no doubt that Aubrey loves his wife, and he appears particularly protective. He places no initial trust in me; nor does he like me. Our final conversation had its adversarial moments. He struggles to control anger when provoked. We might be able to use this.

"Miss Grüner, once you've typed all copies, you may sign the reports, per my usual form."

Pyramis switched off the machine and returned the brass speaking horn to its hook. He then pressed a button beneath the carved desk. In a few minutes, a smartly dressed woman knocked on the door. "Yes?" he called.

The door opened. A petite woman in a bustled silk skirt and white blouse entered. "You called, Herr Doktor?"

"Yes, Miss Grüner, come in," he answered in German. "Here is the next cylinder on Lady Aubrey's case. Please, type out one for us and two for our partners."

"*Ja. Sofort, Mein Herr.*"

She took the wax tube from her employer and left the office. Once the door closed, the mysterious alienist turned towards the balcony, where the bird and black cat waited. He opened one of the doors and spoke to the animals.

"I take it, he's on his way?"

The cat nodded and purred softly.

"Good. Very good. My friends, there is much to do, but we are ready. ALL of us are ready."

As he stroked the cat's dark fur, a gold-and-ivory ring glinted on Pyramis's left hand. Though no one could see it, hidden inside the gold band was an inscription; put there by a long-dead Russian jeweller.

Quia Multi Sumus.

For we are many.

CHAPTER FOURTEEN

Schönbrunn Palace, Vienna

Several miles east of Breitenfurt, at that very same moment that Pyramis spoke to the black cat, two gentlemen arrived at Schönbrunn Palace. Both were exceedingly tall, and servants bowed or curtsied, whenever they walked past. The taller of the two had long raven hair, tied with a crimson ribbon. He wore the uniform of Russian aristocracy: a red, high-collared tunic, decorated with dozens of medals and trimmed in velvet and gold.

His companion was slightly shorter, with auburn hair, worn unbound, that brushed his broad shoulders. He wore English garb: a stylish frock coat, white silk shirt, and crimson waistcoat over merino wool trousers. The visitors were shown to a finely appointed chamber and asked to wait for their audience with the Emperor.

"Do you know about Saint Germain and the others?" asked the auburn-haired Englishman.

"Yes," said the Russian. "Saint Germain and his QMS friends gather round the Sinclair family like buzzing bees, yet their actions are hardly secret. The One has always known their plans, even from the foundation of the world, Hadraniel. All shall come to pass, according to His will. All things will work together towards the One's perfect end."

"How is that, sir?" the Englishman asked.

"You play chess. Surely, you perceive the Great Game the enemy now plays? It began long ago, and the One allows the enemy to set pieces into place. We have seen those moves, Hadra. The King's Gambit, yes? Now, the enemy serves up a countermove to the One. The Poisoned Pawn."

"I'm afraid I don't see, sir. I play chess, of course, but the One's moves and countermoves confuse me. I feel dull in your presence, Prince Samael," said Romanov's companion. "Your eyes and intuition are far sharper than mine."

"Yet your eyes sparkle with great intelligence, Hadra," the elder angel said. "Some moves play out in Vienna, but others in Africa."

"You've been with Lord Aubrey?"

"Presently, he thinks me asleep in my cabin. We must protect all areas of the chessboard, which is why we're here."

"And why West Africa, sir? What's to happen there?"

Anatole started to explain, but footsteps interrupted. "I shall tell you later, my friend. You and I must resume our earthly roles. The chamberlain draws near."

A generously built human approached the two disguised angels. He wore court dress in eighteenth-century style, with a coat of deep-blue wool, trimmed with gold braid; red velvet knee breeches; white hose; and gold-buckled black shoes. He approached the visitors, bowed, then addressed them in German.

"Please, forgive the wait, Excellencies. The Emperor will see you now. Please, if you would follow me."

The disguised angels followed the impressive chamberlain through a series of receiving rooms, each connected to the previous by a single door, and each successively smaller than its predecessor. The final room was painted in creamy white, with a painted ceiling that featured an artist's idea of heaven. Romanov made no comment but shook his head in silence as he surveyed the figures of Odin, Thor, and Loki, taking a meal beside Zeus, Mercury, and Saturn. Within the confused scene, the artist included half-dressed goddesses, cavorting amongst the assembly, their eyes fixed on a central figure: Emperor Maximillian I, dressed in gilded armour, arriving in heaven on horseback. Beside Maximillian, stood his wife, Mary of Burgundy, who'd preceded the great ruler in death.

Naturally, the room was known as the Maximillian, but the man who currently occupied the Habsburg throne bore little resemblance to the fifteenth-century warrior. Though tall and generally robust, this prince preferred cerebral pursuits to military campaigns.

The visitors bowed as they approached the throne. In response, the Emperor spread out his hands and stood. "Welcome back to Schönbrunn, my friends," he told them in German.

"Thank you, Majesty," said Anatole.

"It is always a pleasure to see you, Romanov. And it occurs to me, that we've not finished our chess match."

Anatole Romanov smiled. "Tis an honour to see you again, Franz. Is that why you sent for me? So I could beat you at chess again?"

"No, old friend, no. But if there's time, we'll set the board and revisit that last game." The Emperor turned to the Englishman. "Thank you for coming, Lord Ailesleigh. You've not visited us in four years. Tell me, do English ladies entice more than our Austrian beauties?"

"No, sir," the younger angel blushed. "I beg forgiveness for being so lax in judgement."

"Then, our ladies do entice, eh, Ailesleigh?" teased the Emperor.

"All Vienna is an enticement, sir. May we leave it at that?"

Romanov placed his right foot on the bottom step leading up to the throne. "Majesty, my friend does not avoid your court. Work takes us to other lands, yet we always return to Vienna, yes?"

The younger elohim relaxed, happy for his elder to explain. Known in heaven as Hadraniel ben Ohr, the warrior angel had served beside Samael on thousands of missions. Samael was of an ancient class of elohim called Slayers. He'd defended the One's throne for millennia, beginning with the very first rebellion, when the universe was young. Slayers had authority over all other classes, and when given permission, had power to consign a rebel brother to eternal death.

Hadraniel, on the other hand, opened his eyes during the peaceful, interbellum years. He enjoyed gardening and writing music. He helped Adam in the first human's early days. But with Adam's expulsion and the return to war, Hadraniel learned to fight, instructed by the great Samael. The two elohim had served together ever since.

The younger angel bowed his head to show respect for his disguised superior. "As Prince Anatole says, sir, the beauties of Schönbrunn outshine all others. It is only work that distracts me."

"Well said, my lord," laughed the Emperor. "But ladies aside, I'm glad you've answered my call, for there's a matter I should like to discuss with you." He waved to the chamberlain. "Kaufmann, see that we're not disturbed. Go out and shut the door. Lock it but remain nearby. And no listening at keyholes."

The chamberlain departed. The door closed, followed by a soft *click!*, indicating the turning of a key.

"Now, my friends, come," the Emperor told his visitors. "Let's sit by the fire. My servants have left us wine and fresh pastries. There's much on my mind, and I would sound you out."

Franz Josef left the throne and led them to a sitting area, set with plump-cushioned sofas beside a tall fireplace. Neatly stacked birch logs crackled in the grate, and a long-legged wolfhound slept on a braided wool rug. The Emperor poured three glasses of wine and offered one to each guest. He raised his glass high, saying, "We drink to friendships that last, yes?"

"To eternal life," said Romanov. "A life filled with friends and loved ones."

They drained the cups, and the old man continued. "Anatole, you often talk of eternal life, and it seems you've found it. In all these thirty years, there's not a hint of grey to your hair, nor do your steps slow down as mine have done." He swiped at the white moustache. "Lord Daniel, you are also quite young. We've known one another for over ten years. I grow old, but the two of you remain young. What is your secret?"

"I cannot say, sir," replied Hadraniel in the guise of a Cornish earl. "I've heard old women in the Urals talk of men who never age. They tell strange tales of men that walk through time. Anatole and I are cousins. Perhaps, we descend from such men."

Anatole waved his hand and laughed as any Romanov might. "Old women and their talk! No, my friend, the strength of a man may diminish, but our minds stay sharp, is that not so? We keep them young, Franz. That is the secret to youth. Keep the mind sharp, and the muscles obey. But surely this is not why you summoned us, old friend. What troubles you? What might Lord Ailesleigh and I offer so great a ruler?"

The old man crinkled up his large nose and thumbed at the softly cleft chin. "Yes, that. Tell me, Romanov, you're friends with most of English nobility, correct?"

"I spend time in London as a government adviser. As such, I have become friends with some."

"Which nobles do you mean, sir?" asked the younger angel.

"Aye, there's the rub as you English say, Lord Ailesleigh." He sighed, and the cotton-wool sideburns sagged along with the voice.

"Just one man matters. Duke Charles of Haimsbury. We've met a few times, mostly at public occasions. The opera and the like. His Elizabeth and mine—my precious Sisi—get along well, and Sisi likes Haimsbury a great deal, as do I." He paused, a thick finger running round the rim of the wine glass. "Sisi's having dreams, you see. And keeps thinking about *him*."

"Him, sir? The Empress thinks about Haimsbury?" asked Ailesleigh, clearly surprised.

"I believe the Emperor refers to another man," Romanov told his friend. "Do you not, Franz? She dreams of Rudolf, yes?"

The old man's head bowed, and he gripped the glass, struggling to hold back the flow of tears. "I've tried, Anatole. Oh, how I've tried, but it's all coming out! And it's connected to this wedding somehow. I've had dreams, too. Rudolf's ghost begs me to avenge him, but how can I help, if I cannot make sense of what actually happened?"

"You've summoned Haimsbury for this?"

"Yes," the old man told the disguised angels. "Charles is a man of discretion, with experience in such matters, but without the same restrictions of my police. And without—how shall I say it?—without undue *influences*."

"Influences from whom?" asked Hadraniel.

"From those with the most to lose," replied the Emperor cryptically. "I cannot live forever, though I wish I could. My wife's never recovered from the loss, and it's led her into self-destructive behaviour."

"How so?" asked Anatole, though he already knew the answer.

Franz Josef's white moustache drooped further as he stared into the flames. "She constantly worries about her figure and grows evermore superstitious about her hair. She fears losing it, you see. It's utter nonsense, of course. Sisi's more beautiful than ever, though she recoils at my touch. I'm used to that. She's turned to a mystic for comfort, Anatole. The man's from your country. I wonder, might you know someone who calls himself Father Gregory? No, wait," he continued, scratching his chin. "Not Gregory. Grigor. Father Grigor. Or is it Grigori? Do you know such a priest?"

"Grigor Gregory, and Grigori are all common names in Russia," answered Romanov. "You say he is a priest?"

"A monk or priest. I'm not sure which."

Romanov's dark brows arched high, and the handsome head tilted. "If this priest is a true man of God, then you've nothing to fear. If not, then, he could bring trouble."

Franz Josef sighed. "My information is vague. Sisi calls him Father Grigori. Or perhaps it's Father Grigor."

Ailesleigh leaned forward. "Sir, perhaps I'm overstepping, but isn't this a police matter?"

"Usually, but when I ordered my men to follow my wife, she reacted very badly. I thought she might do herself harm. No, this must be kept secret. Sisi can never know."

"How can we help?" asked Romanov, who already knew exactly what the Austrian ruler would say.

"I thought you might know something of the man. This priest, I mean. He might even be a Romanov, for he bears a resemblance to you—though only just."

The Russian smiled. "My family is quite large. Can you describe the man?"

"Well, sir, he wears his hair long, just as you do, and he has piercing blue eyes that could bore a hole through wood. Your eyes are similar, but always sympathetic and kind. Of course, I've seen you angry once or twice, Anatole. I think, if roused, your gaze could do more than penetrate wood, my friend. It might spear a man to the wall!"

This made the elder angel laugh. "I pray never to be so angry without just cause, Majesty. But tell me, how is Haimsbury involved?"

"He isn't," said the Emperor. "Not yet. I took a chance and wrote to him without explaining why."

"You're asking the Duke about this Father Grigor?" asked Ailesleigh.

"Oh, no. Not about the priest, but about Rudolf's death. I couldn't reveal anything in a letter, so I asked him to wire back with one word. Mozart for yes. Salieri for no."

"So that no one suspects, is that right, sir?" asked Ailesleigh.

"Yes. It was a great relief, when Charles wired back with Mozart, but once he learns my reason for summoning him, he may change his mind."

"Ah, now, I understand," replied Romanov. "Shall I speak to him for you?"

"No, Anatole. No. That's kind of you, but it's this Grigori person I'm worried about. I prefer to leave this monk or priest or whatever he is to you."

"Is he in Vienna?"

"I'm not sure," said Franz Josef. "He was a fortnight ago. Sisi's become despondent again, which makes me think he may be gone."

"Where was Father Grigori staying, sir?" asked Ailesleigh.

"Hotel Metropole. It's in the Morinzplatz."

"Yes, I know the place well. Leave the priest to us, Franz," said Romanov. "When is Haimsbury arriving?"

"A few days from now. He only just left Paris."

"I see," said Anatole. "Do not meet him here. Choose somewhere sacred. A church or chapel. Find a priest you trust and ask him to cleanse it well before the meeting."

"Why?" asked Franz Josef.

"Because your true enemy is not physical, Franz," he told the Emperor firmly. "Cleanse the church first. You must not fail in this."

"I won't. And will you join me?"

Romanov shook his head, his eyes filled with kindness. "Alas, my duties take me to Africa, but if you need me, at any time, wire the Russian embassy here in Vienna. I shall come that very day."

"The same day? But Africa is weeks away! Have you struck some bargain with Mercury? Do you travel with the gods, the way Maximillian does?" asked the Emperor.

Romanov pointed up at the pagan imagery of the muralled ceiling. "That painting is a lie, my friend. It is a pack of lies, concocted and spread by the fallen realm. The entities shown in the murals call themselves by many names. Do not trust them, Franz. As to my wings, they are quite real."

The Emperor's cottony moustache and muttonchop sideburns crashed into a pout. "Real wings? How? Is this another of your riddles? Wait, I have it!" he said, slapping his right thigh and causing the sleeping dog to stir. "You're one of those modern aeronauts, aren't you? A man who flies in airships. Balloons and such. That's how you fly!"

Romanov smiled, the light eyes twinkling. "In a manner of speaking. Talk to Haimsbury, but know that you are never alone, Franz. The One *true* God is still sovereign over all Creation, and he works all things together for good."

The Emperor sighed. "Yes, I'll remember that. But oh, I forgot to tell you the priest's surname. It isn't Romanov, though he certainly has dark hair and piercing eyes. No, it's something else. My memory's not what it once was, but I wrote it down somewhere. He's bearded, like most Russian priests. Mid-twenties, I'd say. He mentioned growing up in Siberia, if that helps," he muttered, fumbling through his coat pocket. "Ah, yes, here it is. It's Grigori, and the surname's unusual."

"Let me guess," said Anatole. "It's Grigori Rasputin."

"Yes! How did you know?" asked the Emperor.

"I know his teacher. Keep Sisi clear of this priest, Franz. His kind is beyond the reach of men."

CHAPTER FIFTEEN

Charles Sinclair arrived in Lucerne shortly before midnight. He slept little, then after a short breakfast meeting regarding investments in the area, he hired a coach to the *Académie des Garçons de l'Institut de l'Aigle*, or in English, the Eagle Institute Academy for Boys. He left the cab and knocked on Seth Holloway's door. He invited the archaeologist to accompany him to Vienna, without mentioning Adele's part in the plan, of course. The handsome viscount readily answered yes and quickly packed a bag. By half past ten, he and Sinclair boarded a train at Lucerne Railway Station. They changed trains at Innsbruck, enjoyed luncheon in the dining car, and arrived in the Bavarian city of Rosenheim shortly after six, where they booked into the nearest hotel.

Refreshed by a good night's sleep, the two men shared an early breakfast, hired a special and arrived at Breitenfurt shortly after seven in the evening. Dr. Helmut Kepelheim, a longtime inner-circle member and Martin's cousin, met them at Breitenfurt Station. Charles and Seth left their bags in Kepelheim's coach whilst they visited Cordelia.

The Retreat's campus lay nestled on a gentle slope, at the northern edge of the Vienna Woods. Charles and Seth meandered along the visitors' sidewalk until they reached the main doors.

"It certainly is a lovely setting," said Holloway as they approached the entrance. "These woods are famed for their beauty. Of course, one hears tales of Slavic folk, who live hereabouts. I'd just ignore them, if I were you. Most stories are hyperbole and lack any evidence."

"Slavic folk?" asked Charles.

"Refugees from Russian pogroms. But people like to talk about strangers. They tell slanderous stories."

"Such as?"

"Lycanthropes, vampires, that sort of thing. There's no scientific foundation to them, other than local prejudice. Most Slavs are decent, hardworking people."

"Have you made a study of these stories?" asked the Duke.

"Somewhat," answered Holloway. "When I was a boy, we'd sometimes vacation here, at a resort on the outskirts of Penzing. Mother still talks about those days sometimes. They involved no arduous work or long hours in the sun. It's idyllic, really. I imagine Cordelia's quite content here."

"Let's pray she is," Charles said as they passed through the doors. Breitenfurt's foyer looked more like a hotel lobby than a hospital admissions area. A man in uniform stood behind a grey-and-white reception desk.

"*Guten abend, meine Herren*," he greeted them in German. "If you're visiting a resident, I'm afraid our visiting hours are over," he added, also in German.

Charles pretended he knew nothing of the local language, despite being fluent in German. "Do you speak English?"

The desk attendant smiled in the same patient, patronising way a teacher might smile at a child. "Yes, sir. I speak English. Visiting hours are over. They end at six. Is on sign, mein Herr."

"Oh, but I'm sure you'll make an exception for the Duke of Haimsbury," said Holloway, deciding to act as Sinclair's assistant. "His Grace has come all the way from London. It's been a very long, very tiring journey. Over forty hours, with few stops. Surely, you won't turn him away?"

Sinclair lowered his head to hide a smile. Already, Seth was proving to be an insightful and very clever detective. And though the viscount also spoke fluent German, he'd made no offer to translate.

Charles took up the masquerade. "If you'd allow me to visit, it would be worth a great deal," he said, hinting at financial reward. "I am expected at Schönbrunn Palace this evening and only wish to speak to my cousin's wife, Lady Cordelia Stuart, the Countess of Aubrey. I'd be most grateful, if you'd allow me to see her."

"Ah, yes, the Lady Aubrey," answered the gentleman, his hand out for the implied gratuity. He was fortyish, with silvering temples set against a field of raven hair, a handlebar moustache with similarly grey inclusions, and a thick-set body. Not that he looked fat. Just thick, as though his ribcage were wider than usual. The impressive height made up for the broad torso. Charles estimated the man at six-and-a-half feet tall. A large man to act as guard dog.

"May we see her?" the Duke asked again, placing a ten-mark gold coin into the man's hand.

"I see if she wish to see you, sir," said the guard.

Charles continued. "She will want to see me. Also, I should like to talk to Dr. Pyramis." The guard dog started to object, but Charles held up his hand, his tone changing. "I've come a very long way to see my cousin's wife. As you can see, I can be pleasant when I get my way. You do *not* want to see my unpleasant side. Not after so long a journey."

"But, sir, I..."

"No," declared the Duke firmly. "Do not *dare* to interrupt me again. You will escort me to Lady Cordelia's room, and you'll notify Pyramis that I'm coming to see him. Am I clear?"

Seth's left brow arched in surprise as he gazed at Sinclair. It wasn't often the congenial Duke behaved as though he owned the room. *Well done, Charles!* he thought, wondering what other talents lay inside the investigator's bag of tricks.

Holloway was about to find out.

"I understand, mein Herr, but I cannot promise. I ask if the lady wish to see you," the desk authority told the Englishmen as he pocketed the coin. "The doctor never sees anyone without appointment. It is out of my hands. Our patients include many nobles. We make exceptions for no one."

Now it was the Duke's eyebrow that arched. He removed his gloves and set them on the gleaming desk. "Then plan on providing us overnight accommodations, for I will not budge until I get what I want. You and Dr. Pyramis can explain to the Emperor why you've delayed my arrival."

He turned to Seth and whispered, making sure the pitch and volume allowed the obstinate gatekeeper to overhear their conversation. "Lord Paynton, tell my driver to go to Schönbrunn immediately and inform Franz and Sisi why we're delayed at Breitenfurt. Have him send a telegram to Lord Aubrey and let the earl know Dr.

Pyramis refuses to meet with me. Ask Paul if he wants me to remove his wife."

Holloway nodded. "At once, sir." He started towards the door.

"Wait! Please!" cried the man behind the desk. "Is funny thing. I remember now. Doctor is here this evening. If you be kind to wait, Herr Duke, I find him and ask for you to see Lady Aubrey."

Charles smiled, but only slightly. "I'm pleased to hear it. What is your name?"

"Scholz, sir. Gerhardt Scholz. I am evening steward."

"Thank you, Scholz. I'll mention your cooperation to Dr. Pyramis, when I see him."

The man bowed at the neck, clicked his heels, and then hastened from the large reception area, towards a stairwell near the far side of the lobby. Charles noticed several well-dressed figures beyond a set of French windows. Residents exercising before supper.

As they were now alone, he turned to Seth. "It will disappoint Major March to learn he's been replaced as my equerry."

The boyishly handsome viscount laughed and ran a hand through the thick red hair. "Must we tell March? He's a rather intimidating chap, but I'm not sure you need either of us. You're quite forceful on your own."

"Scotland Yard training," the Duke replied with a smile. "Supervising hundreds of policemen taught me a few things."

"Charles, tell me again why we're stopping here. Is there some emergency? After all, Paul left just a week ago. And Beth's planning to stop on her way to Vienna."

"No, Beth won't be able to visit now. She's travelling with Drina, and their route takes them through Frankfurt. We're here because Paul wired me. He's worried about Delia, and so am I. I just want to make sure she's all right before we get too involved in the Emperor's plans."

"Any idea what the Emperor wants?"

"No idea at all. The last time Beth and saw him was in Paris. Must have been six months ago. He and the Empress joined us at the opera. They seemed happy."

"Sisi's a world-famous beauty."

"Have you met her?" the Duke asked.

"A few times. She and my mother are close. They both love to write poetry. You know, Sisi always reminded me of Beth's mother, only with dark hair. She's obsessed about her looks."

"A bit like Trish, from what I've been told."

"Yes," sighed the viscount. "Is this assignment about her?"

The Duke started to answer, but the return of Scholz forestalled it. The burly attendant approached, accompanied by an attractive woman in a navy dress and matching jacket. She wore no insignia. Were this anywhere else, you'd assume she was on her way to meet a friend for dinner.

"Your Grace, forgive us for making you wait," said the woman. "I'm Mrs. Fischer. Would you like to visit Lady Aubrey? She's in her apartment, recovering."

"Recovering from what?" asked Charles as he and Holloway followed Fischer to the stairwell.

"Melancholia takes many forms, Your Grace," said the nurse as they ascended the steps. "Lady Aubrey's treatment plan is tailored to her particular type. In her case, the doctor's prescribed long walks through the woods each afternoon. These often leave the countess somewhat weary. But a good, healthy sort of weariness, my lord. Quite good. We turn here, sir. My lady's apartment is on the left, near the end."

As they reached the apartment, Charles prayed silently. And though he had no way of knowing it, Seth Holloway did the same. The former atheist had come a long way since finding Christ in December of '88.

The nurse knocked. After a moment with no answer, she knocked again. "Lady Aubrey? You have a visitor."

"Yes?" came the hesitant reply.

"You have a visitor, my lady," the nurse repeated. "May I unlock the door?"

They heard footsteps, then a click sounded. The panelled white door opened slightly. Cordelia's face appeared in the narrow space. "I have a visitor?"

"It's Charles, dear," said the Duke. "I've brought Lord Paynton. May we come in?"

Cordelia Stuart looked like a lost lamb. Her eyes were swollen and red, as though she'd been weeping. "Charles? Yes, I suppose so."

The nurse pushed slightly on the door and led the two men into the apartment. "Shall I remain with you, my lady?" she asked the countess.

"I don't know," muttered Delia. "Is it more proper if you do?"

The Duke needed to be alone with Delia, and he gently took her arm and led the countess away from the nurse. "I've come on behalf of Paul," he whispered. "He asked me to look in on you."

Her eyes slowly focused. A smile widened the pale face. "Paul's my husband, isn't he?"

"Yes, dear, he is. And I'm his cousin, which makes me your cousin, too. And you remember Seth Holloway?"

"Seth. Yes, I think we danced together once, long ago," she said. "I'm a countess, is that right?"

"You're very much a countess," the Duke told her.

Haimsbury turned to the nurse. "We'd like tea and coffee. Sweet cakes, too, and biscuits. Fruit and cheese, if you have it. My friend and I plan to remain for a nice long chat, then afterward, I'll meet with Dr. Pyramis."

The nurse curtsied and left. The Duke had noticed the woman's slight frown of irritation, but he didn't care. He needed time to assess Cordelia's condition, and if he detected any detrimental changes in her frail manner, any sign of mistreatment or threat, he intended to remove her that very night.

It was a fine plan, but his entire visit was watched.

By a yellow-eyed raven.

And a blue-eyed cat.

CHAPTER SIXTEEN

King's Court, London

"My, but isn't it all so very grand, Viktor?" asked Stephen Blinkmire as he and Count Riga entered the new home's foyer. "Are those marble trees? Might they be oaks?" he asked the Romanian exile. "Oh but wait. I'm such a dunce sometimes. Here now, Viktor, take my hand. I can see your back's bothering you today. Walk slowly, now. Don't rush." Then to the underbutler, the gentle giant asked, "Do you need any help with the cello, Mr. Willoughby? I'm a bit stronger than you, I should imagine. Here, let me carry it."

Stephen Blinkmire originally hailed from Ireland, and so retained a slight brogue to his deep voice, but varied interests and a broad vocabulary marked the eight-foot giant as far more than grand in stature, he was also grand in intellect and interests.

"Viktor, I think King's Court is even outshines Branham Hall, though it hardly seems possible," Blinkmire continued to his smaller companion. "Mr. Miles, are we to meet Chief Inspector Baxter down here, or shall we continue up the stairs?"

John Eric Miles had grown to admire these two men. As members of the 'Castle Company', they'd helped to save Duchess Elizabeth's life in 1889. And because of their bravery, Stephen Blinkmire and Viktor Riga had forever earned a place in the Stuart-Sinclair household. In fact, they'd been living at Branham for over four years.

"Chief Inspector Baxter will meet you in the Loudain Room, sir," said Miles. "It's this way. Just up the stairs and to the right."

Miles and Willoughby escorted the visitors through the magnificent marble-tree boulevard; up the central staircase, with its prophetic scenes of a future Jerusalem; and into a long rectangular room, named for one of Charles Sinclair's hereditary titles.

Cornelius Baxter smiled as his friends entered. "Welcome to King's Court, gentlemen. Allow Willoughby to carry that instrument, Mr. Blinkmire. You're a guest. You needn't worry about such things."

"Oh, I don't mind," said Blinkmire. "I'll just leave the cello by those chairs. Is that all right?"

"That's fine, Stephen. Thank you," said Riga as he put out his hand in fellowship. "Ah, Chief Inspector, how very good to see you. And in such a magnificent setting!"

"It's always an honour, Count Riga. Are you all right, sir?" asked Baxter. "You're flushed. Shall I send for one of the nurses?"

"Oh, no, Mr. Baxter, that's kind of you, but I shall be fine momentarily. My back's somewhat out of sorts today, and we had a rather odd experience on the train coming in from Branham. Of course, I'm not getting any younger. Any rail journey causes my back to complain, but there was a stranger who forced his way on board when we stopped for water at Maidstone. He shoved a book at us and insisted we give it to Her Grace!"

Baxter's dark eyes narrowed as he frowned. "This stranger shoved a book at you? A book for Her Grace? Now, that is troubling. Here now, Riga, let me help you to sit. Willoughby, set the count's cello by the piano for now. Mr. Blinkmire, do take a seat. You'll see a special chair near the fireplace. The Duke had his furniture maker design it with your particular needs in mind."

Stephen gazed at the oversized wingback. The chair was upholstered in hand-dyed lambswool, woven in a tartan pattern of deep blue and green, with red-and-gold accents. The Irishman smiled as he eased into the comfortable chair.

"The Duke did this for me? Why, it's splendid! Simply splendid! Not only is it sturdy, but the upholstery pattern is the County Antrim tartan. That's my birthplace! How very, very thoughtful!"

"Truly our Duke is a kind and generous man," said Riga as he sat close to his friend on a sofa, covered in similarly styled lambswool. "And the chair seems amply built. One might even say capacious."

Baxter smiled. "Capacious? Might that be your word of the day, Riga?"

"Yes, it is! Capacious. A fine word. And His Grace's heart is capacious beyond all description. There are no words for it, my friends. He treats us all like royalty. But come, Mr. Baxter! Come sit with us and explain why you've invited us here. Then, together, we might discern whether any of it's connected to the man who boarded our train."

Neil joined the two men in the pleasant seating area. He sat opposite Blinkmire, in a smaller wingback. A butler's table stood within their circle, laden with refreshments. "I'm sure you're hungry after your journey," Baxter told his friends. "I'll pour. Tea? Coffee?"

"Oh, yes, thank you, but are we all here?" asked Blinkmire. "I see five cups set out, Mr. Baxter."

"Kepelheim and Stoker are joining us," Neil answered with a glance at the mantel clock. "They should have arrived by now. I wonder what's keeping them?"

In answer, the doors opened once more, admitting Miles with those very gentlemen. Abraham Stoker was modestly tall and wore somber but stylish clothing that fit his generally somber, Irish temperament. In the five years since first joining the men and women of the Stuart-Sinclair inner circle, Bram had come to love the fellowship and all the intelligent conversations. He especially enjoyed the circle's approach to life. They believed, that behind almost every material-world action, lay a hidden, spiritual impetus. Bram also believed in a realm beyond natural, human sight, and found acceptance and edification within the family's circle.

Since entering that fellowship, Bram had made two immediate and dear friends. Dr. Edward MacPherson, who served as the circle's spiritual guide; and Martin Kepelheim, a somewhat unremarkable looking, highly complex, multi-layered tailor. Shorter than Stoker by three inches, the portly tailor often surprised strangers by spouting archaeological and ecclesiastical wisdom beyond that of most scholars—all the while, sewing buttons on a bespoke suitcoat.

Stoker and Kepelheim shook hands with their friends, then assumed positions within the modified circle meeting. "It's good to be with all of you again," Stoker began as Baxter handed him a cup of coffee. "Count Riga, I've not seen you for months. Not since Christmas. I hope Easter was pleasant?"

"Oh, it was very pleasant," the Romanian replied. "Mr. Blinkmire and I enjoyed services at Branham Chapel, followed by a quiet dinner at Anjou Sheep Farm. Of course, with the fête coming, the estate's carpenters and blacksmiths are at it, hammer-and-tongs. And I do not say this metaphorically. Literal hammers and literal tongs.

There's to be no theme this year, but the bandstand and display centres are looking quite grand. I'm happy to be in London, for I shan't miss the noise!"

"Nor will I," Blinkmire added, sipping tea from his over-sized cup. "The book, Viktor. We promised to hand over the book."

Riga nodded. "Ah, yes, the book. I mentioned this to Chief Inspector Baxter already, but to explain to Kepelheim and Stoker, let me tell you what happened to us today. We came aboard the *Rose House,* that's the Duke's smallest train, as you probably know. Whilst on our journey from Branham, we stopped for water at Maidstone, and a very strange gentleman boarded. I say boarded, but he actually barged into our car and shoved a book at us."

"He shoved a book at you?" asked Stoker, taking notes in a leather notebook. (Bram had become an informal secretary during these meetings.) "Shoved? Is that the word?"

"Oh, yes," Blinkmire told the writer. "He shoved it quite rudely into my face!"

Riga smiled. "In retrospect, it seems even more of an odd thing. Our Mr. Blinkmire isn't exactly the first person you'd challenge. But yes, the man shoved the book into Stephen's face and insisted we deliver the book to Duchess Elizabeth. 'It's for Her Grace,' he said with exaggerated sibilance to the words. A most peculiar sort of person!"

"How so?" asked Kepelheim, placing a slice of orange cake on his plate. "Is there more to him than rudeness and a speech impediment?"

"Oh, yes. The man reminded me of a crow, if we must make comparison," said Riga. "Dressed all in black, with a pale countenance. I've seen many dreadful things in my life, but this man's face left my own quite lacking blood, or so it felt. For a moment, I thought I might lose consciousness!"

"Whatever from?" asked Stoker.

"Lack of circulatory support, I should think," replied the count. "But despite the man's demands, I prefer the Duchess never see this book, for this person seemed unholy. I shouldn't wonder if the book is dangerous."

Neil held up the book in question, so that all could see. "Count Riga gave the book to me a few moments ago, and I must agree. Our little Duchess must never touch it. The book's binding and weight feel strange, as though it pulses with something not of this world." He set the book on the nearest table and wiped his hands on a white serviette as though trying to wipe away dirt. "What else can you tell us about this man, Count? Of course, the book isn't why I asked all of you to meet with me today. We'll get to that shortly, but I wonder if your experience might connect with an investigation I'm pursuing?"

"May I?" asked Kepelheim, holding out his hand.

Baxter passed him the book. Martin examined it closely. The cover was red, inscribed with a gold title, written in German.

"It's a riddle," said the tailor. "*QMS - Gesellschaft des Geistes.* Ah, for those of you, who don't speak German, the entire title translates thusly:

'QMS – SOCIETY OF THE MIND
An Examination of Human Blood Lines
And How They Relate To Morality And Longevity
VOLUME ONE:
The Coburg Witch and the Curse"

"Coburg? A witch's curse? That title is most ominous, Mr. Kepelheim, particularly with the upcoming wedding there," said Stoker, who'd written down the title in his notebook. "Society of the Mind? Longevity? Blood Lines? Is this book fable or fact?"

"I fear it's probably fact," said the tailor, "and quite likely based on a tale I once heard years ago. But the bigger question is, why would this man insist our Duchess read it?"

"It's clear to me," declared Baxter. "It's got to be the wedding! The Duke and Duchess are to visit that very city. Coburg. Gentlemen, this book is a threat."

"I fear you're right, Chief Inspector," sighed Riga. "The man's appearance startled Stephen and myself, which is no mean feat, for he and I've been through a great deal of supernatural hardship in our lives. And though his arrival caught us unawares, it was the man's exit that most alarmed us."

"Which was?" asked Baxter, also taking notes.

"The man vanished! *Poof!* Gone in a blink!" exclaimed the count. "My old eyes may not be as keen as once they were, but

Blinkmire can vouch for my claim. Isn't that so?" he asked the giant, who nodded.

"Did the man give you his name?" asked Baxter.

Blinkmire set the oversized, red-and-white cup against his broad lap. "Yes, but it may have been a lie."

"Why would you say that?" asked Stoker.

"Because his appearance was like something from a storybook. Rather like a child's drawing. Tall, thin, funereal to the extreme, but with a stovepipe hat like those worn thirty years ago. He had a slight limp—and six fingers on each hand. As all of you know, I have six fingers on one of my hands, but I've never seen a man with six on both. He wore no gloves, and the hands and face were as white as writing paper. Yet, the man's lips had the deep blush of a red rose."

Stoker shivered as he recorded the description. "I've seen a thing like that. As a boy. His name?"

Stephen set down the cup. "He called himself the Count de Saint Germain. I ask you, how is that possible? Saint Germain is fiction—*isn't he?*"

Martin re-entered the conversation. "I don't think Saint Germain is fictitious, Mr. Blinkmire, and it brings us to the witch tale. I shall need a glass of wine, I think, Chief Inspector. Such accounts as these are best told with ample fortification."

Both Miles and Willoughby had left, so Baxter rang for a footman. It was the underbutler who responded. To everyone's surprise, Willoughby's appearance had gone from well-groomed to uncharacteristically disheveled in a matter of ten minutes.

The servant cleared his throat, straightened his waistcoat, and asked, "How may I assist you Chief Inspector?"

Baxter stared at the underbutler, making a mental note to talk with Miles about his staff. *How has this man gotten unto such a state in so little time? What has he been doing?*

"Mr. Willoughby, have the wine cellars been moved from the old house yet?"

"Indeed, they have, sir. What shall I bring up?"

"Have you a preference, Mr. Kepelheim?"

The tailor smiled, his cheeks pink. "My dear Chief Inspector, need you ask? Armagnac is always welcome, and I believe the Duke put in several casks of the '59 Martell last October. That would do quite nicely."

Baxter turned to the underbutler. "Bring a decanter of the Martell, Mr. Willoughby. Five glasses."

"Very good, sir," the young man answered. Baxter noticed an odd sort of expression flit across the servant's face as he left.

"I take it, Mr. Willoughby is new," the former butler said to Kepelheim. "I'm not yet familiar with all the new staff members, but there's something disquieting about that young man."

"Oh, that gentleman is very new," answered the tailor. "Charles leaves most of the staffing decisions to Miles, and his judgement is usually quite sound. I see what you mean. The fellow seemed preoccupied and a tad out of sorts. Stains on his waistcoat, and a crooked tie? And was that rouge on his collar? Very bad form for a noble house. Might he be violating household rules? The one prohibiting fraternisation twixt men and ladies, for instance?"

"If he is, the man will find himself on the street!" Baxter huffed. "I'll talk to Miles about the boy. For the moment, we await your tale, Mr. Kepelheim. Is it possible to commence, even in the absence of a wine glass?"

This caused the tailor laugh. The sixty-four-year-old's cheeks shivered into happy mounds of pink flesh. "I believe it is, Chief Inspector. But first, I must ask about our Duchess. Is she feeling better? When I last saw Charles, he mentioned slight problems regarding digestion and balance. Our dear one is seldom ill—with one exception, if you know my meaning. Might we have reason for celebration?"

Riga leaned forward, arthritic hands gripping the amber handle of a walking stick. "Have Stephen and I missed an announcement?"

"If you're asking if the Duchess is, well, if she is *expecting* again, then I'm permitted to reply in the affirmative," said Baxter proudly. "The Duke informed the London inner-circle members only last week. I'm sure he intended to tell all of you in person, when next you met."

"Oh, this is wonderful news!" exclaimed Blinkmire clapping his hands happily. "But surely she isn't still travelling to Coburg for the wedding? Rail cars jostle one so, particularly on the older lines. I should think trains would be most unpleasant for a lady at such a time."

"I'm told the Duchess will travel by train. It is the quickest way, but she'll travel on a very luxurious, private train," said Baxter. "The Duke ordered it last year."

"Which Duke might that be?" asked Stoker. "Haimsbury or Drummond?"

"Haimsbury," answered Kepelheim. "Charles showed me the design shortly after the wedding invitations went out last year. He commissioned a French company to build a twenty-car train, based on the *Captain Nemo Special* but with a medical facility and extra sleeping cars. Presently, it's housed near Goussainville. The Duchess will board it there."

"Splendid! Does the new train have a name?" asked Riga.

"Oh, yes," answered Kepelheim. "Keeping to the Verne theme, Charles calls it *The Nautilus*. Victoria used it recently, and we all know how much she loathes trains. Even she praised the interior as finer than the Orient Express. But now to this book." Martin opened the red volume. "You say the man who left it vanished?"

"As though he'd never existed," said Riga.

Baxter shook his head, for he'd been deep in thought. "I wonder if this business of the book has anything to do with the murder in Whitechapel?"

"What murder?" asked Blinkmire. "Viktor and I read the London papers every day, but I don't recall any recent murders that might involve your team, Chief Inspector."

"We've kept the matter out of the press for now, though one East-End rag got wind of it. The reporter followed the Duke as he investigated, so I fear it's likely to be in every newspaper soon."

"Why?" asked Stoker. "Why keep it quiet?"

"Because the dead man was heir to a powerful earldom, and the only survivor is the dead man's cousin, also heir to an earldom. And these murders echo our recent past."

The men grew silent. Kepelheim sighed as he stared at the strange book. "I know about these crimes, Neil. The papers may not talk of them, but all of Whitehall's rife with rumours and questions. I'd be happy to help. You need only ask."

"And I shall ask," the former butler answered firmly. "That is why I've invited you today, Mr. Kepelheim. I shall need help from all you before this is done. If His Grace weren't forced to leave for

Austria, he'd be leading the investigation personally. Now, let's hear about this book. Mr. Kepelheim, the tale?"

"Ah, yes, the tale," muttered the tailor, half to himself. "It is troubling, is it not? I do wish this upcoming wedding were being held elsewhere. A vanishing intruder using the name Saint Germain appears on your train and insists you give our dear one this book—a book whose title speaks of a Coburg Witch? Our precious Lord Robby interacts with something he calls the Piped Piper in a dream, but was it really a dream?"

"Is that why Duke James took the children to Scotland?" asked Stoker.

"Oh, yes. Precisely why, but more lies on the horizon. In just a few days, our Duchess leaves to meet the Queen for a journey to Coburg, the very city mentioned in this book. It forebodes a return to warfare." The tailor looked into the other men's eyes; his jaw firmly set. "Gentlemen, we five must agree to this one thing: No one, and I repeat *no one*, will tell Duchess Elizabeth of the strange man or of this book. Promise me. No one says a word."

Every man nodded, but it seemed as though a shadow had fallen on the room. Martin's voice grew low and serious. "Gentlemen, I further propose we seal our pact with prayer." Every man's head bowed as the tailor continued. "We thank you, oh Lord, for your salvation and protection. We thank you for the bounty and promise of this new home and for every moment of every day to come—no matter what lies ahead. As we walk each day, may we honour you, my King. We ask for wisdom and guidance and pray for clear sight as we face the future. We ask you to protect our Duke and Duchess and all their precious children. Protect Lord Aubrey and his wife and children. Please, heal Lady Aubrey and bring her home to us. Send your true and faithful angelic warriors to fight against the fallen and unravel all their wicked plans. Fill our hands with purpose, oh Lord. And may we continue to lift you up: crucified, risen, and coming again! In Christ's name we ask all these things. Amen."

Each head rose, every man thinking of the dangers ahead, but also of the miracles they would soon witness.

"Tis a fearful thing to fall into the hands of the living God," said Baxter, quoting Hebrews.

"Quite so," replied Kepelheim. "Thank you, my friends. Thank you all. We are a curious band of warriors, are we not? Perhaps, that's intentional, for we press ahead in the Lord's strength, not our own. Now, regarding this book. It is probably best to remove it from the house once we've finished here today. So with everyone's permission, I shall take it to Old Haimsbury House once we're done and conceal it in the library shelves. Only a few of us have a key to that room, making it unlikely the book will be discovered. Is that agreeable?" The other four nodded. "It isn't that we don't trust the Duchess with the book, you understand. Elizabeth is strong. Indeed, her heart is stronger than that of many men. No, it's this the book we cannot trust, nor the man who gave it to you, Riga."

"We never intended to show her the book," said Viktor Riga. "How could we? The thing is evil! But might the book act *on its own?*"

"Oh, my, I'd not thought of that!" the tailor exclaimed. You're right, of course, Riga. Such cursed items sometimes behave as if possessed. Recall the small box our Duke carried back from France several years ago during the Branham Fête. Though tiny, the box contained a demonic spirit that coerced Charles into anger against Lord Aubrey. Yes, I hadn't thought of that. I'll consult MacPherson tomorrow. He has more experience in these matters."

"And the story?" prompted Stoker. "You say you know something of the Coburg Witch?"

"Ah, yes," said the tailor. "Forgive me. As I age, my mind tends to wander. Now, as all good Englishmen know, Coburg is the childhood home of our Queen's late husband, Prince Albert. Twelve years ago, I was honoured to visit Coburg with Duke James and the late Lord Aubrey. The earl and Drummond were engaged in diplomatic talks with Tsar Alexander and Duke Ernst. Ernst was Prince Albert's elder brother, of course. He's since passed, as you all know, and the Queen's son Prince Alfred is now Duke of Saxe-Coburg and Gotha. Tis his daughter who's to marry next month. Now, our trip in '82 was partly political, and partly an inner-circle matter. Whilst diplomats discussed political business, I spent time with locals, getting to know their customs and stories. My German's quite good, learnt from my parents, who emigrated from Austria six years before I was born. Therefore, I had no trouble fitting in.

"Coburg is a fascinating city; though, the term city might be a stretch. I'd call it a large village with two royal residences. Christendom knows it as the cradle of Lutheranism, for Coburg is where Luther translated much of the New Testament, whilst safely housed within the massive walls of Veste Coburg. In fact, Luther composed the famous hymn, *A Mighty Fortress Is Our God,* during his stay there."

"Is that so?" asked Stoker, who'd been raised in the Church of Ireland faith in Clontarf. "We sometimes sang that hymn. Fascinating! I should like to visit Coburg one day."

"You'd find it inspirational, Mr. Stoker, I'm sure. Not only for the Lutheran history, but for the occult tales, which brings me back to the witch," said Kepelheim. "Though Coburg gave birth to Lutheranism, it is also the heart of a much darker, much older faith. I heard the story of the Witch from a palace cook, and she insisted every aspect is true. Even today, Coburg is a somewhat rustic region. It's set in Upper Franconia and crouches lazily upon the green banks of the River Itz, a tributary of the Main. There are local legends of the Main's river gods and nymphs, even tales of werewolves and changelings—but this story is about a witch, or as the Germans call them, *die Hexen.*

"The story of the Coburg Witch reaches back to the twelfth century. It commences during the spring, on the last day of April, known as Walpurgisnacht; the day when witches gather at the Brocken in the Harz Mountains to confer with the Devil. The Witch in this tale was named Valul. She lived along the Itz in a typical hovel, where she dispensed magic spells and potions. Locals blamed her for the deaths of seven maidens, who'd vanished, one by one, month by month, on moonless nights. On the first of May in 1166, the village churchmen arrested Valul and dragged her to Saalfeld Abbey. I should add that the Abbey is long gone now, and in its place stands the Veste Coburg, where Luther wrote his hymn."

"Did you say her name was Valul?" asked Riga, his knobby, arthritic fingers tensing round the walking stick. "Is Valul German? I ask, for it's similar to an old Romanian word meaning wave or tide. Might this witch be connected to the river gods you mentioned? You did say she lived by the river, correct?"

"Yes, I believe you could be right, Riga," said Martin as the drawing room doors opened. Willoughby entered, his appearance still sub-standard; and rather than carry a tray (as Baxter might have done), the disheveled underbutler pushed a wheeled cart, laden with a filled decanter and five glasses.

"Shall I pour, sir?" he asked Baxter.

"No, thank you, Mr. Willoughby. We're quite able to serve ourselves." Then Baxter added in a commanding whisper, "Look to your livery, young man. Your tie is crooked, there's a stain on your waistcoat, and rouge on your collar!"

"Yes, sir. I'll take care of it right away," murmured Willoughby, clearly resentful of the remonstrance. He arranged the decanter and glasses on the centre table. *Remarkable the old man could see anything against this tartan pattern*, the underbutler thought, annoyed by the former butler's superior attitude. Outwardly, Willoughby demonstrated false humility. "Thank you for the advice, Chief Inspector. I shall see to it right away."

Kepelheim took note of the tense exchange and decided to probe the new man's loyalties. "Tell me, Mr. Willoughby, is the Duchess still in residence? Is she receiving?"

"My lady's in a meeting at Queen Anne, Mr. Kepelheim. Something to do with the HBH board of governors. More than that, I cannot say, sir. Will there be anything else?"

"Not presently, Mr. Willoughby. Thank you," Baxter answered. "We'll ring when we're done."

The servant bowed and left with the cart.

"What sort of training are these young men getting today?" Baxter complained as he filled their glasses. "I fear this next generation need a firm hand. Do go on, Mr. Kepelheim. I'll distribute the Armagnac whilst you talk."

The tailor smiled, his soft grey eyes alight. "You are ever the professional, Mr. Baxter. Apparently, Mr. Willoughby is like so many others of his age. Brash and boastful, but then we all transgressed when young. What is it the psalmist wrote? Remember not the sins of my youth?"

"Training begins in childhood," said Riga. "And the Witch, Mr. Kepelheim?"

"Ah, yes, the story. As I was saying, the Witch Valul was arrested on Walpurgisnacht in 1166. She was charged with using witchcraft to murder seven young women."

"Was the charge valid? Had she killed them?" asked Stoker as he tried to get it all down on paper.

"Yes, it seemed she did murder them, and she did so in a most unwholesome way," replied Kepelheim. "She was accused of eating them."

"Like the witch in *Hansel and Gretel?*" asked Blinkmire with a shudder. "Cannibalism? I've never liked that story."

"Wait a moment, Mr. Kepelheim, you said this story is true. Are you telling us the woman did eat them?" asked Baxter, thinking of the women found drained of blood inside the cellars of the Molly-Mae Hotel.

"So the story goes, yes," replied the tailor.

Baxter visibly shivered. "Surely, this is devil's work!"

"Quite so," replied Kepelheim gravely. "The churchmen of Coburg would agree with you, I think. At the time, the medieval legal system was rooted in the Church, which explains why the woman was taken to Saalfeld Abbey. The Abbot pleaded with her to confess her sins and recant all pagan associations, but she refused to do either one. Instead, Valul spat upon the assembled clergy and denied Christ, professing fealty to Satan. Then, the Witch pronounced a curse on the Abbey and all the people of Coburg, as well as their descendants."

Blinkmire swallowed hard. His small eyes blinked rapidly. Count Riga leaned close and touched his friend's muscular forearm. "It is only a story, Stephen."

"That may be so, but witches and curses are real, Viktor! In Ireland, I saw the terrifying, twisted results of such curses, and I'm sure Mr. Stoker has, too. My own monstrous stature may have been caused by a witch's curse."

"Even so, your superior strength's been turned to glorious purpose, my friend," Riga reminded him. "Remember? You carried our little Duchess to safety during the fire and nearly lost your life in the process. And later, it was you who carried our Duke from the labyrinth. Had he remained there in his weakened condition, the doctors say he might have died."

"Yes, I suppose so. Do forgive me, my friends. Forgive the interruption, Mr. Kepelheim. Please, continue."

Martin smiled at the Irish giant. "Mr. Blinkmire, you are a blessing, not a curse. All of us know that, and we're honoured to have you as part of our circle."

"Thank you," whispered Blinkmire. "Nothing makes me happier than this fellowship."

"Hear, hear!" cried Stoker, echoed by the others. "Go on, Mr. Kepelheim. I'm writing it all down for our records."

"Good," said the tailor. "Yes, we'll return to the story—which, as I say, took place in Germanic lands, not Ireland." He took a sip of the Armagnac. "Oh, this is quite nice. '59 was a fine year for Martell. The Columbard grapes were particularly flavourful that year. Hmm. Do I detect hints of apple and violets amongst the spices? Our Duke chooses well, doesn't he?" Martin sipped again, then set the glass to one side. "Now, to the story. As I mentioned earlier, I heard the tale from the Schloss Rosenau cook. She was a loquacious woman, and she'd heard the tale as a girl. The curse I mentioned, so said the cook, was uttered in the form of a singsong riddle. Eventually, children played a game based on the story—rather like 'Ring Around the Rosie' today, which is based on the Black Death. You know, I suddenly remember the cook's name: Frau Greta Winkler. Grey-haired and rosy-cheeked. She loved schnapps. Frau Winkler memorised the Witch's riddle as a girl, and she helped me to write it down. In German, of course. Later, on the return train, I translated the rhyme into English; not an easy task, as the account contained some antiquated phrases. But it's for that reason, it sticks in my mind, even today. I believe my translation went something like this:

'When Day kisses Night,
Sky Wolf Hati and Sister Sköll
Will tempt a Man of Words.
A fool shall leap,
A Raven will laugh,
The Owl will watch,
Time Walker is tested,
The Keeper is chained,
The Many in One arises.
Seven Maids will vanish,
Seven Stars will fall
Two Queens will Die
The King of Shadow will rise
The Wolves will eat,
Darkness Will Come,
And then, the Reign of Men will end.'"

As Kepelheim finished, the others stared, their faces paled, each countenance filled with doubt and questions.

"A fool, a raven, an owl?" asked Riga. "And did you say King of Shadow? Is your translation accurate, Mr. Kepelheim?"

"I believe so," answered Martin.

"I don't like this at all!" declared Blinkmire.

"Nor do I," Riga agreed. "But might this Witch's curse mean something other than what we're all thinking?"

Kepelheim still held the red-bound volume. "If this book contains the same account, then we must discern the meaning and its impact on the Sinclair family. I have no idea how much time may be required for the task, but I believe my translation of the cook's tale is accurate, so far as it goes."

Stoker finished recording the last of the translation. "Shadow King. Surely, we're all thinking it? Duke Charles is the Shadow King, but how did this Witch Valul see so far ahead? She lived in the twelfth century!"

"If she heard from fallen spirits, perhaps she tapped into their foreknowledge," said Baxter.

"And what is this Sky Wolf?" continued Stoker as he read through the scribbled notes. "You called it, let me see what I wrote, now. Was it *Hatti? H-a-t-t-i?* Is that the name of a man or a god?"

"H-a-t-i," said the tailor. "He's a Norse god, worshipped in many parts of Germany. Hati's often represented as a great wolf, or more accurately *a werewolf*, as he's often depicted as half-human. Hati is the spawn of Fenrir, sometimes called *Fenrisúlfr*—born of Loki and a giantess called Angerboda. The wolf Fenrir was so dangerous, the gods banded together to chain him, for in the final days, a time called Ragnarök, the Norse believe Fenrir will break his chains and devour Odin and all the other gods. And then, Fenrir's children, Hati and Sköll, will eat the sun and moon—leaving only darkness. The end of the world."

Blinkmire's large hand went up. "May I?"

"Of course, Stephen," Kepelheim answered.

"I do hate to interrupt again, Mr. Kepelheim, but I've read hundreds of books; perhaps, thousands. A few were accounts of ancient beliefs and myth. There's an Oriental story with similarities, only the twins are jackals, not wolves. One a male, the other female. And though siblings, they lived as husband and wife."

Riga shivered and threw up his hands. "No, no, no! This sounds all too similar to Prince Araqiel and his horrid sister Eluna! And with mention of a Shadow King, I begin to wish with all my heart that we'd stopped our Duke from leaving England!"

"Yes, I made the same connexion," said Martin softly. "I tried to stop him, but our Duke is stubborn. If the strange man on your train is an omen, then I fear Charles is heading into the heart of a centuries-old curse, when he reaches Coburg."

Bram turned to a blank page in his leather notebook and began to jot down questions. "What of this other person mentioned in the book? The Count de Saint Germain?"

"Ah, now, he is a curiosity," said Kepelheim. "Might I have a refill, Chief Inspector?"

Cornelius poured a healthy portion of the Martell into Martin's glass. The amber liquid splashed along the curved sides like a tidal fire. "Take care with this, Mr. Kepelheim. Though spicy warm on the tongue, this wine sneaks up on a man. We wouldn't want you falling asleep during your tale."

"Nor would I," smiled the cherubic tailor. "Count de Saint Germain's tale is quite different from that of the Coburg Witch, but oddly enough, it begins in the same place. Now, some claim the count's beginnings are in Transylvania, Italy, or Portugal. One might be true regarding his *mortal* birth, but I speak of a spiritual rebirth, though not through Christ, and not a happy one. It's said the count still walks the earth, though he entered the world in the early eighteenth century."

"That would make him almost two hundred years old!" exclaimed Stoker.

"Indeed, it would," the storyteller replied. "When asked about his longevity, the count might credit a healthy lifestyle, clean water, and nutritious food. I say his choice of beverages is hardly clean and the food nutritious only for ghouls! Nor are his companions righteous, for Saint Germain is a member of the Blackstone Group, a Redwing affiliate, founded in the mid-sixth century."

"When exactly?" asked Stoker. "Do we know the year?"

Kepelheim smiled at the Irish writer. "We do, Mr. Stoker. In 1853, my younger brother and I embedded ourselves within that hated group. We overheard a high-ranking member refer to the year 536 A.D. as the founding date for the Lords of the Black Stone. I can relate their foundation story in full another time. I've written a monograph on it—for circle eyes only, of course."

"I should like to read it," said the Irishman.

"I'm happy to share it, Mr. Stoker. Just let me know when you wish to have the book, and I'll show you the location in the Duke's new library. The monograph's not for removal, you understand, but we encourage research." He sipped the wine, then gently wiped his mouth with a linen kerchief. "The year 536 is interesting for another reason. That is the very year that Charles Sinclair's ancestor was born. Prince Artorius, born in the year of the Second Dragon War."

"Dragons!" muttered Blinkmire. "I truly do hate dragons!"

"As would any man, who's been through dragon fire," said Kepelheim. "We must wonder why this intruder brought you this particular book, for his physical description fits another's, doesn't it?"

"He looked a little like Albus Flint," said Blinkmire. "Only not as ugly. Also, he was taller and had a limp."

"A limp?" asked Baxter. "Now that is curious. The Duchess recently saw a similar figure near the gates. She described him as having six fingers and a limp. Two visiting children saw him as well and mentioned the limp. I never saw the creature, of course, but might there be a reason for the similarity?"

"Didn't Lord Robby describe this dream-world Pied Piper as limping?" asked Martin. "Mr. Stoker, please add that to your notes. We should research 'limping' with regards to demonic visions or appearances. Now, regarding Saint Germain, most tales say he travelled to Germany in his youth. Blackstone's own archives indicate the purpose was to find and dig up the ashes of the old Coburg Witch Valul. Saint Germain planned to use them in a ritual."

"He knew about the Witch?" asked Stoker.

Martin nodded. "Oh yes. Blackstone's archives say Saint Germain began reading mystical texts as a youth, and amongst these he found a copy of the Witch's trial." Martin opened the red-bound book. He scanned through the chapter headings; the book in one hand, his Armagnac in the other. At last, he nodded and cried out, "Yes, here it is! This explains it, and it must be the reason Blackstone and their spirit masters want the Duchess to read the book. My friends, I will *never* allow her to see this."

"What does it say?" asked Blinkmire, on the edge of his large chair.

Martin cleared his throat. "To begin, the title of this section is *Saint Germain's Ritual and the Pursuit of the Elixir of Life.*"

"Elixir of Life?" asked Baxter. "Is that some sort of liqueur?"

"Hardly," replied the tailor. "No, Chief Inspector, the Elixir of Life is an old alchemical dream, said to mimic the effects of the true source of Life Eternal: Christ's blood. Though most believe the elixir is a drink, others claim it isn't a drink at all, but ancient wisdom contained within a book, sometimes called the Emerald Tablets, but known to Blackstone as the *Sefer Raziel*."

"The Sefer what, sir?" asked Stoker. "Forgive the constant questions. I'm still playing catch-up."

"You must never apologise for asking questions," said Kepelheim. "Raziel, as you may know, is one of the evil angels known as Watchers. They're called Watchers as a classification. It may refer to an office, or even a physical type. It was the Watchers who descended on Mount Hermon before the Flood and took human women as mates. From this unholy coupling, arose a generation of giants—half-human hybrids called *Nephilim*. Raziel never coupled with a woman so far as know, but since emerging from the Hermon Stone in 1879, he's used ritual magic to alter humans, whom he calls *adopted* children. One of these children is the mysterious Prince Rasarit, whom the little Duchess called Rasha."

"I'm all too familiar with his kind!" said Count Riga, his face sagging into a frown. "Rasarit Grigor is a despicable creature. He claims to be Romanian but comes from an older branch of the exiled royal family. I pray he is dead and gone!"

"As do we all, but we've never had confirmation of that," said Kepelheim. "He has vanished from the Earth so far as we can tell. Now, at one time, Raziel the Watcher lived in heaven and worshipped beside God's throne. Legend says he served as a scribe and recorded all the words of God—that is, all the words spoken in Raziel's presence. Legends go on to say that Raziel bound the Creator's words into a book called the *Sefer Raziel*, which he stole from heaven and gave to Adam, Cain, or Noah. Sources vary. Prince Anatole tells a similar story. He and Raziel once served together. They were close friends, but Raziel chose darkness and rebellion. Baxter, do you remember how we first believed Raziel and Anatole were the same person?"

The former butler nodded as he sipped the cognac. "Oh, yes," he replied in a deep voice. "Lord Aubrey despised the prince back then. And wasn't it Romanov who imprisoned Raziel within the Mount Hermon stone?"

"Yes, it was," said Kepelheim. "Our circle's learned a great deal in the past few years. Ever since Charles regained his memory, position, and titles."

"As though his return marked a new beginning," said Riga. "The forward ticking of some eternal clock."

"What if the Duke *is* this King of Shadow from the Witch's curse?" asked Riga. "Shouldn't we send him a telegram of warning?"

Baxter's silvering brows arched high as he pondered the notion. "You're right, Count Riga," he said, scratching out a note to himself. "I'll take care of it as soon as we adjourn. Is there more to this Saint Germain tale, Mr. Kepelheim?"

The tailor drained the last drop of wine and then set the empty glass on the nearby table. "Yes. As so often happens in our meetings, one story leads to another and another, and my mind begins to wander far afield! Here now, we'll get to the story as written in this book. I shall translate the German, but please forgive any errors, for it's written in a very peculiar dialect."

Blinkmire's hand rose once more. "Mr. Kepelheim, might Saint Germain's name derive from German in some way?"

"A sensible question, but the Saint Germain location is actually in Normandy," answered Martin. "Saint-Germain-de-Livet. A lovely little village."

"Our Duke's Sinclair heritage is rooted in Normandy," Riga reminded the group.

"Oh, yes," Martin agreed. "And did you know the word *German* is based in the Latin *germanus?* Some say the word means *root* or *shoot*, others say *spear*. It may be both and considering the warlike attitude of Germanic tribes and the current German leadership, *spear* certainly fits. But it may also refer to an old Teutonic myth. We'll re-visit that another time. For now, let me see what our book tells."

Martin scanned the pages of the long entry. After several minutes, he took a deep breath, pale eyes filling with worry.

"This is not good. Not good at all. Riga, do you remember the peculiar book left with Sir Simon Pembroke a few years ago? It was an oddly bound volume, written in a code similar to phrases written on the walls of the puzzle chamber beneath Old Haimsbury House."

The Romanian's face sagged once more as he pondered the question. "Book? Yes, yes, now I remember! It was left with Pembroke by that funereal solicitor, Albus Flint."

"Your memory is sharp as ever, Riga, and yes, Flint left the book with Pembroke. I must call on our Branham baronet soon. Simon fellow seldom leaves his house these days, due to gout. Age ravages all of us eventually."

"Except for this Saint Germain fellow, apparently," Stoker interjected. "What about the Pembroke book? You say it was in code?"

"Yes. We've deciphered most of it now, thanks to Ailesleigh and Romanov. It contains several English words amongst the symbols. Sinclair and Fire. Do you remember?"

"Oh my yes!" exclaimed Blinkmire. "And shortly after, our Duke was taken from us. I remember finding him inside the labyrinth on that crisp autumn day. He was thin and weak, and there were ravens flying above him. I thought they might kill him. What a day that was!"

"Martin, why do you mention that Blackstone book?" asked Baxter, ever seeking to make sense of the world. "Is it only because of this Flint person? We don't know for certain that he's the man from the train, do we? I don't remember anyone mentioning Flint limping or anything about six fingers."

"No, nor do I," said Kepelheim, his eyes clouding with worry. "I bring it up, because this new book contains similar phrases, written in an obscure German dialect, mixed with Latin here and there. Let me offer a sample. Again, this is an *ad hoc* translation."

The tailor's plump fingers held the thick volume in both hands as he stepped closer to the warm fire. Every man leaned towards the crackling blaze, for a deep chill ran through all their bones. Despite the bright flames, the room's light dimmed.

"Does anyone else feel that?" asked Stoker. "A sudden coldness? The old wives in Clontarf would have said someone walked across my grave. It's a supernatural chill."

"I feel it, too," said Baxter.

"As though a ghost gripped my hands," whispered Riga. "May the Lord preserve us!"

"Please, Mr. Kepelheim, read," Blinkmire said. "I think, something wants to keep us in the dark, but we mustn't allow the enemy to stop us."

"No, my friend, we must not," the tailor replied with a determined glance. He settled a pair of eyeglasses against the bulbous nose. "Though the book claims an older publication date, this part is written in a modern style called *vers libre*. Free verse. It makes my task easier, for I needn't worry about rhymes. Here, on page 333, it reads thusly:

"'Childless, friendless, hag Valul,
Offer life to grant life.
He comes. Son of Normandy.
Saint Germain, though not his name.
Ashes to ashes, black offering in claret wine.
He walks. He roars.
Alchemical miracle!
Elixir of Life. Elixir of Death.
Hybrid of Mountains.
The crooked walls.
Maze of Time waits.
He fails. He plots. He waits.
Comes another.
The Forever One arises.
Normandy's Truest Child.
Lost but found. Dead but risen.
He walks the Maze.
Time after Time after Time.
Mirrors Crack. Chains abound.
King of Shadow.
Free Man of Sainted Clarity.
King Amongst the Dead.'"

As Kepelheim spoke the final words, the fire leapt so high it nearly singed his trousers. And at the very same moment, all the lights blinked off, then on. Every crystal on the chandeliers shivered and clinked as though brushed by invisible hands.

"Are you all right?" Baxter asked the tailor. "Here now, let's get you away from the fire. I've never a fire jump like that!"

Riga shivered, his humped-back pressed deeply against the chair's cushions. His face was pale as death. "Heaven protect us all! I wish we'd thrown that book into the river."

"Yet we have it in our hands," Martin whispered.

"What does it all mean?" asked Blinkmire.

"We've heard that final line before," said Baxter. "The line 'King amongst the dead'. It's from a Tennyson poem."

"*The Passing of Arthur*," said Stoker. "I've read it many times."

"And I've heard Duke Charles murmur that phrase from time to time," said Baxter. "As though it preys on his mind. Does this book connect the Witch and Saint Germain to our Duke? Man of *sainted clarity?* Could that mean St. Clair? Later spelled as Sinclair?"

"I fear it does," Martin whispered, his eyes on the strangely animated fire. "We must lock this devilish book away. The thing is evil."

"Man," Blinkmire whispered. "Man. Mr. Kepelheim, could you read that last part again? There was something about the word *man*."

"If I must," said the tailor, a deep ache within his heart. He feared for the Duke and purposed to send his own telegram before leaving King's Court. "It says,

'The Forever One arises.
Normandy's Truest Child.
Lost but found. Dead but risen.
He walks the Maze.
Time after Time after Time.
Mirrors Crack. Chains abound.
King of Shadow.
Free Man of Sainted Clarity.
King Amongst the Dead.'"

Stephen Blinkmire leaned over to glance at Bram Stoker's notebook. "I'm glad you're taking all this down, Mr. Stoker. Normandy is obvious, as is the quote from Tennyson. And we've unlocked the idea of Sinclair. He was lost for a time, but then found. Presumed dead, then recovered. But doesn't the name Charles mean *Man?*"

"Oh, my!" exclaimed Riga. "Stephen, you're right! But not simply man. No, it's the French form of the old Germanic word *karilaz*, which means *free man*. The stanzas describe our Duke's life and his passage through the Time Maze. But how could it be written in this book?"

"Because it comes from a fallen spirit with the ability to see into our futures—or perhaps it manipulates them," said Kepelheim.

Stoker shook his head. "Faeries and the *droch fhola*. Bad blood. Evil spirits, my friends. We must pray against them."

"I agree," said Riga. "Mr. Kepelheim, if the remainder of this horrid book is like this section, then we must remove it from this house immediately. The Old House won't do, for it might be discovered at some future date. We dare not let the Duchess or her children ever find it."

"Yes, you're right," said Martin. "I can take it to one of Prince Anatole's homes. The one on Pall Mall is closest. Even if he's away, Romanov's servants will know how to bind such a book and render it harmless. However, the question remains: why would Blackstone want the Duchess to see the book?"

Baxter made final notes regarding the group's decision and then poured the last of the Armagnac into their glasses. "For the present, we keep all this quiet, but alert Duke Charles right away. I'll wire Duke James, so he is up to date. As to the matter I planned to discuss, we'll table it, but only for the moment."

"What matter?" asked Riga.

"A criminal investigation. I'd hoped to enlist your aid in dealing with the murder in the East End, but we'll meet again tomorrow and discuss it then. Mr. Kepelheim, if you'd deal with the book?"

"Of course," said the tailor.

"Very good," Baxter answered. "As for me, I've an appointment to keep. I'm interviewing the Lords Garashed and Stratbourne regarding their sons."

"Garashed?" asked Riga. "I know him."

Baxter's thick brows crept upwards as he smiled. "I'm aware of that, Count Riga. I thought you might go along with me."

"I am at your service, Chief Inspector," Riga answered. He stared at the book in Martin's hands. "That creature knew we'd be on the Duke's train. He planned all this. It's beginning again, isn't it?"

"So it is," whispered Baxter. "But we'll be ready, for the Lord is on our side."

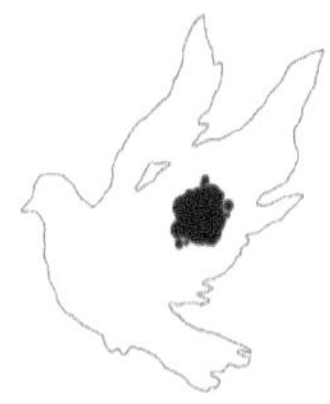

CHAPTER SEVENTEEN

St. Stephen's Church, Vienna

It was bitterly cold that morning. The tall spire of St. Stephen's Cathedral pierced the cerulean-blue canopy above the busy Stephensplatz like an architectural spear. The grand old edifice was the brick-and-mortar centre of Vienna's beating heart. The entrance was formed from a pair of Romanesque towers, flanking a massive doorway called *die Riesentor*, Giant's Door. According to legend, whilst digging the church's foundations in 1443, builders discovered the thigh bone of a giant. Believing it a sign of luck, they hung the mysterious artefact above the entry. Recently, however, the bone had disappeared—whereabouts unknown—adding to the building's mystique.

Dominating the steeply pitched roof, ruled a pair of great eagles made from 230,000 white, green, yellow, and black tiles, creating the unmistakable mosaic of Habsburg Imperial dominion. The double-eagle emblem—one turned eastward, the other to the west—represented over six centuries of Habsburg hegemony. Some said the eagles depicted the union of Austria and Hungary; others implied a higher purpose, that the eagles revealed both *temporal* and *spiritual* rights to rule all of Europe. As mother church to the Roman Catholic Archdiocese of Vienna, St. Stephen's echoed this notion, for it served as spiritual hub to a temporal empire.

Two visitors approached the church that morning, each trying to stay warm. An icy wind cut through their woolen scarves and leather gloves. Both were handsome and both well-dressed; their bespoke clothing fashioned from the finest materials. The tallest led the way from the hired coach, with the second close behind. Once at the Giant's Door, the tallest knocked. No one answered, and the door failed to yield.

"Looks like it's locked," he told the shorter man. "The sign says *Abgeschlossen*."

"Closed," said the other. "What now, Charles? Shall we try round the back?"

Sinclair shrugged. "I'm not sure. He promised to be here. The telegram was clear on that. Ten o'clock at St. Stephen's."

"Perhaps, he closed it because of our meeting. Though I suppose it's actually *your* meeting."

"I've a bad feeling about this, Seth. We've been followed ever since we left Breitenfurt. Do you still have a pistol?"

"Naturally," the auburn-haired viscount answered. He pulled back the black vicuña coat and revealed the metallic gleam of a Webley bulldog in a brown leather holster. "I've become a fairly good shot, too, thanks to your instruction. Assuming we get in, I hope you'll let me come along. After all, Della asked me to keep an eye on you. It's a bit difficult if you move beyond my sight."

"Welcome to the art of spying, Lord Paynton," replied the Duke with a smile. "To quote my Uncle James: make your plan, then plan to change it. I'll knock again. If no one answers, we'll try another door."

Sinclair lifted the heavy iron knocker and let it fall several more times. He could hear a deep, thudding echo reverberate through the enormous space beyond. Several minutes passed. He raised the iron to knock again, but one of the doors opened a tiny crack; just enough for a face, shadowed by a grey cowl, to peer through.

"*Wir haben geschlossen*," the man said in German.

The Duke passed a small card through the narrow opening. "You'll open for us," he countered in English.

The monk read the card. He looked up to examine the visitors' faces. "You are Duke Charles, yes?" he asked in English.

"I am, and I've brought a friend."

"You come alone. Is order."

"Sir, I come with my friend, or I do not come at all," Haimsbury insisted. "You may explain that to the Emperor."

The cowled man turned away and whispered to a second unseen man in Latin, not German. *"Alius homo venit etiam. Ego facio eum in?"*

Holloway stepped close to the opening and called out, "*Dic domino tuo quod, ambo intus ueniamus uel relinquemus!*"

The cowled face returned, the shadowed eyes wide with surprise. "You know Latin?"

"Of course, I do," Seth told the monk. "What educated man doesn't? Let us in, please. It's freezing out here, and you're wasting valuable time."

The massive doorway creaked slowly inward on groaning metal hinges. The two men passed through the Giant's Doorway and into a cavernous nave. Faded palm branches were tacked to the ends of pews and on walls. A few lay strewn on the black-and-white floor. All were remnants of Palm Sunday celebrations, commemorating the day Christ entered Jerusalem to the joyous shouts of thronging crowds; a day when the city paved the Miracle Worker's path with supple green branches and cloaks to cushion the donkey's hooves. The remains of these brittle, broken palms signified Christ's rejection.

Seth bent down and picked up a branch from beneath a long oak pew. He removed one of his gloves and felt along the crackling, spear-shaped leaves. They crumbled in his fingers. "Death comes to all things."

The cowled porter bowed and left. A second man approached and bowed his head. "*Guten Morgen, Herr Duke. Verzeih das Chaos. Unsere Reinigungskräfte sind noch nicht da,*" he said, his voice resonant. "*Verzeih Bruder Weber. Er hatte Befahle.*"

"That was Brother Weber?" asked Sinclair in English. "Of course, we forgive him. As you say, he was only following orders."

"You know German, but English is better, yes?" asked the deep-voiced gentleman.

"Yes, please. Our native language is easier, particularly as we're both quite tired this morning."

"*Natürlich!* Of course!" said the other, smiling. "I speak English well, my lord. I studied in England when I was much younger and much thinner. King's College. You are His Grace? The great King in Shadow?"

Charles Sinclair's sea-blue eyes sparkled as he managed to find a smile. Deep dimples creased his smooth cheeks. "Yes, I'm Haimsbury. And this is the Viscount Paynton. I take it you're Archbishop Gruscha?"

"Yes, my lord, I am. Welcome to Vienna."

The Archbishop was heavy-set with fleshy cheeks and gold-rimmed spectacles. He wore a simple, black cassock and pectoral cross. He smelled of lavender water and musty old books. "Forgive the confusion. We put up the sign to keep out tourists and told our cleaners to come this afternoon. To keep your meeting private, you understand. If you would follow me? We'll go through to a private place."

"Thank you, Excellency. The Emperor's telegram instructed me to come alone, but Lord Paynton has my complete trust. He's helping with the investigation."

The Archbishop pursed his lips and softly exhaled. Charles could hear a faint buzzing sound. The action reminded him of a trumpet player, preparing to play by setting his mouth against a cool brass instrument. After this peculiar bit of contemplation, Gruscha said, "I see. Yes, very well, Your Grace. If you insist, then I've no choice but to concede. My instructions said you would be alone, but I shall take you both through and allow *him* to decide, yes?"

"A logical solution," Charles answered.

"Logic is the foundation of faith," replied Gruscha. "Come, gentlemen. Follow me."

The three men passed through the tiled nave to a transept area. "How should we address you?" asked Sinclair after several steps. "It's my understanding the Pope made you a cardinal recently. Do you prefer we address you as Archbishop or Cardinal?"

"Call me as you wish," the plump cleric replied genially. "I am not so high as full Cardinal yet but was honoured to be created Priest-Cardinal by Pope Leo three years ago. Here, in Vienna, I am Archbishop."

Seth Holloway scrutinised their host and the building, trying to remember all he'd learnt about spy-craft and field agent rules. He'd promised Adele he'd look after her father, a man who might—if God so willed it—become Seth's father-in-law one day.

Will she really marry me? the viscount wondered as he walked. *Keep your mind on the job! Stop thinking about her!*

Charles slowed his pace to match that of the moon-faced Archbishop. As Gruscha spoke, the gold spectacles rode up and down on the soft cheeks in a wave motion. "Isn't our church breathtaking, Your Highness?"

"Exceedingly so," replied the Duke. "Excellency, why do you call me Highness?"

"You are a Royal Duke, yes? But also Shadow King? It's the right form, I hope?"

The words Shadow King drew Seth from his introspective survey of their surroundings. As he did at the Retreat, Holloway assumed a secretarial role. "His Grace is a blood royal, descended from English, Scottish, and European kings, including the Plantagenets, Stuarts, and Valois, Excellency."

"Thank you for explaining, Lord Paynton," said Sinclair, "but the Archbishop needn't call me Highness. Your Grace is sufficient. I only use the other titles when required. Let's keep them locked away for the moment."

"Locked, but never forgotten, yes?" asked the pudgy churchman.

"I suppose so," Charles muttered. "The cathedral's architecture is breathtaking. How old is it?"

"It has stood here since the twelfth century."

"Really?" asked the Duke. "And Vienna? I know very little of your history; other than the Ottoman wars, of course."

"Ah, yes, those," Gruscha replied with a sigh. "Terrible time! But the city held its own. And Vienna is older than you might guess. The Illyrians, Celts, Romans, and even Giants laid claim to this land."

"Giants?" asked Charles with obvious surprise. "Not real giants, surely?"

"Oh, yes. Real giants. Some say, they descended from the Cyclops Cadmus."

"Cadmus?" asked Seth, suddenly interested. "I'm an archaeologist and linguist, Excellency. I'd love to see any evidence you have for that."

The churchman smiled, the golden spectacles riding the round cheeks. "I cannot promise, but I'll ask if the records might be made available for you, Lord Paynton. Did you know that you passed through a Giant's Door?"

"Our driver mentioned it," said the Duke as they walked beneath the heavily gilded transept.

"It is named for a gigantic thigh bone, discovered during construction; but many other bones were found as well. Some think the bones lost, but we keep them in a dry, cold place." Gruscha stopped and pointed upwards. "See there, my lords? Above us, stands the Spire of St. Stephen's. Its belfry contains twenty-two bells. And do you see, just over our heads? It is the largest bell. It hangs from the tallest spire and rings with the deepest voice in all Christendom! The spire is one-hundred-and-thirty-six metres tall, my lords. Is your St. Paul's so tall?"

"I'm not sure," said Charles, "but your steeple is a great marvel."

"Oh yes, and the deep-voiced bell I mentioned is also a marvel," the Archbishop continued proudly. "It is called the *Pummerin* and was cast from the metal of over two hundred, captured cannons, following the second siege of Vienna by the Turks in 1683. Hence the name *Pummerin*, for the sound of the cannons. *Boom! Boom! Boom!* The name means boomer."

"Quite sensible," said Holloway, "but two hundred cannons? The bell must weigh ten tons! How can a man ring such a massive bell?"

"Not ten, sir, *twenty* tons," beamed their guide proudly. "But you're right. No single man is strong enough to make it move. A mechanical device pulls the clapper. The bell remains stationary. It does not swing."

Charles smiled, thinking of his friend Stephen Blinkmire. The eight-foot giant would find the beautiful cathedral soothing and satisfying; and he might even succeed in ringing the great bell.

"If you look ahead, my lords, you will see the magnificent choirs. Beyond these, and to the right, lies the tomb of Friedrich III. You have seen it before, yes?"

"I'm afraid this is my first visit to your cathedral," Charles admitted. "When I visited in '91, I saw only the grounds of Schönbrunn Palace. My uncle and I attended the Emperor's congress on colonial expansion into Africa that year. I fear three days of intense meetings consumed all of our time."

"Then, you must tour the city, Your Grace. Enjoy our rich history."

They passed through the Apostles Choir and up a short flight of steps into a semi-circular apse, formed from carved, red Adnet marble. Here, every surface boasted mysterious symbols and figures; many quite disturbing.

"My lords, here we are. Friedrich's final resting place."

Seth moved round the massive tomb, examining the carvings with the careful eye of a scholar. Sinclair approached the sepulchre but hesitated. He was compelled to touch it, but a strange dread overwhelmed his thoughts. He had never before visited this church, yet everything about the tomb seemed familiar. Without moving to the other side, he instinctively knew what motifs were carved there.

Touch me, a seductive voice whispered inside his head. *Feel my face, Charles. Become one with me. The Blood of Eternity binds us together.*

The Duke removed his right glove and stepped forward. Though his heart warned against it, the long tapering fingers moved in defiance of their owner's will, and his skin made contact with the red marble. That old, familiar electric shock passed through the fingertips and up his arm.

The voice whispered again. *Come find me, Charles. I am lost. Find me!*

"Charles, are you all right?" asked Holloway. He took his friend's forearm. The simple action broke the hypnotic connexion to the cold tomb. "Charles? Talk to me."

The Duke blinked. He'd been far away, lost in another world. He could hear a deep, rhythmic booming, as though the Pummerin were sounding out the seconds.

Where am I? How much time has passed? Minutes? Hours? Days?

"Charles?" Seth asked again. "You've gone pale. Here, now, lean on me."

"Sorry," Haimsbury muttered. "I'm all right. Just tired."

"Sometimes, the tomb speaks with its own voice," the Archbishop whispered, his words echoing in the red marble chamber. "I've seen visitors grow weary and even faint in its presence, as though Friederich steals all their energy. Others hear voices. Perhaps, these are just stories, yes?"

"Yes. Strange tales," Sinclair answered. "In my case, it's ordinary fatigue. Train travel, without stopping."

"You came directly from London?"

"By way of Paris and Lucerne," Seth explained. "Two long days spent on trains and in bouncing coaches. We had an errand in a nearby village, so it was long past midnight, when we finally reached Schönbrunn. Our rooms there are beautiful, but a trifle noisy. It sounded as though everyone were partying."

"Easter celebrations," Gruscha answered.

"Easter was days ago," said Sinclair. "Does Vienna follow the Eastern Orthodox Calendar?"

"No, we follow Rome, but our festivities often last for weeks. Duke Charles, your friend is right. You are quite pale. Are you well enough to continue, or shall I convey your regrets?"

"Thank you, but lack of sleep is familiar ground to a policeman."

"A policeman?" asked the Archbishop.

"Scotland Yard. Fourteen years on crime-ridden streets in London's East End. As you studied at King's College, I'm sure you're aware of the dangers in Whitechapel."

"Oh yes."

"I rarely slept for most of those years. You're right about one thing, though."

"What is that, Highness?"

"The carvings," Charles explained. "The tomb's figures are very strange."

Gruscha nodded. "Oh, yes. Sometimes, on a quiet night, I have stood here, praying against unseen forces that hang about this corner of the cathedral."

"What sort of forces?" asked the Duke. "Palpable? Audible? Visible?"

"No, not visible, and not always audible," Gruscha told them. "But palpable, yes. Your Grace, do you believe? Forgive me for prying, but have you faith in the Redeemer?"

Sinclair smiled. "Excellency, I believe firmly in Christ, as does Lord Paynton. You might say our faith was forged in fire. Why did the carver choose demonic shapes for the lower part of the tomb?"

Gruscha struck a professorial pose, as though instructing a university class. "An excellent question. The mason's name was Nikolaus van Leyden. A Dutchman. See the many coats-of-arms along the corners? These represent Friedrich's dominions. In all, the carvings total two hundred and forty, precisely. I know, for I've counted them."

"Is the number significant?" asked Sinclair, the mathematician in him instantly churning through possible permutations of the number.

"I've never been asked that before," said the Archbishop with an endearing smile. "But I find it interesting. A stone puzzle, you might say. I've looked for clues in records from the period, but nothing explains it. It remains a mystery. As to the figures, you'll find the Apostles represented, along with monks, and our Saviour. All those who intercede for the dead at the Last Judgement."

"Ah," said Charles, "as a Protestant, I trust in Christ's blood for salvation. *Solus Christus*. Christ alone."

The Archbishop smiled again. The golden spectacles rose up along the plump cheeks. "I understand, Highness. The Saviour knows your heart."

"Christ knows all men's hearts," replied the Duke, deciding it was futile to dispute the title Highness. "Tell me, Excellency, why did Herr van Leyden include these other, disturbing figures? Do they represent Purgatory? Evil?"

"Oh, no, not at all! These are the evils overcome by Emperor Friedrich. Those of the Turk and many others who fought against him. I should like to tell you more, but the ten o'clock bells sounded several minutes ago. My delight in your company causes delay. Follow me, sirs. Your meeting will take place in the vestry."

They left the sarcophagus and walked towards the High Altar. Gruscha stopped to genuflect and make the sign of the cross, then led the Englishmen up the steps of the *Wiener-Neustadt* choir and through a connecting door. Beyond, lay the vestry, an irregularly shaped room, coloured by prisms of light as the sun's rays passed through a set of tall stained-glass Gothic windows. In the centre of the room, stood a cloth-covered table, set with a chased silver teapot and three china cups, each piece painted with the red-and-gold Habsburg eagle.

Gruscha pulled out one of the chairs. "Highness, if you would care to sit? I will tell the Emperor you are here."

The plump Archbishop bowed and left the visitors alone.

Seth plopped into one of the chairs, but Charles began to walk round the space, examining it carefully.

"Looking for clues, Holmes?" asked the viscount. "I doubt there are any. I've seen a lot of vestries in my time, and they're nothing but dusty books, ledgers, and clerical clothing."

"Is this a confession, Lord Paynton?" asked the Duke, smiling.

"Hardly," Seth laughed. "I've a second cousin, who's my age, and we're quite close. Laurence planned to study law, but then shocked our entire family, when he entered the priesthood."

"Church of England or Catholic?"

"England, but any sort of church would have been a shock," Seth answered as he picked up one of the ornate teaspoons. "Laurence was raised atheist, just as I was. His father, like mine, only believed in what he could touch and measure. Laurence's father died last year. I've no idea what faith my uncle might have chosen, if any. And, as you know, my old dad studied the religions of ancient cultures, but never believed in God or a real Saviour. Not till a few years ago. Now, both he and Mum are Christians, I'm happy to say."

"And your cousin? Is he saved?" asked Sinclair.

"I'm not sure. Probably. I should ask him."

"Yes, you should," answered his friend. "Before it's too late."

"Yes," murmured Seth. "I'll write to Laurence and set a time to talk, face to face." He rubbed his hands together. "At least, there's a fire in here. March weather's been up and down like a see-saw. Warm one minute, freezing the next. Then, there was that strange fog last Sunday."

"Yes," the Duke whispered as he examined the books. "A lot of people died in that fog."

"Charles, is it my imagination, or has it grown steadily colder since we left Lucerne?"

Charles muttered a 'yes' and continued surveying the room. The vestry's high ceiling had the same smoke-finished patina found in many old buildings. A cheerful fire crackled in a tiled hearth on the south wall; the brick-face mantel was stained from constant use. The northeast wall housed a pair of tall cupboards, presumably wardrobe presses for priestly vestments. Another held four masterfully carved, oak bookshelves. Each was filled with hundreds of books, stacked high and tightly packed; the title on every book's spine gilded. The lettering revealed stamped dates, reaching back to the twelfth century.

Church records, thought Sinclair.

"I'll wager this place is a treasury of European history," he told Paynton. "I'll also wager Martin would enjoy spending a week in here."

"A month wouldn't be too long," said Seth. "Della loves history, too, and she's very good with languages. I suppose it's an inherited ability."

Charles wondered if Seth knew the truth of Adele's birth: that her mother was Charles's late sister, Charlotte Sinclair, stolen as a baby and raised as a harlot in Paris. "I imagine so," the Duke muttered. "What's this?" he asked, reaching for an unusually coloured book. All other bindings were dark blue. This was crimson red. *1420* was printed in gold on the spine; the precise year the Plantagenet Twins were born in France. Yet, one of the blue books also had *1420* on its spine, neatly tucked twixt *1419* and *1420*.

Why repeat the year, and why in red?

That familiar electric buzz ran along his hands and arms.

Find me, whispered a voice.

Charles shut his eyes and prayed silently.

A man's voice broke the silence. It was human, and unlike the previous whispers, this voice was friendly, alive with a mix of German and French overtones.

"Might history be another of your many interests, Your Grace?" asked the voice.

Seth stood at once, for he recognised the speaker.

Charles turned towards the doorway and bowed his head in deference. "Your Imperial Majesty. It's a pleasure to see you again."

"None of that bowing and scraping, Haimsbury. And it's good to see you again, too," said the other. "And you've brought Lord Paynton with you! When Gruscha told me Charles brought an extra man, he failed to mention that man was you, Seth. Tell your parents hello from Sisi and me. It's been far too long. We must get together and catch up. Please, gentlemen, sit."

Emperor Franz Josef had a large head that was almost devoid of hair, save for patches of wispy white tufts along each temple. As if to make up for the loss on top, the sides of his flat cheeks boasted great mounds of cottony white, formed into mutton chop whiskers, connected by a bristle-brush moustache. At sixty-four, his face held a roadmap of fine creases and age lines, that told a story of warfare, woe, and bitter disappoint, interrupted now and then by moments of beauty and joy.

He reached for Haimsbury's hand. The grip was firm and friendly. "It's good to see you again, Charles. Thank you for coming. Sorry we didn't greet you men last evening. Sisi and I retire early. I hope Kaufmann saw to your needs."

"He did, and our rooms are delightful, Your Majesty."

"Good. Shall we have tea?"

The three men sat, the Emperor and Duke opposite one another. Franz Josef untied the ribbons of a woolen cloak and draped it across the chair's tall back. "These days, I keep a heavy wrap close. Sensitivity to cold is an old man's malady. Would one of you mind pouring? Not that I think either of you is inferior, you understand. It's just, there's a nagging weakness to my upper arm these days, and I find lifting anything heavy bothersome."

"Allow me," offered Seth. The viscount poured the steaming rose-amber tea into three cups. "Sugar? Milk? I see lemon as well."

"Two sugars, no milk," said Charles, his mind on the book marked *1420*.

"One cube and a squeeze of lemon, if you don't mind, Lord Paynton," the Emperor answered. "Did Gruscha give you the tour? He's quite proud of our cathedral. He attended here as a boy, you know."

"Our tour was all too brief," Charles explained. "What we did see is beautiful. Next time, I'll bring Elizabeth, and we'll take the full tour."

"Will the Duchess attend the wedding next month?" asked the Emperor.

"Oh yes. Beth leaves in a few days to meet the Queen in Belgium. Drina's presently in Luxembourg. She asked me to convey her best wishes and many fond hugs."

The old man smiled. "Alexandrina is a kindred spirit."

"Will you be there, sir?" asked Holloway.

A shadow crossed the elderly ruler's face, a sadness that added years. "I fear not, young man. My wife and I are invited, of course, but recent politics make our attendance problematic. More's the pity."

"What politics?"

The old man sighed. "Anarchists, murder, envy. If you choose to investigate my problem, you'll understand." A silence followed, and they sipped their tea. Charles decided to let Franz Josef proceed at his own pace.

After a moment or two, the Emperor continued with more small talk. "You must visit Belvedere Palace, if you find time. The orangery is the finest outside of Versailles. One tree produces a delightfully sweet orange, with very few seeds. It came from Jaffa, I think. We're redecorating the Belvedere, but most areas are accessible. My brother's son, Franz Ferdinand, will move there next year. He's my heir now."

"Not your brother?" asked Haimsbury.

"Karl is next in line, of course, but he's abdicated in favour of his son. It's logical, I suppose, given my brother's age."

The Emperor grew silent again, his breathing steady as he stared at the steaming teapot. His guests sipped their cups. After several minutes, the old man spoke again. "Forgive me if I seem strange. I'm not sure how to begin. I'm glad you came together, for what I'm about to ask will toss you into the firing line. If you say no, I promise it won't affect our friendship. Not at all."

"Thank you, Majesty," said Paynton. "You and my parents have been through many adventures together. No matter where the conversation leads, you can count me in."

"Count me in as well," said Charles. "But I hope you're about to reveal specifics, as your letter included none."

"That was intentional. Oh, but forgive me!" exclaimed the Emperor, his face suddenly animated. The rheumy eyes rounded, and the mutton chop whiskers seemed to dance. "Forgive me, Charles, I should have asked right away. How is Lady Aubrey?"

"It's kind of you to think of her, Franz," Charles said with a knowing glance at Holloway. "Delia's slowly improving, but the path before her is long. I'm sure you understand."

"Oh, yes, of course, I do. Losing a child is like losing an arm or leg. I say this as a father, of course; but for a mother, it's quite different, I think. Mothers never truly break the bond, do they?"

"Most don't," said Charles, remembering his late wife's coldness. She'd ignored the living Albert for months, then pretended to mourn his death. Charles still carried a painful scar upon his heart. "Fathers bleed, too," he whispered.

Franz stared at the Duke. "You know such pain?"

"I was married before, but my wife left me for another man. She died in Ireland, making me a widower. Amelia and I had one child together. A son. Albert died at one year old of smallpox."

Franz slowly nodded. The muttonchops drooped. “Then you understand. No, it never leaves you.” The Emperor began to stir his tea, the pale eyes fixed on the slowly moving spoon. “Life seldom goes as we expect, does it?” Then, finding the past too painful, he changed the subject. “Tell me about this bombing in London. It was last month, yes?”

Charles began to wonder if the old man might have forgotten why he'd sent the mysterious letter and assumed the visit merely friendship.

No. Franz is shrewd. He's working up to the truth.

“We know very little about the man behind it,” the Duke answered. “The blast was relatively small and happened at a time when very few people were near the Observatory. Presumably, the man wanted to destroy the main building, though I can't imagine why.”

“Do you know the man's name?” asked the Emperor.

“Bourdin, or so we presume. It's likely he used an alias. Evidence links him to a wider circle of anarchists, possibly even the Black Hand.”

The Emperor shuddered. “The Black Hand! They are a very dangerous lot. Be very careful of them, Charles.”

“Always, sir. And I hope your Secret Police are keeping a careful watch on you, Franz.”

“They do, but God's will be done. If he chooses to take me, then I am taken, no matter what I do. Death awaits us all, Charles. That grand tomb is evidence of that.”

“But till that day, we must live to the fullest. We make every day count, Franz.”

“Yes, of course, you're right. Forgive me, my friends. My mind travels in a thousand directions these days, and I am often maudlin. But Lady Aubrey is better? Might she and Lord Aubrey be at next month's wedding?”

“No, neither will attend, I'm afraid,” Charles replied. “Paul's been called to a foreign assignment, and Cordelia's doctors want her to stay until late May, at the very least. Seth and I visited her on the way here. She seems to have acclimated, though sadness still dominates her thoughts.” Charles decided to omit the truth of Delia's condition: that she imagined herself haunted by the spirits of her late father and dead child; that she still had visions of her brother William, floating outside her windows. William Wychwright was sentenced to ten years in prison but managed to escape in transit from ICI headquarters to Newgate. His whereabouts were still unknown. Charles said nothing of it to Delia.

The Emperor sighed. "Lady Aubrey is a gentle soul, I think. I'll visit, if that's permitted. Sisi might even join me."

"Will Empress Sisi be attending the wedding?" the Duke asked. "I'm sure Beth would enjoy seeing her again."

"No," the Emperor replied softly. "As I said, politics prevent us both. I fear we'd not be welcome."

"Why?" asked Holloway. "Surely, Austria and Germany are allies?"

"Yes, we are on paper, but this drive of Wilhelm's to subsume all German-speaking states into a single kingdom has placed us in opposition. Don't mistake me. I like Wilhelm, but his policies and mine are like oil and water. And some of his friends are even worse, Lord Paynton. Much, *much* worse. These days, he and I dare not occupy the same room. It would upset the entire wedding."

"I've never met Wilhelm," said the viscount. "Have you, Charles?"

"Oh, yes. Several times. At the Palace, but also at Cowes yacht races. The Kaiser and Bertie have quite a rivalry going there. Wilhelm's obsessed with winning. Perhaps, it's to overcome his physical limitations. He has a withered arm, Seth. Caused by something that happened during the birthing process. Do you remember how Paul's son, Ian, very nearly came into the world upside down? In breech position?"

"Vividly," Seth answered. "I was there, remember? Is that what happened to Wilhelm?"

The Duke nodded, half his mind on the red book as he stirred the tea. "But unlike Ian's case, the physician couldn't turn Wilhelm and had to break his left arm to bring him into the world. As a result, Wilhelm isn't the strapping warrior Germany expects of a leader."

"It's more than that, Charles. Wilhelm is *seltsam*," said Franz Josef. "How do you say it in English? Not right in the head. *Verrûckt.*"

"I'm not sure I'd go that far," said the Duke, "but you know the Kaiser better than I. The Queen speaks of him with great fondness."

"Because Wilhelm's her favourite grandson," explained the Emperor. "Is Bertie going to this wedding?"

"The Crown Prince? Of course. Most of Europe's royals are attending," replied Seth.

"Including England's Shadow King," stated Franz without blinking. "You should be Crown Prince, Charles, not Bertie."

"I've no desire to be King, sir."

"But you cannot hide your blood. Good heavens, it is bluer than my own! Still, have it your way," he sighed, then sipped more of the tea. "I should like to see Drina again, though. It isn't often one can watch two grandchildren marry one another. I'm sure Drina's pleased. We've sent gifts, of course. Sisi and I wish Ernst and little Ducky all the happiness in the world."

"Ducky?" asked Charles.

"Ach, it is what we call Princess Victoria Melita. A silly pet name. Do you gentlemen have pet names?"

"My mother always calls me Digby," Seth answered with a faint smile.

"Digby?" asked Sinclair. "Really?"

"Oh, yes. As a boy, I was always jumping into pits and digging out buried treasure. Boyish curiosity overwhelmed my patience, hence, Digby. Beth's nickname for you is far more dignified."

"What is that?" asked the Emperor.

"She calls me Captain," Charles answered smiling.

"Captain? Is this why you were made Lord High Admiral of England's Navy?"

"That's just a ceremonial title, Franz. Nothing more. As to Captain, my wife has her own reasons for it, but it always makes me very happy, when she says it. I call her my little one."

Franz Josef laughed, his eyes bright. "Now, this pet name makes sense. The little Duchess! But you'll explain this Captain name another time, yes?"

"Yes, I promise."

Another silence followed. Charles assumed the Emperor would eventually come round to talking of his true purpose, and the intervening small-talk helped to overcome a natural reticence—or perhaps fear. Whatever the reason, it must be deeply personal. An affair? No, Sisi had known about her husband's wandering eye for years. Though he loved his wife dearly, as with many royals, Franz Josef kept an official mistress. Even Sisi knew that.

Might the Empress be having the affair? Charles decided to give the older man a slight nudge. “Sir, the letter you sent implied a need for haste. You asked me to come as soon as possible. Is there a political reason behind it? Franz, are you in danger?”

The Emperor’s face sagged again; the white whiskers slumped. “You’re right. How I wish our meeting could be only about nick-names and weddings, but there’s another reason why I cannot go to Coburg next month. Prince Philipp of Saxe-Coburg will be there, and he may be involved in...”

“Involved in what?” asked Haimsbury. “Franz, what’s this about?”

The old man finished the tea, using two hands. Charles noticed the hands trembled. The Emperor swallowed the warm liquid. Then, with tremulous voice, he leaned closer to the Englishmen and whispered, “It is about *murder.*”

“Murder?” echoed Haimsbury. “Whose?”

“My son’s. Do you remember it?”

“I remember reading about it,” Charles replied. “And our family discussed it. Seth?”

“Who doesn’t remember?” said Holloway. “I knew Rudolf, though not well. We shared an interest in science and antiquarianism. He had diverse interests and even studied alienism at one point. My sister’s good friends with Rudolf’s widow, Princess Stéphanie. Your son died at a hunting lodge, didn’t he? Early ’89?”

“Yes, in Mayerling, thirtieth of January. Perhaps, even the twenty-ninth. No one knows the precise time.”

“I’m very sorry, Franz,” Charles told his friend.

“Rudolf’s death is why my nephew is now the heir,” said Franz. “Sisi never recovered. If only she...” The Emperor let the sentence trail off, unable to voice the pain. “Not all men find happiness, but if I could resolve the questions about my son’s death, perhaps my wife’s broken heart would heal. So much darkness resides in her now, Charles. So much regret.”

“Feel free to share your heart with us,” the Duke said. “I promise, it will go no further, unless you sanction it.”

“Yes, yes, I know. I trust you both. You and your inner circle know how to keep secrets.”

The Duke smiled. “I imagine you refer to our intelligence service. The ICI.”

"Charles, you needn't be coy with me. I've known Drummond all my life, young man. We're close in age and have shared many adventures. You should ask him about India sometime. I'm quite aware of your family's inner circle and why you are England's Shadow King."

"It isn't how I see myself, sir."

"Nevertheless, it is how you are viewed by the world. Newspapers never tire of printing your photograph and sharing your adventures. And it's why I suggested you come here openly and stay at Schönbrunn."

"I'm glad you did, sir. It avoids dangerous speculation."

"Good," said the Emperor. "How much do you know about my son's death?"

"Only what the circle's Vienna chapter reported. After receiving your letter, it occurred to me Mayerling might be discussed, so I looked up the notes in our archives. I also asked Martin Kepelheim about it. As you're aware, Martin's head of Austrian enquiries."

"And?" asked Franz.

"The police reports call it suicide, but as an experienced detective, I find that unsatisfactory. Our circle detectives agree. Would it surprise you to learn we called it murder?"

"No," the Emperor said, "but did your men name the murderer?"

"They listed several suspects, but five pages of our report are missing. Martin's trying to locate them. Why investigate now, Franz? Rudolf died five years ago."

"Is there an end to murder investigations? I might ask why those five pages are missing."

"Yes, sir, you might," replied the Duke.

"Will you take up the case?" asked Franz Josef.

"Seth, what do you think? It could prove dangerous."

"Isn't that why I'm here? To watch after you?" laughed the auburn-haired viscount. "I've been in tight spots before, Charles. Egypt and Arabia aren't exactly England."

"Then, we'll begin today," Haimsbury told the Emperor.

The old man's face relaxed, and tears filled his pale eyes. "Thank you! My dear friends, thank you! Oh, you relieve my mind. I give you *carte blanche* to speak to anyone, and that includes me and my household. Soon, it will be obvious that you're here professionally, but I pray that truth remains out of the press until you've completed your work. The newspaper hounds are necessary, you understand, but I prefer to keep them on a leash. Like my hunting dogs."

"It must be a miraculous leash!" exclaimed Seth. "The English press refuse to be collared. Though, they dearly love our Duke."

"Not always," Charles noted. "But I've grown used to dealing with them. Don't worry, Franz, we'll find a way to misdirect the dogs and keep them sniffing elsewhere."

"Excellent," said the Emperor. "Keep watch on your shadows. Black Hand cells are everywhere, even Vienna. And other trouble-makers creep along our streets; some are close to my throne." The Emperor sat heavily against the wooden chair and took a deep breath. "I suggest you begin with Mizzi Kaspar."

Sinclair called up the name from the inner-circle report. He'd filed it neatly inside his orderly, mental library. "The actress? She was one of your son's mistresses, I believe."

"Actresses often collect wealthy patrons. Mizzi Kaspar hosted many important men in her private rooms. Not all are trustworthy. I know, for I've kept an eye on her through my own spies," he added with a sly wink.

"Perhaps, we should recruit you into our circle, sir."

"James has mentioned it, but no, it is too much for an old man."

"Then, it's our loss," the Duke replied. "Does Miss Kaspar still work in the theatre?"

"Oh, yes. She's presently rehearsing at *Theatre an der Wien*. She lives in a very fine house, purchased by my son, I might add. Sisi asked me to evict the woman, but how can I? Kaspar holds the title deed in her own name. Besides, I like to know where she is. The address is in a box file. Here, let me show you."

The Emperor stood, wincing at arthritic pain in his knees and hips. He slowly crossed to the bookshelves, where he removed the red book with *1420* stamped on the spine and returned to the table. "Forgive my boldness for using such an important date to hide the contents. Very few read these old ledgers, save for the newest ones, of course. Any history older than twenty years is soon forgotten. And so, I've stored all my evidence in this box file. It is why I asked to meet you here. And I trust Archbishop Gruscha with my life."

As Charles opened the false book, that same electric tingle ran down his hands and up through his arms. The red leather binding disguised a hollow interior, filled with handwritten pages, police reports, medical notes, and newspaper clippings. Most included notes in small, spidery script written along the margins in black ink.

"Is this your handwriting, sir?"

The Emperor nodded. "I'd trust this file to no one else."

"Yet you place it into my care."

"And I do so with joy! Charles, you're the most trustworthy man I know."

The Duke reached for the old man's hands and shook them. "I'm honoured by your faith in me, sir. I promise to guard this file with my life. Lord Paynton and I will uncover the truth behind Rudolf's death. We promise."

Suddenly, every muscle in the old man's face relaxed in a single movement, as though years of tension fell away in unison. He wiped away tears. "Thank you, Charles. On behalf of Sisi and myself, thank you. Promise to be careful. My son was often foolish and chose friends poorly. I believe, one or more of those friends may have been involved in his death—if not directly, then through mistaken entanglements. Prince Philipp is not the only royal on that list."

The Duke placed a comforting hand on the Emperor's shoulder. "We'll uncover the truth."

"No matter what that truth is, Charles. Even if..." His voice broke, and the old man's thin lips quivered beneath the bristle-brush moustache. "If such a truth isn't one I wish to hear, you must promise to be honest with me."

"No matter what, I'll tell you everything, Franz. I promise."

The three men said farewell, and Archbishop Gruscha escorted Haimsbury and Paynton to a side exit, close to the choir. As the Englishmen hailed a cab, Charles noticed a tall man in a stovepipe hat, watching them from a nearby corner.

"And so it begins," he whispered to the viscount.

"You mean that odd man watching us?"

"Yes. Come on, let's return to the palace and read through this evidence. Take us back to Schönbrunn," Charles told the inner-circle driver. The two peers climbed into the chilly interior and shut the doors.

Once the horses started trotting, Seth pointed to the man on the corner. "Do you suppose that chap plans to hail a cab and follow us, or should we have invited him to share with us?"

"Oh, I'm sure he'll find a way," Charles said, using a small mirror to watch the receding stranger. The man began to walk towards a waiting hansom.

The Duke noticed he limped.

CHAPTER EIGHTEEN

West Africa – Kumasi City, Ashanti Kingdom

If Charles Sinclair could draw a line connecting his coach to Paul Stuart's present location, that line would stretch nearly three-thousand miles long. At seventy-two degrees, the morning was cool for Africa's Gold Coast, but the sun shone brightly on a wide veranda, owned by Major Sir Frederick Hodgson. His wife, Mary Alice, was the daughter of Sir William Alexander George Young, former governor to the Ashanti people. Mary Alice spoke the local language well, and often translated for visiting dignitaries. Short of stature with flaxen hair, she reminded Stuart of his own wife, the beautiful Cordelia. The earl ached to be with her.

Mary Alice poured cinnamon tea into three porcelain cups. "I trust you slept well, Lord Aubrey?"

"Much better than well; thank you, Lady Hodgson. It's been almost a fortnight since I slept in a real bed. I appreciate your willingness to host me at such short notice."

"You're always welcome, my lord, but usually British diplomats are given suites at the palace; particularly those with peerage titles."

"If my title were higher, perhaps," he answered, "but in my case, another man with a higher title sailed with me. Prince Anatole Romanov of Russia."

"Really? Where's he staying?" asked Hodgson. "He's welcome here, if he requires billeting."

"I rather doubt he does," Aubrey said politely. "In fact, I saw him just twice, though we sailed together for thirteen days."

"Inscrutable sort of chap," muttered Hodgson. "But then Russians always are."

"Romanov's helped our government navigate some choppy political seas," said Aubrey. "I imagine that's why he's here, but I didn't see him disembark. He may have sailed on."

Lady Hodgson smiled and handed the guest a plate of honey-filled pastries. "Lord Aubrey, rumour says you've come to negotiate with King Prempeh. Is that right?"

"Is that so?" the earl replied vaguely as he stretched out his long legs across the veranda's flagstone floor. "I'd certainly like to talk with him whilst I'm here. Has either of you met him?"

"Once, and only briefly," answered Major Hodgson. "The new king is young, and so has a court of young advisors. Most are suspicious of Englishman, particularly those of us with military titles. Mary Alice lived here with her father for years, as you know. She and the king's mother get along well enough. Perhaps, you might try a feminine door. It could prove easier to open."

Paul laughed as he stirred a sugar cube into the strong tea. "Surely, my reputation hasn't travelled this far."

"If you mean your exploits in France and Egypt, then I fear those tales *have* preceded you, Lord Aubrey," answered Mary with a delighted smile. "King Prempeh is only twenty-four, with no daughters for you to persuade, but you're handsome and speak Ashanti well enough. Both will lend you credit with the king's mother. Ashanti women have a great deal of influence, as you may already know. Heritage rights descend through matrilineal lines; therefore, mothers control family life. Royal mothers hold even more control, particularly when her son's still learning."

"I understand, but what is he learning?" replied Aubrey. "His mother's teaching him to distrust everything the British say. Thus far, he refuses to consider any compromise. Does his mother speak English?"

"Oh, yes," replied Mary. "She's conversant in several languages, including French and English."

"True, but you must speak to her in Ashanti first," the major warned. "If you hope to gain influence, I suggest you use all your charm and wit, Lord Aubrey. I imagine that's why Rosebery sent you, instead of a crotchety old diplomat."

Aubrey smiled as he poured himself another cup of tea. "Charm is but one arrow in my quiver, Major, but if I cannot convince the king to accept England's terms, then I shall have to resort to a less pleasant option. Let's pray it doesn't come to that."

"Less pleasant? What sort of option is that?" asked Lady Hodgson. "Oh, do forgive my manners! I shouldn't slice a cake without offering some to you. It's lemon, sweetened with native honey."

"No, thank you," Paul answered politely. "It looks delicious, but breakfast filled me up. You've a marvellous cook. Is she English?"

"French, actually," replied his hostess. "And your other arrows? I've heard some in government talk of your previous exploits, my lord. I wonder, if such an arrow might be..."

"Leave the man be, Mary Alice!" Hodgson interrupted. "My dear, remember, Lord Aubrey's not only a peer, but he's also one of England's top spies. Indeed, the very top! Do you really think he's going to reveal the details of his assignment to us?"

Lady Hodgson answered without hesitation. "If he plans to sow discord, then I pray he does reveal them, Frederick, for I've no wish to live through another war! We've only just recovered a semblance of calm in Kumasi. New buildings are finally going up, and there's even a church that's opened, just down King Street. Oh, that reminds me, Lord Aubrey, there's a baptismal service on Sunday. Six new converts! We'd be pleased if you'd come with us."

"If I'm still here, Lady Hodgson, I'd like that. Thank you."

Having arrived long past midnight, the earl had slept late. Already, the sun stood high over the distant palace. The long, grand avenue twixt the royal complex and the Hodgsons' veranda provided a perfect view of the magnificent Garden City.

"The day's quickly lost, my friends. I should call at the palace and see if the king will receive me," said Aubrey.

"But you can't just stroll up to the gates and expect to be let inside," Mary Alice told him. "My husband will send word to the mother first and gain permission."

Paul smiled. "No need. A friend has already done that."

"What friend?" asked Frederick Hogdson.

"I'm not to say," answered the Scotsman. "Suffice to say he is of very high rank."

Hodgson laughed. "Well, that explains Romanov's presence, I suppose! I should have guessed you'd have it all in hand."

Aubrey rose and kissed the woman's hand. "Thank you for the hospitality, dear lady. Major, I hope to return in four hours or so. Perhaps, you and I might take a tour of the lake?"

Hodgson grew serious. He nodded and began massaging the bristly moustache, as if trying to make it grow longer. "Yes. Yes, I suppose we could do that. Let me send a runner over to my friend Arnie's house."

"Arnie?"

"Lieutenant Arnold Ramsfield. I'm sure you know him. First cousin to Dickie Patterson-Smythe."

"Yes, of course, I know Ramsfield," replied Aubrey. "His son and I were at Merton at about the same time. We played polo together once or twice."

"Then, it's a plan. Mary, we'll want you along, of course. This isn't to be some men's outing."

"Even if it were, I'd still go," she said with a firm but bright smile. "Just to make sure no one gets into any trouble."

After saying goodbye to the Hodgsons, Paul took a hat against the ever-present sun and set off walking towards the palace. He could have ordered a sedan chair or a horse-drawn carriage, but preferred a less showy arrival. The British had been living and working amongst the Ashanti tribes since early in Queen Victoria's reign. Consequently, some parts of the capital city might have passed for an English village or market town: Brick homes with gabled roofs and broad porches, yards filled with English flowers. Yet, these sat comfortably alongside handsome Ashanti structures of mud-brick with flat roofs, the yards lined with date palms and beehives. The English idea that progress could only be achieved by Anglicising the natives troubled the earl.

As he walked along the gravel avenue, Stuart remained alert and cautious, observing local customs as he interacted with locals. He'd chosen his clothing carefully, appearing as a simple traveller. Most British diplomats wore court dress when calling on a sovereign, but here such overt ornamentation sent a strong and angry message. English diplomats usually meant a new English war. And unlike his predecessors, Paul hadn't come to force the King to abdicate. Instead, he hoped to broker a better deal; one that allowed both sides to win and prosper. And avoid another war.

He'd reached King Street, a colonnaded avenue, lined on either side with graceful date palms. The walkway reminded him of similar approaches in Cairo. He strolled casually, behaving like a tourist. Elegant women passed by, dressed in colourful silks made from Kente Cloth, a hand-woven material, dyed in specific patterns, proprietary to each clan or family. The tradition reminded him of Scotland, where tartan plaids were designed and defended by clans, and even septs within those clans. Only a few Stuarts had the right to wear the King's Red. As a direct descendant of James I of Scotland, Paul had that right, as did his son and daughter.

Don't think about them, he reminded himself. *Just get on with the job. Be efficient and speedy, but get it done right.*

He remembered the look on his wife's face as he said goodbye. *Cordelia,* he thought with a pang of regret. He'd ordered the postman at Breitenfurt to forward his wife's outbound letters to King's Court in London, care of Duke Charles; otherwise, the precious letters might be lost twixt Austria and Africa. He'd written to her every day whilst on the voyage, posting heartfelt notes each time the ship docked for supplies. Paul ached to hold her, longed for the day when she could come home to him and their children. For now, he must concentrate on his assignment. One more job for England, then he'd retire.

The earl had reached a tall gate. He approached one of several armed guards. Paul had visited Africa before and spoke the *Twi* language well. And so using the local dialect, he asked permission to speak with the queen mother, explaining he'd brought her a gift.

The guards whispered to one another, then motioned to a larger man, several yards beyond the gate. The massively muscled guardian carried no rifle, but a curved blade hung from his belt. He wore a golden helmet, crowned in the centre with the horns of a bull, and projecting outwards was a sweeping semi-circle of black, brown, and white hawk-eagle feathers.

Paul recognised the uniform of a high-ranking military commander. Only the tallest warriors served as palace guards. Military commanders were taller still; but as the elegantly dressed soldier approached, he realised that the pale-skinned visitor stood taller yet. Paul's six-foot-three advantage forced the stern-faced soldier to look up several inches.

No matter. If looks could kill, then Aubrey would be dead.

The experienced spy smiled in his most innocent fashion. Paul bowed low and said, "I come from England's true King to speak with Ashanti's truest ruler."

This took the beefy guardian by surprise. Even in Africa, everyone knew England's sovereign was a woman, not a man. What did this stranger mean by 'King'? Had the old woman died?

"King?" asked the man in Twi.

"King," Aubrey repeated in the same language. "And that true King sends greetings. I am cousin to this great King, and I speak for him."

The impeccably dressed soldier turned to the smaller guards and spoke quickly in the dialect of the Akan peoples. They talked for many minutes. Paul waited patiently, sometimes offering a brief smile to passing ladies. Most of these wore Kente cloth and golden ornaments gleamed from their braided hair. More gold dressed their wrists and upper arms, and strings of ivory circled the slender throats. Even the sandals glittered with gold ornamentation.

Welcome to the Gold Coast, thought the earl.

Finally, one of the smaller guards opened the gate.

The commander motioned to Paul and said in English, "Come, cousin of true King. The lady queen mother will speak with you."

CHAPTER NINETEEN

Kumasi Palace

This wasn't Paul Stuart's first visit to the Gold Coast. He'd come here in 1875 on a diplomatic mission with his father, the nation's preeminent negotiator, Robert Stuart, 11th Earl of Aubrey. During that visit, Paul learnt to speak basic phrases in *Twi*, a language used by nearly all Ashanti tribes. Robert Stuart cautioned his willful son regarding cross-cultural contamination. The Gold Coast had seen Europeans crowding its shores since 1471, beginning when Portuguese sailors came ashore twixt the mouths of the Volta and Ankobra Rivers. In the centuries since, the locals adopted both good and bad habits from the pale Europeans; including how to barter the lives of men, women, and children from enemy tribes. Perhaps, if Europeans had never landed, such inhuman practices might never have been devised.

Today, as he waited for an answer to his request, Paul remembered his late father's words, spoken on their voyage back to England. He and Paul were standing together on the quarterdeck of the HMS *Swiftsure*. Rob Stuart's silvering, black hair was tousled by the sea's salty breeze in a profile that sent society ladies to the nearest fainting couch.

The gentle diplomat had turned to his heir, and with a soft voice and ageless eyes, said, "Son, one day you'll return to this land on your own. When that day comes, you must lift up Christ, no matter the mission. Though there are Christian churches here and there, most are enslaved to animistic ideas and ancestral worship. Diplomacy isn't cultural, nor is it political. It is always, always, *always* spiritual," he told his son. "Never forget that. Not for one second. Your enemies are not the Akan and Ashanti peoples. If they seek to harm you, remember they are pawns, used by the fallen realm in a very old, very long war. Think of diplomacy as a game of chess. If you're ever presented with a tempting pawn, consider your next move carefully, for it's probably a trap. Remember, pawns are often poisoned."

Poisoned pawns. Robert Stuart was wise beyond his years, and since then, Paul had learnt such lessons all too well. In some ways, Cozette du Barroux had been a poisoned pawn. Beautiful, easy to know, easier to love, willing to love him in return, but most assuredly a velvet trap whose sweet jaws closed upon his unsuspecting heart. He'd fallen in love with Cozette; yet despite his feelings, he'd followed orders and left her in Paris, unaware that his child already grew inside du Barroux's body. Only later, would he discover he'd become a father. And years after that, Paul would learn Cozette's true name: Charlotte Sinclair, his cousin, and probably the woman he'd have married, had no one kidnapped Charlotte as an infant.

A poisoned pawn.

As he waited, Paul studied the lounge's decor: a collection of fertility statues, lining the walls. The idols' eyes stared back at him with anger and accusation.

You left her, they seemed to say.

Paul sighed. *Why does Charlotte's face still haunt me? Why can't I let her memory go?*

Because of Adele, he realised.

Adele Marie had her mother's eyes, so very like those of Charlotte's brother, Charles Sinclair. To avoid telling Della the truth, Paul had forfeited his parental rights. He'd given up his daughter twice. First to his own father, who'd adopted the sweet toddler without a moment's regret; and then to Charles Sinclair, Della's blood uncle, who'd adopted her in April of '89. Nearly five years ago.

In December of '88, Paul married Cordelia Wychwright. At first, he thought it gallantry, but in truth he'd fallen in love. Since that day, Delia had given him two healthy children, but lost two others to miscarriage. Then, they lost Liam, taken to God's throne at just six days old. Now, Cordelia was sequestered behind velvet walls, designed to heal her mind. But would she heal? Was Cordelia another poisoned pawn? Was Adele?

Those old familiar guilt pangs pierced his heart. He stuffed them down with thoughts of an ice block. He counted to five. The trick worked, and he breathed normally again. He'd write another letter tonight, if for no other reason than to remind Cordelia of his love. God willing, he'd conclude this business and sail home in a few days.

"My lord?" a woman's voice called, tearing the earl from his thoughts. She was young and beautiful, dressed in gold-trimmed Kente cloth. Her small head was wrapped in the same material, and a string of multi-hued glass beads encircled a small waist. A pair of gold-trimmed sandals hugged her supple feet. She smelled like a garden, and a blend of spicy florals filled the air as she moved close and bowed. "You are the Lord Aubrey, yes?" she asked in English.

He smiled and offered a slight bow, the long chestnut hair falling across both shoulders. "Yes, miss. I'm Aubrey. Have you a message for me?"

"You are to follow me, my lord. I take you."

Without hesitation, the earl trailed after the exotic beauty, passing through one room, then another, until finally arriving in a courtyard garden. He'd waited for nearly an hour. The sun had long since passed its zenith and hovered over the western palm trees. In the centre of the garden, stood a mahogany table, set with white linen and an English tea service. Tall vases of colourful flowers decorated the sitting area, adding to the delightful scent.

"You sit?" asked the young woman.

"Of course, thank you," Aubrey replied in courtly manner. "Will you also sit?"

She smiled, radiating a beauty that comes only from an innocent heart. Paul wondered if she might be a princess or a nobleman's daughter. "I sit later, yes," she told him. "Thank you. I speak your words for the *Asantehemaa*. Is our word for queen."

"Queen? King Prempeh's wife?"

"No," the girl giggled. "Asantehemaa is mother to king. I hear her music. She come, my lord. You stand now."

Stuart rose again, his eyes on an ivory-framed, ebony door to the far north of the courtyard. As it opened, drummers and pipers played, and several young women, dressed similarly to Paul's guide, performed a delightful dance as vanguard to the primary entrant. That entrant did not fail to impress. Set amongst rows of musicians and singers, rode a magnificent woman, robed in gleaming gold cloth and endless chains of gold and ivory. Far too important to walk as mortals do, the queen mother was carried on an embellished litter, supported by golden staves that rested on the shoulders of well-muscled men.

As the singers arrived at the table, they surrounded the earl and draped gold-imbued cloth round his shoulders and chains of gold around his neck. Paul knew he must accept the gifts and prayed nothing about them invoked local spirits.

The men placed the litter on the ground, and two others lifted the queen mother from the interior and carried her to the table, where she sat into a specially woven chair, decorated with ivory beads and golden bells. The legs and seat of the wicker throne creaked as the middle-aged woman relaxed into its embrace. She waved to her men and ladies, who bowed and left the garden, returning inside. Only one man, the tall commander Paul met earlier, remained near the door. The long, curved knife still hung from his belt.

Dive in, thought the Scotsman, remembering his late father's advice. *Let's see what chess moves the enemy has for me today.*

The queen mother spoke in Twi, her voice strong and commanding. The younger woman turned to Paul and interpreted. "Great queen mother Yaa Akyaa say you come here for nothing. Ashanti people not English. Ashanti people not French. Not Spanish. Not Dutch. We Ashanti."

The earl had understood the queen's words perfectly well but decided to work through the interpreter for the moment. *Sometimes, feigned ignorance is a strength*, he told himself, thinking of his wise father.

"Your Majesty, I am honoured to meet you. You are known the world over as the greatest queen of all Africa, and your son, King Prempeh is the strongest warrior. My English Queen knows this."

After the girl translated the earl's words, the old woman answered in English, her tone angry. "Queen? Where is English Queen? She no come. Let her come! Then, we talk."

Paul was warned this might be the queen mother's response, but England had no plans to send their Queen to these shores. Even if she were willing, Victoria's advanced years and health made a long voyage impossible. Nor would the Prince of Wales agree to come. Prince Edward Albert, known as Bertie to family and friends, detested diplomacy. Besides which, the philandering Crown Prince had a tendency towards sexual escapades. It was probably best to leave the official royal family out of all negotiations.

Still, Paul could use an *unofficial* royal. He had discussed that possibility with Charles previously. The Duke expressed a sincere interest in following such a plan.

"Queen Victoria cannot come, Your Majesty, but I could bring our true King," he told the Ashanti royal in clear, precise Twi.

The Asantehemaa's eyes rounded in surprise. A smile widened her face, and she began to laugh. "You know Ashanti tongue?" she asked in English.

He smiled in return, using that dimpled flash of white that always made ladies swoon; and even here, that famous smile worked. "I endeavour to please, my lady," he told her with a courtly bow. "And so I speak your tongue."

The Asantehemaa slapped the cloth-covered table and declared in English, "You are man worth knowing, Lord Aubrey! Bold and direct! Pretty, too. Tell me about the true King."

"Your Majesty, in January of 1890, Duke Charles Sinclair became Shadow King of England as well as Reserve Emperor of India and all England's territories. He was hand-picked by Queen Victoria to serve as Shadow King. On the eleventh of January, he was anointed with holy oil and crowned by the Archbishop of Canterbury. Indeed, his blood is more royal and more true than any other ruler in Europe. I am honoured to act on HIS behalf."

"You act for this King?" she asked. "Not for old Queen?"

"I act for both, but I speak directly for King Charles. And I've brought you a gift, sent by His Majesty: a pair of magnificent Arabian stallions, chosen from the King's own stables. His horses are prized for their bloodlines, for they are like kings themselves."

"You bring horse kings? To my son, or to me?"

"To you, Your Majesty. I have other gifts for your royal son, of course, but I speak to you first."

She nodded to the younger woman and told her in Twi to leave. The girl bowed and crossed the courtyard to the door. She spoke to the guard, who opened the door. Both left.

Paul now sat alone with the most powerful person on the Gold Coast of Africa. If he succeeded in this mission, then he could help the queen's people avoid a fourth and surely final war with England; a war that would destroy the Ashanti nation forever.

Half an hour flew past, with Aubrey continuing to converse with the powerful queen mother of the Ashanti Empire. It was three o'clock by Paul's pocket watch, when a quartet of female servants joined them, carrying steaming hot baskets and golden bowls of local delicacies. Along with traditional English cuisine, they enjoyed yams, fish, plantains, flat bread with onions, roasted guinea fowl, water buffalo, boiled eggs, and lastly honeyed fruit and a chocolate drink.

As they finished the meal, the queen ordered the women to prepare the earl a sleeping chamber. Aubrey accepted the invitation and asked that someone go to Major Hodgson's home and collect his luggage. This was done, and by nightfall, Stuart had settled into a spacious bedroom on an upper floor of the palace.

His room looked east and offered spectacular views of the rain forest. From the balcony, he could see flocks of birds, bound for Lake Bosomtwe, thirty miles to the southeast. Paul opened the windows to let in the cool breeze.

The bed stood one foot off the floor. It was dressed in silks and animal skins and perfumed with precious oils. He imagined his cousin in the same room, perhaps one even finer, being fêted and fussed over as England's Shadow King. It had taken some time to explain the unusual office to the queen mother, but she eventually understood how much power and influence Paul's regal Cousin Charles enjoyed in England. The earl emphasised how thoughtful and generous King Charles might be, and that his only desire was for an equitable and peaceful balance, where both sides—English and Ashanti—might benefit. He warned the queen that some in England's government had grown impatient; that these men might force her son's hand through military means. The queen laughed at this, saying war was tried before, three times; yet she still ruled.

Then, after their meal, the Scotsman took the powerful ruler to see the gift the Shadow King had sent her: two Arabian stallions, presently housed at Major Hodgson's stables. Paul climbed into the saddle and demonstrated the clever horse's tricks, learnt at Sinclair's new Spanish-style riding school. The stallions leapt into the air and kicked with all four feet, as though flying. The old queen marvelled at such tricks and asked Aubrey to teach her men to ride in such a way, no doubt hoping to use them to military advantage over rival tribes.

Or against the English.

In the previous three wars, England's troops had assaulted the Ashanti and neighbouring tribes with traditional weapons and tactics. But ever since Sudan, the British Army employed a far more efficient way to rip a man apart: The Maxim Gun. These killing machines could fire six hundred rounds per minute and turn the tide of war by producing a *red tide of terror*. Paul shuddered at the thought, praying God would help the Ashanti rulers to imagine a better option for their people. If King Prempeh and his mother agreed to grant England sole rights to their ports, then Prempeh could sit securely on his throne. If not, British soldiers would pour through their settlements like a crimson flood. Prempeh and his mother would be deported; or worse, they'd both be dead.

As Stuart watched the palm trees sway, he sighed. Was this mission another poisoned pawn? Had he promised the queen too much? Did he dare bring Charles into the matter? He longed to talk with his father, just one more time. And what of his own son? Would Ian work for England one day? Would he serve as an agent for the inner circle and put his life on the line, over and over?

The earl knelt beside a small chair; his hands folded on the seat. And bowing his head, Paul Stuart began to pray.

CHAPTER TWENTY

Dusk's deep blues and purples had long since fallen across Kumasi, bringing with it a night chorus of chirping crickets, singing cicadas, and the distant cries of baboons. After an hour of prayer, Paul had drifted into a restless sleep. He tossed and turned, dreaming of Cozette and reliving the moment of her death—over and over again. Sometime after eleven, his eyes popped open. His muscles were tense, and every nerve registered high alert, but the troubling dream hung about his thoughts as he lay in the scented bed, surrounded by a veil of misty mosquito netting. Paul forced the dream aside and listened.

What woke him? Animals?

No. Voices. Conversation. Words.

Somewhere nearby, two men were arguing in Twi, and a third spoke in English. Then, someone shouted. He could hear men running. Paul wanted to rush to the balcony, but first he needed to discern the reason for the shouting. More arguments in English and Twi. More running, only this time closer; from the courtyard just below his balcony.

Finally, his brain shouted *action!* Paul pushed the filmy cloud of netting to one side. He latched on a pair of boots, buttoned up his shirt, and crossed to the balcony window. The Scotsman moved slowly, taking great care before emerging into the open. Experience made him wary of open invitations to a bullet.

A silver moon hovered over the palm trees. Below, he saw streaks of yellow light, where half a dozen men criss-crossed back and forth on the courtyard below. They were palace guards. Something worried them. Something had happened. Every nerve began to tingle, and the experienced spy readied himself to act.

He returned to the bedchamber and found his shoulder holster. Paul needed no light. He could disassemble and reassemble any firearm in pitch blackness, so he lit no lamps to give himself away. He made sure the weapon was fully loaded, then buckled the holster into place and pulled his arms through the sleeves of the linen jacket he'd worn earlier. After whispering a prayer, the earl ran a hand through tousled long hair and tiptoed from the bedchamber.

He followed a spice-scented corridor to a short staircase. Along the way, statues of fertility gods watched from niches. Carved totems stood guard alongside portraits of a crucified Jesus, the queen mother, and King Prempeh in a strange imitation of the Trinity. The Ashanti king was shown sitting beside the Golden Stool, the *Sika Dwa Kofi,* or 'the stool born on a Friday'. The throne was believed *to be a god itself*, for it descended from heaven and fell into the lap of the Empire's first ruler, King Okomfo Anyoke. The magic stool was the repository of all the Ashanti's ancestral dead: Past, present, and future. To control the stool, meant you controlled access to the dead.

It was a powerful image.

As Paul reached the courtyard doors, two men rushed towards him, their curved machetes raised. "Kill him!" shouted one in an Akan dialect. Paul sidestepped the attack and spun the attacker round, then pulled the man upwards, with a pistol to his head.

"Drop the knife, or I shoot you dead," Aubrey told the man in Twi. "The same for your friend, if he moves one foot! Do you want to die?"

The trapped thief dropped the blade. The second man followed. "Are you friend to True King?" asked the second man. "The British King Man?"

Paul said nothing, for he heard the scuttle of approaching feet. Dozens of palace guards rushed in from all directions, armed to the teeth with rifles, knives, and handguns. He recognised the tallest as the man who stood guard during his luncheon with the Queen.

The guard asked in English, "You okay, Highness?"

Paul nodded, then tossed the man he was holding to one of the shorter guards. "Yes, thank you. Take these men, and then we talk."

"Yes, Highness. Queen want talk, Highness. King talk. You come, yes?"

"I come, yes," answered the earl.

The palace guards took custody of the rival tribesmen, and Paul followed the tall guard to a private room. His guide bowed. "Queen come. King come. You wait, yes?"

"Of course. I wait, yes."

The guard left Paul in a rectangular chamber. A single window allowed the moon to cast pale beams upon a pair of chairs, set against the opposite wall. As with the upper corridor, he noticed rows of filled niches, containing figural representations of Ashanti gods and ancestors. Portraits of past kings dominated another wall, beginning with Osei Tutu, who'd established the Golden Stool monarchy, all the way through the current and thirteenth ruler, King Prempeh. Each painting was skillfully wrought and looked as though it could hang in a Parisian gallery. Candles and gold beads were laid before each painting, like offerings in a Catholic church, echoes of French and Portuguese influences.

I'm standing inside a chapel, he realised. *These thrones are part of an earthly assembly. The paintings represent the presence of the ancestors and the tribal gods. All this is an imitation of God's throne room.*

The doors opened, and the queen entered, followed by her son. King Otumfo Nan Prempeh, the first of his name, had ruled a united Ashanti Kingdom since March of 1888. *Odd,* thought the earl. *Prempeh took the throne just as Ripper began to terrorise London. And Prempeh is their thirteenth king. Charles would find the number a disquieting coincidence.*

A cold chill ran along his spine. Paul rarely had spiritual visions or intuitions like Beth and Charles, but now he did. A peculiar tingling ran along his back and coursed down to his hands. *Something is coming. Something terrible.*

He prayed silently as he waited for the royal family to speak. Once Prempeh assumed his throne, the queen began in English. "All is now well, Highness Paul Stuart. Two men from Fante tribes come. They try kill you. They pay great price. This my son, Prempeh, ruler of all Ashanti. True king of land you call Gold Coast."

Paul dropped to one knee; his head bowed. "Oh, great King Prempeh, I bring greetings from Her Majesty, Queen Victoria of England, Scotland, and Ireland—Empress of the British Empire."

"We welcome you, Highness Paul Stuart. You are blood of true King, yes?" asked Prempeh in English. He'd clearly dealt with Her Majesty's representatives before.

"I am blood of Charles, Shadow King of England."

"What is Shadow King?" asked Prempeh.

"Only true blood can make you King, is this not so?" asked Paul, still kneeling. "England's rulers have strayed from the true blood ties."

"Strayed? What is strayed?"

"May I stand, sir?" asked the earl.

The king nodded. Paul rose and put his hands together, the palms pressed closely. "See this? How my hands and fingers touch? Now, I make them stray." He moved the hands apart, the fingers fanning outwards. "England's rulers have blood that is far away from first blood. Charles is like this," he said, putting the hands back together, the fingers locked. "Charles is old blood. Ancestral blood that speaks, just as your ancestors speak through your blood. Shadow King's blood is true."

Prempeh nodded and pointed to the portraits. "I am true blood. Why the stray blood? It come from war?"

"Sometimes. King Charles is peaceful and wants only to bring prosperity to your people and to ours."

Prempeh glanced down at the magnificent golden stool to his left. Every square inch gleamed with metallic glory: The curved seat, where the *nsamanfo*, or ancestor spirits rested. And beneath that seat, stood a central pillar on a rectangular box that must never touch the earth. Finally, the chair bore a set of hand-crafted bells, used only by the gods, to warn the king of impending danger.

Aware of the legend, the earl silently thanked the Lord God Almighty for keeping the bells silent. He could sense angelic presences—but not all the spirits were good.

"This Charles," began the queen mother, "he is good man?"

"A very good man," answered Aubrey. "He is a beacon of light."

"Then, we meet this man!" declared the king. "Bring him here, Highness Paul Stuart. If he is blood to you, then he come, yes?"

Paul bowed. "If that is your wish, then he will come."

The queen stepped forward and touched the earl's head with a gold-embellished rod, used as a scepter. "We name you *Adamfo Pa,* good friend to us. Bring the true blood King on your ship of steam. You stay till he come."

"I shall write to him today, but the true King will not come unless I sail with him on the ship of steam."

"Why is this?" asked the queen, an edge to her voice.

"He and I are blood," he said, putting his hands together again. "I am guard. I protect him on the ship."

"But you here. Who protect him now?" the king asked from his raised throne.

"The Creator of all protects him, but King Charles and I are truest blood, made so by the Creator. He will not come, if I am here."

"Ah! Then, you must go," decided Prempeh. "Write the words and send them. You celebrate fullness of *Mawu* with us. Yes?"

"Mawu is the moon?" asked Aubrey.

"What you call moon, yes," the queen mother replied. "She watch over you and ship of steam till you bring True King." She smiled, her teeth rows of strong, straight pearls against the radiant mahogany skin. "Sleep now, *Adamfo Po*. Rest. We talk tomorrow."

The earl bowed deeply, the chestnut hair falling once more across his shoulders. He knew better than to speak again, for he'd been dismissed. He backed away and kept his head down as the queen, king, and golden stool (carried on a velvet cushion), vacated the audience chamber. Finally, the burly guards also departed. One man remained, the tallest guard in the magnificent hat.

"Come, *Adamfo Po*, I take you."

By the time Paul Stuart returned to the peaceful bedchamber, *Mawu* had risen high over the tall palm trees. Once asleep, he dreamt of a pale-skinned woman with large blue eyes and iridescent hair that flowed like shimmering moonlight upon a perfect body, a ghostly version of his absent wife. Paul clutched at the bed's tasseled cushions in his sleep. Even in the land of visions and dreams, he longed to be with Cordelia.

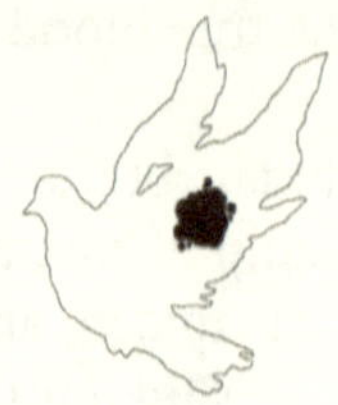

CHAPTER TWENTY-ONE

Brussels, Belgium - Hotel Metropole, 10:13 pm.

Lady Gemma Rosalind Smythe-Daniels (née Finchley) was thirty-two years old and recently married to inner-circle member Sir Percy Smythe-Daniels. Following the death of Gemma's brother Andrew, 3rd Baron Finchley, Gemma inherited half the Finchley estate, but the title passed to a second cousin. Since her husband served the Sinclair family, Gemma had joined the household as Elizabeth's travelling companion.

Some might describe Lady Smythe-Daniels as pleasantly rounded with a slim waist and well-formed arms. She had a flawless complexion, large grey eyes, a pretty mouth, auburn hair, and a soft voice. That evening found the baronet's wife weary from the long journey. She still wore her travelling dress but decided to see to the Duchess's needs before joining Percy in their own rooms.

"The hotel's quite nice, isn't it?" she asked the Duchess.

Elizabeth Sinclair sat before a warm parlour fire, reading a newspaper she'd found on one of the tables. "It's beautiful, not to mention miraculous that we secured reservations. The Metropole's not open yet, not officially."

"I imagine the Duke's name convinced management to open their doors early," answered Gemma. "And speaking of doors, Percy and I are in the adjoining suite. If you need anything, just ring." She placed a silver handbell on the Duchess's bedside table.

"I'm sure that won't be necessary, but it's a comfort knowing you and Sir Percy are close. What about Miss Grayson?" Beth asked, referring to her lady's maid. "I've not seen her since she unpacked my trunk. Did the hotel provide her a room?"

"Oh, yes. Grayson's right across the hall," Gemma answered. "Will you want a bath before retiring? Travel always leaves me feeling the need for one. I noticed a fine porcelain tub in the *en suite*. I could ask Grayson to fetch your special soaps, if you want. I think they're in the small blue case."

"Are they?"

"Of course. Everyone knows you don't like to travel without them," laughed Gemma. "I do love your soaps and perfumes, Elizabeth. I may visit your perfumer and have my own scent created. Which shop do you use?"

"Guerlain," answered the Duchess. "It's on the *rue de Rivoli*. Gabriel Guerlain and his wife Clarisse are geniuses. They've achieved the perfect combination of ingredients. Paul and Charles always call it raspberry-and-vanilla, because those scents strike the nose first, but there are other, more subtle notes as well."

"Such as?"

"Sorry, Gemma. I promised to keep their secret," she whispered. "I'm not sure the Guerlains are accepting new customers, though. I'll write you a letter of introduction and ask."

"That's very thoughtful, Beth. Oh, I am so tired! Warm water sounds lovely. I may take a bath, once Percy's returned."

"Has he gone?" asked the Duchess.

"You know my husband. As soon as he checked all our rooms, he left to tour the hotel grounds, no doubt looking for signs of trouble. Typical Percy."

"Wonderfully typical," Beth answered. "I always feel safe with Sir Percy nearby. Your husband reminds me of Charles. He gets that same look in his eyes when switching to his *inner-circle* persona. Very businesslike and commanding."

"It's one of the first things I noticed about him," Gemma answered happily as she crossed back through to join the Duchess. "And by that, I mean Percy. I never thought to marry, but God brought me an extraordinary husband, didn't he? Did you know Paul and I once courted?"

Elizabeth patted the sofa. "Come sit. Yes, I knew. Paul told me about it after I turned sixteen."

Gemma sat beside her friend. "I knew nothing about the arrangement twixt you and Paul back then. Truth be told, I don't think he ever really saw me as a future bride. We got on very well together—still do, but I think it was more a friendship than anything else. I wish Cordelia understood that. The last time we spoke, she seemed quite jealous."

Beth reached for Gemma's hand. "You mustn't let Delia's comments worry you. She doesn't mean them. Not really. Her mind works against her heart sometimes."

"Yes, I know," replied Smythe-Daniels with a sigh. "Where do we go tomorrow?"

"Frankfurt, assuming the railway connexions work as planned. If not, we'll overnight in Cologne. Charles made arrangements in both cities, just in case. Oh, I pray he's all right! He promised to write. I'd hoped to find a letter waiting when we arrived. Regardless, I shall write to him."

"Where's Charles staying?"

"At the Schönbrunn. I stayed there once with Grandfather, back in the autumn of '86. It's a breathtaking palace, though I doubt Charles will have time to sight-see."

"Beth, why is Charles in Vienna? Percy's been very hush-hush regarding the Duke's visit."

Beth sighed. "I'm not permitted to know either, Gemma. He's doing a favour for the Emperor, I think. But regardless of the reason, Charles promised to meet us in Coburg." The Duchess stretched outwards and arched her back. "You'd think, after three pregnancies, I'd grow used to backache. Wait until you're with child. You'll see. Travel always makes it worse."

"Shall I fetch Dr. MacAlpin?"

"No, leave Henry alone. He's exhausted. I don't think travel agrees with him either." The Duchess took a deep breath. "I shall need larger clothes again soon. This one's growing so very quickly." She reached for Gemma's hand. "I'm glad you're with me. Not just as companion. I'm glad you and I are friends."

"I'm glad, too," said Smythe-Daniels. "What's that you're reading?"

"A local paper. I found it on a table, next to the sofa. It's called *Le Libertaire* and seems to advocate violence against the ruling authorities. Its tone's rather militant. Is this the sort of thing the Metropole's management want guests to read?"

"Percy says there's unrest all over France. After the end of the Paris Commune, many of the *communards* escaped to Belgium. You can find anarchist sympathisers everywhere now."

"Charles sometimes talks about it. Do you suppose the man who set off the bomb at the Observatory held the same beliefs?" asked Beth. "This paper praises someone called Joseph Déjacque. I can't think why, but the name sounds familiar. Paul may have mentioned him once, years ago. Déjacque's portrayed as an anarchist poet, of all things. How can one combine the two? Gemma, do you think there are anarchist sympathisers here, in this hotel?"

"Of course not," said Gemma flatly. "The Duke would never have put us here, if there were. Charles is a very careful man, Beth. He would never put you in danger."

"Of course, you're right. Charles and I've talked about the rise in anarchy a few times, and it isn't going away. If we don't address it now, our children may face the possibility of revolution. Honestly, I sympathise with some of their complaints. If you and I'd been born into poverty, we might agree with all the socialists. I wonder, might some of our neighbours feel this way? The people living in Whitechapel, for instance? Should I talk with our hospital staff about it?"

Gemma folded the newspaper and set it aside. "It's impossible for us to understand all the thoughts of those living in poverty. What is it the Lord said? That we'd always have the poor with us?"

"Yes, but shouldn't we show compassion to those less fortunate? Once the Coburg wedding is over, I'll discuss it with Charles. I want to make sure all our staff and tenants, and all those working in our manufacturing houses are well treated and well paid."

"Beth, Percy and I've talked to everyone on your staff, from the kitchens, butlery, pages, maids, and sculleries, to every groundsman and tenant. All love you, and as to payment and provision, you and Charles pay higher wages and give far more freedoms than any other household in London; save, perhaps Lord Aubrey's."

"That's a comfort to hear, Gemma. Regardless, I plan to review all our policies with Miles and our head steward, Mr. Templeton." The Duchess closed her eyes, wincing as though in pain. "I shall take that bath you offered. The warm water might help my back."

"How far along are you?" asked Gemma.

"Sixteen weeks or thereabouts. What did you do with that anarchist paper?"

"It's here," said her friend. "Let me throw it away."

"No, I'll take it with me. I want Charles to see it."

"Shall I find Miss Grayson, then, and have her run a bath?"

The Duchess tapped her rounding abdomen. "Yes, I think so. I wonder if my waist will vanish entirely one day, the way Drina's has?"

"There is no chance of that," said her companion. "Beth, might you be carrying twins again?"

"I doubt it," replied the Duchess. "One set of twins is beating the odds, as my husband says. I just pray he's born full-term and healthy."

"You're not thinking of Delia's miscarriages, I hope?"

"Women do lose babies, Gemma. Poor Delia! Imagine miscarrying two children, then watching your six-day-old son convulse and die. It's no wonder her mind is broken."

"God watches over you and all your children, Beth. Those already born and those yet to be. And he's also with Delia. Those sweet babies are with the Lord now. That must comfort her."

"If only it would, but you're right. God keeps watch on all our children." Elizabeth reached out for her friend's hand. "Help me to this tub then. My feet are tight as drums already, and we've just begun our travels."

"Let's give those feet a rest, then, shall we?" Gemma said sweetly.

Beth spent half an hour in the raspberry-and-vanilla scented water. Gemma made sure the Duchess emerged safely, whilst Grayson laid out a blue silk night dress, trimmed in white Battenberg lace. The two women helped Beth into nightwear and placed the silver bell within reach.

"My room is just beyond that door, should you need anything," said Smythe-Daniels. "Percy and I are light sleepers. We'll hear the bell. Should you need anything, Beth, just ring. Anything at all. Even if it's just to talk."

"Thank you, Gemma. I will. Oh, but would you mind finding my lap desk? I'd like to write to Charles. Whatever he's doing now is probably dangerous. The last thing he needs is to worry about me."

"I know just where it is," said Gemma with a sisterly smile. "He'll be glad for the letter. Give Charles my best and let him know you're in safe hands with us. Tell him Lord Salperton's here to look after your medical needs. With all of us keeping watch, you're safe as a newborn lamb."

"Thank you, Gemma. I'm glad you're with me. But go on, now. I'll be fine. Spend time with your husband. And tell Miss Grayson to go to bed. We all need rest."

"I will. Goodnight, Beth."

"Goodnight, Gemma."

The companion curtsied, then disappeared through the connecting door, shutting it softly.

Taking up her pen, the Duchess began to write:

> My Darling Captain,
>
> Our party left Dover yesterday morning in clear weather and arrived in Brussels by six. The crossing was tolerable, though a storm tossed the steamship a bit. My stomach handled it with modest complaint.
>
> The Metropole is a beautiful hotel, Charles. Thank you for arranging the reservation. As you know, it's not officially open to the public yet. The manager, M'sieur Garnier, is most accommodating and speaks English quite well. He's placed us in lovely apartments on the top floor with spectacular views of the city.
>
> So that you are up to date, I shall list the members of our entourage (which changed by the hour as we prepared to leave London). The members of our group are:
>
> Myself, of course.
>
> Dr. Henry MacAlpin (per your orders)
>
> Sir Percy and Lady Gemma Smythe-Daniels.
>
> Captain Crenshaw and six ICI agents.
>
> Miss Jane Grayson, my new lady's maid (you met her the day you left for Paris)
>
> Hamish Granger, for driving and other matters
>
> Also, per your insistence, we've brought along Mrs. Paget to act as cook, should we need one. She's a dear lady and has never been to the continent; meaning, she's all eyes and constant chatter. Remember how well she and Auntie Drina got along last Christ-

mas? I'm sure they'll enjoy talking and playing cards on the train. We're meeting the Queen at Verviers, on our way to Cologne. As you know, she's coming up from Luxembourg, using one of your new ICI trains.

And best of all, our darling Adele will meet us there, too! Thank you for agreeing to let her attend. She's so very happy (as am I). Della's travelling on Drina's train with Tory and our sweet Uncle Reggie.

And per your request, Grandfather has taken the children to Glasgow. He so enjoys their company. He's a wonderful great-grandpa, don't you think?

I miss you terribly, Captain. Do be careful. Oh, and give my best to Lord Paynton and to Emperor Franz and Empress Sisi. Tell them I hope to see them again one day soon.

Until we meet in Coburg, my darling, please know my heart is never far away from your own. A golden line connects us, you see. And that line will last forever.

I'll write again tomorrow, dear heart.

All my love,
Your Beth

PS – I'm feeling quite well, so don't worry.

Elizabeth finished the letter by drawing a heart round her signature. She folded the pages into a pale pink envelope, then set the lap desk aside and switched off the electric lamp.

As she settled into the soft satin sheets, the Duchess gazed up at the room's coffered ceiling. How many children went to bed hungry tonight? How many mothers lacked milk to feed their infants? How many fathers could not buy bread?

The idea of starving children bothered her. The Duchess wondered if England might soon see the same kinds of work riots Belgium had suffered in recent years. Did London's boroughs conceal nests of incensed anarchists, who even now plotted the next bombing? She'd built a hospital in Whitechapel, but was it enough? Should she do more?

"Lord, if I am to do more, I ask that you show it to me, please," she whispered into the darkness. "You've given Charles and me so much. It's our duty to use those resources for your kingdom. Help us to be good and honourable stewards of your bounty."

Weariness overtook her, and Beth closed her eyes. Outside the windows, on the brick-lined *Place de Brouckère* she could the sounds of voices, carriage wheels, horse hooves, music, and public house revelries. The square stood on the ruins of an old convent; destroyed by French revolutionaries in 1796 and razed to the ground by anarchists. That supernaturally driven mob slayed men, women, and children with one singular aim: to remove the head of government and all who supported them.

They were *an-archos*. Without ruler.

An ironic truth, for supernatural events inevitably have a root in the plots of Archons.

A tapping sound caught her attention. Beth assumed it to be water in the pipes, settling or knocking in the bath next door.

But then, she heard a voice.

Come find me, it whispered seductively. *Come find US! We're very close. Just below, watching.* The tempter whispered in a deep, deliberate tone, almost penitent, hinting of velvety darkness and secrets.

Elizabeth never travelled without a Bible, and she reached for it now. Holding the book close, she shut her eyes and began to pray. "The Lord is my Shepherd; I shall not want..."

As if response, outside her window, a great white owl alighted above the busy square to keep watch from atop a streetlamp. Its round, unblinking eyes were icy blue. Occasionally, the owl flew over the hotel's roof, then circled slowly over the square, and back to the lamp-post.

The Watcher had seen chaos here before, a hundred years earlier. He'd seen war and mayhem far too many times. He remembered the old convent that once stood on this spot, and the nuns who prayed and sang here. He also remembered a battle that nearly defeated him—right here, ten thousand years ago, when he'd fought against a friend; a friend who rebelled.

Now, that same, cruel entity was returning.

The owl shut the strangely blue eyes and began to commune with his Maker, asking the One for guidance.

Something was about to happen.
Sen-Sen was cracking.
Something was coming.

Legion had found a way out.

CHAPTER TWENTY-TWO

Vienna, Austria

Charles Sinclair sat inside the royal box at *Theatre an der Wien*, a grand Empire-style edifice, built by Amadeus Mozart's friend Emanuel Schikaneder in 1801. Just over the theatre's main entrance, visitors could view a memorial sculpture called *the Papagenotor*, depicting the mythical birdman Papageno and the Three Boys. The boys represented child spirits that worked for Sarastro, high priest of Isis and Osiris. All were characters from the infamous Freemasonic opera, *The Magic Flute*, which Schikaneder co-wrote with Mozart.

That evening, the Duke and Lord Paynton occupied the prominent and plushly appointed royal box, courtesy of the Emperor. The air smelled of lilacs and gardenias, the scent wafting from the delicate petals of six floral sprays draped along the box's apron. That evening, the theatre was mounting a special performance of Mozart's *Flute.* Scene VII had just begun, with the hero Prince Tamino, standing outside the Temple of Ordeal, listening to the instructions of two armoured choristers singing of the difficult trials awaiting. If traversed correctly, the Temple's path would lead Tamino to ultimate enlightenment and apotheosis—a strong Masonic theme indeed.

The duet *Der Welcher wandert diese Straße voll Beschwerden* (in English, *He who walks this path, weighed down with cares*) took its inspiration from Martin Luther's hymn, *Ach, Gott, von Himmel sieh darein* (Oh, God, look down from heaven). Of course, neither the long-dead Mozart nor that evening's performers could have known how the idea of a human forced to walk an otherworldly maze to fight a monster might disquiet the gentleman now sitting in the royal box. Since Charles Sinclair spoke fluent German, he understood every lyric and every horrid implication. For a moment, memories of the Time Maze and Legion, the terrifying keeper, at its heart, crushed the Duke's spirit with such ferocity, that he suddenly left the box to find cleaner air in the corridor beyond the velvet curtain.

"Charles?" called Holloway as he followed his friend into the gaslit corridor. "Are you all right?"

"Yes," Sinclair whispered, his face turned to the wall. "Actually, no. I'm not."

"It's probably the flowers," suggested the viscount. "The perfume's too strong. It's giving me a crushing headache."

"I just needed air. Sorry to worry you, Seth. Perhaps, we should have waited till tomorrow night to come. It's been a long journey."

"I'll not complain, if we go back to Schönbrunn."

The Duke took a deep breath. He whispered a silent prayer. Leaving now was admitting defeat. No. He'd stay and do his job. Legion's taunts wouldn't pull him from God's true path.

Just one day at a time. That's all. Follow the Shepherd. Now, get back in there and smile.

"We should stay," he said. "Unless you prefer we go back? That headache you mentioned."

"It's not that bad," Seth answered with a smile. "Besides, I'm to stay close, remember? I promised Della."

"Yes, I remember." Charles said. *Seth's loyal, I'll give him that. Points for Paynton.* "Come on, let's go back in."

The well-dressed peers returned to their seats, with Charles in the chair closest to the stage. Below them, the stalls glittered with Vienna's finest: elegant men in bespoke evening suits and ladies in sartorial splendour with feathers, jewels, multi-coloured sequins, silks, satins, velvets, and enough perfume to fill a vat.

A slight shift in the ambient light and a soft fluttering sound caused Charles to turn round. The air had changed; the heaviness gone. Something had altered the atmosphere.

Not something. Someone. A third man had joined them.

"May I join you?" asked the newcomer.

"Good heavens, Ailesleigh!" exclaimed Haimsbury as the Cornish earl entered the royal box. "I'd no idea you were in Vienna. What brings you here? Who sent you?"

Lord Daniel Aaron Porter, 17th Earl of Ailesleigh (better known in the heavenly realms as the warrior *elohim* Hadraniel ben Ohr) had golden brown eyes and rich auburn hair, streaked with darker shades of sable. He was the same height as Sinclair, a smidge above six-foot-three, and the broad-shouldered physique cut quite a figure in white tie and tails. Ailesleigh's hair was longer than the last time they'd met. Previously he'd cut it short, but now it brushed the disguised angel's shoulders in poetic splendour.

"I hope I'm not intruding?" asked Ailesleigh, shaking the Duke's hand. "Good to see you again, Lord Paynton. I'm here on business. Imagine my surprise to learn you both were here tonight. It cost me fifty marks to convince an usher to lead me up here. But it's worth it."

"You heard about our visit?" asked Holloway. "How? It's supposed to be a secret."

"Dr. Holloway, Vienna has no secrets. Not in diplomatic circles," answered Ailesleigh. "But in this case, I heard it from a colleague. Prince Anatole. He and I are attending the Coburg wedding next month, and he asked me to call on the Russian embassy for him."

"Is the prince in the city?" asked Charles.

"No, he's dealing with a minor problem elsewhere," said Ailesleigh. "Ambassador Kapnist mentioned you'd be here. He and I were in a meeting this morning. Old Kapnist has spies all over the city, and he told me the famous Duke of Haimsbury and a fellow peer were in the city. I don't think Kapnist knew that friend was you, Lord Paynton. I just saw Kapnist in the lobby on my way in. He'll probably try to corner you and ask for money during the next interval. He's always broke."

"We'll keep our wallets close then," laughed Seth as he shook the newcomer's hand. "It's good to see you, Ailesleigh. You've missed the big setup to Tamino's test, but I imagine you've seen the opera before."

Daniel smiled. "Many, many times. In many theatres. I hope I'm not intruding?"

"Not at all," Charles said. "As you've paid fifty marks to get here, we can hardly refuse. Besides, it isn't our box. The Emperor arranged for us to use it, but with all the flowers and bunting, you'd think Franz and Sisi were here."

Ailesleigh laughed and took a chair. "It's your visit that's behind it, Charles. You've become quite a celebrity."

Indeed, word had spread. England's Uncrowned King had come to Vienna on his way to attend the royal wedding in Coburg. As a result, when the two peers had entered the main lobby earlier, Charles and Seth passed through a gauntlet of society ladies and courtesans, eagerly vying to make their acquaintance. Acting as an equerry, Seth ran interference, reminding each seductive woman that His Grace was happily married, and that his only reason for visiting Vienna was to enjoy the museums, not to taste its more *sensuous* pleasures.

"You could have kept your visit quiet," suggested Ailesleigh. "After all, staying at the Schönbrunn is hardly hiding. Reporters keep watch on all the activities there. You might as well have taken out an advertisement in *Weiner Zeitung*."

The Duke smiled as he glanced across the crowded theatre. An elderly woman in a feathered hat waved. Charles politely nodded. Another woman in the box opposite raised a black silk fan, allowing it to fully open—then, she quickly closed it and tapped the handle to her rouged lips. She smiled.

Seth placed a hand on the Duke's forearm. "Don't respond to that one, old man. She's just invited you over for a kiss."

Charles turned towards his friend. "How can you tell that from a simple wave?"

"She didn't wave," Ailesleigh chimed in. "Don't you read fan signals?"

Haimsbury shook his head. "I've no idea what you're talking about."

Seth laughed. "Finally, I can teach you something! It's an old idea that's fallen out of fashion in England. Beginning a century or so ago, a lady who wished to communicate with a gentleman didn't send notes, she used her fan. Resting it on the right cheek means *yes*. The left means *no*. Spreading the fan whilst held in the left hand means *come and talk to me*. Touching the mouth with the handle is asking for a kiss. As I said, don't wave back."

"Really? I wonder if Beth ever used fan signals?"

"Not with me," Seth answered. "And she rarely uses one anyway. That woman opposite has the look of a predator, so stick with me. I'll look after you."

Charles shrugged. "Perhaps, I should have kept my visit secret."

"Then why come to the theatre?" asked Ailesleigh.

"It's a notion Adele and I discussed last summer. Have you ever read Edgar Allen Poe's *Purloined Letter?*"

"Oh, yes," Seth answered. "In fact, Della and I read it out to one another a few weekends ago. Funny, she talked about applying it to spying. She's very clever."

"Yes, she is," Charles echoed, noticing the light in Seth's eyes when he mentioned his daughter's name. "But hiding in plain sight is sometimes the best way to conceal yourself. If we make a great show of our visit, then any quiet discussions we have on behalf of our client will be ignored. People will assume we're here to enjoy the opera, not to interview suspects."

"Client?" asked Ailesleigh, feigning ignorance—after all, he knew all about the Emperor's request. "Might someone *royal* be this, uh, client?"

"You might say that," Sinclair answered as he waved to another woman; this time, one sitting close to the orchestra pit and without a fan.

"And is the Emperor aware of your *Purloined Letter* conspicuity?"

"Conspicuity sounds like one of Count Riga's words of the day," laughed the Duke. "As to the Emperor, it was his idea for us to stay at the palace. Hardly conspicuous."

"Obviously," Ailesleigh joked. "Dr. Holloway, are you part of this purloined-letter investigation?"

Seth shrugged. "I do as I'm told."

"Charles gives the orders?"

"In part," Seth admitted. "The rest is because of a promise. I'm enjoying it thus far. I'd no idea sleuthing, as Della calls it, included attending the opera in a royal box."

"Seth's filling in as Watson to my Holmes," Charles explained. "Adele's become a theoretical investigator in the manner of Mycroft, and she sent Seth to keep an eye on me."

"And you're Holmes?" asked Ailesleigh. "I like that."

"Do you like it enough to join our expedition?" asked the Duke.

"You'd allow me to sleuth along with you? Oh, yes. I enjoy sleuthing, assuming it means what I think it does," replied the angel. "Are we talking about detective work?"

Charles nodded. "We are, and my first question is this: As our presence here is known, why did the theatre decide to mount *The*

Magic Flute? Two days ago, the newspapers were advertising *Die Fledermaus* as tonight's offering. Yet we're watching *Flute*."

"What does your Holmes intuition say?" asked Ailesleigh.

"It says the change was deliberate. In his introduction, the manager mentioned something about an orchestral issue, but his manner struck me as disingenuous. Have you noticed how *Flute* echoes my own recent history? I've tried to forget it all, but the Time Maze returns again and again in my dreams."

"You're referring to Tamino's journey through the labyrinth?" asked Daniel. "Yes, it's eerily similar to what you endured. I wasn't there, of course, but Anatole's related bits of it to me now and then. From your stories, I mean."

Charles knew Ailesleigh's true identity, of course, and marvelled at the elohim's ability to assume different roles; not just as the Earl of Ailesleigh, but as the faithful servant Fenwick. Hadraniel played each and every part well. How might Seth react if he knew the truth of the spirit entity behind the smiling guise; that an angel was hiding in plain sight?

Just then, a hand parted the velvet curtain of their box slightly. They could hear a uniformed usher, speaking to another man in German. "*Auf diese Weise, Eure Hoheit. Ich blaube Duke Charles ist auch hier.*"

The curtains opened wide, and a very tall gentleman entered and bowed. "Good evening, my friends. I apologise for arriving late."

"Well, this is another surprise!" said the Duke happily. "Ailesleigh told us you were elsewhere tonight, Your Highness, but you are always welcome. You're just in time to join our new sleuthing club."

Anatole Romanov handed several gold coins to the usher. The servant bowed and muttered a quick *Danke sehr, Mein Herr* and left them alone. Charles Sinclair had known the Russian prince for many years, yet Anatole Romanov remained mysterious and multi-layered. His height reached six-foot-eight. Black hair fell down a straight back and ended at a trim waist. But the image of Russian royalty was a façade, in the same way the Lord Ailesleigh *persona* allowed Hadraniel to interact with humans. Both angels had spent millennia behind various clay masks; sometimes, guiding God's chosen; other times, spying within the fallen realm's councils.

The spirit being masquerading as Romanov had hundreds, perhaps thousands of names, including Samael, a warrior prince and wielder of fire swords. Anatole had served as chief guardian to Charles Sinclair since the day he was born. The Duke had come to trust and admire the enigmatic elohim. However, Romanov's presence nearly always presaged trouble.

We're coming, the limping Piper had told his son. *Tell your father, we're coming—that we're already here.*

"Join us, please," the Duke told Romanov. "It's nearly the interval, and we're deciding how best to begin our mission."

The angel smiled. The ice-blue eyes twinkled. "It is why I've come, Charles Robert. I should enjoy being part of this new sleuthing club. And I like the idea of starting a mission. Somewhat like angels, no?"

Seth laughed. "I get the joke. Messenger angels, right? If only we had such powerful beings to help us, but I imagine ICI investigations require more brains than brawn. That's a happy truth, for I'm not as skilled a boxer as you and Aubrey, old man."

"Old man?" asked Charles, smiling. "Just remember you said that when you're asking my help. But you're right. Brains are paramount to solving crime—reasoning through all the information at hand."

Romanov's eyes glittered. "You've seen the 1420 ledger?"

"You know about that?" Seth asked, his freckled face open with surprise.

"Twas I who suggested it to the Emperor," replied Romanov. "As to investigation stratagems, I find a steady hand and keen eye are also required. Let us consider this opera. *The Magic Flute* echoes the Duke's recent trials, yes?"

"You know about those, too?" asked Seth.

Ailesleigh provided the answer. "Anatole and I work very closely together. You might say we are also sleuths."

Romanov laughed. "In Russia, it is *sphion*, a spy. Or *shyschik*, as you say, a sleuth. Or *sledovatel*, an investigator, yes? Daniel and I serve in all these ways, do we not?"

Ailesleigh nodded, a soft smile lifting the corners of his smooth upper lip. "I'm honoured to say we do, yes. What did you wish to say about the opera?"

"Ah," said Anatole, "allow me to explain. There is a strange, twisting plot, rather like the undulating serpent seen at the beginning. We see broadly drawn archetypes: The beast, which is the serpent. The innocent maiden, Pamina. The hero, Prince Tamino."

"Is our Duke the hero in this comparison?" asked Ailesleigh.

"As regards the Time Maze, indeed, yes. It is interesting, that Tamino means 'lord' or 'master', and Charles means 'free-man', used for former servants. Terms that are alike, yet opposite."

Seth was intrigued. "And the opera has its own opposites. Opposing archetypes, I mean."

"Like the wizard Monostatos?" asked Charles. "He is depicted as overtly evil. His opposite is Sarastro, the wise man who helps the hero."

"Indeed," said Romanov. "Numerically—and you will appreciate this, Charles Robert—we have repeated groups of three, symbolic of a Freemasonic metaphor. Three ladies, three spirits, three priests."

"Three slaves," said Ailesleigh. "If this is sleuthing, I like it. It's rather like solving a puzzle, isn't it?"

"That is more apt than you might imagine," said Romanov.

"And Papageno?" asked Holloway. "He's an odd little creature. Is he a hybrid archetype?"

"Papageno is difficult to categorise, when using mythical archetypes, Lord Paynton, but hybrid is a good guess," said Romanov. "Neither man nor animal, and unable to find a mate."

"You're right," said Paynton. "This sleuthing is like an addictive puzzle. What else?"

Romanov took a moment to smile at a waving child. The girl sat with her parents near the centre of the stalls. She had golden curls and a sad expression. Seeing the prince, she began to laugh and wave her small hands. The angel waved back and asked the One to watch out for her. He foresaw difficulties in the girl's future.

Turning to the men, the angel answered the viscount's question. "Forgive me. I can never resist a child's smile. The 'what else', Lord Paynton, is Princess Pamina, our damsel in distress. However, in this case, it is her own mother, the Queen of the Night, who places her in danger. Now, consider these archetypes. The Priest Sarastro and the Queen of the Night. In the opera, one is good and one evil. Sarastro serves Isis and Osiris. He possesses a powerful talisman called the Circle of the Sun. The Night Queen believes this talisman is hers, and she tricks her daughter into recovering it. As part of her plot, the Queen gives Prince Tamino a Magic Flute—hence the opera's title. To Papageno, she gives bells. Both instruments play a role in the battles to come."

"Might the Queen represent the Moon?" asked Seth. "If Sarastro owns the Sun, so to speak, then might the Queen own the Moon?"

"One might say that," Romanov replied, his eyes on the Duke, who'd gone quite pale. "You look unwell, Charles Robert. Shall I send for someone?"

Haimsbury's troubled gaze was riveted on the stage, but his thoughts were far away. *Music. Moonlight. Maze.* These three words had triggered horrid memories that shook his soul. Suddenly, he wanted to leave—to find his wife and children and shut them away, where they'd be safe from Music, Moonlight, and that horrid Maze!

I should be with Beth. What has Prince Rudolf's death to do with me? And why are these two angels here?

A gentle hand touched the Duke's shoulder. "Charles Robert?" asked Romanov's deep voice. "Charles?"

He snapped back to the present. "Yes, sorry, Anatole. My mind wandered. Lack of sleep, I imagine. You were saying?"

"It is of no importance. Perhaps, we should simply watch and listen."

The men and angels relaxed into their chairs, whilst on stage, the Three Spirits—represented as boys, but sung by young women—conveys Tamino to Sarastro's temple. The hero, Prince Tamino, tries three different doors, but only the centre way opens. A priest appears (called The Speaker in the playbill). He assures Tamino that Sarastro is good, not evil, as the Queen of the Night has claimed. He wishes only to help the Princess Pamina.

Tamino plays his flute, and to his surprise, all the animals obey him. Tamino responds with the aria *Wie stark ist nicht dein Zauberton* (How strong is thy magic tone).

Charles tried to watch, but his mind was elsewhere; drawn back to the Time Maze. He could hear the incessant ticking and the scuttling rats, smell the damp air, feel the stone floor beneath his shoes—the heartache of weary, endless walking.

He relived each of the locked rooms.

I watched Beth die. She had twins, then she died.

Somewhere beyond the inner turmoil, a gentle voice broke through the spell. Anatole whispered, not audibly, but into his mind. *She didn't die, Charles Robert. Not truly. The real Duchess is very much alive, and she bears two more sons within her. Two great oaks. Twins! Think on that, my friend. The One is with you. You are NEVER alone.*

Hadraniel's voice followed, using the lilting Scottish accent of the ever-faithful Fenwick, the servant who'd looked after Charles in Theseus's Castle.

Don't relive it, sir. Legion wants you to slip back there. He uses the music to lure you into an endless spiral. Don't let the past drag you into his trap. Press ahead and follow the Shepherd. Listen to Him, sir, listen!

"Mein Herr?" called a new voice. It was an usher. "Sir? Your Grace?"

The Duke broke from the strange reverie and took a deep breath. "Yes, of course. Sorry. What is it, young man?" he asked in English.

"A message for you, my lord."

"Thank you," answered the Duke as he took the folded note. "Does the sender require an answer?"

"No, sir."

Charles gave the man a coin. The usher bowed and left, shutting the soft curtains.

"Who's it from?" asked Seth.

Charles held up bit of paper. "I'm not sure, but it's certainly elaborately folded. Like a paper puzzle."

"That's because it's locked," said Romanov.

"Locked?" asked Holloway. "Wait, I remember! The Elizabethans used to fold secret messages into very elaborate forms, didn't they? It's a clever way to keep the contents safe from enemy eyes. I've never seen a modern version. Is this the first leg of our investigation, Holmes?"

"Perhaps," muttered the Duke. "Let's see what it says."

The fascinating missive was carefully folded, over and over, until it formed a square, then the package was tied with a black ribbon to hold it in place. On the exterior, written in bold black ink, it read:

HRH Duke of Haimsbury and Branham, personal.

Charles sorted through the many folds and unsealed the message. "It's a paper labyrinth."

"Strangely apt, considering the opera," said Holloway.

"Hmm, yes," the Duke whispered. The note opened into a creased sheet of cream rag linen. Inside, were instructions, penned by the same bold hand:

Come to the Don Giovanni Salon after the curtain.
I'll introduce you to Vienna. – An old friend.

"Seth, would you ask that usher to come back? I think he's loitering near the entrance to our box."

The viscount left and spoke briefly in German, then returned, leading a different usher from the first. This one was younger, no more than twenty. He bowed and asked in accented English, "You need me, Highness?"

Charles had grown used to being addressed as Highness and answered, "You speak English? Good. Tell me, young man, what is your name?"

"Hans, sir. Hans Brünner. My father, he is conducting the orchestra tonight. Herr Jacob Brünner."

"Your father's an excellent conductor," said Haimsbury. "Did you happen to see who sent this letter? Another usher delivered it, but might you know who wrote it? A man? Woman?"

"Ja, Highness, I know. I see, yes? Was woman. She is with man, also. They come together. I see them many times."

"Do you know their names?"

"No, Highness. Not so, but maybe. I hear things, yes? Someone talk to man. Call him *Herr Doktor*."

"Interesting," said Haimsbury. "And this room, the Don Giovanni Salon. Is it large or small?"

"Very large, Highness. There is party, after last curtain. Many great peoples come. If please, sir, I give answer for you."

"My answer?" Sinclair mused as he glanced at his three companions. "Well, as this party will be attended by many great people, how can we refuse? Please, tell the sender we shall be pleased to attend." He passed two *gulden* to the lad, who grinned broadly.

"*Danke sehr*, Highness! Thank you! Is most kind!"

As the curtains closed behind the departing usher, Holloway took the note and read it. "Do you think this has something to do with our mission?"

"I've no doubt it does," replied Charles.

"But it might prove dangerous?"

"I don't doubt that either. There's a deep mystery opening before us, Watson. Are you in or out?"

"Most definitely in, Holmes," Seth answered. "Ailesleigh? Prince Anatole? In or out?"

"We are both in," answered the Russian, a twinkle to his eyes. "It is fortuitous we arrived when we did."

Charles placed the note into his pocket, saving it as evidence. After all, this was an ICI investigation. If he uncovered a plot involving the two deaths in Mayerling, then he'd need forensic evidence that would stand up in a court of law. Assuming it ever came to that.

"Lord Paynton, consider this your first lesson in police work," he whispered. "Those whom we hunt, will also hunt us. When you flush out your prey, you place yourself in danger."

"And if our blind is compromised? If the prey sees us?" asked Ailesleigh.

"No matter. We are still under God's protection. He is our shield," Charles replied. "We have until the final curtain, so let's enjoy the rest of the opera. We're supposed to be here as tourists, remember?"

The opera unfolded with more scenes resonant of Sinclair's time in Legion's Maze. And as with his own experience, the two lovers, Tamino and Pamina, faced a series of ordeals. The Duke wondered what inspired Schikaneder and Mozart; what muses whispered to them?

The Queen of the Night echoed the personality of Princess Eluna. And Sarastro, the solar high priest, initiated members into a great Brotherhood of the Sun through a ritual that would surely delight Eluna's conceited brother-husband, the fallen angel Araqiel.

As the curtain fell on final bows, the Duke's hands began to tingle with the same electric charge that so often foreshadowed spiritual encounters.

Just who am I meeting at this party? he wondered. *Lord, you are the Good Shepherd. I will follow where you lead.*

CHAPTER TWENTY-THREE

Gold Coast, West Africa

After spending the next day with Major Hodgson and the Ashanti queen, Lord Aubrey was invited to a ritual few Europeans had ever witnessed. Stuart and Hodgson were instructed to eat no meat, then bathe and prepare themselves by allowing a team of female servants to anoint their hair and hands with fragrant oils meant to purify their thoughts and deeds. As night fell, the women dressed the men in special clothing, scented with the same special oils.

As they left for the ritual site, the full moon began to rise above the horizon. The men were blindfolded and led along a path covered in flower petals. As they walked, their bare feet crushed the flowers, sending a heady scent into the cool night air. They proceeded along the flower-strewn avenue, flanked by white-robed priests whose ebony arms and faces glistened in the pale moonlight. They walked like ghosts amongst the living, never speaking a word. The blindfolded foreigners could hear sounds of the forest at night: the mad laughter of striped hyenas, the chittering talk of mangabey monkeys, and the disturbing cries of the aposor, often called bushbabies for their perfect imitation of a human child's cry.

Paul also recognised the rustling of a much larger predator, passing through the underbrush. A leopard? Lion? Hyenas, or a pack of wild dogs, looking for an easy meal? Aubrey prayed that he and Hodgson weren't on the menu.

When at last their blindfolds were removed, Paul blinked to clear his eyes. They stood beside Lake Bosomtwe, its still surface a black mirror. Within that sleek, dark water-glass, floated the face of *Mawu*, goddess of the moon: creator of the earth, animals, and all Ashanti peoples.

A priest approached and spoke to them in Twi. Major Hodgson's knowledge of the language was rudimentary, so Aubrey interpreted.

"What was that?" whispered the Major as they reached a blackened formation near the edge of the forest. "Did he say something about a sacrifice?"

"It's a ceremony for Mawu, the moon goddess," Stuart explained. "And yes, there's to be a sacrifice, but not us, at least that's not implied. Probably grain and fruits. My father and I watched a similar ritual about twenty years ago. The priests released blood into the fires."

"Whose blood?" asked Hodgson nervously. "Ours?"

The earl kept a close eye on the priests. "I'm not sure. Back then, a young woman cut her forearm and let the blood drip into a golden bowl. If I understand the history correctly, such blood rites are now forbidden. It's possible these priests are running a secret cult."

"A cult?" the Englishman whispered tensely. "Paul, could it be the queen isn't as pleased as you thought? We're in the middle of nowhere. She could have us killed and blame our deaths on a cult of crazy priests."

"Yes, that's possible," whispered the earl.

A young woman approached. She was dressed in a gauzy white sheath. A six-inch wide, lunar crest of pure gold, hung from her mahogany throat. She was ethereal, exquisitely beautiful, like a river nymph come to life. Paul stared at her intense eyes and delicate features. Each of the Gold Coast tribes had unique physiognomies. Ashanti women possessed a regal bearing unlike all others. The memory of the slender girl's beauty would stay with the Scotsman for the rest of his life.

She smiled and knelt before him, speaking softly in broken English. "You no fear?"

"No fear," he declared, silently praying her question had nothing to do with the sacrifice of two foreigners.

Again, she smiled, the straight white teeth set off by the glorious sheen of her skin. "Mawu like you, Aubrey of England. You talk to true King, yes?"

"Yes, I will talk to England's true ruler, King Charles."

"You bring back, yes?"

"I will bring him back."

She stroked his cheek and ran her fingers through Stuart's chestnut locks. "Pretty," she said. "Is called *haar?*"

"Hair," he whispered. "It's called hair."

"I like. Mawu like. I speak for her."

"You speak for the moon?" he asked, pointing up at the pale round orb that floated above the glassy lake.

She nodded. "Mawu talk. I hear. You watch, yes? Big magic now. Big magic."

The girl pulled Paul to his feet. The earl obliged, allowing the young priestess to guide him to the edge of the bonfire. She was taller than Cordelia; five-foot-six or so. Like Paul, she was barefoot. The six-foot-three Scotsman towered over her as they approached the crackling pyre.

"You watch. Tell King we strong. Tell him, Mawu is strong. She wait for him."

"I'll tell him everything that happens," promised Aubrey, praying in silence. *Lord, please, help me to be a witness of your power and glory. I beg you to intercede for all who stand here now. Free them from these pagan chains.*

The drumming began. Men and women danced to the infectious beat. The jungle sounds seemed to coordinate and complement the percussive invocation, for the monkey chatter served as syncopation to the persistent drums. Teams of white-robed priests brought basket after basket of grain and fruit to the fire and threw them in, bowing afterwards as they awaited Mawu's pleasure.

"Mawu like you," said the young woman. "She want King close. Like Lisa."

"Lisa?" asked the Scotsman. "Who is Lisa?"

"He Mawu's man. Brother. He shine in day. Yellow King. She shine in night. White Queen. Your King come and meet Mawu. Join with us."

Paul thought carefully before answering. If the girl's words meant what he feared they did, then this cult wanted Charles to come to Africa and share in a fertility ritual as a representative of the sun. Was this what the Ashanti royal family wanted? Was the queen part of this strange moon cult, or were they witnessing palace intrigues beyond the royals? Might one of these priests hold greater power than the queen?

Lord, what do I say?

"King Charles will come, but he will not be Lisa. The King is more. His God is more. His God is greater."

She frowned. "He no be Lisa?"

"No. King Charles knows a very powerful God. He will talk to him first."

Her smile returned. "King Charles talk to his god. He come. Mawu happy. You watch. Listen. Hear Mawu speak."

She moved away, and Paul remained where he stood, fearing any other action might be misunderstood. *Lord, why am I here? My wife needs me. I should be with her, not in Africa watching this pagan ritual! Please, show me why I am here!*

The drumming grew louder. The priests and priestesses danced wildly round the flames, their arms and limbs rising up and down with the rhythm as they cried out to their goddess. Paul looked back at Hodgson, making sure the territorial governor was still unharmed. The major nodded. The poor man looked decidedly confused.

Paul had been just nineteen years old, when he and his father made the brief tour of the Gold Coast in the summer of 1875. The third Anglo-Ashanti War had just ended, and Robert Stuart was sent to negotiate a settlement with King Mensa Bonsu, tenth ruler of the Ashanti Empire. Both Paul and his father attended numerous rites and celebrations but saw nothing like this. Nothing.

This must be a secret ceremony, he reasoned. *How much power do these priests hold? Are they for or against the current rulers?*

The sharp cry of a bushbaby broke his concentration. Paul's head turned. The drumming had quickened, as if responding to the animal's unsettling cries.

But it wasn't a bushbaby. Not this time.

A group of white-robed priests had entered the clearing. Their dark, bare feet pressing into the floral carpet sent nauseatingly sweet incense into the cool night air.

Perhaps it was what they carried that sent the Scotsman's stomach into knots. Not a bushbaby.

A human baby.

A crying infant, wrapped in a sheath of gauzy white and held aloft by the lead priest. Paul could see tiny hands and feet, wriggling beneath the cloudy cloth. Was this to be a blood offering? Did the men intend to prick the infant's skin and drain a few drops as appeasement to the goddess, whom the the Ashanti believed created all life?

Blood is the life.

Or had the ceremony turned dark? Had it twisted to a more sinister purpose?

All the priests began to chant. Paul listened carefully, silently thanking the true Creator, that he knew enough of their language to discern the priests' intent. The baby was a gift; offered to the flames, to appease and invoke the sun god, Lisa, twin and consort to Mawu.

Aubrey didn't stop to think.

Not for one second. He acted.

A desperate cry burst from his mouth.

"STOP!" he shouted in Twi. "No! You cannot do this!"

Every head turned to stare in his direction. The beautiful young woman frowned. The tallest man, presumably the high priest, shouted angrily in Twi, speaking so rapidly that Paul caught only parts of it, but the tone was unmistakable.

Four armed guards surrounded the foreigners. One thrust a long, curved blade into the earl's face.

The chief priest stepped close, the baby still in his arms. "Why say stop?" he asked in fairly clear English.

"Because Mawu will be angry if you kill this child," replied Paul with as much confidence as he could muster.

"Mawu be happy," argued the other. "Why you say angry?"

Paul whispered a prayer for guidance, then said, "Because the King Charles will not come, if you do this thing, and Mawu wants to meet him."

The priest's regal back straightened. A series of quick computations passed through his strong features, as he considered all possibilities. "The true King no come?"

"He will not come," answered the earl firmly. "Not if you kill this child. King Charles does not want such things. He will be very angry."

The priest beckoned to the beautiful young woman who'd previously talked with Stuart. He spoke to her in Twi, then handed her the squirming infant. The girl approached the earl, saying, "Mawu say she King's now. You take girl to King Charles, yes? Tell him, she safe, yes?"

Paul took the infant without a second thought. "I take her?"

"Take. She go to the King Charles. She gift."

The logical side of Paul's brain wanted to argue, but his heart knew he had no choice. If he refused, the baby would die. "Yes, I'll take her to the King Charles. Tell me, what is your name?"

"Abena," she answered. "Abena Mawu."

"Like the Tuesday Moon?" asked the earl.

She smiled. "Yes. I serve Mawu. She speak. I hear. Mawu happy you take baby."

He pulled back the gauzy fabric and glanced at the child's face. To Paul's surprise, she looked more European than West African. Ever since the fifteenth century, foreign colonists had intermarried with local women, producing offspring called *mulattoes* by the Spanish and Portuguese. The term was a corruption of *muwallad* or *muladi*, words used in the Peninsula to mean *born of two tribes*. Originally, the term referred to a mixture of Spanish and Arab blood, but since those early days of Portuguese colonisation, the Spanish, Germans, French, and English had arrived and intermixed with locals, resulting in entire tribes and family groups with light skin.

"Where is her mother?" he asked, wondering if her skin colour marked her for sacrifice. "Is this baby Ashanti?"

The priestess smiled. Her manner was unsettlingly cool, as though the idea of killing an infant were routine. *How many others may have died in such a way?* he wondered.

"Not Ashanti. Baby mama dead. Baby papa dead. You take, yes?"

"I take, yes, but you must not kill any more people. No babies, no children, no adults, no one. The great and powerful God of King Charles will be angry."

Doubt shadowed Abena's face, and she spoke to the priest in Twi. Paul could see a flicker of doubt in the tall priest's eyes. He repeated her words to the entire congregation. A murmur passed through the assembly.

Abena Mawu turned back to face the earl, offering another of her spectacular smiles. "We no kill the human peoples. But you bring the King Charles *and* your God to us. Then, we talk, yes?"

"I will bring them," he told the woman. "The King Charles and his God."

Paul held the baby close as Abena led him back to the area closest to Hodgson. The two men witnessed the remainder of the ceremony without incident. Fruits, grains, and a golden cup—filled with a priest's blood, willingly offered—were cast into the flames. The indifferent moon watched from the midnight heavens; her pale face reflected in the lake's black waters.

Stuart remained one more day with the Ashanti people. He sent a coded telegram to ICI headquarters in London, instructing them to forward his report to Haimsbury at once. As the morning of the final day dawned, the earl bid farewell to the queen mother and her son, King Prempeh. Both rulers reminded Paul of his promise to bring the true King Charles to Kumasi very soon. Paul explained that his cousin was presently in Austria, and their earliest departure would be late summer.

To Stuart's relief, they accepted his words.

Lord Aubrey left the Palace compound, along with three unexpected passengers: a six-day-old baby girl, a quarter-caste wet-nurse and an English-German governess. By nightfall, their ship entered the open sea, bound for Portsmouth.

Now, how to explain it all?

CHAPTER TWENTY-FOUR

11:30 – Vienna, The Don Giovanni Salon

Charles Sinclair stood near the entrance to a magnificent salon, accompanied by Paynter and Ailesleigh. Romanov had gone ahead without explaining why. Even in human form, the warrior possessed an otherworldly, out of sync manner. As usual, he'd defied all convention and worn fashion of his own choosing, harking back to Muscovite uniforms of a century earlier. He'd chosen a military costume of red silk, decorated down the front with horizontal rows of braided gold thread. A bright blue sash ran from his left shoulder to the right hip. On the sash, he'd pinned the Star of St. Petersburg, a high-ranking chivalric honour equal to the Order of the Garter in England. A pair of neatly folded, white gloves hung from the gold-edged belt. All told, the Russian was far more splendid than any man in the salon, with one exception: Duke Charles of Haimsbury.

As the Duke would be attending several royal and high-society events whilst away, his former butler, Chief Inspector Cornelius Baxter, instructed Sinclair's valet to pack the Duke's royal orders, medals, and sashes. Tonight, Charles wore the Order of the Garter Star, accompanied by six ribbons of the Haimsbury Regiment and two from the Lord High Admiralty. The canvas for the impressive regalia was a silk black cutaway coat and rolled-collar waistcoat fashioned from gold Paisley. A deftly tied French bow of the same gold silk wrapped round his throat to set off the crisp white shirt beneath. A gold chain and Haimsbury crest fob hung from the waistcoat's pearl button, with the Duke's Sir John Bennett resting neatly in the watch pocket. Charles looked every inch a King.

"Shall we mingle?" he asked his companions.

Prince Anatole had the clearest view of the crowds, for he stood a head taller. “This is a high-class soirée, but I sense danger, Charles. Stay close.”

“There must be a hundred people in here,” answered Haimsbury. “Too many witnesses for major trouble.”

“One hundred-and-sixteen,” corrected Romanov. “That is the number of humans.”

Charles stared at the disguised angel. “Do you include yourself?”

“Of course not,” he smiled. “Be careful.”

“Always,” replied Haimsbury, “but if I’m to meet the note’s sender, we’ll need to work the room. Seth, go right. Ailesleigh, take the left. Anatole, I’ll leave you to your own discretion. I’m going to try my hand closer to the middle. I recognise someone.”

“Shouldn’t I go with you?” asked Seth. “I did promise to look after you.”

“Tell Adele I ordered you,” laughed Haimsbury. “Besides, I’m armed, remember? See if you can get to know a few of these people. Ask questions about Rudolf.”

Ailesleigh whispered before leaving, using Fenwick’s voice: “The Prince and I are never far away, sir. Should you require us, just pray.”

He and Paynton left to follow instructions.

Alone with Romanov, Charles turned to the disguised angel. “You only mentioned the number of humans. I presume there are other types as well?”

“I cannot say how many others there are, for the population varies. Yet there is a dark presence. An old intelligence, somewhere nearby. Ah, good evening!” the Russian said as a pleasantly plump woman approached them. “Lady Farnsworth, it is always an honour. I was sorry to hear of Lord Farnsworth’s passing.”

The flaxen-haired widow was tall, with fine features, bright blue eyes, and a claret mouth. Her ample curves were modestly wrapped in a sweeping gown of midnight-blue crepe, adorned with white rhinestones.

“That’s kind of you, Your Highness,” the widow said to Romanov. Then she asked in a whisper, “Is this Duke Charles of England? Anatole, would you introduce me?”

“Of course,” answered the prince. “Charles, allow me to introduce Lady Marguerite Farnsworth. Her husband, Lord Michael

Farnsworth, died of consumption last year whilst at a sanitorium here in Vienna. It is a tragic loss to diplomacy. Marguerite is my fourth cousin, by way of a cadet branch of the Romanov family, the Vershinin. Cousin Marguerite, may I introduce His Royal Highness, Prince Charles, Duke of Haimsbury."

The Duke took the woman's hand and bowed slightly. "An honour, Lady Farnsworth."

The handsome widow curtsied and lowered her head in deference. "The honour is all mine, Your Highness," she said in perfect English. "I'm Austrian by birth, but my late husband was English, as you've probably guessed from the name. We lived near York. Michael died at the Wienerwald. They specialise in consumption treatment. I've always been so very healthy, yet poor Misha—that's what I called my husband—well, he was never robust. I live with my brother now, near Belvedere Palace."

"I'm sorry for your loss, Lady Farnsworth," said Haimsbury.

"You must call me Marguerite, Your Highness."

"Only if you call me Charles," he answered with a bright smile. "The salon's certainly crowded."

"Yes, it is," she said, turning to wave to a passing gentleman. "I'm familiar with most of Vienna society, but many of these people are strangers. No doubt they're all hoping to glimpse England's Shadow King."

"In my heart, I'm a simple policeman," he laughed.

"A policeman?"

"It's a long tale, Marguerite."

"I look forward to hearing it," she replied. "You and Anatole are friends?"

"Very good friends," answered the Duke.

"Charles and I've known one another for many years," Romanov said, stepping aside to let a heavily laden servant pass. As he moved, the long black hair swept across the Russian's face, causing the widow to laugh.

"Anatole, you really must tie up that hair, or else cut it. Though I can't imagine you with any other style, can you, Duke? My cousin's always been the epitome of chivalry and charm. Rather like the old Russian princes, minus the beards, of course."

"I prefer a clean face," whispered the disguised angel. "But, alas, the Duke and I must leave you, Cousin. We're to meet an old friend."

"Do stay out of trouble," the widow replied with a wink. "Duke Charles, I hope we'll meet again."

"As do I," said Haimsbury with a slight bow.

Once Lady Farnsworth departed, Charles stood silently, observing the well-heeled members of Vienna's elite classes. The Don Giovanni salon was an immense, rectangular room, each wall filled with colourful scenes from the titular Mozart opera, including several paintings of the infamous gigolo with two of his conquests, Donna Anna and Donna Elvira. One panel depicted a duet twixt Giovanni and Donna Anna's father, the Commendatore—a General who is slain by the predatory Italian. The artist painted the dead father in hues of pale blue and chalky white to emphasise his ghostly presence. The mouth was open and stretched, as though the baritone-bass voiced an impossibly low note. His hands reached out towards Giovanni, fingers elongated in similar fashion to the mouth, as though indicating abilities beyond the human. The final panel depicted the moment Giovanni is pulled down to Hell.

The crowded salon rang with clinking glasses and conversational voices in several languages. The air smelled of cigars and champagne, mixed with the heady scents of men's cologne and ladies' perfume.

A liveried servant approached the two visitors, carrying a tray of filled glasses. "Champagne, meine Herren?"

Romanov shook his head, but Charles took a delicate flute of the bubbly wine, saying, "Danke. *Sprichst du Englisch?*"

"Ja. I mean, yes, my lord."

"Good," answered the Duke with a bright smile. He concealed his mastery of German, for the pretence allowed him to eavesdrop on unguarded conversations. "I wonder if you might help me. I've received a note, you see, and..."

The question was interrupted by the arrival of a woman in scarlet. She was Elizabeth's height. Intricately arranged red tresses gave the impression of greater height. Crimson taffeta capped her shoulders and a glittering bustier outlined a modestly ample bosom. As with most women, her waist was tightly cinched. A swag of red silk hugged the broad hips, whilst yards of taffeta gathered into a large bustle at the back.

The woman took his hands and squeezed them boldly. A pair of rouged lips spoke his name. "You are Duke Charles, yes?" she asked huskily.

"Yes, do we know one another?" Charles asked, gracefully withdrawing his hands from her grip.

"No, my lord, but your face is famous. The pictures do you no justice, sir. You're far more handsome in person. You received my note?"

"Your note? Ah, yes, I did," he replied.

"Then, come with me. We've been waiting!"

She pulled on his hands, trying to guide him through the crowd. Charles resisted. "And you are?"

The woman stopped and laughed. Only now, did he realise she'd said nothing to Romanov. In fact, she'd behaved as though the Russian weren't even there.

"I'm Countess Maria von Reichstadt. I am nobody special, Highness. Just one of many nobles here tonight. Come, come! I introduce you to my friends!"

"Both of us?"

"Both?"

"Yes, both. Prince Anatole?" he asked, turning to his right—where Romanov had stood just seconds earlier. Charles found only empty air. The evasive angel had vanished. *Where has he gone? And why?*

"Come, Highness! Come!" she said, pulling with greater strength.

"Yes, all right," he answered, half his mind on Romanov's vanishing act, the other on the peculiar woman. The countess led her victim from the main salon to a more intimate space, equally crowded, though smaller. In one corner, stood an oval table, hosting a dozen or so individuals. All wore expensive clothing. Most were strangers, but Charles recognised two.

His muscles tensed.

The two troublemakers had altered their appearance since their last meeting—he with golden locks instead of raven, and she with equally blonde hair to replace the previous auburn. No matter. Charles would know Prince Araqiel and his evil sister, Eluna von

Siebenbürgen, anywhere. The familiar tingling coursed along his forearms and hands.

Where is Anatole? Should I pray and ask for help? Where is Ailesleigh? And what of Seth? Dare I bring him into this viper's nest?

The scarlet woman dragged her victim to the table's edge. "Come, Highness! Come! Meet my friends. We've been waiting to meet you. Yes, all of us have waited so long."

"I know two of them already, Countess, and I've no wish to speak to either. Araqiel and his sister are not my friends."

"You know them?" she asked, teasingly. "Such a surprise, then, yes?" The flirtatious woman patted his hand as she introduced him to the curious circle. "Pay heed, everyone! We speak English now, to honour our guest. This, as you must surely know, is..."

"It's Charles Sinclair, England's very own King of Shadows," Araqiel interrupted with a toss of the golden curls. "We're old friends, aren't we, Charles? I wondered if you'd recognise me with my improved look. Do you like it?" he asked with another toss of the golden mane. "Luna loves it, don't you, my pet? That's why she's copied me. My sister and I were just discussing this evening's opera. It's a delicious coincidence, don't you think? The plot's about a royal human, forced to walk a long maze of trials in search of enlightenment. Most intriguing, don't you think?"

"Yes, quite a coincidence," muttered Sinclair.

"Do sit with us," Araqiel continued. "It's been years since we last talked, and I've so much to say. I promise not to bite. Well, not yet, anyway."

"The table's already filled," replied Sinclair, seeing no empty chairs.

"Nonsense, we'll make room for you. Boy!" Araqiel called to a young servant. "A chair! Mach schnell!"

In less than a minute, a plushly upholstered chair was placed twixt Araqiel and his sister. Charles stood behind the chair, wondering what game these two now played. Did he dare sit? *I'm never alone,* he reminded himself. *Fine, then. I'll play. See how you like playing the Lord's game.*

Eluna mischievously kissed his hand. "Don't worry, my darling. We're only playing cards. Do you know poker?"

"A little," he said, pulling the hand away. "I'm surprised. Isn't poker an American game?"

"They claim it," she purred. "but the American version is really just the French game of Poque. The goal is to have the best combination of cards. If your hand is bad, you pretend it's good. You bluff. It's great fun, and we sometimes fight. Ara doesn't like to lose, and he's already lost three times," she whispered, laughing at her dragon brother. "Here, let me introduce you to our company. We're like your inner circle."

"I prefer the true version," replied Sinclair, taking the empty seat. "I'll just watch."

"Good, Charles. Good!" cooed the mischievous princess. "You already met Countess Maria," she began, pointing to the woman in scarlet. "Do be careful. Maria's a shameless harlot and will try to seduce you. She is married, but her husband doesn't care. He encourages it. Isn't that true, Count Ernst?"

The man beside Maria shrugged. "My wife's free to choose."

"As are we all," said Eluna. "This is Count Ernst von Reichstadt, Charles. We call him a sometimes husband. They live apart, you see, and enjoy a liberated marriage. I'm sure you disapprove."

"I cannot choose for someone else, Princess."

She laughed, the dark eyes glinting sparks of fire. "You're playing coy. How sweet! Sitting next to Ernst is his close friend, Lukas Wagner. He descends from Richard Wagner. A great-nephew or something like that."

"Third cousin, twice removed," the man corrected.

"Is there a difference?" laughed Araqiel as he drank the last of his wine; or rather, what looked like wine.

"Stop interrupting, Ara, or else I shall tell all your secrets!" complained Luna. "As I was saying, Lukas descends from Richard Wagner and is just as musical. It runs in the blood," she said, touching Sinclair's hand. "Lukas and his musical blood compose for the theatre. He writes for the magician."

The youthful composer had green eyes and auburn hair. He reminded Charles of London's Fabian agitators, who idly lounged in Whitechapel's music halls. Wagner had a sensitive expression, as though ready to compose an aria. His fingers moved rhythmically, and the languid expression gave him a sleepy look.

He's probably on morphine or some other intoxicant, Charles surmised.

"I compose and play piano for the Great Kasadya," explained Lukas in strangely accented English. "He's performing tomorrow night. You should come, Duke Charles. Vienna's crowded with illusionists, conjurers, and magicians, but I tell you, Kasadya is real. He does the impossible. I've no idea how, but he performs miracles. He even summons ghosts, without a spirit cabinet. They just appear—*poof!*—out of nowhere!"

Eluna stroked the Duke's forearm. "I've seen Kasadya work. I tell you, he is wholly unnatural."

The Duke stared into Eluna's dark eyes, wishing he could make the unwholesome creature vanish forever. *One day, Lord. One day. Vengeance belongs to you. You will repay.*

"How is he unnatural?" Charles asked. "Is it his talent or material composition that supersedes the natural?"

Eluna signalled to a servant for more champagne. "It is both, of course. Here, let me continue the introductions. I've left off with our talented friend, Herr Hans Lechner. Hans used to write poetry, but now spends all his money and all his nights with us. Poor Hans hasn't written a line since! I think he enjoys himself too much. Is that not so, Hans? And one day soon, all your stingy grandpapa's money will be yours." She turned to Charles. "The old man owns Lechner Chocolates. Everyone loves them, except for Ara. My brother dislikes everything these days. He pouts. But isn't our Hans sweet, Charles? Look at those pretty eyes."

Hans Lechner was small and boyishly handsome, with pale skin, even paler eyes, delicate hands, and a beardless face. "It's an honour to meet you, Highness," said Lechner. "You're even more beautiful than Eluna told us."

Charles had no idea how to reply, so he merely smiled.

The man sitting next to Lechner nudged the pale man's shoulder. "You mustn't say such things, Hans. You'll embarrass us. The Duke is handsome, not beautiful." He stared at Haimsbury as though memorising every feature of his face.

"Ah, yes, he's very handsome, Max," Lechner added with a sigh. "A regal nose, firm jaw, confident posture. He has the look of Adonis, particularly the eyes. Such a unique colour."

The man next to Lechner cleared his throat and reached out. Charles shook his hand. The grip was strong, like a vice. A cold shiver ran through the Duke's spirit. "And you are?" he asked.

The mystery man rose, clicked his heels, and bowed his head. "Count Maximilian von Hoffbauer at your service. I live at Ehrenburg Palace in Coburg. I understand you are enjoying a little rest in Vienna before attending next month's wedding. Is true?"

"Yes. Have you a position at the palace?"

"Oh, yes. I am *der Oberststallmeister*. You understand this title? You speak German?"

"A little," Charles answered carefully.

Hoffbauer was stocky and broad-shouldered, with straw-coloured hair, cut very short. He wore silver spectacles, positioned at the tip of a broad nose. Blonde mutton-chop whiskers framed a round face, dominated by a mobile mouth. Charles could smell pipe tobacco and something else; a sickly-sweet blend of strong cologne and burnt opium. Overly large pupils made the blue eyes look almost black. His intoxicated manner mirrored hundreds of men Charles had arrested in Whitechapel.

But one other detail nagged at the Duke. The name. A man listed as Maxim Hoffbauer featured prominently in the Emperor's 1420 book, always with the marginal notation, *Vertraue Nicht!* Do not Trust!

The German's lips widened into a slick sort of smile. "You needn't speak German, Highness. We all speak English. Taught by the Kaiser's mama and grandmama, you know."

"And for that we English are grateful," Charles replied diplomatically.

"Maxim is Master of Horse at Ehrenburg," said Eluna. "He is master of many things."

Hoffbauer threw out his chest proudly. "The title is honourary, you understand. Given to noble friends. I do not saddle or look after horses. No menial labour, though I enjoy riding. Have you a horse master, Highness?"

"In England, the Master of Horse is called an equerry. Mine is head of the Haimsbury Regiment, but he also looks after security in my household."

Araqiel finished the glass of 'wine' and wiped his mouth, clearly enjoying the tense conversation. "You have a brand-new house, don't you, Charles? I hear it's filled with symbolism."

"What sort of symbols?" asked Lechner eagerly. "Statues? Are they Roman? Greek?"

"Most of the art's based on the Bible, actually," answered Charles.

"The Bible, bah!" Eluna shouted, insulted by the mention of a book she despised. "Are we playing cards or not?"

Hoffbauer looked down at his poker hand. "I believe, I win," he said, spreading the cards on the table. A ten, knave, queen, king, and ace—all diamonds. "Ah! A royal flush. You bring me luck, Highness. I shall enjoy getting to know you better as time allows. Perhaps we hunt one morning next month in Coburg?"

"I look forward to it," replied the Englishman carefully. Charles would need to keep a close eye on Hoffbauer.

"What about me?" asked the man beside Hoffbauer. "I'd like to be introduced."

Eluna smiled. "Dear Peter, how could I forget you? Charles, this is Peter Schilling. You may have noticed him in the orchestra tonight. Peter's the most accomplished violinist I have ever known, and I have known plenty," she laughed. "He is a virtuoso of the strings and a fine fellow, too, though a little strange. I like men who are strange."

Schilling reached out to shake the Duke's hand. As Charles took it, that familiar electric sensation ran along his entire arm. And at the very same instant, Romanov reappeared. Charles hadn't seen him coming, yet the angel stood just two feet from the card table. And though he looked solid and real, the crowd milled about Anatole as though unaware of his presence.

Something was about to happen. Eluna had called Peter Schilling strange. What did she mean? Was he a disguised devil? What of Kasadya, this magician? Who was he? *What* was he?

Why was I invited here?

"It's a pleasure to meet you," Charles managed to tell Schilling.

The violinist's well-formed lips widened into a beguiling smile. Perfect teeth gleamed within a scarlet mouth. The bridge of a Grecian nose supported oval spectacles, set with forest-green lenses that obscured the eyes. Brownish-black hair fell two inches beyond the shoulders.

The man sent chills down the Duke's spine.

"Your Highness, it is my honour," said the musician. "You know, I very recently visited England and was honoured to play a night of Schubert for your Queen. Do you enjoy music, Highness? Shall I play for you?"

Charles had no idea what to say. Had he blundered into another of the fallen realm's traps? Had a rebel spy used the Emperor's invitation to devise an evil plan?

Lord, help me to see clearly.

"If time permits, I'd enjoy that," he managed to reply. "Will you be in Vienna long, Mr. Schilling?"

"Not long, no," replied the other. "I'm a vagabond, meaning I travel where I please. England, Germany, Austria, even the *Gold Coast of Africa* from time to time," he added, emphasising the very place where Paul now worked. "I hope you'll forgive my rudeness, but I see an old acquaintance. Another traveller, from a more northerly clime than my own. I really must say hello. We'll meet again, Highness. I promise."

The man in green eyeglasses bowed, and as he stood, Charles noticed a creaking sound; metal groaning against leather. As he walked away, Schilling limped slightly, as though the left leg were weak.

"Poor Peter wears an ankle brace," explained Hoffbauer. "He claims the injury was caused by a bad accident a few years ago, but I've heard rumours of dabbling in the dark."

"Dabbling?" asked Charles.

"Some say Schilling struck a deal with the Devil to obtain his remarkable talent. That he traded gifted fingers for a weakened ankle, but does it matter? The man plays like an angel!"

Eluna leaned close and stroked Sinclair's hair. "The longer length suits you, my love."

"I'm not your love," he bit back angrily, moving out of her reach. "Did you tell that countess to send me a note?"

"Perhaps," whispered the princess.

"Do not send for me again. I'm done with your games. I'm finished with you and your mad brother!"

Eluna von Siebenbürgen sighed. "Then we must find a new play-thing for our games. Perhaps, that handsome man who came with you tonight? Lord Paynton. He's very pretty. Such sweet eyes and freckles. Shall we play with him?"

Sinclair pushed back the chair and straightened his waistcoat, as if brushing away her words. "Excuse me, everyone. I've an early appointment tomorrow morning. Good evening."

The card players remained, but the scarlet-gowned countess rushed after the departing Englishman, trying to change his mind.

"Highness, forgive us! Have we offended you? Eluna is too much sometimes. We rarely meet new people, and our manners are clumsy. Forgive us, please!"

He paused to look her in the eye. "If your apology's sincere, then I forgive easily. Thank you for the invitation. It was—enlightening."

The Duke bowed, just to be polite, and crossed into the main salon. Romanov had moved again. Now, the Russian was in a deep conversation with Ailesleigh. What were the two angels discussing?

Why am I here, Lord? To run from evil or confront it? Have I done right by leaving the table? Should I go back?

Charles thought of Ephesians. In the sixth chapter, St. Paul explains that a believer's true enemies aren't made of flesh and blood, but are spirits: powers, principalities, and rulers in high places—the fallen angels who currently run the world.

He could almost hear Adele whisper to him: "Stop, Holmes! The game's afoot! Time to start sleuthing!"

He glanced back into the card salon, praying inwardly. *Lord, forgive my anger. Help me to make decisions according to your will alone. And as I do, please, keep my Della safe. Keep all my family safe. Hold my wife and all our children in your mighty hand.*

He noticed Schilling talking with someone near the eastern edge of the main salon. *Where's Seth?* Hoping Ailesleigh might know, the Duke took a direct path towards the disguised angels.

"Has either of you seen Lord Paynton?"

"Ah," said Romanov. "He is talking with a fellow scientist. I take it you found no clues at the card table?"

"Nothing that makes sense," Charles answered. "How is any of this connected to the Emperor's investigation?"

"Eluna and her card playing friends are distraction. You're here for the actress," replied Ailesleigh. "Ah, I believe this is the real clue."

An usher approached and bowed. A gold badge identified him as the *Leiter Platzanveiser,* the Head Usher.

"Yes?" asked Romanov. "Have you a message?"

The grey-haired servant carried a bit of paper on a tray. He offered the note to the prince. Romanov read it quickly, then passed it to Charles. "It is tomorrow's playbill," he said.

The Duke read the contents. The playbill listed the next evening's performers. "The magician headlines tomorrow, this Great Kasadya. Who sent this?" he asked the servant.

"A lady, sir."

"A titled lady? In a crimson dress?"

"No, Highness. An actress. She wish to speak to you, sir. Backstage."

"Give us a moment," answered the Duke. "If you don't mind waiting over there whilst my friends and I discuss this?"

"Of course, Highness. I wait." The man bowed and left.

As quickly as the usher departed, another man arrived. He was auburn-haired and freckle-faced. Those freckled cheeks were flushed, and the hair thoroughly out of order.

"What happened to you?" asked Ailesleigh. "If I didn't know better, I'd say you'd just enjoyed an intimate conversation, but having seen the gentleman with whom you spoke, I must assume otherwise, Lord Paynton."

Seth laughed as he ran a hand through the tousled red hair. "No intimacy with that old gentleman, Ailesleigh. Not that sort. Professor Glitsch is an expert on Sumerian digs. He and I were talking about some of our circle's recent mysteries. And before any of you asks, I said nothing out of turn. Besides, Glitsch may already know some of our secrets. He's good friends with Martin Kepelheim and knows all about our inner circle."

"And the reason for your present state?" asked Romanov teasingly.

"What state?"

"The redness of your face," said Charles, "and the rouge on your cheek. Is Dr. Glitsch prone to kiss his colleagues?"

"Kiss? No, of course not," answered Holloway, his face reddening further as he rubbed the rouged spot. "No, after talking with Glitsch, I ran into a family friend, that's all. Lady Sylvia Montfort. And before you ask, she's over sixty and forever kissing any man who says hello. Is that tomorrow's playbill? Strange they're not continuing *Flute*. It only just opened."

"Do Austrian theatres generally mount an opera one night and offer a magician the next?" asked Ailesleigh.

"Hardly," said Holloway. "The cost of changing costumes, sets, cast, and orchestra is very expensive. Most theatres barely break even. Doing this is very poor management."

"Perhaps, the magician draws more crowds than opera," suggested Ailesleigh. "Which begs the question, why mount the opera at all?"

Charles had a very bad feeling. "Since tonight's opera mirrors my weeks inside the Time Maze, it's probably because we attended."

"I don't know, Charles. That's a lot of money lost, just to make a point," said Holloway.

"So it is," replied Sinclair. "Who's this Great Kasadya, Anatole?"

"I know only the fellow's name, nothing more, though it does remind me of another name—one from very long ago," replied the Russian.

"Kasadya," muttered Holloway as he read through the bill. "What sort of name is that? Russian? Daniel, you enjoy etymology and language. Do you know anything about it?"

Ailesleigh glanced at his superior. "Well, Kasadya might be a corrupted version of Kasadye, with a final *e* instead of an *a*."

"Kasadye?" asked Holloway.

"Perhaps," answered Ailesleigh, casting his fellow angel a knowing glance. "May I?" he asked as he reached for the playbill. Daniel turned it over. "The text is in German, of course, but a rough translation reads:

Come, one, Come all, and be amazed!
The Great Kasadya and his assistant
will augur the dead and astound the living!
Known for impossible feats of magic
the world over.
This is not illusion.
This is REAL.
ONE POWER, MANY FACES.

"One power? Many faces? Real illusion? I find this troubling," Ailesleigh muttered. He held the paper up to the light. "There's nothing hidden behind the ink. Nor is there another page sealed inside. Still, the page feels heavier than it should."

"Daniel, what are you not saying?" asked Haimsbury.

"Nothing. Not yet, at least," he answered, returning the playbill to the Duke. "Like Sherlock Holmes, I require more data. But the usher awaits an answer, Charles. Shall we visit the sender or not?"

"I think, we must," replied the Duke, the nervous tingling subsiding. He glanced towards the card table. Eluna laughed as she and her brother held court with their coven of strange acolytes.

Charles motioned to the usher.

The four friends were about to enter the shadowy regions of Schikaneder's backstage maze.

CHAPTER TWENTY-FIVE

The usher gave his name as Gerhardt. The playbill's sender, he explained, was rehearsing in the building next door. To reach it, their path took them through a long passage, lit by gas lamps. They descended into a long tunnel beneath the streets, then climbed up again to a rehearsal chamber called a black box. Its dimensions mirrored those of the mainstage and wings. Every wall was painted in dull black paint and softened with black velvet curtains from ceiling to floor. In one corner, a flamboyantly dressed man played piano for dozens of singers and dancers; the cast of next month's operetta, *Die Fledermaus* by Richard Strauss.

The usher and noblemen entered the chamber to the strains of the famous drinking song, *Im Feuerstrom der Reben*, In the Firestream of the Grape, led by Count Orloff, played by a mezzo-soprano in a trouser role. As Orloff, the singer danced across the black-box floor, extolling the virtues of drinking to excess and hailing champagne as the King of Wines.

"This way, sirs," whispered Gerhardt. "Please, my lords, keep to the edge. The singers react badly when disturbed."

They stayed close to the walls, then passed through a locked door. The usher led them up a flight of stairs, where they turned left into another gaslit corridor. They stopped at a door marked *Privatgëlande: Nur Darstelle.* Private: Performers Only.

"Are we permitted here?" asked the Duke.

The usher smiled. "*Ja,* Highness. Is fine. Is private rooms with food and drink. The lady, she wait inside."

The door opened to a cavernous space that smelled of sweat and talcum powder, mixed with Turkish cigarettes and cheap gin.

Though beautifully decorated, the room was obviously used by actors, quite possibly when meeting friends and lovers.

"You sit, meine Herren?" the servant asked.

"What of the woman?" the Duke asked warily. Romanov and Ailesleigh showed no sign of worry. Seth toured the room, examining posters and photographs.

"The lady will come. She with Kasdaya. Please, to sit, yes? I find her."

The tingling returned and shifted into a higher frequency. *Something's about to happen.*

Romanov's eyes scanned the space, glaring at one long section as he if saw beyond the drapes and wall coverings.

Charles chose one end of a leather sofa. Ailesleigh took a seat nearby. Seth and Romanov remained on their feet. The Russian lingered beside a table littered with burnt cigarettes and wine glasses.

"Kasadya," Anatole muttered, followed by unintelligible words in another language.

Charles could hear singing. It sounded distant, as though from a second black box. He recognised the music as Mozart's *Don Giovanni*; a pivotal scene in Act II, where the slain Commendatore appears to Giovanni in the form of a ghostly statue and sings *A cenar teco m'invitasti* (You have invited me to dine). Giovanni thinks himself clever and agrees. He orders his servant to set an extra place at the table. The statue refuses *mortal* food and suggests Giovanni dine with him instead. He extends a hand towards the heartless gigolo. The prideful Giovanni refuses to appear weak, and he takes the hand, finding it freezing cold.

The Commendatore is Death. He offers the vainglorious human one final chance to repent and save his soul. Giovanni refuses and pulls away.

Moments later, demons drag Giovanni to Hell.

As the opposing singers rehearsed their roles, Charles was drawn back to the Time Maze. In a waking dream, he again stood inside Legion's lair. A piano softly played the first measures of Beethoven's *Moonlight*, but then, the left hand added motifs from *Don Giovanni.* Charles faced a massive obsidian statue, not Mozart's Commendatore, but the 1st Duke of Branham, surrounded by two lines of statues in the misty space.

I'm at Branham, he realised.

The Branham duke's cold eyes stared down at the human, and he extended a marble hand. It had six fingers.

"Come," he said in a booming, operatic voice.

Against his will, Charles reached out, his arm controlled by some unseen force. He stared into the obsidian statue's face. It had changed, no longer the Branham duke. Now, the horrid thing was the very image of himself. Duke Charles Sinclair: with his curling hair, his face, his proportions, his clothing, even the Sir John Bennett watch.

Charles tried to scream but failed. He knew the statue couldn't be him—not really. It must be the devil who controlled the Maze. It must be Legion! But no matter how hard Charles tried to stop it, his hand moved closer and closer to the cruel statue's hand.

As though Death itself drew him in.

Strains of *Moonlight* and *Don Giovanni* combined into a mad duet. His fingertips were mere millimeters from oblivion, ready to touch, ready to fall into the abyss!

Then...

Something warm touched his shoulder and rescued him from the internal nightmare. Charles nearly collapsed. His right arm was cold as ice.

"Take care, Charles Robert," said Romanov. "Do not let the music entice you."

"I was there. I was back *there*," whispered the Duke.

"A piece of you went there, yes. A bit of your mind, but Legion cannot control your soul, Charles. Here, allow me." He brushed the human's eyes and touched the affected hand. Skin and muscles warmed. The dizziness vanished. "Is that better?"

"I want to go home," the Duke said in a small voice.

"Yes, Charles, I know, but the fight is here, and the woman approaches."

The dressing room door opened to a tall figure in a pink Georgian dress and powdered wig. She giggled. "*Mein Herr?*" she asked, lifting her wide-hipped skirts to sit into one of the chairs. "*Du bist der Herzog, ja?*"

"I'm Duke Charles. Do you speak English?"

"Ja, I do." The actress removed her wig and jewellery.

"You're Miss Kaspar?" asked Charles.

"Ja. Mizzi Kaspar. I speak to you, yes? Not others."

"These men are my friends," Charles replied. "Prince Anatole Romanov, Lord Paynton, and Lord Ailesleigh. I prefer they remain. You may speak freely. I trust them with my life."

"I see. Just talk, then, yes? Nothing else," she said, removing the costume's white silk gloves. "You are Charles of England, yes? You are King?"

"I've been called that," Charles answered, growing frustrated with her games. "Miss Kaspar, why did you send me a playbill for tomorrow night's performance? Because of Kasadya? Is there something about him I should know?"

Beneath the powdered wig, Mizzi Kaspar had a luxurious mane of finely textured dark hair. She began to brush the long locks, her light eyes unfocused. "Kasadya is friend. He is most powerful. I meet him long ago, with Rudolf."

"Prince Rudolf?" asked Holloway. "The Emperor's son?"

The hairbrush stopped. She heaved a dramatic sigh. "Ja. The Prince. Why are you here? Is for Kasadya or Rudolf?"

"Both," replied the Duke.

"Why you come here—now, tonight?"

Charles tried to be patient, but her attitude was puzzling. "We came to see the opera. No other reason. And we've come to your dressing room because you insisted. These men are witnesses to that fact."

"*Vielleicht,*" she answered in a singsong voice. "Perhaps."

Someone knocked. The usher opened the door. He spoke to the caller, then turned to the visitors. "Herr Kasadya wish to meet with you. Is welcome?"

"If he wishes to join us, yes, of course," Romanov said smoothly. "I should very much like to meet this *magician*."

The usher bowed low as Kasadya entered. The magician was quite tall. Charles guessed his age at thirty. He moved nimbly, with the grace of a dancer, though the Duke noticed slight hesitation on the left foot.

He has a limp.

Yet, despite the handicap, the overall effect was one of wonder. His face and body were beautiful. Each aspect chiseled with precision, almost like a statue. He had almond-shaped eyes with turquoise irises, a straight nose, full lips and flawless skin. His hair was a rich chestnut and matched Anatole's for length, ending at the waist.

The magician bowed, sweeping the right arm along the floor in knightly fashion. "I am Kasadya," he told the visitors. The accent's origin was unclear. Not German, English, French, Romanian, or Russian. He stepped closer, the limp more obvious. "You are King Charles?"

The Duke's left brow arched into a high question mark. He focused on the magician's eyes and answered without a single blink. "I am *Duke* Charles."

"But some call you King, yes?"

"Some do. I prefer Duke. Your accent's unusual, Herr Kasadya. Where is your home country?"

The magician laughed. "Is interesting question, King Charles. No, you say is Duke? No matter," he chattered as he kissed the actress. "Nowhere is home. I travel. I wander here and there. You meet my friend, yes? Schiller."

"The violinist?"

"Oh yes, he is fine musician. Peter and I are like brothers! How you say? Inseparable! When Peter play, he pull a man into dreams. Is this not true, King Charles?"

The other three observed the tense encounter. Ever the faithful assistant, Seth had taken out his notebook and begun writing it all down. Romanov said nothing. Ailesleigh's posture shifted. He sat on the edge of the chair now, as though ready to spring.

Something is coming. He is coming. That's what the Piper told Robby. Is this it? Is it Kasadya?

Remarkably, Charles seemed calm and in control. "That's an interesting way to describe music's effect. It's true that some compositions have power to influence our minds and even our spirits. Some may elevate us to the heavens, whilst others drag us to the brink of despair. But music is also an aspect of worship. It is one of our Creator's many gifts."

"Creator! Is funny," laughed the magic man. "You have interesting view. And you?" he asked Romanov. "You are famous Russian—in the flesh, yes? The Prince Anatole? I have longed to meet you. Indeed, I wait millennia!" He hobbled towards Daniel's chair; the limp growing more profound as he neared the disguised angelic warrior. "And this is the Earl of Ailesleigh, yes? You look very good—for your age."

"A gift from my Creator," answered Ailesleigh boldly.

Kasadya smirked, then looked at Seth. "And this one? The red-haired friend? I've seen you before, I think. Viscount Paynton, yes? Digby, perhaps. I call you Digby."

Seth jumped to his feet, ready to challenge the man. Charles intervened. "My friend is young, but it's clear you're much older, Herr Kasadya. Much older. How do you know my friend's nickname?"

Kasadya began to play with Mizzi's gloves. "Do I? Digby. Is funny. You, King Charles. Someone calls you... *Captain*. I am right, yes?"

Now, it was the Duke's turn to challenge the rude magician, and Anatole who intervened. The disguised angel approached the limping interloper. Charles watched as Romanov's height began to increase. He stepped close, growing taller. He loomed over the magician and whispered into his right ear. The language was neither German nor Russian. Charles made out a few of the words. They sounded like *usemi, alu, ezeru, dalkhu, naparsudu*.

Sinclair stored the phonetic sounds in his eidetic memory to ask Romanov about them later. Whatever their meaning, Kasadya's carefree manner, even the beautiful face, fractured and fell into a twisted mask of utter loathing. His fists clenched, and he whispered a tense reply into Anatole's left ear. Again, the words were strange. Something like *sarum, daku, sanannu,* with each *s* a sibilant *HISSSSS*.

The loyal angel stepped back, and his right brow arched. His mouth widened into a victorious smile. "Is that so? Clearly, you have lost your edge, Kasadye. Your manner tells me all I need know. Be warned. I see you the truth of you, Kasadye. We *will* meet again—and soon."

"It is Kasadya," the magician corrected with false bravado. "Kasadya, with an *a* at the end. Not an *e.*"

"Vowels do not change truth. I know who you are. I know your true name," the Russian replied. "Miss Kaspar, I suggest you and the Duke speak in private. We shall wait here."

The actress's eyes had a sleepy, drugged look to them. She set down the hairbrush. "Dimmy?" she asked, looking at the magician. "Is all right?"

"Yes, my darling, is quite all right. You go. Let me talk with these others."

Charles turned towards Holloway. "Lord Paynton will accompany me. He can interpret."

Seth had no idea what Sinclair meant, but stood, adding, "Yes, that's what I do. I, uh, interpret."

Mizzi led the two Englishmen through to another dressing room. Once inside, she locked the door. This room contained rows of dressing tables, mirrors, and metal chairs. Each table was covered in stage makeup, glue, moustaches, wigs, and tubs of beeswax. Mizzi took a chair near one of the tables and selected another hairbrush. Charles wondered if the familiar activity helped to calm the woman's nerves. Or perhaps she was drugged with opiates, for the pupils were large and black.

"Is Rudolf," she began in German. "You want to know about him, yes?"

"Yes," answered Charles. "You've noticed my friend is writing," he said in perfect German.

"I thought you no speak German," she said sleepily.

"I'm fluent in several languages, but somewhat lazy."

"Ja," she muttered. "I talk English, if you like."

"That's fine. My friend will take notes. He's a university professor and researches crime. He's writing a monograph on unexplained deaths."

"Professor? You teach death?"

"Well, yes," said the viscount in English. "I teach modern and ancient languages, too, as well as history. As an archaeologist, I study death," he added, thinking of Adele and wondering if she'd be pleased with his progress. "I'm writing a monograph. A little book. Please, just converse normally. If you prefer German, Charles speaks it well enough that he shouldn't need me too often. I'll just take notes if that's all right?"

"Notes?" she asked, dragging out the 'n' and slurring the word.

"*Notizen schreiben,*" said Holloway. "*Ich schreibe ein Buch über Kriminalität.*"

"*Ja, ich verstehe*. I understand."

"Then, we'll talk in English," Charles said. "Tell me what you know about the night Prince Rudolf died."

"Not only him die," the actress explained. "The Baroness, too. Mary Vetsera. Both dead."

"Were you there?"

"No. I work."

"Do you still live in the house the prince bought for you?"

"Ja, is mine. In my name," she said proudly. "Rudolf never like Kasadya."

"Rudolf and Kasadya knew one another?"

"Kasadya was there that night. He help to..." she began, suddenly paling. "No. Not there. No. I say no more! Go! You go! *Geh raus!*"

"But you asked to talk with me," Charles argued. "Miss Kaspar, why are you afraid? Has someone threatened you? Was it Kasadya?"

"No! Dimmy love me. He never hurt me. Not Dimmy."

"Dimmy?" asked Seth, still writing.

"Demetri. His name Demetri. I call him Dimmy."

"I see," Holloway replied, making a note of the magician's first name. "Demetri? Or Demetrius?"

"I not know!" she cried. "Leave! Leave me!"

"I can protect you, Miss Kaspar," Charles began, his voice soft and convincing.

"No, you talk to *them*. I send for you, but *not me!*"

"I don't understand," Charles said. "Who sent for me? Gerhardt told us it was you."

"No! Not me. Sun, moon, lies, lies, lies! Blood and fire! Leave me! He come and pull me down. I cannot go there again! Go!"

A heaviness fell across Sinclair's spirit. The woman was terrified, perhaps drugged—but who was behind it? He passed his personal calling card to the actress. "Keep this. I want to free you from whatever chains bind you. No tricks. I want to help. I'm staying at the Schönbrunn."

She stared at the gold-edged card, her eyes barely focusing. "Poor Rudolf," she said, the prince's name catching in the throat. "Come tomorrow. See Kasadya, yes? But leave now. Please, go. Please."

"We'll come tomorrow night. Thank you, Miss Kaspar."

The actress nodded. She picked up the brush and began stroking the long hair. The ritual reminded Charles of Beth. Every night, she removed the pins from her hair and brushed out the curls. *One hundred strokes*, she would say. *One hundred strokes to keep it soft and shiny. Tory insists on it.*

Mizzi Kaspar couldn't be older than thirty, yet her hands trembled like an old woman's as she pulled the brush through the thick strands. Was it opium? Or might it be syphilis? Some actresses took multiple lovers, making it easy to catch the dreaded disease.

Did Rudolf have syphilis? Nothing in the Emperor's book mentioned the late Prince's health. Could the court's ruling be correct? Had Rudolf killed himself, rather than face a degraded body and mind? Had syphilis driven the late prince mad?

"Miss Kaspar, if you need anything, send word. Until tomorrow, then," he said. "Come, Seth. I've had enough of this place for one night."

The Englishmen took their leave. Kaspar remained at the mirror, brushing, brushing, brushing the hair. After a few minutes, Demetri Kasadya entered and sat beside her. The magician kissed her cheek and took the brush.

"Let me do this," he whispered. "You did well, my love. Tomorrow, we'll have another chance at our King without that annoying entourage, yes? King Charles of the Time Maze. Soon, he'll open all the doors and free us. He'll free me, yes?"

"Time Maze?" she echoed, her voice growing faint.

"Time, my darling. Time, time, time! And this particular human knows how to unlock it."

"Lock?"

"Yes, locks. Locked rooms and locked Time. King Charles possesses immense power, but we must find some workable weakness, if we're to convince him to join us. Every human has one. Finding it just takes a little TIME."

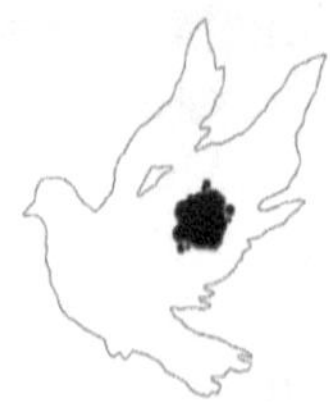

CHAPTER TWENTY-SIX

Breitenfurt Institute

It was almost tea-time, but Cordelia Stuart had no wish to return to the main building. Since arriving, she'd longed to take a walk on her own, and Pyramis had finally given permission. Dressed in pale blue chiffon with low-heeled cream shoes, the countess idled her way along a leaf-strewn path at the edge of the Vienna Woods. Another resident had warned Delia about the woods. She'd told haunting tales of faeries and sprites that gathered in the trees at night, but it was daytime. What could possibly harm her now?

The young woman felt the urge to dance as she approached the clearing. Within the mounded area, stood an old well. As a girl, Delia enjoyed reading the Brothers Grimm, and the book's illustrations included picturesque clearings such as this. She approached the stone well, careful to avoid stepping on too many flowers. All round, lay pristine beds of bluebells, yellow narcissus, fiery red valerian, celandine poppies, and violets. She stooped to pluck one of the violets and placed the fragile blossom in her hair.

"Very nice," said a man's voice.

Delia turned to find Vano Pyramis, smiling at her.

"Oh!" she exclaimed, her body tensing. "Who are you?"

Pyramis bowed. "I'm your doctor, good lady. Have you forgotten me already?"

Delia puzzled through the stranger's words. She felt oddly out of sync with the world, caused in part by a new medication, prescribed by Pyramis's partner, a Greek by the name of Panemorfí. His surname was certainly apt, for the gentleman had the face of a beautiful god. Indeed, he was admired by the entire nursing staff. Panemorfi's sole flaw was a slight limp.

"I've forgotten you?" she asked, her words a little slurred. "You're a doctor? Do I need a doctor? Am I ill? Is this a hospital?"

He stepped close to assess her eyes. The pupils were large and glassy. "This is Breitenfurt Retreat. It is a place of rest. Do you remember coming here, Lady Aubrey?"

"Lady Aubrey? Who is that?"

"Why, she is you, my lady," he told her. "Here now, let's sit on this bench for a moment. I should like to enjoy the music of the woods with you."

Delia obediently sat, and the skirting of the sky-blue dress folded round her like a bashful flower. She wore no hat, and her maid had skillfully arranged the strawberry blonde waves into a long braid, set with glittering sapphire pins. Her lace-gloved hands were clasped demurely against her lap. Cordelia Jane Stuart looked picture-perfect, yet something about the eyes told a different story. As before, the countess had regressed into a world of imagination and fantasy.

"I don't know a Lady Aubrey," she told him. "Why do you call me that?"

The alienist produced a small, cabinet photograph of two men, facing one another. Their features were similar, though one's hair was longer.

"Do you remember these gentlemen?" he asked her.

Delia touched the frame. "I'm not sure. The one on the left looks familiar. Who is he?"

"Charles," Pyramis told her.

"Charles," she repeated wistfully. "Did he visit me?"

"Yes. Do you remember what he said to you?"

The countess sighed. "He asked if I like it here. I do, but not all the time. I want to go back to Windermere. There's to be a party soon, and I'm to have a new dress made."

"How very nice. What else did Charles say?"

"He brought someone else along, didn't he? A man with red hair and lots of freckles on his face. Freckles on men are becoming, but not on ladies. Mama doesn't like my freckles. She uses buttermilk to remove them. She scrubs and scrubs." Delia brushed her pale cheeks, the gaze far away. "Will Charles be at the party?"

"Is the party in Windermere?" She nodded. "Then, I cannot say. Lady Aubrey..."

"Please, don't call me that. I'm Lady Delia. I don't know who Lady Aubrey is. May I go home?"

"Soon, my lady. Might I ask, how old you are?"

Her eyes narrowed, and she gently slapped his hands. "That's an impertinent question! Mama would call it naughty, but I'll answer, if you wish. I'm sixteen, and there's to be a dance in a few weeks. Oh, it will be so very nice! All the young gentlemen of the Lake District will be there. And the ladies, too, with silks and satin in every colour, filling the ballroom. I love to dance, don't you?"

"Indeed. Perhaps, we might share a dance?" suggested the alienist as a second gentleman joined them. "Ah, Gregory. You remember Lady Delia. I'm very glad you've come. There's to be a dance soon. Lady Delia's looking forward to it."

Gregory Panemorfi smiled, his beautiful face alive with wonder. "A dance? How marvellous. I love the way you British ladies glide across a dance floor. However, at present, my wobbly ankle makes dancing difficult. I do enjoy walking, though. Might I have the pleasure of a walk with you, Lady Delia? My ankle continues to heal, but it would be helpful if I could lean on someone's arm whilst enjoying the afternoon air."

Cordelia responded just as Panemorfi anticipated. Her naturally gentle disposition rose to the forefront, and she reached for his arm.

"Then you must lean on me. Allow me to be your helper."

The clever alienist helped her to stand, then took her arm. "We shan't be long," he told Pyramis. "You and I shall talk further later. I've left a note on your desk. Please, read it."

Gregory Panemorfi's slight limp caused him to drag the left ankle, but the pressure he exerted on Cordelia's forearm seemed light as air. As they strolled, she babbled on and on, discussing flowers, the lake, and the Vienna woods. Panemorfi knew a great deal about flora and fauna, and Delia liked his laugh.

"You're very nice for a doctor," she said as they reached the edge of a large lake. "It's peaceful here, don't you think? The lake reminds me of home. Did you know Coleridge and Wordsworth composed poems there?"

"In the Lake District, you mean?" asked the handsome alienist. "I should enjoy seeing your home, Lady Delia. I've not travelled nearly as much as I'd like—you might say I've been bound to one place for a very long time. Only recently, have I found modest freedom."

"Bound? How?"

"Locked inside," he whispered. "Shuttered away like a prisoner. It is a long tale."

"How terrible! That reminds me of a poem by Coleridge, and I believe he wrote it in Cumbria. I wonder if Charles has ever read it?" she added in a vacant whisper.

"Charles?"

"Who?" she asked as she plucked another wildflower. "Do you know his work?"

"Whose work, my lady? Coleridge or this Charles person?"

"Coleridge, of course," she laughed, her mind switching from one reality to another. "I'm not sure who this Charles person is. Coleridge's Christian name was Samuel."

"Oh, yes. I'm a great admirer. He used medicinal aids whilst working. As a physician, I understand the efficacy of roots and plants. Do you have a favourite?"

"A favourite root?" she asked, stepping closer to the lake's steep bank.

"No, my lady. Do you have a favourite poem? By Coleridge. Do you prefer one work to another?"

"Once, I memorised *Christabel*," she told him. "It took me a month to set it all to memory. I recited it at one of Mama's soirées, and again for Papa's Parliamentary colleagues and their wives. *Christabel* would make an interesting song, don't you think? Although, it is very sad, and a little frightening. The malevolent spirit, I mean. Do you suppose ghosts are real?"

"Ah, now that is a most intriguing question, my lady. The study of supernatural entities is one of my passions. If I remember rightly, Christabel was the daughter of a baron, yes? Like you?"

Her face paled. "Paul," she whispered. "I remember someone with that name. He helped me once, rather like the way Christabel helped Geraldine. What place is this?"

"The locals call it Breitenfurt Lake, but I suppose we may call it whatever we like—even Lake Christabel if you wish."

"No, I shouldn't like that. Did Christabel die? I think she may have. Geraldine may have... Well, she may have lured her, you know. To her death, I mean. I'm never quite sure. Am I dead? Did someone lure me to my death? I sometimes feel dead. Like all of my life has drained away."

As he leaned closer, Delia could smell the faint scent of bergamot oil on his skin and something else. Nutmeg? Sage? The man was quite handsome, but another face slowly dominated her thoughts: a handsome man with clear blue eyes and a kind, dimpled smile.

"He has long hair," she said, wondering why she did.

"I saw a man with long hair recently," answered the mysterious alienist. "Might we sit? There's a bench beyond the little willows. It's my ankle, you understand. Sometimes, it aches."

"Oh, yes, of course! Here, let me help. Lean on me."

Together, they took their places on the wooden bench, side by side, his hand on hers. "What happened to your ankle?" she asked. "I hope that isn't too forward, Doctor. I'm not prying, merely concerned. Is it a new injury? You seem so healthy otherwise."

"Relatively new," he told her, the sun intensifying his turquoise irises. "It happened in a battle."

"You served in a war? Was it in Africa?"

"No, this war is older and covers far more territory."

"I don't understand," she whispered. "I'm afraid I don't know very much about politics."

"Few know of this war," he said with a smile. "But warfare is a constant in certain realms. It's rather like Christabel's story. As Christabel prays near the oak tree, she finds a bedraggled maiden and offers to help her."

"Geraldine, yes?" she asked, growing sleepy.

"Yes, but Geraldine is a cunning liar. She entices poor Christabel into doing terrible things. Do you know the name means *beautiful Christian?* Coleridge is demonstrating the constant war I mentioned by pitting a faithful believer against a tempting spirit. It's like Fanu's novel, *Carmilla.* Or Poe's moving poem, *The Sleeper.*"

"You're very well read," she marvelled.

"I read everything mankind composes, and sometimes, my mind bends towards their pen, moving the metal nibs along clean linen paper to produce chilling ends."

She smiled. "That sounds like a poem, Dr. Panemorfi. Do you write, too?"

Panemorfi smiled, and his countenance glowed with a light so bright that it seemed that Sol himself resided there. "I dabble," he answered, laughing. "I'm also a musician. I play violin and the piano, amongst other things. Do you enjoy music?"

"Very much," she whispered, her eyelids heavy. "I don't really play well. I prefer to sing."

"Perhaps, we could plan a duet? I will play, whilst you sing. Have you a favourite composer? Mine is Beethoven, but I doubt you perform any of his songs."

"Oh, but I do! Beethoven composed some very beautiful art songs."

"So he did," the strange doctor told her. "Have you ever sung *In Questa Tomba Obscura?*"

"No," said Cordelia. "Is it for soprano?"

"Contralto, but I could alter the key for your voice. It is a poignant piece. Beethoven wrote it for the Contessa von Rzewuska. The theme is reminiscent of Coleridge and Poe."

"The title again?" she asked, a peculiar and uneasy darkness passing through her thoughts. She kept picturing a pale baby. His eyes are closed. The tiny face still.

"*In Questa Tomba Obscura*," he answered. "Beethoven set Carpani's poem to a painfully slow score. It's about a man who seeks out his dead lover, but she wants to be left alone. The lover and her dead companions desire no discourse with the living. They wish only to unfound and unharried."

Delia began to tremble. "No, that's a lie. The dead don't stay unfound, nor do they stay dead. They visit us, all the time. Father, and even my brother visit, though I'm not sure if William's alive or dead. No one will tell me. But, also, there's another, who..."

"Yes?" prompted the alienist.

"I dream about him sometimes. He's so very tiny, with fingernails and lashes like those of a doll."

An owl flew past and landed near the edge of the dark lake. It had pure white feathers and ice-blue eyes. The abnormally large bird stared at the two, sitting upon the bench. His head tilted to one side; the pale eyes fixed on the dreamy countess.

Cordelia blinked and shook her head, as though waking from a dream. "I shouldn't be here. I want to see Paul. Where's Paul?"

"Paul?" asked the other, unaware of the owl.

"He's my husband. Where is he?"

Panemorfi's turquoise irises contracted, and the pupils grew large and black. "Paul's abandoned you, Cordelia. You are dead to him. You are nothing but a ghost like *Christabel* or Poe's *Sleeper*. You've no need of such a faithless husband. Trust only in me."

The owl stepped close. It hooted loudly.

Panemorfi's attention snapped towards the bird. His cruel mouth widened into a snarling square, and the dark eyes flashed bright red. "We must go," the alienist whispered to Cordelia. "I've other patients to see. Here now, take my arm."

The owl flapped its wings, and a flock of migratory birds appeared from nowhere, bringing a sudden wind. The owl stretched—its bird-form lengthened, the shape liquefied into a figure, invisible to human eyes, like a vacancy in reality.

"I want Paul," the countess whispered, her chin dropping as she began to weep.

"Yes, of course," muttered the evil spirit using Panemorfi's skin. He started to stand, but a sharp pain ran along his left leg, causing him to stumble. "Ahh! We must go now. It's too crowded here. Come, help me back inside."

She shook her head. "No, I want to go home. I need to see my baby's grave. I want to visit his little tomb and let him know how much I miss him. Poor little Liam! Why did he die?"

The weeping came full force now. Delia cupped her palms aside her cheeks to hide her face, and so she didn't see what happened in the next few seconds. The tall figure within the void extended a long arm and *PULLED* Panemorfi into the vacant field.

The limping alienist vanished from human sight.

A hand touched her shoulder. Delia glanced up to find one of the nurses. "Wake up, Countess."

"What?" Delia murmured sleepily. "Mrs. Fischer?"

"Yes, my lady, it's Fischer. I've been looking for you everywhere. Tea's ready. Here, now, let me help you back to the main building. We're all on the south veranda."

"But I've been with Dr. Panemorfí. Didn't Dr. Van tell you? We took a walk along the lake."

"Pardon?" asked the nurse. "My lady, Dr. Panemorfi's not been here for three days. I think you must have nodded off."

"But he was here! Then a white owl came, I think, and... Oh, I'm not sure." Delia turned towards the lake, trying to sort through the strange conversation.

Music. Poems. Death.

Have I been dreaming?

"We have no white owls at Breitenfurt, my lady, I'm sure you've been dreaming."

"Yes, you're right. I must have dreamt it."

The nurse smiled. "The woods have that effect on me, too, but it's time to wake up, yes? Cook's prepared roast pork, potatoes, asparagus soup, and a trifle to follow."

"I'm not hungry, Mrs. Fischer. May I write to Paul? I want to see him so very much. I miss him. He told me to send the poem if I needed him. I just need to remember which one."

"Of course, you may write," said Fischer as they left the lake. "We'll make sure the earl receives your letter as quickly as possible. The postal trains twixt here and England are notoriously slow, you understand."

"Yes, so you've said. I'll write anyway. Perhaps, I could send for Charles. He said he'd take me home."

"Charles?"

"Charles Sinclair. He's a very dear friend of mine. Like a big brother," she continued. "Yes, I'll write to Charles. He'll take me home."

They left the lake and climbed the leafy path towards the main building. As the two women vanished over the rise, the white owl flew out of the dimensional doorway and soared over their heads.

Once Delia was safely inside, the large bird transformed into a well-dressed man. The tall figure snapped his fingers, and in half an instant, Anatole Romanov returned to Vienna.

CHAPTER TWENTY-SEVEN

A train, not far from Coburg, Bavaria

It was long past nightfall, as the private train sped towards its destination. The *Captain Nemo II* hugged the rails as it cut a swathe through picturesque gorges, sleepy villages, and magnificent valleys of ancient Saxony. The rhythmic chug-chug-chugging of the iron-horse wheels had lulled most of the passengers into a pleasant sleep. Inside one of the lounge cars, a dark-haired woman dozed on a leather chaise. Beside her, sat a well-dressed gentleman, reading a book.

The sleeping woman's dark curls gleamed beneath the flickering gaslight. The silken bodice of her travelling dress rose and fell as she dreamt, and petite fingers moved as if playing a piano. Her head jerked, and a soft moan escaped her lips.

The reader shut the book and reached over. "It's all right, Beth. Go back to sleep."

"Moonlight," she whispered. "Charles. Oh, no!" Her arms flew up, reaching towards an invisible phantom, but she grasped only air.

A gentle hand touched Elizabeth's shoulder. "It's all right, dear. It's only a dream."

"A dream? But it seemed so real, Henry," she sighed, wiping her eyes.

"Do you want to talk about it?"

Elizabeth Stuart Sinclair sat up higher, and MacAlpin helped support her back with two cushions. "Forgive me for falling asleep. Did you ask me about a dream?"

"Yes," MacAlpin answered. "I'm a very good listener. Dreams are part and parcel of my profession."

"Are you analysing me now?" she asked, managing to smile. "It was just a dream, Henry. Nothing more. Where have Gemma and Drina gone?"

"Gemma's resting in the next car, and the Queen's playing bridge with Mrs. Paget and some of the circle agents. I think our Drina enjoys being the centre of male attention."

"And she usually wins," Beth said, stifling a yawn. "Are we almost there?"

"No idea, but possibly. Are you hungry? What about toast? I could ring for a porter, if you want."

The Duchess laughed, casting off the disturbing dream. "I am, actually. Not toast, though. Have we any chicken? I've been craving chicken for days."

"A fine craving, too, nutritionally speaking. I'll see what I can muster." He started towards the dining car, then stopped. "Wait a moment. I can press a buzzer rather than go myself, can't I?" He crossed to a small fireplace and flipped open a wall-mounted brass cap that concealed a white button. "It could be a minute or two before anyone answers the bell. Most of the crew are with Her Majesty."

"Then, don't bother them. A glass of water and a few biscuits will do," Beth said, willing to compromise.

"Then, allow me to fetch them for you, my lady," he said, kissing her hand. Salperton left through the forward door.

Alone, Beth moved to a seat nearer the window. Regardless of what she'd told Henry, she wanted to sort through the dream. Charles had told Beth a little about the awful weeks he spent inside the Time Maze. Strangely, during those same weeks, Elizabeth had often suffered persistent dreams, where she walked the same darkened passages as her husband. Impossible though it seemed to everyone, she and Charles had remained connected to one another—even across time, space, and reality.

Now, she'd travelled there again. Elizabeth had dreamt of those same tunnels. Why? She prayed the dream were nothing more than memory, but she had an awful dread that Charles might be in trouble.

Henry returned, carrying a small sheet of yellow paper. "David Anderson's on his way," he told the Duchess. "Mind you, he left a winning hand, but didn't seem to mind. Fine fellow, that Anderson. He's fetching us a pot of tea and some biscuits. I asked him to add rye toast as well. If you won't eat the toast, then I shall." He handed her the yellow paper. "This was waiting for you at that last water stop. It's from Charles. I thought you might want to see it right away."

"Charles? Oh, yes, thank you!" she cried out happily, and opened the folded telegram. "He says he's all right. He and Seth are investigating a possible murder but doesn't explain whose. And he visited Cordelia. He says, she seems no better. Henry, how long does it take for a grieving mother's mind to heal after the loss of a child?"

The alienist took the chair nearest the Duchess and crossed his legs casually. "Well, there's no typical answer. It varies. Some women heal easily, though I cannot say *easy* is the right word. Losing a child is never easy. In Delia's case, her mind was already bruised when Liam died. That complicates recovery. Dr. Pyramis has his own methods and seldom fails."

"Do his methods differ from your own?" she asked.

"Oh, yes. Pyramis uses lithia water to speed healing."

"What is lithia water?" she asked.

"It's a type of mineral water. It seems to have a positive effect on some patients."

"Some?" she asked. "But not all?"

He shook his head, idly fiddling with the crease in his trousers. "No, not all. Truth be told, I'm worried about our Lady Aubrey. I've written to her six times since we left but had no reply. Has she written to you?"

"No, I've received nothing," the Duchess sighed. "I've written every day, Henry. I told her about Paul's journey to Africa, although he may have already told her. I'm worried about him as well."

The viscount reached for her hand. "Never fear, dear friend. Your cousin is quite good at his job. Even when we were at Oxford, Paul was forever dashing off to hither and yon on government business. And as to your equally capable husband, I'm sure he's fine. The Lord looks after him. You mustn't worry. Your job is right here," he said, lightly touching her waistline. "Charles relies on you to help this little one grow."

She placed her hand on his. "I think we'll call this one George, for his great-grandfather Branham."

"Just George? No other names considered?"

She laughed. “If you’re asking if there’s another baby needing a name, I think it’s just the one. But this baby’s growing so quickly, Drina keeps asking if I’m carrying triplets!”

“I doubt that, but might it be twins again?” he asked.

“No, I don’t think so, but you’re right. I mustn’t worry about Charles. My job is to take care of his son.” Her eyes took on a wistful expression. “You know, I sometimes feel it’s my sole purpose on this earth—to deliver Charles’s children into the world, I mean. I’ve been dreaming about these children for years. Only...”

“Only?” he asked softly. “Only what, dear?”

“Only,” she whispered, her eyes on the passing German countryside. “Sometimes, I dream about death.”

“Everyone dreams of death now and then,” he assured her.

“Perhaps, but mine are specific. I’ve dreamt it since I was a girl. I’m standing beside three graves with no names on the headstones. Henry, what might that mean?”

“Well, they’re not prophetic, if that’s what’s worrying you. Darling, let’s not think of death. We’re on our way to a celebration of life. A wedding! Even our stodgy old Queen is pleased as punch. Two of her grandchildren are marrying. Surely such a match will secure Europe’s squabbling throne rooms, don’t you think?”

“I fear it may prove to be the opposite,” she said as David Anderson entered with their tea. “Good evening, Mr. Anderson. I’m delighted you came along with us, and the Duke will appreciate your expertise once he meets us in Coburg. My husband’s still learning what ribbons and sashes go with which occasion.”

Anderson bowed his head and began to serve the tea. “His Grace’s rising importance makes it an ever-increasing problem, my lady. But it’s a lovely problem to have. Sugar?”

“Two, with milk. Anderson, when did we stop? Did I miss a station?”

“Half an hour ago, ma’am. I believe my lady was napping when we stopped,” he said. “Did Lord Salperton deliver the Duke’s telegram?”

“Yes, he did, thank you. Are we still on schedule?”

“We’re running a little late, my lady, but the engineer promises to make it up.”

“Thank you.”

Anderson bowed again and left.

Henry reached for the Duchess's hand. "I should have told you, but we ran into a slight delay at the water stop. A minor mechanical issue that's now repaired. Also, there might be a slight problem with our next hotel. You could be sleeping on the train tonight."

The Duchess offered a weary but genuine smile. "Then, it's a good thing my husband designed his train with such comfortable cars, isn't it? But I am puzzled, Henry. Charles arranged for hotels all along the route. Why should we need to sleep on board?"

"Bad luck. Whilst at that last water stop, we learnt of a fire at our Nuremberg lodging."

"A fire? Was anyone injured?" she asked.

"No, just smoke damage to some of the rooms. Well, to our rooms, actually. Captain Crenshaw and Sir Percy aren't happy about it. They exchanged several wires back and forth with the hotel. Management are trying to arrange for another hotel. We're to stop at the next station and send a follow-up telegram."

"Let's pray they find one, Henry. I don't mind sleeping on a train, but I shouldn't want our Queen to do so."

The physician smiled. "England's Shadow Queen doesn't mind?"

"Very amusing. Shall I toss you into the Tower?"

"Perhaps not right away," said Henry, smiling. "Let me finish my biscuits first, all right? I'll go talk to Crenshaw and ask if they've made any other decisions."

After MacAlpin left, Beth quietly sipped her tea. She was thinking about the first time she'd been with child; or rather, with children, Robby and Georgianna. What miracles they were! To think, that God used them to guide their parents through the treacherous challenges of the Stone Realms still amazed the Duchess. The twins had spent years learning to navigate the maze whilst in dreams. Beth dreaded such a future for her children, yet both had seemed healthy, brave, and exceedingly bright when she and Charles met them.

"Lord, keep them safe!" she whispered as the mountainous scenery flew past. "Keep Charles and Seth safe. Protect Paul and help Delia to heal. Please, bring them all home."

CHAPTER TWENTY-EIGHT

Mayerling Lodge, Vienna Woods

The picturesque village of Mayerling, Austria was a sleepy market town, nestled beside the Schwechat River, within the Vienna Woods. In January of 1889, the rural community became notorious for one thing: Death. That fateful year, Crown Prince Rudolf of Austria allegedly committed suicide after murdering his young mistress, Baroness Mary Vetsera, at Mayerling hunting lodge. The sudden death of the Habsburg heir forced Rudolf's father, Emperor Franz Josef, to name his brother Karl Ludwig heir. Almost immediately, Prince Karl abdicated the honour to his only son, Franz Ferdinand. At the time, no one realised how the Mayerling Matter would lead the world to war.

Shortly after Rudolf's death, the grieving Emperor converted the lodge into a convent for the Discalced Order of the Carmelites (*discalced* referred to shoeless or sandaled feet). That spring morning, as Sinclair and Holloway left their carriage, they were met by a pleasant woman dressed in simple robes made of finely woven brown wool. She wore brown leather sandals, and her head was modestly covered in a cream-coloured *coifette* or cap, overlaid with a heavy black veil. A large cross hung from her neck, and a rosary belt from her waist.

She bowed before speaking. "Good morning, Your Highness, Lord Paynton. Welcome to Mayerling," she began in perfect English. "I'm Mother Thomas. I serve as Prioress here. Yes, I know," she added with a wry smile, "Thomas is a man's name, but I wear it proudly, as it harkens back to that first Thomas, who sought proof of our Lord's miracles. I'm a sceptic, you see. I grew up in London, and before finding my vocation, I read chemistry at Oxford. Do come inside, won't you?"

The two peers followed the woman into the great foyer to the former hunting lodge. The interior was dark and quiet.

"I pray we've not disturbed your routine, Mother Thomas," Charles said as they entered. "I presume the Emperor told you of our visit?"

"Oh, yes, and it's a great honour to have you visit, sir. We receive the London newspapers, and I've watched your remarkable story with keen interest. I'm aware of your position as Shadow King and agree with it. I also know you read mathematics at Cambridge. England could use a ruler who understands numbers, particularly now."

Charles wasn't quite sure how to respond. "I enjoy puzzles as well as equations. I suppose that's what led me to criminal investigation. Do you know why we're here, Mother Thomas?"

"Oh, yes. I've arranged all the rooms for your inspection. I confess to doubt, regarding your success. It's been five years since the incident, and the rooms and grounds have since been altered; not only by us. The Emperor had made changes before we arrived."

"I appreciate the candor, Mother Thomas," said the Duke. "We've no expectation of discovering anything new today, but it helps to see the location. The Emperor did say our visit is for training purposes, I hope? My organisation isn't opening a formal investigation. Lord Paynton is a recent recruit, and as he and I were in Vienna, I thought we might use the opportunity for him to learn."

"It's always best to teach with a 'hands-on' approach," said the woman. "The rooms are this way."

She led them up a carved ash staircase with white-washed walls, devoid of portraits or ornamentation. "When we arrived, the lodge was filled with hundreds of statues and oil paintings," Mother Thomas explained. "They were removed to Vienna several years ago. Good morning, Sister Augusta. Don't mind our guests. They're touring the shuttered rooms."

Sister Augusta gave no audible response but leaned in to whisper to the Prioress. Mother Thomas told her, "Oh, I don't know. Let me ask. Your Highness, will you and Lord Paynton be staying for luncheon? We meet at one on the dot. Sister Augusta runs the kitchens, you see, and needs a head count."

"That's kind of you to ask," the Duke answered politely, "but I'm afraid we must decline the invitation. We have an appointment in the city this afternoon."

"There's your answer, Sister Augusta. But arrange tea for our distinguished guests. Set it up in the aviary. We'll send them in to enjoy it once they've finished." The kitchen nun bowed, then descended, allowing the guests to continue their climb.

Schloss Mayerling was similar in design to other castles Charles had seen since returning to his family: Slate or stone floors, plaster-and-timber walls, arched doorways. The primary differences were nuns and lack of ornamentation. Sweet incense perfumed the air with pleasant spices, as their guide led the men down a broad corridor, where she removed a key from the pocket of the woolen tunic.

"We call these the shuttered rooms, because we keep them locked at all times. They've not been altered since the incident; though, of course, the linens and soiled fabrics were laundered, and the floor's been cleaned. I wasn't here back then, but the former servants talked of blood-soaked carpets and stained coverlets. Forgive me for such frank language, Highness, but as you work with serious crimes, I imagine very little shocks you."

"I'm sorry to say that's true," Charles answered.

She opened the door. "I'll leave you to tour at your leisure. We're about to have mid-morning prayers, and afterward, I'll be speaking to our ladies in the garden. The aviary is on the west side of the Priory. We'll serve tea there."

"Thank you, Mother Thomas. You're very kind."

"I pray you find nothing out of place, gentlemen. May God guide your efforts, your eyes, and your hearts."

With that, the Prioress left the Englishmen alone.

Charles entered first, quickly memorising the layout. "Shut the door, Seth. I prefer no passing nuns overhear us."

Holloway did so, then followed his companion into the rooms. The apartment consisted of a small entryway, a spacious parlour, two bedchambers, and a bath. Heavy damask draperies obscured the sun, making the room quite dark. Seth pulled back the curtains, noting thick layers of dust. As the fabric moved, pyramidal shafts of yellow light brightened the walls and filled the air with billowing clouds from the past.

"The Prioress certainly told the truth. These women clearly don't come in here much. Look at this dust!" said Holloway, coughing and fanning the air. "Charles, what are we doing here? The Emperor's 1420 book has detailed descriptions and even diagrams of the castle as well as this apartment. Is there some advantage to seeing them in person, five years on?"

"I'm not sure," answered the Duke as he examined the corners and cupboards. "I cannot fathom why Franz called us in on this. The story's a vague puzzle, don't you think?"

"How so?"

"To begin, let's examine the elements," Sinclair began, assuming the role of teacher. "The official story goes this way. Prince Rudolf had a reputation as a philanderer."

"Not unlike most royals," said Seth. "Present company excluded."

"Thank you," his friend replied with a smile. "Despite having a beautiful wife and daughter, Rudolf kept several mistresses. We met one last night. Mizzi Kaspar."

"She's an odd one," said Seth. "Did she seem frightened to you?"

"Terrified," replied the Duke, "but also drugged. In fact, most of the people we met seemed influenced by narcotics. Kaspar was only one of Rudolf's mistresses. By all accounts, there were scores of others. Now, a few months before his death, the prince took up with an impressionable young baroness named Maria Vetsera; seventeen years old and by all accounts somewhat impressionable. However, before we fixate on the mistresses, let's consider the man's politics."

"He had none," said Holloway, taking a seat near the window and opening his notebook.

"Not true. He may have played the fool, but it seems the prince had a serious side and was quite liberal in his views. I talked with Kepelheim about the suicide theory before leaving London. Martin firmly believes Rudolf died because of politics, not because of a fatal romance."

"I don't follow."

"Think of what happened at the Observatory, Seth. An anarchist set off an explosive to demonstrate his hatred for all rulers and autocrats. Such beliefs are rife throughout Europe. England's constitutional monarchy allows her people freedom within the law, yet some wish for more. Here in Austria, the monarchy is far more absolute, but a future Emperor Rudolf would have broadened his people's rights. He envisioned a democratic society, governed by elected officials. Martin says the prince wanted to restructure the entire system. Rudolf's egalitarian approach might have ensured European peace."

"I can see how that would be fine for Austria-Hungary, but how does that benefit Europe?" asked the younger man.

"Because Europe's countries are irrevocably linked, not only by treaties, but through bloodlines. I love our Auntie Drina with all my heart, but the Queen's children and grandchildren control nearly all of Europe's thrones. Drina orchestrated these liaisons to foster peace, but you and I know how families fight. It would take very little kindling to ignite a European fire-storm, if not from human choices, then due to demonic influence. Spiritually, anarchy is the desire to remove all rulers, to be *an-archos*. But human rulers don't actually run the world. Our politics are merely an echo of spirit-realm realities. Until Christ returns, this world is run by *arche*, *exousia*, and *kosmokrators*."

"You're talking about Ephesians six, right?" asked Seth.

"You've been studying," smiled the Duke. "Our battle isn't against flesh and blood, but against spirit beings: powers, principalities, and rulers of darkness—spiritual wickedness in high places. Drina hoped to promote peace by filling Europe's thrones with her family, but it's doomed to failure. Why? Because of spiritual wickedness."

"Yes, but you have clearer spiritual vision than the Queen, Charles. Mightn't you be able to change all that? You could talk to her. Or better yet, you could take the throne."

"Yes, I could do that, but it wouldn't alter the truth," the Duke replied. "Scripture is clear. All human governments are under the influence of fallen spirits and will be until the time of Christ's return. No, Seth, my position as Shadow King isn't to prevent war. It's for another cause entirely."

"What cause is that?"

The Duke sighed. "Most is still a mystery. I've seen glimpses of it, but the future remains sheathed in mist. The Lord will make it clear, though—step by step, day by day, as he leads me along his chosen path."

"How do you know when you're on the *right* path? I hope the question doesn't make me sound sceptical. I'm still learning, Charles. I want to be a good man—a good Christian. Not only for myself, but for my future wife."

"Do you love her?" Charles asked pointedly.

"Her?" repeated Holloway with a subtle smile.

"You know what I'm asking. Do you really love Adele?"

Seth lowered his eyes. "Yes, I do."

The Duke nodded. "Good. Then I'll say the same thing to you, that James said to me when I asked for Beth's hand. So long as you love Della and keep her safe, then I grant permission. Of course, that permission depends on my daughter's choice, so I have to ask: does Della love you?"

The viscount sighed. "Honestly, Charles, I don't know. I like to think she does, but love takes many forms. For example, Beth loves you profoundly, and your attachment is eternal and inexplicable. She loves Paul as cousin and lifelong friend. She loves Henry and even me, but just as friends. Elizabeth's dear to all of us. And regarding Henry, I'm aware that Della loves him, although I cannot say just whether it's as a friend or something more. Do you know?"

"I know Della loves you both; more than that I cannot say. I'm sure she'll make a decision soon, and when she does, I'll be pleased to offer her hand to either one of you, without reservation."

"I really do love her, Charles," the viscount sighed again. "How do I follow Christ's footsteps? Is there a secret?"

Charles sat beside his friend. "A man could spend an entire lifetime trying to answer that, but I find it easiest to think only of the day ahead. I look to my feet, see where Christ's light shines, and try to find the narrow path where his lamp glows. The choices made today will determine what choices you're given tomorrow. Do the best you can with today's work. Study God's word and let its light lead the way."

"You make it sound so easy, Charles, but it isn't," the other countered. "No, forget I said that. I'm letting worry lead me into darkness. You saw how my mother's been acting. I'm worried she's getting worse. They blame it on that last trip to Damascus, but the truth is, ever since she and Dad stayed in Normandy a few years ago, Mum's not been herself. I've prayed with her, but it doesn't really help. Dad's thinking of sending her to a retreat."

"Not Breitenfurt," the Duke answered quickly. "I've no confidence in that place."

"Now that I've seen it, neither do I," said Seth, who'd begun to twiddle his thumbs, trying to settle a restless mind. "I could take her back to London, if you want. But it may not help if Paul's not there. I think Delia's mother is the cause of most of her problems. If Connie hadn't accused Delia of negligence, if she hadn't claimed Dee caused the boy's death, then all this might have been averted."

"I'm sure you're right, but Paul must approve any changes to Cordelia's status."

"Have you contacted him in Africa?"

"I cabled the British Governor there," Charles answered. "No answer yet. Once Paul's back in England, I'll make sure Delia goes home. Let's get back to our crime. What are our options?"

Seth sat up straight, ready to resume the mission. "Here's one: was Rudolf a victim or a perpetrator?"

"It might be both," said Charles as he stood, "but probably victim."

"If victim, was it murder or suicide? Was he a victim of a confused mind, for instance?"

"The Emperor's book contains a great deal of evidence that casts doubt on suicide, regardless of Rudolf's state of mind."

"I agree," said Seth.

"If murder, what was the motive? Romance, revenge, or politics?"

Seth shook his head whilst writing. "I'm not sure we have the complete picture yet."

"Did you know Rudolf visited England in '87?" asked the Duke.

Seth glanced up. "Really? I don't remember that. I may have been out of the country then."

"I was with the Yard in '87," Charles explained. "We were asked to work with Special Branch during Rudolf's visit. I was stationed outside the very room where Drina invested Rudolf with the Order of the Garter, an honour very few foreigners receive."

"Yes, but it's given to Shadow Kings and Scottish earls," the viscount noted.

"Yes," the Duke answered, smiling. "That year, Prince Rudolf visited the House of Commons and spent time with Salisbury, learning how a constitutional monarchy functions. I believe the prince would have modernised Austria-Hungary. His death removed all such possibility."

"So tell me, Holmes. Have you any theories?"

"Theories? I'm not yet sure, but my detective's nose begins to twitch, Watson," he said. "According to the Emperor's book, his son came here to hunt, correct?"

"Yes, but since he brought a mistress, he clearly planned to enjoy himself in other ways."

Charles nodded. "He also brought two friends to join in the hunt. Prince Philipp of Coburg and Count Josef Hoyos."

"He may have brought that magician, too, Charles. Demitri Kasadya. Mizzi mentioned it, remember? Or she very nearly did. She caught herself just before admitting it."

"We'll need corroborative evidence, but add Kasadya to our suspect list."

"Got it," Seth declared, underlining the magician's name. "And? Go on about that weekend."

"After hunting a few hours, Rudolf mentioned being unwell. He'd caught a cold. The manservant's testimony mentions that fact several times."

"A cold's an odd thing to emphasise."

"I thought that, too," agreed the Duke. "Following luncheon, Philipp excused himself, saying he had to return to Vienna for an important state dinner."

"That's not unusual," said Seth. "Vienna hosts hundreds of society dinners every year."

"As does London, but why didn't Rudolf attend the dinner as well?" asked the Duke. "Surely, a slight cold wouldn't have stopped him."

"Now you mention it, that is odd," said Holloway. "He didn't go, yet Coburg did? What was this dinner all about, Charles? Why did Philipp of Coburg insist on attending?"

The Duke had brought the 1420 book along, and he opened to one of the scrapbook-style pages. "Here we are. The Emperor's pasted in a newspaper cutting with notes in the margins. Kaiser Wilhelm was visiting, and the dinner was to celebrate his birthday. It looks as though the festivities went on for days."

"Days? Wait, if Wilhelm spent days in Vienna, why didn't he come here? Everyone knows Wilhelm loves to hunt!"

"I find nothing here to indicate whether he came to Mayerling, but when I see Wilhelm at the Coburg wedding, I'll ask him. I can interview Prince Philipp at the same time."

"That could prove dangerous, Charles," said Holloway.

"I'm used to that," smiled Sinclair.

"Yes, well, Della won't be happy."

"Then, don't tell her," Charles replied.

"Is this how it's going to be? Secrets and danger?"

"Always," the Duke replied with a slight smile.

"All right, then. Go on," the viscount said, his pencil at the ready. "I'm taking it all down in shorthand."

"You make a very fine Dr. Watson," laughed the experienced investigator. "Now, let's consider the evening of the twenty-ninth. January, 1889."

Seth glanced through his list of dates. "Rudolf and the Baroness are here, at the hunting lodge, with only Count Josef Hoyos for company, right?" asked Seth. "Philipp of Coburg has already left?"

"Probably, but what if someone else were here? Kasadya, for example. Also, I think the Emperor's notes mention an argument twixt Rudolf and Hoyos about someone named Count Karolyi." Charles opened the book. "Here it is. I'll do my best to translate the German: 'My son talks of being compromised. He grows impatient and irritable. Talks of shadows and spies. He's accused Kaspar of working for Germany, but he talks also of Count Karolyi. Both spy for Germany.'"

"Spies? Charles, are you saying Franz Josef believes that *actress* spied for Germany? Mizzi Kaspar doesn't seem intelligent enough to spy."

"She's an actress, remember?" replied the Duke. "And theatre work allows her to entertain and seduce all kinds of men."

"Including Shadow Kings?"

"Never," Charles replied. "Others, yes. I love but one woman. Still, Mizzi's to be pitied. That creature Kasadya has her enthralled. I wonder if the magician knows Prince Philipp? Even with the dinner appointment, Coburg could have returned before Rudolf died. It took you and me over an hour to drive here from Vienna. Yet, we're supposed to believe Philipp came all this way to hunt, spent a few hours, left to attend a state dinner, then returned to Mayerling just in time to eat breakfast? The roads twixt here and the Palace are narrow and dangerous at night. Why risk it?"

"When you say it out loud, it sounds preposterous," said Holloway. "Why come back for breakfast at all? If he drove all that way just to see Wilhelm, why didn't Philipp stay at the palace and eat breakfast with the Kaiser?"

"Perhaps, he attended the dinner to build an alibi," said Charles. "But here's another oddity, Seth. Why did Count Hoyos sleep in the gardener's cottage? According to the police report, the prince invited the count to stay in the lodge, but he refused. Did that provide Hoyos with an alibi?"

"Yes!" said Seth, scratching notes. "I see where you're going with this, Charles."

"Good," the teacher smiled. "Now, we're supposed to believe the manservant was the only servant in the house. Not even a cook or cleaner, which reduces our witnesses even further."

"That is strange," said Seth, taking down the Duke's words. "Why just one servant?"

"Quite. Now, according to this solitary servant, sometime after eight the following morning, Count Hoyos returned to the lodge, expecting breakfast. At the same time, Philipp of Coburg returned from Vienna. The servant tells them his master's still asleep. He cannot rouse the prince, though he's tried for *over an hour*. This manservant says he's worried for his master's health and fears the prince might have succumbed to coal-gas fumes. Yet, despite such a dire possibility, the servant has refused to break down the door. He's waited over an hour to ask permission from his master's guests!"

Charles set down the book and stepped closer to his friend. "Think about that claim, Seth. The only responsible party left inside the hunting lodge refused to break down his master's door, despite trying to rouse him for over an hour! Imagine one of our staff in the same situation. Miles or Kay or Anderson. He's received no reply to persistent knocks. He's tried for an hour or more without an answer. Would any of our servants delay for so long?"

"Hardly! They'd have broken it in after ten minutes, if not sooner," Seth said. "Good old Baxter would have kicked it down after five minutes, especially if he suspected coal-gas fumes!"

"Of course, he would, yet Rudolf's servant did not. He waited *over an hour*."

Seth wrote down the words and underlined 'over an hour'. "I begin to think the local police did a very poor job."

"Or they deliberately covered it up," suggested the Duke. "Now, once the door was broken down, the three men—the servant, Hoyos, and Coburg—finally break down the door and find Maria dead. However, each witness tells a slightly altered version. One claims Vetsera was poisoned, others say she'd been shot in the head. Rudolf is either poisoned or shot. Still another version described him as lying on his side, facing Vetsera, with a bullet wound in his back. Another says the bullet entered his head. Yet another claims the men broke into the bedroom and found the prince alive, sitting on the edge of bed with the pistol in his hand! Seth, I begin to think most, if not all of these testimonies, are fabricated."

"Which makes our task that much harder. Do you know who did it? Did someone murder the baroness and Rudolf?"

"We have no post-mortem to advise us. The dead baroness was whisked away in a coach, with a broomstick down her coat, to keep the body upright so that everyone would think her alive. To this day, no one knows where she's buried. Prince Rudolf was hastily delivered to the palace, but no medical examination was ever conducted. The funeral happened shortly after. All evidence gone. If I didn't know Franz, I'd suspect him of covering it up."

"He may have been so shocked, he couldn't think clearly," Seth suggested. "Losing a child scars a man."

"Yes, I know," Charles whispered. "That scar never fully heals."

The Duke took a deep breath, noticing the old familiar tingling had begun again. Through the room's dusty windows, he could see half a dozen nuns working in the distant vineyard. Others toiled nearby, collecting vegetables and acorns. "Don't you think it strange that Franz built a convent here? It's as though..." Charles stopped. The electric hum within his nervous system heightened.

Something's coming.

"Seth, we're still looking for a human solution, but these rooms tell a dark tale. History may never prove me right, but I think Baroness Maria and Prince Rudolf were murdered by intelligences far beyond our own. It isn't so much who killed them, as *what.*"

Seth shut the book. "Who or what? Human or other? Perhaps, the answers lie elsewhere. Shall we take in a magic show?"

"Kasadya?" asked Sinclair. "Oh, yes. Let's see what this conjurer can do."

CHAPTER TWENTY-NINE

That evening

Once they'd finished in the Mayerling apartment, Seth and Charles took tea with the nuns, but refrained from offering any observations on their findings. The Duke considered stopping by Breitenfurt again; after all, the retreat was just half an hour to the southwest, but he needed to write his preliminary report and submit it to the Emperor first. Time was short. He could sense it slipping away, like the hands on his childhood Arthur clocks: the King against a fiery dragon.

Victory or Defeat? Tick, tick, tick.

So rather than visit, Charles sent a telegram to Martin Kepelheim's brother, asking him to look in on the countess. Less than fifteen minutes later, the Duke received a reply from Helmut. Herr Kepelheim was otherwise occupied but promised to send his best inner-circle agent, Sir Leopold Mison, an intimidating bare-knuckle boxer, nicknamed 'Mison the Bison'. Mison would visit the retreat that very day and throw around his considerable weight as needed.

By half two, Charles and Seth had returned to Schönbrunn Palace. After hearing the Duke's initial findings, Franz Josef thanked the men for confirming his suspicions. The two peers then enjoyed a late luncheon in their rooms, where Charles discovered three telegrams waiting: one from Paul Stuart, another from Duke James, and one from Elizabeth.

Naturally, he read his wife's message first.

> DEAREST CAPTAIN – Thank you for your telegram. I'm glad all is well. We reached Nuremberg safely. Staying at Schindlerhof, as planned. They'd

> suffered a small fire that left smoke damage to our original rooms, but all is well. The owner cleared another wing, just for us. Tory and Adele left Paris two days ago, aboard your *Nautilus* train. Instead of meeting them in Frankfurt, we will see them in Coburg on Friday. Give my love to Seth, but remember, my heart is saved only for you. I am counting the minutes till we're together again, Captain. All my love. – YOUR BETH

"I love you, too, little one," he whispered as he folded the priceless paper into his pocket. Drummond's message had similarly cheering news.

> CHARLES – In case you don't know, all the children are with me in Glasgow. We had a break-in at the distillery, but nothing was damaged or stolen. I've taken Baron Ned Wychwright with me. As you and I discussed, he's to learn the distillery business. Ned's two girls are with us and are presently working puzzles. Georgie is playing piano, and Robby is reading aloud to the other children. He takes after me. Paul's children, Ian and Abbi, are also here. This old castle sings with young voices again! Tis very pleasant, son. Very pleasant. Give my love to everyone at the wedding and tell my sweet Princess how much I miss her. Watch yourself, Charles. You're always in my prayers. – Your old UNCLE DRUMMOND.

Charles smiled as he finished Stuart's happy missive. Since coming aboard as Haimsbury-Branham estate manager, Ned Wychwright had become indispensable to the Sinclair and Stuart families. And since his divorce was finalised, Ned had taken Christ as Saviour, as had both his little girls.

The Duke read the third, a typically short note from Aubrey.

> CHARLES – On ship back to England, but not alone. Bringing you a gift. Much to report, but all went well. Hope to see you in a month. – PAUL.

It was typical for his cousin to drop hints with little to follow. Not alone. Something about a gift; yet all went well, which was a blessing.

With the visit to Mayerling behind him, Charles decided to spend a few hours resting. He drifted off within minutes and enjoyed a restorative, dreamless sleep. At seven, he ate a delicious meal, then dressed for a second visit to the *Theater an der Wien*; this time, to see the mysterious magician perform his act.

He and Holloway arrived at the theatre shortly before nine. Lord Ailesleigh sent word that he'd be late and not to expect him before the curtain. As on the previous night, the stalls and boxes of the popular theatre were filled with blindingly bright colours and lively conversation. Everyone who was anyone clamoured to be there, including Vano Pyramis. The alienist sat on the opposite side from Charles, in a very expensive box, accompanied by two beautiful women and a well-heeled gentleman, whose name Charles would later learn was Gregory Panemorfí.

As they entered the lobby, Paynton and Haimsbury passed through a silken gauntlet of upper-class wives, widows, and marriage-age daughters. The Englishmen shook a hundred gloved hands and offered a hundred excuses for not remaining to talk. After fifteen minutes this way, Charles and the freckle-faced viscount finally reached the gracefully curving ironwork staircase to the Emperor's royal box. As they took their seats, a young woman in the adjacent box leaned over the bordering rail and tapped the viscount's arm.

"Hello, Seth."

Holloway's eyes widened, and a genuine smile creased the freckled cheeks. "Good heavens, Gemma! I'd no idea you were still in Vienna. This is a lovely surprise," he said, tapping the Duke's shoulder. "Charles, allow me to introduce my sister, the Countess Gemma von Burgau, wife of Count Karl von Burgau. Gemma, this is His Grace, Duke Charles of Haimsbury."

Lady Gemma was a softer version of Seth, with golden red hair and a splash of pale freckles across alabaster cheeks. Those cheeks rounded into happy apples as she said, "It's a very great pleasure, Your Grace, but I've heard the correct form of address is Your Royal Highness. Beth's always struck me as a future Queen, and I can see why everyone calls you King. You're very regal, sir. It's a great honour to meet you, Your Grace."

"I'm not sure how to respond to such lavish praise, Countess, but I'm honoured to meet you as well," said the Duke. "I understand you and Beth spent time together as children."

"Oh yes, we did," replied the soft-voiced countess. "We got together as often as our families could manage. My elder sister's name is Ruth. She and I love horses almost as much as the Duchess does. Every summer, Ruth and I would escape the dull life at Torden Hall and catch a train to Branham. Them, the three of us—Beth, Ruth, and I—would spend days and days galloping and gallivanting round the county. It was a rare time of freedom. Sometimes, Lady Victoria chaperoned, but whenever possible, we'd run off by ourselves. We called ourselves the Kent County Riding Club. Such times we had!"

"I can imagine," Haimsbury answered with a huge smile. "I'm always happy to hear about my wife's childhood, and Beth's mentioned the Riding Club many times. It's clear she has fond memories as well. I'm surprised you slipped Tory's chaperoning, though."

"It was easy enough, once we discovered the trick. You just get her talking to one of the cooks. Mrs. Stephens had only just started as head cook back then, so it was easy. Both women are delightfully loquacious. However, Mr. Baxter was the new head butler. Slipping Tory's net was simple but slipping *his* was nearly impossible!"

"No one escapes Baxter's eye," the Duke agreed. "He's a detective now and works for my Intelligence Branch."

The countess smiled. "Yes, I know. Beth wrote to me and revealed all. She also said my brother works for you."

"No, no, I work *with* him," clarified the viscount.

"Is there a difference?" asked Gemma. "But never mind! Seth wouldn't explain, no matter what the answer was."

Charles noticed the playbill in her hand. "Are you an admirer of magic acts, Countess?"

"Not really. My husband enjoys the odd bit of prestidigitation. He tries to figure out the tricks at home. I suppose he's an amateur illusionist. And you, Your Grace? Are you an admirer or sceptic?"

"Neither," replied the Duke. "Tell me, have you seen this fellow Kasadya perform?"

"No, not yet, but he's becoming quite famous in Vienna. And call me Gemma, please. Everyone does. My husband's round here somewhere, probably in one of the smoking salons. Karl doesn't smoke, but he loves to gossip. He's worse than an old woman sometimes, but I love him dearly." She paused a moment, pondering whether to say the next sentence. "Your Grace, talking of gossip, there are rumours flying round Vienna about your visit. Forgive me for prying, but as I say, my husband loves gossip. Karl says you and my brother are investigating a murder. Is that true?"

"Hardly," replied the Duke with a thoroughly disarming smile. "Tell your husband his sources are mistaken. We're here to visit the Emperor and tour the city. Nothing more."

"That's odd. Seth's been here dozens of times."

"Exactly. He's acting as my guide," said Charles.

"All the way down to Mayerling?" she asked.

"My cousin's wife resides nearby, at a retreat. Whilst there, we called on the Carmelite convent at Mayerling, as possible supporters of their work."

The look on Gemma's face mirrored one her brother often wore. "Ah, yes. I see. I'll not ask anything more. It's clear you two are keeping secrets, but I don't mind. Our father raised us on secrets. I didn't go into antiquities or linguistics, but I've spent lots of time on foreign digs. Mum's the word."

"Your father's an interesting man," Charles told her. "I can only imagine what secrets he keeps."

"I try not to ask," she answered. Gemma used a jewelled fan to cool her face. "It's always so hot in here. I see others have started using fans, too, and not just for ventilation. They're used to convey secrets. Did you know that?"

"Actually, yes," said the Duke. "Seth informed me last night. Sadly, gentlemen aren't allowed to take advantage of such a signalling system."

"Oh, but you're the recipients of them!" she laughed. "I wonder, though, do you know that gentleman across the way? Two boxes to the left of the stage. He's been looking at you with a very intense expression."

Charles turned his eyes towards the box in question and recognised Cordelia Stuart's doctor. "I cannot profess to know him well, but we've met. His name's Vano Pyramis. I've no idea who the other gentleman is."

"I know who he is," said a new voice from the rear of the theatre box. "Good evening, everyone. Sorry to be late."

It was the angel Hadraniel, disguised as Daniel Porter, 17th Earl of Ailesleigh. The messenger was resplendent in a black European-style cutaway and crimson waistcoat. He kissed Gemma's gloved hand. "A pleasure to see you again, Countess."

"You know each other?" asked Seth in amazement.

Gemma's freckled cheeks lifted, forming crinkles near the corners of each eye as she laughed. "Oh, Seth, do keep up! Lord Ailesleigh was at our wedding."

"I missed your wedding, remember?" asked Holloway. "Dad had me delivering artefacts up from Egypt for the British Museum exhibits. I sent you a gift."

"I knew that, silly," laughed Gemma. "I was just testing you. I saw you below, Lord Ailesleigh. Weren't you with that handsome Russian fellow?"

"If you mean Prince Anatole, yes, he came with me," the disguised angel explained as he joined the two Englishmen. "He should be here shortly. He stopped to talk to a friend."

"You said you recognise the man with Dr. Pyramis," Seth reminded Ailesleigh. "Who is he?"

"Ah, now that is an interesting question," said Ailesleigh as he removed his gloves. "He calls himself Gregory Panemorfí. It's Greek for beautiful, which I suppose applies in his case, as his female patients find him attractive."

"I'd not call him beautiful," muttered Seth Holloway. "I suppose he's handsome enough, but certainly not beautiful."

"Well, I think he's beautiful," Gemma argued with a happy sigh. "Do you think him untrustworthy, Lord Ailesleigh?"

"Let's just say I've seen him in other settings using another name entirely, and it's a name some would call impossible."

"How very interesting!" exclaimed the countess. "It's a shame Karl isn't back yet. He'd love all this. So if not he's not really Panemorfi, who is he? And before you answer, let me tell you what I've heard about Dr. Panemorfí—from Karl, you understand. The man has quite a reputation, and I say this as the beneficiary of a very chatty husband and mother-in-law. The local gossip says he's had a hundred mistresses, though I'm not sure if that includes just Vienna or all of Austria. Surely, the number's impossible, isn't it? Here,

Your Grace, use these," she said, handing the Duke a pair of opera glasses. "They make long-distance viewing much easier."

Using the gold-trimmed lenses, Charles took a closer look at the opposite box. Vanu Pyramis sat with an auburn-haired companion. The woman beside Panemorfi had dark hair and resembled Elizabeth, though not nearly as beautiful. Gregory Panemorfi certainly mirrored his name. He had the kind of features found in images of Greco-Roman deities: a straight nose, high cheekbones, flaxen hair, and turquoise eyes. Panemorfi and Pyramis were apparently sharing a joke, and their lady friends were laughing.

But there was something else. Behind Panemorfi, deep in the shadows, Charles perceived the outlines of two others. A male and a female. The woman waved. Charles shuddered. It was Eluna von Siebenbürgen, which meant the male shadow must be Araqiel.

Panemorfi's eyes turned from his companion and towards his observer. The cold gaze pierced through the magnifying lenses of Haimsbury's opera glasses, startling the Duke. The beautiful man's perfect features began to morph and shimmer as though made of smoke; as if another face were trying to come through the first, like a mask dropping.

Ailesleigh touched the Duke's hand and whispered, "Not now, sir. Let it go. There's much to explain about this one, but your instincts are correct. Remember, this wrestling match is not against flesh and blood. Wait for the right time to act." Then more loudly, the earl said, "Ah, the curtain's rising! I believe the manager's about to speak."

Charles lowered the glasses and returned them to Gemma. "Thank you. I'll have to purchase a set of these. They provide very clear vision."

"Feel free to borrow them anytime," she answered.

The black proscenium curtain parted, and a thin gentleman in evening dress stepped through the opening. He had wavy white hair and a pointed Viennese beard. A pair of gold-rimmed *pince-nez* hung from a silk cord about his neck. He smiled at the full house, no doubt mentally counting the take for the night.

"*Wilkommen, meine Damen und Herren,*" he began. "You forgive, yes, if I speak the English for our esteemed guest?" He gazed up into the royal box. "Tonight, we are having not the Emperor, but a royal guest from the great land of England. Please to welcome His Royal Highness, Prince Charles of Haimsbury!"

The house lights brightened. Every audience member rose and began to applaud. Even the orchestra stood and turned towards the royal balcony, placing Sinclair in the limelight once again. He'd slowly grown accustomed to the public's fascination with his life but preferred the country seclusion of Branham Hall or Rose House. The Duke bowed gracefully to the elite audience. A man sitting near the orchestra pit, held up a Kodak One camera and snapped half a dozen photographs.

"You'll be in the morning papers," Seth told his friend. "Must be nice to have so many admirers."

Gemma's husband returned at last and slipped into the seat beside his wife. Twenty-five years her senior, the kindly gentleman was shaped like a potato, with sagging cheeks and jowls that caused the greying moustache and chin beard to droop over the lower lip.

Once Sinclair resumed his seat, the count leaned across and said in English, "Is pleasure to meet you, Highness. I am Count von Burgau. You call me Karl, yes?" He shook Haimsbury's hand, then turned to the Duke's two companions. "Guten abend, Seth. Hello, Lord Ailesleigh. Is full house. No room for more, I think. Everyone say, come see great Duke of England! Come see next King! And so, we come. Gemma love it so, and me, too!"

"It's a pleasure to meet you, Count," Charles answered.

"Good to see you, Karl, but let's be quiet now," the red-haired viscount admonished his brother-in-law. "We don't want to miss what the manager's saying."

Von Burgau laughed. "Koch never say nothing worth hearing." He lifted the lid on a box of chocolates. "You try, Duke? Is made by Einem. Has liqueur fillings. So nice! I order bottle of Krug, too. It be here in shakes of two lamb."

"Two shakes of a lamb's tail," his wife corrected.

Down on the stage, Jacob Koch, the white-haired manager, bowed once more to the Duke, then continued his introduction in English. He described that evening's headliner as a miraculous man, who'd astonished the crowned heads of China, Egypt, Ceylon, and India. His magical feats had no rival, and before the night was over, every man and woman would believe in things supernatural and entirely unfathomable.

"But first," Koch added, "we have our beloved Fraülein Gitta Schumann to sing for us. Tonight, she choose to sing from Bellini's tragic opera, *Norma.* Here is Gitta Schumann with *Casta Diva.*"

The rail-thin manager bowed to the Duke, then exited stage right. A few seconds later, a lithesome woman of modest age entered from stage left. Her bearing was straight-backed and regal, and she wore a glittering black gown. The flaxen hair was piled high on the crown of her head and set with rhinestones. The maestro raised a white baton, and violins took up the plaintive strains of the opening measures.

As the soprano sang, Gemma leaned over to speak with Haimsbury. "It's a pity Beth isn't here. *Casta Diva*'s one of her favourite arias. Strange that Schumann would perform the song before a magic act, though."

"Why?" asked the Duke. "I've not seen *Norma*, but the music's certainly beautiful. What's the opera about?"

"Oh, the usual. Love, deceit, sacrifice. But then aren't most of them?" Gemma said as she passed the chocolates to the others. "These really are amazing, Your Grace. You should try them."

"No, thank you," answered Haimsbury politely. "That's kind of you, Countess, but I had a large supper earlier."

With the chocolate box in her lap, Gemma continued to explain. "Bellini's *Norma* is set in a Britain dominated by Rome but filled with pagans. The title character's a Druid priestess. Like most operas, there are bedroom shenanigans involving Norma and a Roman Proconsul. I can't remember his name."

"Pollione," said Seth.

"Ever the teacher, aren't you?" his sister countered, smiling. "But I think you're right. It is Pollione or something like that. Now, this aria is an invocation to the Druid moon goddess. Norma's about to enter a forest temple to ask the goddess for prophetic news, but as high priestess, she must be chaste to succeed. That's the dilemma, you see. Norma's given birth to several children, fathered by the Proconsul."

"She not so chaste, then, yes?" said Count Karl.

"Eat your chocolates, dear," his wife whispered, then turned back to the Duke. "That's what the aria's all about. Norma's plight. *Casta Diva* means 'chaste goddess'."

"Really?" asked Charles. "A chaste moon? How is a moon goddess chaste?" He referred to Eluna, of course, who presented herself as a moon deity. The female shadow in the opposite box moved into the light and waved again. There could be no doubt. It was Eluna. She smiled, as if she could hear the Duke's comments. Charles stared directly at her and added, "In fact, I'd say the moon is sex mad, or perhaps just mad."

"Mad?" asked Gemma. "I've never heard that before. Do you know something about the opera I've not read?"

"No," the Duke quickly answered. "Forgive the interruption, Countess. You were saying?"

"It's Gemma. Call me Gemma. Do you know that woman, Your Grace? The one in Box Seven? She's been trying to get your attention."

"She's an... *acquaintance,*" Charles replied.

"I am knowing these acquaintances," Karl von Burgau interrupted. "My wife not allow me any."

"You don't need them," his wife whispered. "I'm all you need."

"Please, don't misunderstand," Charles countered. "I've known the woman for fifteen years, in one form or another. You might say, she's constantly inconstant."

"Like moon, yes?" asked Karl.

"Yes, Count. Like the moon," Charles replied with a sigh. He'd have to face her again eventually, but he dreaded it. *Follow Christ's steps one by one*, he reminded himself. *Stay focused. Tonight, the goal is to learn more about Kasadya.*

The soprano finished the aria, and after an appreciative round of applause, she curtsied—first to the audience, then to Duke Charles. She exited into the stage-right wing.

A moment later, the main curtains lifted to a darkened stage. Minutes passed. The audience tensely watched for signs of the main attraction. Then, slowly, one at a time, tiny shafts of coloured light appeared across the mainstage area. The lights danced like delicate faeries in faint moonlight. The audience *ooed* and *awed* at the dazzling display.

Charles wasn't fooled. A logical truth lay behind the phenomenon. There had to be a trick.

The faery lights amplified and brightened. Their numbers grew larger and larger until the entirety of the stage flickered with ethereal dancers.

Then, everything went black!

All light vanished in the same instant, leaving only darkness. After another, anguished interval, a precisely aimed shaft of white light penetrated the blackness. And from this light, emerged a tall man. He just appeared, as though he'd entered from another world entirely.

Like passing through a portal, thought Charles, trying to work out the mechanics behind the trick. *Trap door?*

"Good evening," said the Magician in English. "I am the Great Eternal Kasadya, and I bring you LIGHT!"

He shouted the final word, as though commanding the elements. In response, every lamp inside the theatre and in the boxes began to pulse with multi-coloured shimmers. Murmurs of shock ran through the audience.

Ailesleigh leaned over and whispered to Charles. "This one is a liar. Do not trust your eyes. Kasadya is but a suit of flesh. He lies about everything, even his name."

"Suit of flesh?" asked Sinclair. "Daniel, are you saying he isn't human?"

"Not in the least," the angel declared. "I see beneath his lies, but so can you, I think. Keep a close watch. As Adele would say, the game is afoot, Holmes."

"I wonder what she'd think if she knew the truth about you?" Charles whispered to the heavenly warrior.

"We shan't tell her," Ailesleigh smiled. "Not yet, at least."

For the next thirty minutes, Charles watched the 'suit of flesh' perform a series of familiar magic tricks. He made one woman float, sawed another in half, and pulled great wads of German bank notes from a third woman's handbag. The Duke had seen tricks like these in Whitechapel's music halls. If this 'suit of flesh' represented a fallen-realm spirit, why pretend to be so unabashedly normal?

But the act was far from over. After this series of mundane tricks, the lights dimmed again, and a team of workmen cleared the stage. Darkness followed, then as before, Kasadya stepped out of a white spotlight and asked for silence.

Now, he told them, he would speak to the dead.

Charles had seen tricks like this before. Many stage conjurers fooled audiences by claiming to produce a loved one's ectoplasm, or an entire ghostly figure, but only within the confines of a spirit box. In '86, the Duke investigated the murder of one such magician. The man had convinced a vulnerable widow to pay him a hundred pounds, so she could talk to her dead husband. When she discovered the truth behind the smoke-and-mirrors trick, the distraught widow pulled the pin from her hat and used it to stab the man's eyes over and over. He bled to death, all over the stage.

But Kasadya used no spirit box, so how would he produce ghosts? Still favouring his left ankle, the conjurer limped towards the stage apron and looked directly at the Duke, saying, "Tonight, I have a message for someone. A dead woman asks me to tell her son's future."

"This should be good," Seth muttered.

"Hush," his sister admonished. "I want to hear this."

"She is coming through," said Kasadya. "Silence! Everyone, please, silence! The dead speak only in whispers." The magician's head bowed, and a shroud of silence fell upon the theatre.

Charles sat back against the chair. Across the way, Eluna and her brother were enjoying champagne and chocolates with Pyramis and Panemorfi. Two others had joined the miscreant party: Mizzi Kaspar and the handicapped violinist Peter Schilling.

Kasadya murmured nonsensically, as if conversing with the other side. At the same time, Sinclair's hands began to tingle. He could smell roses and sandalwood. The air was thick with the pleasant scent. He pictured his mother, sewing embroidery and sitting in a flowered chair by a window. He sat on the stool nearby, reading a book about stars.

Ailesleigh leaned close. "Don't let it take you."

On stage, Kasadya cried out, "Concentrate! You must all concentrate! She is here! She wants to speak! Close your eyes, please. I require silence to work. She is coming through!"

Two feet to Kasadya's left, a second spotlight cut through the darkness, aimed from above. It fell upon a void, a shadow. The light actually *bent* around a field of black, shaped like a woman, sitting in a chair.

"Who are you?" asked the magician. "Tell me your name."

The reply was hesitant, but feminine. "Angela."

A shock ran through the Duke's nervous system. Ailesleigh placed a hand on his friend's forearm. "He's lying," he whispered. "That is not your mother."

"Yes, yes, I know, but how?" asked Sinclair.

"Suit of flesh, remember?"

"Talk to me, Angela," said Kasadya. "Do you bring a message?"

The magician paused a moment. The woman-shaped shadow stepped closer, followed by the bending light. The magician began to contort and shake. He opened his mouth to speak. The sound was female, as though the woman were trying to pierce through the shadowy veil by using his mouth. She spoke in a strange language, but to the Duke, she very clearly said, *Charles*.

Then Araqiel stood, dressed in all his satin finery. He raised his hands, proclaiming, "I hear her! I will translate!"

The audience gasped. Women shut their eyes, and some grew faint. A few required smelling salts.

Araqiel probably knew Kasadya well and planned the trick in advance. Charles waited for the arrogant prince to begin spouting a string of lies, but instead, he heard a small whisper.

He knew the voice. He'd heard it many times as a boy.

Charles.

Mother? he thought.

In the background, Araqiel and Kasadya were talking back and forth as if one translated the mutterings of the other, but Charles heard the sweet voice of Angela Stuart Sinclair—whispering into his mind.

Darling son, you must become King. You are the True Blood. Not a Shadow. My sweet, sweet son, you are Truth.

Ailesleigh leaned close. "Tis a liar's voice, sir. Don't listen!"

Ignoring the voice proved difficult. "Liar?" he asked.

"You're hearing one of many lying spirits, sir. That is not your mother. Lady Angela is with the Saviour."

Somewhere from another world, Charles could hear Seth Holloway laughing with Gemma. "I've seen this act before. One man claims to speak for the dead, and another translates. This fellow's no better than a drawing room palmist!"

Charles, do you hear me? asked the pseudo-mother's voice. *Listen! You must take the Crown!*

Someone nudged his elbow. It was Holloway.

"Charles, are you all right? You've gone pale."

"Yes, yes, I'm fine," the Duke managed to answer. He could still hear the lying voice, though the words grew becoming indecipherable. They blended with the theatre's noise, but he could still smell his mother's perfume.

Charles wanted to scream. He stood and straightened his waistcoat. "Excuse me, everyone. I need air. No, what I mean is, I've just seen someone I know. He and I need to talk. Please, forgive me. I shan't be long."

"Shall I come, too?" asked Holloway. "Della did say I should keep watch over you."

"No, that's all right. Keep an eye on Eluna and her brother. I don't trust them, and neither should you."

The Duke left the theatre box to find a way back to the lobby. He did need air—clean air. As he passed along the upper level, he met an usher. The uniformed man acted as though he'd expected to meet the peer.

"For you, mein Herr," he said as he passed Haimsbury a note. It was written in an older version of inner-circle code and translated as: YOU ARE IN DANGER.

"Who gave you this?" asked the Duke in German.

"Is prince, mein Herr." the young man replied. "I speak your English. You come, yes?"

"A prince? Yes, I'll come. Take me to the man who sent this."

The usher led the peer through a gilded door and down a flight of carpeted stairs to a smoking salon. The room was empty, save for one occupant.

Not a woman, but also not a man. Not exactly.

"Hello, Charles," said the note's author. "Come and take refreshment with me. And don't worry about tipping the usher. I've already paid enough for us both."

"Alphonse Theseus," said Haimsbury as he took the chair opposite the hybrid entity. "It's been what? Four years?"

"More than four, but I have good reason for the long absence. Coffee? The Viennese make a delightful espresso; a recipe stolen from invading Ottomans centuries ago. I've ordered pastries and caramels, too. I've developed a sweet tooth of late."

"We noticed your clinic was shuttered," said Charles. "A lawyer said you'd relocated to America. I tracked you to New York, then all clues to your whereabouts dried up."

"It's a very long tale, filled with sorrow, but I shall give it to you in full another time."

"Then, why send for me? And why here?"

"Therein hangs a tale," Theseus replied. "I hoped the circle's cipher might intrigue you. I didn't wish to announce my presence to the others."

"Others?"

"You've seen them. Eluna and her mad brother. But also Kasadya and his brother."

"*His* brother? I'm not sure what you mean," Charles answered. "And how do you know our code?"

Theseus laughed. "You'll probably change it now, but I assure you no one else is aware of it. Nor have I shared it."

"If it's still secret, how did you learn it?" asked Sinclair.

"An old friend gave it to me. A woman who seeks a rapprochement of sorts."

"I can't think of any woman who might..." Sinclair started, but then his voice changed to anger. "Do you mean Diedra Kimberley?"

"Expertly deduced, Holmes."

"Where is she?"

"That is the wrong question, my friend. Forget Kimberley. Her reward will come one day, but not at your hands. Think of her no longer. Tonight, I've come to offer advice."

The Duke sat back against the club chair's leather; his arms crossed. "Advice on what?"

"On your enemies," answered Theseus. "The Time Maze offered up some of its secrets, but not all. Cigar?"

"No, thank you. What secrets?"

Theseus lit a match to the cigar's tip. The brief flash of light showed age lines in the hybrid's usually young face. He'd altered somewhat since Charles last saw him in late '89. The dark hair was streaked with silver, and the skin near the eyes was creased with age lines.

"You look older," said Charles, pouring a cup of espresso.

"Ah, yes, that," smiled the other as he blew out the match. "Just an illusion. An older face helps me fit into society. I've been working with Dr. Pyramis."

Charles's eyebrow arched. "If true, then Delia's leaving."

"I shan't argue with you."

"No? Why?"

"Because Vanu Pyramis has another partner, who's far more trouble than I, and he convinced Vanu to join an occult organisation you despise."

"Redwing?" asked the Duke.

"No, not exactly. *Die Herren von dem Schwarzen Stein.* The Lords of the Black Stone, or as your circle call them, Blackstone. You should probably send Lady Aubrey home, but until then, I can keep an eye on her, if you like."

"I do not like," the Duke responded quickly. "Seth will take her home."

"I thought the viscount was acting as your daughter's eyes and ears?"

"And how would you know that?" asked Sinclair.

"Charles, I know a great deal! I've watched nearly all of your life through the seeing stones."

"You've done what?" shouted the human. "That is totally out of bounds!"

"No, no, you misunderstand me. I'm not spying on you. I merely want to help you."

"Help me?" the Duke gasped, nearly spilling the coffee. "I don't need your help."

The hybrid sighed. "Charles, I seek only friendship and fellowship. Truly, I want to help you."

"Listen to me, Alphonse. I want to believe there's good in you somewhere, deep down, but it's difficult, given your past."

"And yet, what I say is true," countered the hybrid.

"Then, explain. You have one minute."

The halfling took a deep breath and swiped at the long, silvering mane. "Since that day at the Time Maze gate, I've been forced to examine my life and contemplate the notion of truth. The One's dreadful power that day terrified all of us. Not just me, but Araqiel and Eluna."

"Nothing terrifies them," the Duke declared. "But one day, even they will bow the knee to the Almighty."

"You're probably right. Did you know, when you walked the Maze, we watched your progress through the seeing stones?"

"I thought you might," said Sinclair.

"Yet my eyes saw a truth, that the others missed," Theseus confessed. "The One is far greater, far more powerful than I ever dared imagine. Watching you shook my theological foundations, if you must know. The way the One helped you through each phase of your journey fascinated me. He really did work all things together for good."

"Are you quoting scripture, Alphonse?" asked Sinclair.

"Does it surprise you? The fallen realm know the Bible far better than humans," replied the alienist. "But seeing the words *come to life* is unsettling, when you're on the wrong side." He paused for a moment; the dark eyes thoughtful. "You once tried to win me to your side, but then I assumed myself wiser. I've walked the earth for millennia and met many travellers, some fallen, others loyal to the One. That is why I'm here. You might call it penance."

"Do you seek absolution?" asked the human. "Only God can forgive you, Theseus. Seek him, not me."

"I don't think he'd listen. I thought, perhaps, helping you might be a place to start. I cannot say if my actions will make any difference to my final ending, but I'm determined to try. To begin, let me tell you what happened *after* you escaped the Maze."

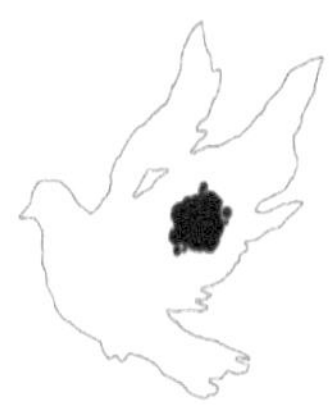

CHAPTER THIRTY

Coburg, Germany – Ehrenburg Palace

It was long past nine, when Beth's train arrived at Coburg station. The Duchess was glad to be in a non-moving room. Her body ached, and her stomach complained. This pregnancy was proving to be very like her first.

Duke Alfred, ruler of Saxe-Coburg and Gotha, met them at the station with an entourage of coaches, servants, drivers, and twelve long waggons. Alfred was Queen Victoria's second-born son, and the prince embraced his mother with a polite kiss to the cheek.

"Mama," said Alfred happily. "*Wilkommen in Coburg! Ich freue mich dich weider zu sehen!*"

"English," the Queen admonished. "Not all in our party are fluent. I'm very pleased to see you, Affie. Where's Victoria Melita? She is here, I hope?"

"My daughter's with friends at Rosenau," he answered. "You'll all be staying at Ehrenburg. The wedding's to take place there, and we've plenty of space. Did you bring your hunting dogs, Mama? We're to hunt boar once all the men arrive." He saw the Duchess and exclaimed, "Oh, my, Elizabeth! Look how beautiful you are! My dear, you grow prettier each time I see you. My son talks endlessly of his visit to Branham last year. Alfie and your daughter are fast friends. Is Adele with you?"

"Hello, Alfred," replied Beth. "Della's coming with our Aunt Victoria on a separate train. She's written glowingly about Prince Alfie, but then it's your daughter who's the star, isn't that so? It's good of you to invite us. I love weddings."

"As do I," said the duke. "Is Drummond coming?"

"I'm afraid not," the Duchess answered. "Grandfather's in Scotland. He's taken the children there for a holiday."

"And Charles?" enquired the older gentleman as he helped his mother into one of the coaches. "Careful, Mama. Beth, you sit beside her. I'll ride opposite. What about Charles?" he repeated as they settled into the interior.

"He's in Vienna on business," the Queen answered for Elizabeth. "We're not to know much about it. Intelligence matters, you see. Ah, but we've a great deal to decide before the wedding, my dears. Let's have a nice talk, all right? But only about children and romance. No politics."

Henry MacAlpin joined the duke and two ladies, whilst Hamish Granger, Sir Percy, and Captain Crenshaw made sure all the trunks and luggage made it onto the waggons. Once all was secure, Percy joined his wife in another coach, and the circle agents found spots beside drivers to keep watch for highwaymen. Coburg footmen took positions in the rear of each coach. The first driver snapped the reins, causing the horses to trot along a cobbled avenue. Soon, the long caravan began the climb towards Ehrenburg.

The winding road took them past a blackened spot, marked with a sign that read *der Hexebaum*, the Witch Tree, where local legend claimed a sorceress named Valul (of Martin Kepelheim's tale) was burnt to death.

Beth shivered as she read the marker. "What does that mean?" she asked Alfred. "Is it a Witch's Tree?"

"I'm not sure," the duke told her. "As you know, my family and I moved to Coburg only last year. Servants and locals insist the marker is true. The story claims a witch was burnt on that very spot in the 1500s. You know, Beth, it's quite strange, for it's supposed to have happened at about the same time that one of our Coburg ancestors gave refuge to a man we know quite well in England. Martin Luther."

"Really?" asked Queen Victoria. "There's a Coburg witch connected to Luther's story? I don't remember your father ever speaking of it. Surely, the village had no such thing as witches, not even then."

"Coburg is filled with very superstitious people, Mama," replied Alfred. "Yes, I know, Papa was of a scientific mind. He never liked to talk of superstitions, but Coburg has a rich history of supernatural encounters. Not only this witch. There's also a tale of Luther battling a demon."

"Nonsense!" said the Queen.

"I thought that, too, Mama, but I found corroboration in a history book at the castle. It was written by one of the guards who looked after Luther whilst he lived at Veste Coburg."

"Where is Veste Coburg?" asked Henry, who'd been rather quiet. "Is *Veste* another word for castle?"

"Not exactly," explained the Queen. "Schloss is castle. Veste is a fortress. In fact, Veste Coburg's where Luther wrote his most famous hymn. Albert took me there once and showed me the rooms where Luther stayed. There's a black mark on the floor where a demon *supposedly* stood, but it's just an old ink stain."

"Perhaps," whispered Alfred, "but to paraphrase the Bard, there are more things in heaven and earth than are dreamt of in your philosophy, Mama."

This made Henry laugh. "Well said, Your Grace! I doubt Shakespeare knew just how true his words still are." He turned to the Duchess. "Beth, you're shivering. Why don't I find a rug and we'll leave off talk of witches and demons. I think sleep is a better tonic for all of us."

Alfred produced a woolen blanket from one of the storage boxes, and Henry tucked it beneath Elizabeth's chin. The party processed up the hill towards Ehrenburg Castle, which dominated the lower plateau of the royal complex. After half an hour of bumpy travel, the coach finally stopped, and the footmen jumped down to open the doors and unload the trunks.

Once inside, Henry helped the Duchess up the long staircase, to an apartment she'd soon share with her husband. MacAlpin helped Beth settle, then said goodnight.

Henry was given the apartment across the hall. Elizabeth's maid took a small room nearby. Granger and Crenshaw found space on the next floor up, whilst Sir Percy and Lady Gemma took the apartment nearest Henry.

After everyone left, Beth took up a pen to write a heartfelt letter to her husband. She filled three pages on both sides, and then asked her maid to take it down to the castle's postbag. Midnight had long since passed by the time the Duchess dressed for bed. She dreamt of the Time Maze tunnels again, only this time, it was she who found the centre, where she met a man who looked exactly like Charles.

The doppelganger wore a heavy chain round his left ankle, that caused him to limp. He sat before an enormous piano, playing *Moonlight Sonata* over and over as he laughed about Time and its many cracks.

CHAPTER THIRTY-ONE

Vienna – A smoking parlour at Theatre an der Wein

"You promised to tell me what happened after I left the Maze," Charles reminded Theseus.

"I can tell you what we all saw," the other replied. "It was a terrifying light show, so bright it very nearly blinded us. Then—*poof!*—you were gone! Spirited away by an unseen force. Araqiel said your blood allowed you to find a hidden key; that you escaped on your own. But I believe you had help."

"I simply vanished?" asked the human.

"Indeed. You disappeared in the blink of an eye! It's a very keen trick for a human, don't you think?"

"I don't remember any of that," the Duke told him. "But afterwards, I lay in a weakened state for many weeks, and even now, most memories remain veiled. I sometimes dream about the Maze, but once awake, it's gone. All I have are faint impressions."

"Yes, I had a similar reaction when I walked through it," said Theseus. "You have no idea who helped you?"

"None."

"And what of the passages?"

"What about them?" asked the Duke.

"Who guided you through the trickier sections of the Maze? It's true, your blood is eternally linked to something greater, but you possess neither the strength nor knowledge to defeat Legion on your own."

"Legion?"

"Don't pretend with me, Charles. You know his name. Who else was with you at the end?"

Charles found the question intriguing. If the elemental members of Blackstone watched his ordeal through the 'seeing stones', then why didn't they see his manner of exit? The Duke had only a vague impression of angelic battle, but had no intention of providing what Blackstone lacked, and so decided to say nothing at all.

"It's clear you don't know either," Theseus suggested with a smile. "A shame, for I've often wondered how you and I differ. As Maze Walkers, I mean. I told you about the other human that successfully finished the Maze, didn't I? Francis Rákóczi of Transylvania?"

"Yes, I believe so," Sinclair answered, half his mind distracted by a visual oddity in the far corner of the room. The air there seemed to ripple, as though an unseen figure resided just beyond sight. *Kasadya? Araqiel?* "Didn't you say this Transylvanian took a different name after leaving the Maze? What was it again?"

"I'm glad you remember that much, at least," said the halfling, unaware of the visual disturbance. "He calls himself the Count de Saint Germain now. I mention this because Saint Germain's currently in Vienna. And I believe he's on your list of suspects."

"Suspects?"

"Don't be coy, Charles. Your meeting with the Emperor is well known amongst my kind. We have spies inside the cathedral, the palace, and in all sorts of places. Your conclusion is correct, by the way. Prince Rudolf and Baroness Vetsera were murdered. Shall I tell you the murderer's name?"

"Even if you did, I'd need to find evidence to support it. But why help me?"

"Because I want to be your friend!" exclaimed Theseus. "There are very few of us in the world, Charles. You and I are part of a rare breed."

"If you mean I'm a hybrid, then I beg to differ. I am not," the Duke insisted.

"Not in the traditional sense, no, but your emergence from the Maze proves your blood is compatible. Charles, you are a Time Walker! And, I suspect, your wife and children are as well."

"Leave my family out of this."

"They are in it, whether you like it or not. Let me help, Charles. I really do want to be your friend."

"Very well. Who murdered Rudolf?"

The alienist smiled, his white teeth gleaming. "I could give you name of the human participants, but that would only reveal the puppets. The puppet-master is a spirit."

"Who?" asked the Duke.

"Saraqael ben Chosek," declared the hybrid without a blink. "He murdered that naive young woman, then fired a pistol into the prince's brain. Not with his own fingers, you understand. He used a flesh suit for that. Could you explain such a plot to His Excellency? Can a human court indict a fallen Watcher?"

The Duke sat quietly, half his mind working through the new information, the other trying to discern what caused the strange phenomenon to his right. The glimmering vacancy slowly took shape. Charles could make out a tall entity, yet its identity eluded him.

Is it Saraqael?

"Why would Saraqael care who inherits the throne of Austria-Hungary?" Charles asked the hybrid.

Theseus poured himself another cup of espresso. "War, Charles. Sara wants the world embroiled in war."

"Why? Just for the bloodshed?"

"In part. The fallen realm believe the right amount of human blood might break the chains holding back Chaos. To do that, Sara needs to alter the future."

"What future?"

"The oaks and willows. The trees on the hill."

"My wife's dream?"

"No, Charles, your wife's *vision*. Saraqael and Chaos fear such a future."

"Who or what is Chaos?" asked Charles.

"A monster that sleeps in chains, far beneath the Earth's deepest prisons. You might say, he dreams, and those dreams are given life by the actions of fools like Saraqael."

"Saraqael's no fool. He's devilish. Clever. He killed my father, but he's no fool," Charles whispered. "He once used the human guise of Prince Aleksandr Koshmar. Does he still use this name?"

"From time to time. I asked if anyone helped you through the Maze. Saraqael helped Saint Germain through it. And if Sara was allowed to enter Legion's domain, it may mean they're working together. That, my friend, would be a very dangerous fellowship."

"I remember only a little of my meeting with Legion," the Duke said, keeping watch on the unseen visitor to his right. "The name's mentioned in the Bible as a collection of demons, cast out by the Lord at Gadara. Surely, those same demons aren't living inside your Time Maze?"

Theseus laughed, the dark eyes glinting. Strands of silver-streaked hair fell across his face, and he brushed them back behind his ears. "Forgive me, but that is quite funny, and you've no idea why. You're correct regarding the Bible, but the Legion mentioned in the gospels is hardly the same entity you faced inside the Maze."

"No?"

"Not at all. Allow me to explain. The English word is based in Latin, from the word *legere*, meaning choosing or gathering together. Roman armies used it to denote a group of soldiers, gathered beneath the same banner—a choice and a gathering—usually numbering six thousand or so. Now, the entity at the centre of the Maze is something else. In fact, his original name isn't Legion at all. He just likes to use it. And he is anything but a demon. Far from it! The Time Maze Legion is a child of Chaos; first offspring of the first Dragon. Like Chaos, he destroys all organisation and structure, Legion can even disorder Time. He feeds on it. Indeed, he's already luring your son into his dark world. That is why I'm here, Charles. That is why I want to help."

CHAPTER THIRTY-TWO

HSM Valiant - Paul Stuart's Journal

Today is the 8th of April, Beth's birthday. As I write this, my darling sweet cousin is probably in Coburg. I long to be there, too; though not alone, with my beloved wife—sharing slices of raisin cake and dancing till dawn. My beautiful Cordelia Jane. It is she whom I miss most. With God's mercy, we'll reunite very soon.

When I left for my mission to the Ashanti people, I had no idea I'd return with a baby in my arms. Dorada, the wet nurse provided by the Ashanti Queen speaks English quite well and works beneath the careful eye of Johanna Brückner, a former teacher for the German missionary camps. Brückner is twenty-six and recently widowed. Her husband was killed when Moslems raided their village. Dr. George Brückner was a fine man and a devout believer. His widow is a forthright, efficient woman, who skillfully supervises the wet nurse, whose name is Dorada, Spanish for Golden. She is quarter-caste, with light olive-skin and brown hair, born of a Spanish father and half-Ashanti mother.

The child given to my care is also multi-ethnic. I'm told she's one-quarter Ashanti, one-quarter German, and half English. She was taken by the moon cult after her mother was killed in an inter-tribal skirmish—perhaps from the same tribe as the men who tried to kidnap me. I asked if the baby's father might be found, but Frau Brückner says he died three months ago.

The baby would surely be dead without God's intervention. No child deserves such a fate, yet this secretive moon cult believes they have a right to sacrifice human life to their cruel deity. When I asked the Ashanti queen mother about it, she denied any knowledge of such a cult within her palace and blamed it on neighbouring tribes.

I only know that an innocent life was spared. But for what purpose? And why give her to me? Or rather to Charles, for she's a gift for England's Shadow King, after all.

Frau Brückner suggested I call the baby Hope, for she represents hope for the future of West Africa. The woman has no way of knowing how the name fulfills a prophecy. During the voyage down from France, I enjoyed the company of Prince Anatole Romanov, who offered me advice, which only now makes sense. He said I would find Hope in Africa, and this Hope would lead the Sinclair-Stuart families to our destiny.

Did Romanov know about the infant? Had he foreseen it?

Strange, too, for the entity who appeared in my coach near Vienna told me to avoid going to a moon ritual in Africa. If he knew my plans, why try to keep me from saving this baby? I can only conclude the two entities—Romanov and this Prince Kasadya person—are on opposite sides.

I'll admit, Hope has won my heart. She often sleeps in my arms in sweet contentment. I cannot imagine life without her now. How do I explain her to my family back in England? Will Charles keep her as a gift? Could I bear to part with her, if he does? After losing Liam, my arms feel full again. Perhaps, Hope will also enliven my dear wife's heart. I miss her so! Cordelia Jane is my lifeline. Without her, I would simply fade into nothingness.

And so, I end this entry by writing of my beloved. Strange, for I began it with Beth, a woman I once thought to marry. God knew better. Elizabeth belongs to Charles, just as I belong to Cordelia.

I hear Hope calling. My arms reach out for hers.

Three days more, and we dock in England. Praise God Almighty for his tender mercies.

And for this gift of Hope.

CHAPTER THIRTY-THREE

Theatre an der Wein, Smoking Salon

Inside the private salon, Alphonse Theseus continued, a lit cigar in his hand. “Charles, you have power beyond your imagination. Your escape from the Maze shocked Araqiel, but it delighted Eluna, as you might imagine. Once you vanished, they left the seeing-stone room. Only I remained. Now, I cannot say whether others aided your escape, but after you vanished, I saw an elohim return and challenge Legion. You call him Prince Anatole, but we generally call him Samael. He returned and engaged Legion in a fierce battle. I watched in fascination. Samael and Legion were evenly matched, but then Shelumiel arrived. He’s an immensely powerful warrior, who stands beside the One’s throne. With combined strength, they placed an adamantine chain around Legion’s left ankle. The chain doesn’t stop him from roaming the earth. His mind is still free to travel the earth through human suits.”

“He travels the earth?” asked Charles, still perceiving the shimmering phantom in one corner of the salon.

“Oh, yes,” Theseus said easily. “Legion travels through fit extensions. We call them flesh suits. Do you know what I mean by that?”

“He inhabits human victims.”

“Yes, but not without an entry point. A human must grant permission for full habitation through occult dabbling. Free-will rules may be bent but never broken. A spirit knocks, and the human must choose to open.”

“Are you describing possession?”

“Not always a full possession. Sometimes, Legion merely influences the human. He whispers to them.”

“He uses them.”

"Oh, yes. He can also influence humans through dreams, another source of temptation."

"How?"

"Have you never awoken from an erotic dream with no idea of its origin? Perhaps, you've dreamt of a beautiful woman you met just once, or of a scenario without a known reference. When you awake, the dream hangs about you, influencing your thoughts. Now, you're a strong man, Charles, therefore such dreams might not worry you. But whilst you might shake it off, another man would succumb to that dream woman and long to return to her. Hence, a portal is opened."

"Surely, that's bending the law."

"Is it?" asked Theseus. "The One uses dreams, why can't his enemies? Chaos sits within his prison, dreaming, but Legion sits at the root of all dreams. Think of him as an upside-down tree, whose roots rise to the surface and draw energy from the wellspring of human life. Have you seen the Black Book used by Blackstone?"

"Once," replied Sinclair, still sensing the presence. "Albus Flint left a copy with an old friend of the Branham family. Sir Simon Pembroke. Poor man nearly had a heart attack over it."

"Flint does enjoy frightening humans. And you saw it? You saw the book?"

The Duke nodded. "Leather binding with a tree on the cover."

"Not exactly a tree. And the leather binding is human, tanned from the hides of witches. The flesh of condemned men may also be used, but only if he's hanged at a crossroads. The book's outer decoration shows two trees. One sits above the ground, the other below it. The trees are supposed to represent the hidden spring that feeds all life. This life-giving spring comes from dead ancestors, who live below ground and communicate with the living above. Ah, but the truth is far different. The image of the double-tree is a double-cross. It represents the fallen realm, who feed upon humankind, sucking out energy and bending rules to deprive humans of their free-will choices. They sap the very life from our veins, Charles! In Legion's case, he eats away at our future. Time is his delight and his sustenance."

"Our energies? Our futures?" asked Charles. "You cannot include yourself. You're not human, Theseus."

"I am half human," argued the hybrid. "If you insist on including my paternal side, may I not claim my mother's?"

"Perhaps," the Duke whispered. "How does Legion feed on Time?"

"In this image, Legion *is* the lower tree. He sits there, like an ancient locust and feeds on human choices. He corrupts and ruins. He even uses fallen-realm comrades to accomplish what he cannot. Legion's soldiers roam the earth. His human suits, I mean. And his demons may cross, back and forth, from below to the above world. So may some Watchers."

"I thought the Watchers were imprisoned," said Charles. "Those from before the flood, in Tartarus. Those after, in stones and mirrors."

"You've been reading Dr. MacPherson's new book," the halfling remarked. "Yes, I've read it as well, and he's correct about most things. As he writes, the Watcher class of elohim can be loyal or fallen. But not all are in prison. Today, they run throne rooms and even board rooms. Remember your Bible? The separation of mankind into lingual tribes after Babel?"

"Yes, what of it?"

The alienist's smile vanished. His eyes searched the room, as though expecting to find an intruder. "Odd. Do you feel a strangeness to the air? A chill? A sense of something new, as though someone opened a window?"

Before Charles could form his lips into an answer, his spirit was taken. The Duke left the room and found himself in his own library at King's Court, back in England. In the blink of an eye, Charles had left the salon and entered a new conversation—this time, with an old friend: Aleister Fenwick, the servant-form used by the angel Hadraniel.

Fenwick allowed his startled passenger a moment to compose himself.

Charles gasped for air. It felt as though all oxygen had left his lungs. He was dizzy and struggled to make sense of his surroundings. "Fenwick? Is that you? Wha—what are you doing here? Where are we?"

"I've brought you to London, sir. Your library, in fact. King's Court. I like the new name, sir. And the house is magnificent, particularly the marble trees."

"Yes, yes," answered the human, still gasping. "The trees on the hill. Am I dreaming?"

"Not actually dreaming, sir. I've taken your spirit on a journey. It's Theseus, sir. He isn't to be trusted. Though his heart leans towards repentance, it shows no sign of genuine contrition. He fears the final judgement, and that fear drives his current actions. Theseus realises he's chosen the wrong side, but part of him will always rebel."

"How can you know that?" Charles asked.

"I cannot, but the One sees his heart. Theseus's pride hasn't died. It still lives and will lead him into even greater error soon. I know you tried to witness to him, sir. The compassion you feel is noble, but despite your witness, Theseus will never accept the True Son as Redeemer."

"Was it you who watched us in the salon?"

"I hope I didn't frighten you, sir. I'm surprised you could see me."

The dizziness subsided, and Charles began to breathe more easily. "I saw you as a void in reality. Your various forms grow evermore mysterious, Hadraniel."

The angel smiled. "The Lord's ways are mysterious, sir. I merely follow orders. I've been quietly communing with Prince Samael whilst watching the magician perform. He and I agree. The creature is trouble."

"Creature? Then, Kasadya isn't human?"

"Not at all, sir. He is one of Legion's extensions; perhaps more. Keep your wits about you, sir, and remember, you are never alone!"

With that final word, the human's spirit rushed back to the salon and returned to his body. Theseus was only now finishing the question about a strange sensation to the room. Sinclair's flight to London had happened in less than a blink.

He took a deep breath to clear his mind. The visual phenomenon had vanished from the corner. No matter. Charles remembered Fenwick's promise.

You are never alone.

Christ, the Shepherd is always nearby.

"A strangeness?" the Duke asked after finding composure.

"Yes. As though something invisible stands nearby," answered Theseus. "I'm imagining it, I suppose. Perhaps, Kasadya conjured up one of his minions to keep an eye on me. He doubts my allegiance, Charles. And so he should, for I despise that creature."

"Creature?" asked the human. *Fenwick called Kasadya a creature, too. Coincidence?* "Creature implies something other than the norm, and by that, I mean human."

"You've gained insight, Charles," the hybrid told him. "I wish it were down to my tutelage, but alas, it's more likely your ancient blood rising to its fullness."

"Be careful, Theseus. Do not ascribe that which is worthy to your false belief in the merit of my blood, for I will not hear it!"

"Yes, yes, forgive me," the other murmured, his eyes looking ages older. "I return to the old ways. I want to gain new sight, Charles. It's so very difficult, you understand. What's that old adage? A leopard cannot change its stripes?"

"Spots," the Duke corrected. "And it's more than an adage, Alphonse. You're quoting the Bible again. Jeremiah 13:23. 'Can an Ethiopian change his skin, or the leopard his spots? Then may you do good, that are accustomed to do evil.' All of us are born sinful. It's part of our human inheritance from Adam. Changing or removing that black spot is impossible without a contrite heart. You must truly believe yourself a sinner. You must confess your sins to the Lord. And you must turn away from them."

"How can I turn from them, when they wrap round me like an unholy death shroud?" asked the hybrid. "I admire your courage, Charles, but courage can fail. I like you a great deal, and I wish we could be true brothers. For now, all I can do is warn you. Be careful in the next few weeks. Steer clear of Kasadya and his kind."

"What kind is that?" asked the human.

"HIS *others*," Theseus admitted. "Legion's others. He'll want my blood for this, but I'll tell you how to recognise his extensions. Watch for someone who limps. Not all with such an injury will be Legion's puppets, but many will. Particularly, if that person favours the left ankle or leg. Remember, Samael and Shelumiel placed the chain on Legion's left leg? For now, that great chain stops him from escaping, and so he uses human suits. Yet, the massive weight of that chain will always bleed through, and the suits will limp."

Fenwick had told Charles the same thing. Had he met anyone who'd limped? Yes. The violinist Peter Schilling. The woodland Piper who frightened Robby. The shadowy man in the tall hat—the one Beth saw at King's Court gate. He limped. What was his name? Beth had told him. Justice Ravenhill. Had he seen anyone else? Perhaps, but his brain screamed for rest. He needed sleep.

"You say I should watch for that sign over the next few weeks. Why the next few weeks?" Charles asked Theseus. "What is Legion's plan?"

"I'm not sure of everything, but a fallen-realm prophecy says Legion will escape in the Last Days. I believe those days are close. He and Chaos will use any means to stop the One's prophecies from coming. Watch for his limping suits."

"And Saraqael?"

"That one wants to rule all the realms. He's been trapping his Watcher brethren and storing them inside elaborate sarcophagi. For what, I'm not sure, but Raziel is missing—as are Turiel, Bataliel, and Bazaliel. All these once worked with Legion. And all once trusted Saraqael, much to their regret. Sara is clever. Recently, he's been tutoring a young mystic, for what purpose I cannot say. Saraqael's dressed the man in monk's robes, cut from self-absorbed piety, no doubt. But beneath the false robes lies a cruel heart and a thirst for hedonism. The monk is Russian. Think of him as an explosion waiting to happen."

"Do you know his name?"

"Oh, yes," said Theseus. "Father Gregory Rasputin."

CHAPTER THIRTY-FOUR

By the time Charles returned to the royal box, the magic show had ended. He'd hoped to visit the dressing room area and interview the Great Kasadya, but the mysterious magician managed to perform one last trick: he vanished from the theatre. Lord Ailesleigh showed no surprise, and Seth complained of weariness, if not utter boredom. Holloway referred to the performance as sophomoric sorcery and paltry prestidigitation.

Yet Kasadya had limped—though he claimed the malady resulted from a hunting accident. Charles thought him a liar. Had Kasadya summoned up his mother's voice?

Of course, not. His mother was in heaven.

Was the magician in league with Araqiel? Most assuredly. Kasadya concealed his occult abilities beneath a mask of mundane magic. Charles felt sure they'd meet again.

Before leaving, the Duke asked the theatre's manager for a way to contact the magician. Herr Koch handed him a calling card for the performer's legal representative.

The name on the card was *Albus Flint.*

After bidding goodnight to the von Burgaus, the Duke and his companions returned to Schönbrunn. The moon stood directly overhead as the coach pulled into the palace drive. Charles stepped out, as did Holloway. Ailesleigh remained in the coach, explaining he had an appointment to keep elsewhere. Charles wondered what warfare awaited the faithful angel.

The following morning, Charles delivered a final report to the Emperor. When he learned his son was murdered, the old man's rounded shoulders sagged.

"It is as I thought," he said. "Might the killer be a friend? Or one of these spies?"

"It's possible, sir," the Duke told him. "I could remain here and continue the investigation, if you wish. I could interview the servant."

"No, he's left Vienna," the Emperor explained. "His last testimony is included in the book. I'm sure you read it."

"Yes, sir, but if you know where he's gone, then..."

"I've no idea, Charles. It is my own fault. I've left this too late. No, you must leave for the wedding. I mustn't keep you."

The Duke placed a compassionate hand on the old man's forearm. "I won't give up, Franz. I promise. I'll be seeing some of the suspects in Coburg. Count Hoyos and Prince Philipp. I might even discuss it with the Kaiser. I'd like to know why Wilhelm wasn't invited on the Mayerling hunt."

The Emperor glanced down at the typed report in his hands. "Rudolf's life is summed up in just a few pages." He wiped tears from his wet cheeks. "No, we'll leave it alone, Charles. Sisi and I are resigned to a childless life. No more sons await us. I have my nephew. I pray he has more sense than my son did."

"I'll keep looking," the Duke promised "If I learn anything new, I'll write to you. In code. Do you still have the copy my uncle gave you?"

"Yes, I have it. It's locked away in my rooms."

"Good. Keep it, just in case. Franz, I'm here, if you need anything else. Just ask."

"Thank you, Charles. You're a good friend. Keep the 1420 book. Perhaps, the information will prove useful to you in future."

The Emperor wiped away the remaining tears, as though wiping away pain. Then, in typical male fashion, he stuffed it all down and put on a mask of strength. "Now, before you leave, I have a gift. A small thank you for all you've done."

Franz Josef rang a silver bell to summon his chamberlain. The impressive servant entered and bowed.

"Mein Herr?"

"Kaufmann, bring the Duke's gift."

The servant slipped back through the door. Charles could hear a sort of *click-clacking* sound, as if a dozen fingernails tapped out syncopated rhythm on the wooden floorboards. Kaufmann returned with a footman. The second man held two leashes. And attached to each braided leather leash was the collar of a black-and-tan dog.

"Dachshunds?" the Duke asked, laughing at the animals' eagerness. They didn't jump, but pawed at Sinclair's shoes, pleading for attention. "Dachshunds are my gift?"

"Actually, they're for the Duchess, but the breed will hunt whatever you pursue, be it animal or human. Kaufmann, where is the other?"

"Coming, Highness," answered the chamberlain.

There were more tapping sounds on wood, followed by the entrance of a third servant, also holding a braided leather leash, though not attached to dachshund. A large, lean dog with greyish fur and ice-blue eyes. Without a single word of command, the animal crossed to the Duke and sat beside him, as if claiming his new owner.

"Ach! He knows he is yours, Charles!" the Emperor explained. "The dachshunds are eleven months and will make fine hunters. Your master of hounds will know how to train them. And this fine specimen is a two-year-old Weimaraner. He is fully trained for bear, boar, even stag. And he runs like one of the old ones. Like the *älfer*. His feet are soft, so you never hear him coming. I call him Ghost."

"Ghost?" asked Charles. "A fitting name for a stealthy hunter. Does he answer to English commands?"

"Oh, yes. He was trained by an Englishman. Drina suggested the present last year, you know. She said you needed more dogs. Ghost comes from a long line of champion hunters. Take him to Coburg with you, Charles. Make Wilhelm jealous!"

"I will," the Duke answered, taking the Weimaraner's leash. "Thank you, Your Highness. I'm sure my wife and children will claim the dachshunds, but I'll keep Ghost as my own."

The remainder of that final day was spent touring the city and buying gifts for Beth and Adele. Seth purchased a leather-bound set of Mozart sonatas for Della, and Charles bought a sapphire necklace for his wife as a belated birthday gift.

The following morning, as he arrived at the railway station, Charles received a telegram from Paul, sent from Pontevedra, Portugal, including a few coded lines:

> CHARLES – Four days more, then back in England. Much to tell. Leave Delia at Breitenfurt. I've sent a trusted friend to keep watch on her. A friend with

> WINGS. All is well. God is good. Praying for you. See you soon. – PAUL.

As he folded the telegram into his pocket, the Duke smiled. *God is very good*, he thought. He, Ailesleigh, and Seth Holloway stood beside their hired train, seen off by Lady Gemma and Count Karl, who insisted they take chocolates and sandwiches for the long journey. Gemma gave Charles a bottle of perfume as a gift for Elizabeth.

Several of the Emperor's footmen stowed all the luggage. The dogs were secured in strong crates with instructions to the porters regarding handling. It was time to say farewell to Vienna.

"Well, gentlemen?" Charles asked Ailesleigh and Paynton. "Our bags are loaded. The dogs have settled. Shall we board our train?"

"The next fortnight should prove very interesting," said the disguised angel as he climbed the short flight of steps.

"Is Romanov joining us?" asked Charles, who led the way.

"Not immediately," replied Ailesleigh. "He's coming with the Tsar and the Russian entourage. It is a very large group, as you might imagine, and they travel quite slowly. I expect we'll see them all in a few days."

"Then, we're off to Coburg. It's been far too long since I've held my wife," the Duke said, a glimmer in his eyes. "Coburg will be a most welcome sight."

"Welcome and welcoming," said Holloway with an endearing grin. "Ehrenburg Palace is a grand old place, but after sleuthing our way through Vienna, I look forward to two weeks of dinners and dances. And we'll see Adele again."

The Duke smiled. "I'll give my daughter a full report on your resourcefulness. You've made a very fine Watson."

The head porter made sure everyone in the party was safely settled before lifting away the wooden steps. He made a final survey of the platform, looking both ways along the smooth tracks to make sure no one was left behind. Satisfied that all passengers had boarded, he tapped on the Duke's window.

"Is all your party on board, Herr Duke?"

"We're all here, Mr. Meyer," he told the man in German.

"*Sehr gut*," said Meyer with a polite tip of his cap. He signalled to the engineer's assistant, then after looking round one more time, he boarded the train himself.

In the engine compartment, a middle-aged driver removed the external brakes, drained the moisture build-up in the water lines, released the Johnson bar and cylinders, switched on the headlamp, blew a loud whistle to signal forward movement, then—and only then—slowly opened the throttle. The sleek train began to huff and chuff and puff, inching forward on the iron rails, headed for Coburg.

Jacob Meyer was a veteran of the Vienna Railway System, and he loved to watch the mighty iron horse showed its muscle. He leaned out of the electrics-car window, a smile on his beardless face. He breathed in the air. As he did so, a chill shuddered through all his limbs. He felt cold and hot all at once.

Jacob pulled a checkered kerchief from his pocket and wiped beads of sweat from his forehead and neck. He felt dizzy, odd and out of sorts. The thirty-seven-year-old had spent twenty-two years on the railway, but never once had a train's movement affected him so adversely.

I need a drink, he thought as he leaned against the wall of the electrics car. *A bite to eat would help.*

Jacob was indeed very hungry. He craved meat. Something undercooked. Rare. Very rare.

Something juicy red with blood.

As he stumbled towards the Duke's car, Meyer heard piano music. He knew the song well. His daughter often played it. Beethoven's *Moonlight.* But though he tried, Jacob couldn't quite picture his little Heidi's face. Nor could he recall his son's name. Or his wife's.

All personal information began to vanish, replaced with something new. *Moonlight*. How lovely to live in a world with just the moon to guide us. A world without Time. A world without humans.

"Jacob!" shouted the engineer's assistant from the connecting doorway. "*Gerhardt will dich sehen!*"

"*Ja, ich komme!*" called the porter in return. "*Ich komme!*"

The dizziness had passed. The middle-aged porter tucked the kerchief back into his coat pocket. He smiled as he walked towards the cab. The left foot dragged a little now, causing him to limp. No matter. Somehow, the impediment felt normal, even powerful.

As he limped towards the engine, Jacob began to whistle.

The tune was *Moonlight Sonata.*